A LESSON IN KILLING

Mrs. Eddington had been surprised to see him, but not threatened. Adults just weren't threatened by a kid with scrawny legs and flyaway hair. Too bad he didn't have freckles. That would have been icing on the cake. Moving behind Mrs. Eddington, making small talk about the Science Fair, he had slipped the length of duct tape over her head and tightly around her throat, slapping the ends onto the back of her chair. Her hands had jumped to her throat, just as he predicted. He had come prepared with several lengths of tape stuck loosely inside his jacket. He had to move fast. He knew he had only a few seconds before she recovered enough to angrily unpeel the tape. He dove for the floor and fastened a piece around each ankle, anchoring her to the chair. She started screaming, but the door was closed and the music program in the gym was gearing up. The next piece of tape went across her mouth. Not only did that shut her up, but it increased her panic, which played right into his hands. Hands. Her hands were the most difficult to deal with. That was the tricky part. Unfortunately, adults were stronger than he was. He had anticipated that, and brought out the hacksaw . . .

CHAMELEON

Shirley Kennett

Pinnacle Books
Kensington Publishing Corp.

http://www.pinnaclebooks.com

PINNACLE BOOKS are published by

Kensington Publishing Corp.
850 Third Avenue
New York, NY 10022

Pinnacle and the P logo Reg. U.S. Pat. & TM Off.

First Kensington Hardcover Printing: November, 1998
First Pinnacle Printing: June, 1999
10 9 8 7 6 5 4 3 2 1

Printed in the United States of America

CHAPTER

1

Columbus Wade was on his hands and knees rummaging in the kitchen cabinet, the one with all the glass bowls in it. He was sure he had seen a gallon jar on his scouting mission the day before. There it was, and now the problem was to get it upstairs without Nanny noticing. He extracted the jar as quietly as he could, his small fingers grasping the screw-on lid because his hands couldn't span the entire jar, but it clinked against the lemonade pitcher.

"Columbus, what are you doing in there?" came Nanny's voice from the living room. She had shut off the volume on the TV. How she heard that tiny clink over the talk, talk, talk of the TV was beyond his understanding. But it was as predictable as Pop having two eggs for breakfast.

"Nothing, Nanny," he answered, keeping the hated quivers from his voice.

"Is that a good nothing or a bad nothing?"

"Just nothing," he said.

He eased the gallon jar back into the cabinet in case she didn't go for it. A long moment passed in silence. He knew Nanny was considering whether it was worthwhile getting up, which meant putting aside her lap table with its diet root beer and magazines with fancy cupcakes on the front, pushing down the foot support of her recliner, and probably getting the shoes she had kicked off her swollen feet caught in the foot support. Then she would sit there getting red-faced, unable to get her feet down, and would finally call Columbus to pull out her stuck shoes. In the meantime she would have missed the last round of her quiz show.

The TV talk started up again, and Columbus thought it was certainly good to be five years old. Last year Nanny would have come in to check on him. Now she gave him just that little edge of independence—after all, he would be in school next fall—and he took full advantage of it. He was better at things, too. He had waited until her favorite show was on to make his trip, and his timing had paid off.

Upstairs, he eagerly carried the gallon jar to the hall bathroom to fill it with water. The jar wouldn't fit upright in the shallow sink, so he could only run the water into it partway. He dried off the outside so it wouldn't be slippery—a lesson learned on a previous ill-fated mission when he had been a baby of four—and carried the jug to his room. He had cleared a spot on his dresser for it. He made several trips to the bathroom, bringing a glass of water each time, until the jug was full to the very top.

Columbus walked over to the window. There was a strong glare from the sun shining on the snow outside, but his eyes adjusted as he looked out at the front yard. It had snowed yesterday, halfway up to his knees, and Pop grumbled about shoveling the sidewalk one last time. It was almost the end of March, and apparently it wasn't supposed to snow in Nashville in March, at least not this much. Nanny just shook her head and said "In like a lamb, out like a lion," which Columbus didn't understand at all. But she helped him put on his boots, coat, hat, and gloves, and watched him through the window of the front parlor as he built a snowman. Columbus reveled in that creative act, adding a lump of snow here, chopping off a bulge there. He modeled its face after Nanny's, framed in the steamy warmth. When he came in, she stripped off the wet snow clothes and hustled him into the kitchen for hot chocolate. It wasn't just the bite of the wind that reddened his cheeks. For a time he had held sway over the snow, molding it to his will, knocking it down at his whim, bringing into being and destroying.

The sun had done its work on the yard. The grass was showing in places, and he could see the crocuses along the front walkway, purple spikes pushing up through the white. Water gurgled in the down spouts, washing out all the itsy bitsy spiders, if there were any in March. His snowman had gotten smaller, and it was tilted. Soon it would fall on its carrot nose, which was short and thick like Nanny's.

The sun had power. Columbus wanted power, too.

In the corner of his room under the window there was an elaborate habitat for his pet mouse Robert. Robert had tunnels and wheels and a hiding place shaped like a cave. Columbus lifted the lid of the habitat and looked for the white mouse, which had retreated to its plastic cave as soon as the lid was raised. He removed the shelter, revealing the mouse, with nowhere to hide, huddled in its bedding. Closing his hand over the mouse, Columbus felt the small heat of its body, and the shaking of its fear. A thrill of anticipation tiptoed up his spine.

He didn't know the jar would overflow when he put

Robert in, lowering it by its tail. He screwed the lid on tight, and then went to the bathroom for a washcloth to wipe up the spill.

He looked over the railing, down into the living room, to make sure Nanny was still watching TV. She didn't know what he was doing. Probably she wouldn't like it. Maybe she would make him stop. Columbus suspected that he wasn't supposed to play with his pets like that.

It was a good thing Nanny's favorite program was on.

He pulled a stool over to the dresser and sat down to watch as the mouse swam round and round. In a disappointingly short time, the exhausted animal sank below the water.

"Good-bye, Robert," Columbus whispered. There was no sadness in him.

At any time before Robert sank, Columbus could have taken the lid off, pulled the mouse out, and put it back in its habitat to lick itself dry. He had done that several times already, using a bowl he found underneath the bathroom sink. That had gotten boring. Always there was the need to take things further, to learn more, to experience more, to see if new sensations would trigger the emotions that should have been there and weren't.

Columbus learned that his mouse couldn't live in water, and before that, that his shiny goldfish couldn't live in air. Most importantly, he learned that he had power over their small lives.

He pulled the wet body from the jar and dried it as well as he could with the washcloth he had taken from the bathroom. He put the dead mouse back in the habitat and covered it with the plastic cave so that it was out of sight. No one tended the mouse except him, so no one would notice. Tomorrow he would "discover" the body, dry and curled inside its shelter. No one—Mom, Pop, or Nanny—

would question the death. Mice died all the time. That was, after all, part of the mystery he wanted to understand, and to control.

Even though he felt no grief, he would produce a few tears. It was expected at moments like that, and he was getting better at mimicking the emotional responses of people around him. He had seen a science program about reptiles, and thought of himself as a chameleon that changes color depending upon events or surroundings.

Mom and Pop would console him and offer him a new pet.

He slid his latest video into the slot and settled back to watch. Snack time would be coming up soon. As the cartoon images moved across the screen, he replayed in his mind Robert's last fierce struggle to live.

Where would his curiosity take him next?

At the age of twelve, Columbus Wade still spent a lot of time with his bedroom door closed.

But on this particular Thursday night during his school's spring break, he was out on his bike, pedaling casually toward the school, hoping that he wouldn't encounter a patrol car along the few blocks to his destination. Fortunately, the five inches of snow that had fallen a few days ago had succumbed to plows and milder temperatures. The streets were clear and dry, but remnants of dirty gray snow clung to the curbs like hair fringing the head of a bum. There was a full moon, and its light cast shadows of tree branches onto the street, spread out in front of him, grasping arms that he eluded as he pedaled faster.

Strapped onto the luggage rack of his bike was a small cooler. He had lined the inside of it with thick foam padding salvaged from the school's Dumpster. The night was chilly and there was a strong March wind, but he had worn a jacket. He hated physical discomfort and always avoided it by careful planning.

When he rode into the front parking lot of Deaver Junior High, there wasn't a car in sight. The lot was deserted, as Columbus had anticipated. Just as he was getting off his bike, a car roared down the street, high-schoolers whooping through the open windows. It was an unwelcome intrusion, although he was fairly sure they hadn't seen him in the shadows near the front of the building. The moonlight was bright enough to guide him, but not so bright that he couldn't conceal himself when needed. He pushed his bike behind the bushes near the front entrance. In the rear, soccer goal nets were orange-lit by the building's security lighting, and beyond them he could make out the softball backstops. He walked around to the delivery door, where he had ensured the security light was not working. He knew that the door didn't fit well in its frame, and that the lock was old and ineffective. If he jostled it just right, he could spring the lock and gain entrance to the building.

Once inside, he waited near the door for a couple of minutes, resting the cooler and his backpack on the floor and taking slow, deep breaths through his nose.

Project Brimstone was under way, and the outlook was promising.

He made his way through the darkened halls toward the science lab. EXIT signs glowed with a brilliance not apparent during the day, and there were dim lights at each corner and every twenty feet or so of the hallway.

The hammer and chisel from his backpack took care of the puny padlock on the chemicals locker in the lab. He wasn't worried about leaving his fingerprints; as one of the lab monitors, his prints were all over the locker anyway. The ceiling panel light right over the locker was turned on, so he had enough illumination to work. He reached for the heavy glass jar of acid, with its label that said H_2SO_4 and had a black skull-and-crossbones on it. It was toward the back of the locker, since it was used only for demonstrations by the science teacher, and not by the students. The sulfuric acid would provide an added dimension to his experimentation with cockroaches. He had a science paper due in a week, and he had chosen as his subject the ability of the hardy insects to survive environmental stresses. Columbus didn't believe in passive learning. He conducted his own research wherever possible, even if most of it had to be kept to himself.

He pressed the stem of his Indiglo watch and noted that it was 11:15 P.M. Mom and Pop, or the Cow and the Turd as he now called them, wouldn't be home from their weekly bridge game for another two hours. He had plenty of time.

He had brought duct tape in his backpack to wrap tightly around the ground glass stopper so it wouldn't work loose in the padded cooler on the way home. He set the jar on a counter next to the hammer and chisel, and dug into his backpack for the tape.

"What are you doing, Columbus?"

The voice lashed at him from the darkened doorway of the lab. He straightened up abruptly, backpack forgotten. As he twisted to see who had caught him, his elbow sent the jar of acid flying. It landed with a crash that echoed in the hallways.

A man stepped forward, into the light where Columbus could recognize him. It was Ed Mitchell, one of the teachers at the school. Thoughts raced through Columbus's mind, colliding with each other and leaving him dumbfounded.

"I'm surprised, Columbus. You know chemicals don't leave this room. You should have talked this over with Mrs.

Garfield, and maybe you could have done whatever it is you're trying to do under her supervision.''

Mitchell was calm but very stern. Columbus had never heard him use such a tone of voice. It snapped Columbus back into cunning mode, and he began to get angry. After all, he was certain that Mrs. Garfield would not have approved of the use he intended to make of the acid.

"I'm sorry, Mr. Mitchell," Columbus said. It was hard to keep his voice sounding humble, because he was seething as he thought of the trouble the man would make for him. Project Brimstone was rapidly heading into the toilet, and he'd have to do his science paper on acorns or something.

"Now we've got quite a mess to clean up," Mitchell said as he approached the lab counter. "Help me get out the kitty litter."

Mitchell bent and reached for the cabinet door near Columbus's legs. Inside was a tub of kitty litter, the first line of defense against spills in the lab, something to keep the problem from spreading until it could be dealt with properly.

Somehow the hammer jumped from the counter into Columbus's right hand, and he swung it at the back of Mitchell's head as the man was bent over. Mitchell didn't go down immediately, as Columbus had hoped. Instead, he grunted and fell heavily to his knees, reaching out for Columbus's legs. Columbus almost panicked and dropped the hammer. But he held on, and gave the man a satisfying whump above the ear. Then it was just a matter of swinging again and again, until his shoulders hurt.

CHAPTER

2

Penelope Jennifer Gray mentally crossed her fingers and struck the last match. It flared, and she closed the few inches between it and the corner of newspaper she was trying to light. The wind immediately snuffed the tentative flame out. PJ closed her eyes tightly against both the wind and her misfortune, squeezing tears of exasperation from the corners.

It was the last night of PJ's vacation with her son Thomas. They were staying at a rustic cabin in Big Springs State Park in southern Missouri. Part of the National Scenic Riverways, Big Springs certainly lived up to its name: the park contained a stream that gushed millions of gallons of water a day from a modest-looking cleft at the base of a hill.

PJ and Thomas had gone to the site of the park's namesake soon after their arrival. It was only March, so the flow hadn't reached its late-spring peak yet, but it was still impressive. Where the water rushed from the hillside, its motion was enough to keep ice from forming. Water vapor rose into the chilly air and condensed on their hair and eyelashes. Ferns on the shaded hillside above the spring were lush and green, even that early in the year. The air was heavy with moisture, so heavy that droplets condensed on anything or anyone that held still more than a moment. Moss-covered rocks were washed constantly with the turbulent water of the spring, trapping bubbles of air in the green mats as they were lashed back and forth. Farther downstream, a thin layer of ice remained on the surface while the water moved rapidly underneath.

PJ had been energized by the place and could have stayed all day listening to the water tumbling over the rocks. Thomas had reacted very differently. He couldn't seem to stay near the spring, and could offer no explanation beyond not liking the sound, which he described as a roaring that drowned out his thoughts. He stayed as far away from the spring as he could get, preferring to hike the park's wooded hills instead. So they rose early, dressed warmly, and walked on the trails while the ground was still frozen.

The forest was beginning to awaken from winter. Leaf buds were swollen and small green plants nudged aside last fall's leaf drop as they pushed their way up to the sunshine. Squirrels dug and chattered, chickadees called to each other, and woodpeckers rapped out their staccato searches for lunch under the bark of trees. The sky was a deep, brilliant blue, and the sun warmed their shoulders through the leafless tree branches.

In the afternoon, when the forty-degree warmth thawed the frozen ground and the trails became slippery and unpleasant, they either went back to their cabin to read and relax, or explored the nearby town of Van Buren, where they browsed in small stores with dusty postcard racks and salt and pepper shakers shaped like corn on the cob or a gold prospector and his mule. In the evenings, they ate whole fried catfish in a restaurant overlooking the stream.

At the beginning of the week, PJ felt tension drain from her as though she had gathered it from all parts of her body and set it adrift on a log in the stream. Her job as head of the Computerized Homicide Investigations Project (CHIP) with the St. Louis Police Department had been a challenge from the start. Under the skeptical gaze of Detective Leo Schultz, the experienced detective assigned to CHIP, she had demonstrated that she had the right stuff for the job, surprising not only Schultz but herself as well.

The past week, when Thomas was out of school on spring break, had been their first opportunity to get away since the move to St. Louis from Denver. Thomas had lobbied for a trip to Disney World or the Grand Canyon, but PJ had taken a cut in pay from her previous work in consumer behavioral modeling. Money was tight, as in most single-parent households, and Thomas knew his suggestion was doomed from the start. PJ had gathered information on driving vacations within Missouri, and settled on Big Springs because a picture in the brochure of a cabin with smoke coming out of the chimney reminded her of Rocky Mountain scenery outside of Denver. The cabin had turned out to be delightful, with rough-hewn pine furniture, a huge stone fireplace, open beams in a high ceiling, and a toilet that actually worked, as long as the handle was held down a long time.

The weather in the first part of the week had been glorious, which had been particularly satisfying because PJ had heard that St. Louis had gotten a few inches of snow. It had rained the past couple of days, turning the trails impassable and the town dreary. PJ and Thomas had spent a lot of time in the cabin, and they both felt like two cats rubbing up against each other and getting a static electricity shock. Words were said that shouldn't have been, and PJ wanted to end the vacation on a positive note. She decided a cookout was the perfect thing. She dragged Thomas, sullen and sodden, to a grocery store in town, and bought hot dogs, buns, and marshmallows. By evening the rain had stopped. There was dry firewood in the cabin's enclosed porch, but PJ had neglected to bring in any kindling earlier in the week.

Undaunted, at dusk PJ scraped the wet ashes from the outdoor cooking grill that stood next to the cabin. Having no kindling, she crumpled newspapers and set a full-size fireplace log on top. Her hopes were beaten down as match after match expired in the brisk wind. Even if she had gotten the newspapers to burn, the likelihood of the log catching fire was slim. She wiped her face and stuck her hands into the pockets of her jacket. It looked as though the two of them would be spending their last evening sniping at each other over cold lunch meat sandwiches and untoasted marshmallows.

A pickup truck came down the narrow, winding road that served the cabins and stopped in front of hers. She was familiar with the truck; it belonged to Ellen and Roger Brenner, who managed the cabins. The window on the passenger side rolled down, and in the gathering dark, PJ could barely make out Ellen's rotund face.

"Having trouble with your cooking fire?" Ellen said, with that lilt of hers that took the sting out, so that her words didn't sound like the bald statement of PJ's incompetence that it was.

There was no point in trying to cover up her predicament. "I don't have any dry kindling, and I've run out of matches."

"We figured you might have some problems. Muriel down at the store said you bought hot dogs. We thought we'd just check and make sure you got a good hot fire going. Hot dogs don't do a body good when they're cold." Her face disappeared from the window opening as she turned away to speak to her husband.

"Roger'll be right down to get you started."

PJ was aware that Thomas had come out onto the porch of the cabin and was watching the proceedings. Roger got out of the pickup, opened a box in the truck bed, and rummaged around a minute or two. Then he walked over to PJ, carrying a bundle of dry kindling. He nodded to her. She hadn't heard Roger speak in the week they'd been at the cabin. Apparently Ellen wore the voice in the family.

Roger pulled the log out of the grill and recrinkled the newspaper to his satisfaction. He built a neat pyramid of kindling on top of the newspaper, and then pulled a butane fireplace lighter from his pocket. A flick of his thumb produced a flame two inches long that laughed at the wind and eagerly accepted the offering of paper to burn. The dry kindling flared up quickly. Roger went to the porch and poked through the firewood there, rejecting pieces for no reason apparent to PJ. He returned with three small split logs, which he balanced on top of the kindling. He and PJ watched silently as the logs caught fire. Roger put the fireplace lighter on the picnic table and went back to the truck. He was back a minute later with two long metal cooking forks. PJ felt her cheeks redden, and was glad it was almost dark. If she had gotten the fire going, she and Thomas would have had to scrounge in the dark woods around the cabin for pointed sticks to impale the food.

"Just leave the supplies in the cabin when you're done," Ellen said from the passenger seat. The truck rumbled down the road, presumably to check on the occupants of the only other cabin that was rented that week, which was about a quarter mile down the road. PJ wondered if they had bought hot dogs, too.

Thomas came out and stood next to her. She expected him to gloat about the fire and the cooking forks, but he didn't say a word. He was close enough to touch, so she put her arm around his waist and drew him in. The long bones in his legs and arms were beginning their pubescent growth, leaving the muscular development behind so that he appeared to be limbs attached to a rib cage. Two months from his thirteenth birthday, he was as tall as she was, and he rested his head lightly on her shoulder. She remembered the way things were when she was thirteen. She and her mother had been at odds over everything from chores to clothes to which movies she could see, and her father just sat there, silently and infuriatingly supporting Mom. Since she was a single parent, she knew she was going to carry the load of Thomas's teenage angst. But for this one moment she could feel her son's burgeoning life wrapped around her as though the umbilical cord still ran between them.

A phone ringing in the cabin made PJ pull away. She had brought along her cellular phone, but it had been silent all week. As she went to answer it, she found herself hoping that Bill Lakeland would be on the other end. Bill was the father of Thomas's best friend Winston. She and Bill had recently begun having a weekly telephone chat, mostly about the kids. Bill's voice was warm and self-confident, and she felt that he was a man she could trust with her emotions—a safe haven.

She moved the hair out of her face as she reached for

the phone, pushing the long strands behind her ears, and noticed that she had brought the wood fire smell in with her, in her hair and clothing.

"PJ here."

"Hi, Doc. Got some news for you."

"Oh, it's you." It was Schultz, and news he called about was rarely good. Belatedly she realized that he had heard the disappointment in her voice, and would put his own spin on it.

"You really know how to make a guy feel appreciated," Schultz said. "Especially a guy who's been taking care of your cat while you're out playing pioneer woman. Did you know that critter gets right up on the table?"

"Come on, Leo, I thought you liked cats."

"Let's just say that of all the animals commonly kept as pets, I dislike cats the least. So tell, you waiting for Lover-boy to call?"

"I wish you'd stop referring to any male friend of mine, yourself excluded, as Lover-boy," PJ snapped.

"Christ. Don't get your ass in an uproar. Don't you even want to know why I called?"

She realized that she had been using her voice like a rolled-up wet washcloth, flicking it at him, wanting to hear the "ouch" on the other end. Taking a couple of deep breaths, PJ was silent, waiting him out.

"The news is that somebody killed a teacher at your son's school," Schultz said. "Name of Edward T. Mitchell."

"Ed Mitchell's dead?" PJ had met him at a PTO potluck dinner, and liked him. He seemed to genuinely care about his charges, and often could be found at after-school activities or volunteering in the one-on-one mentoring program the school had started this year.

"Give the woman a medal. She can talk and hold the phone at the same time."

"Could you be serious for just a moment? How was he killed?"

"Struck with a blunt instrument. ME hasn't said yet, but my guess is man's favorite tool."

"Say again?"

"Christ. Women. A hammer. Man's favorite tool."

"Oh. I would have thought . . . Never mind."

"He was hit a lot more times than necessary to do the job. The janitor found him this morning in the science lab. It looks as though he interrupted someone trying to steal chemicals."

"How terrible." She closed her eyes for a moment, picturing the scene that the janitor had walked in upon. "Why was Mitchell in the building during spring break?"

"Principal says he was working on some new pilot reading program. He had put in a lot of his own time on it."

"That sounds like the Ed Mitchell I knew. I don't think Thomas was in any of his classes this semester, but all the kids knew Ed. Does CHIP have the case?" If so, PJ would have to drive back to St. Louis that night.

"Nope. Barnesworth drew the short straw. He was first at the scene. The chief and Wall think he can handle it. Can you imagine that? Picture Barnesworth interviewing those lady teachers. They'll clam up the first time he says fuck or tries to spit and misses, and ends up with a gob on his shirt."

"Please. I haven't eaten dinner yet," PJ said.

"Anyway, the school's calling in some counselors to help the kids deal with it when they go back to school Monday. I'm sure Thomas will be hearing a lot more about it. Probably know more about the case than Barnesworth by Monday afternoon."

PJ sighed. "Well, keep me informed."

"Sure thing, Doc. So, how are you and the kid doing?

You had a weenie roast yet? Kids like that outdoorsy shit. Me, I'd rather get a burger at Millie's and rent a couple of shoot-'em-ups."

"We're doing fine. We're just about to have a cookout." PJ hoped that he couldn't hear the strain in her voice.

"Burn a marshmallow for me, Doc. See you Monday."

After Schultz hung up the phone, he sat back in his chair and folded his arms across his chest. While his boss vacationed someplace in southern Missouri where hush puppies weren't shoes, Schultz was reviewing old unsolved case files, supposedly determining if any were relevant to CHIP. In the absence of a current investigation, it was either case review or compiling crime statistics. At least when he was doing case review, there was always the chance that a fresh viewpoint on an old case would yield results. The promise of field work was the reason Schultz had joined CHIP in the first place, in spite of his misgivings about working for a woman with no law-enforcement experience. He was leery of the computer aspect of the assignment, too. In the nine months he had been involved with the project, both the woman and the computer had begun to prove their worth. Not that he would admit either, unless both hands and both feet were pinned to the wall. Perhaps not even then.

He tried to focus on the folders, but the commotion going on around him was a distraction. After thirty-three years with the St. Louis Police Department, Schultz didn't have a private office, just a desk in a communal work area. Detective Larry Barnesworth, he of the foul mouth and mind, was uncharacteristically working after five P.M., and had been on the phone for the last hour. He was making call after call to his bevy of informants, trying to find out if there was any meaningful street talk about Ed Mitchell's murder. He sounded so oily on the phone that Schultz thought it was a wonder he didn't slide out of his seat.

Schultz also had a low opinion of conducting an investigation with your posterior planted in a chair. Most of the informants Schultz used didn't have phones anyway. If he wanted to talk with them, he had to search them out in bars, flophouses, or lockups.

Barnesworth had half a dozen assistants working with him on the Mitchell case. It was poor publicity for the city to have the kids slipping around on a teacher's blood in school, so the chief had thrown a lot of warm bodies at the case. Every last one of them was gathered in the same room with Schultz, talking, flipping through notes, slamming desk drawers, and generally acting like lemmings waiting to be led off the cliff. Disgusted at the sight, Schultz gathered the folders spread across his desk, bundled them under his arm, and left.

Under most conditions, he could ignore the hubbub and focus intently, at a wordless level, with images flashing one after the other on the screen behind his eyes. Sitting next to Barnesworth was one of the handful of circumstances under which Schultz couldn't concentrate. The others all had to do with his richly textured fantasies, which featured a rotating harem of sexy women.

He went to PJ's office to work. He closed the door of her small office, even though there wasn't much traffic in the hallway to disturb him. The place had been a utility room before PJ was hired. The only thing that still showed the room's heritage was the stained linoleum floor. PJ had painted the walls and put up nature prints. Her choice of decor was anything but relaxing to Schultz. Wild cats eyed him from all parts of the room.

Windowless, off the beaten path of the heating and air-conditioning systems, and directly across the hall from the men's room, PJ's office wasn't exactly a choice location in the Headquarters Building, but Schultz wished it was his.

He opened the folder on a murder case that was almost exactly a year old and spread the contents over PJ's desk. It annoyed him that the chair was set so low—PJ was a shorter than average woman—but he knew better than to tamper with it. Feeling what his mother would have described as nettled, he turned PJ's Mickey Mouse clock around so he wouldn't have to glance at its cheerful face.

As he considered the photos of the late Patrick Washburn, he saw a man physically very like himself: balding, formerly fit but carrying an extra forty pounds that softened all the hard edges, except for the ones on his personality. He noted that the deceased was fifty-four at the time of death, the same age as Schultz was now. Washburn was a widower, not divorced as Schultz was. Washburn's wife, Janice, had died ten years ago in the crash of a small airplane that had been ferrying her and a group of other women with too much time on their hands to Las Vegas for the weekend.

The man in the photos wore custom-made clothing that fitted his position as proprietor of an exclusive art gallery as well as it fitted his generous shape. The suit jacket had been draped across the back of a chair, the tie removed, and the shirt collar unbuttoned, all indicative of a man working late, alone in his office. Papers on his desk showed that he had been working on the gallery's business receipts, a fact confirmed by Washburn's accountant, who said that Washburn turned over the receipts every year by March 5 in preparation for filing tax forms in April.

Washburn had been found in the rear office of the gallery, shot in the back. The shot had not been immediately fatal, and he had crawled several feet toward his desk, where there was a telephone to call for help if necessary. The phone cord had been unplugged from both the wall outlet and the phone base, and was missing from the scene, evidently taken by the killer. Also taken was over two million dollars worth of paintings. The body had been discovered by the gallery's manager, Rebecca Singer, when she came to work the morning of March 3. Singer had been surprised to find that the gallery's sophisticated security system was turned off when she arrived. She was even more surprised by what she found in her boss's office. At least, according to her story.

Washburn had two sons. The younger of them, Henry, had been the pilot of the plane taking the group of women to Las Vegas. He was left incapacitated by the crash which killed his mother, and was in a treatment facility with no hope of recovery short of a miracle. As a suspect, he was pretty low on Schultz's list.

The other son, James, had such an aura of suspicion about him that he reminded Schultz of that character from the L'il Abner comic strip who always walked around with a thunderstorm above his head. From the interviews with Singer and others who knew the family, it was clear that James must have been a disappointment to his father. Washburn had assumed that James would carry on the family business, but James was drawn more to the ladies than to art. He was also a spendthrift who had gotten into minor trouble with the law over bad checks written to cover impulse purchases. But passing bad checks was a long way from murder.

It all boiled down to the reason for the shooting. Was Washburn killed by a thief whose goal was to steal the paintings, or was the theft a cover-up for an intentional murder?

If the reason was theft, there was little chance that the

case would be solved. There was no physical evidence at the scene, and the only apparent witness was dead. The stolen paintings would have been in the hands of a knowledgeable fence for months, and would surface in the international black market years from now, if at all. They could already be in a private collection. The percentage of solution of such crimes was small, and Schultz knew that the insurance company's investigator realistically stood a much better chance of tracking down the paintings than he did.

If the real reason was the murder of Washburn, then Schultz was in familiar territory. One tantalizing fact pointed in that direction: the alarm system appeared to have been deactivated from inside the gallery. According to Singer's story, when she left at a few minutes after five P.M., there were no customers in the gallery. Washburn had walked her to the door and then turned on the alarm right after she left, as was his practice when working alone in the building after hours. If her story was true, then Washburn himself must have turned off the alarm later that evening to admit his killer.

Who would Washburn let into the gallery under those circumstances? His trusted assistant Singer, certainly. His son James, probably. A known customer who requested a private showing, which Singer claimed was not unusual. A lover. Possibly a person with law-enforcement identification.

Schultz scribbled four words on a notepad: revenge, love, power, money. Just the basics, the reasons cops learned to look for in homicide cases, with the exception of those committed by psychopaths, who danced to their own internal rhythms.

Apparently Washburn had been scrupulously honest with his family, his customers and employees, and even, according to the accountant, with the IRS. If there was a motive for revenge, it would have to be something from Washburn's distant past, not his recent dealings.

Love? Washburn was a man who wouldn't let go of the memory of his wife. If there was a jilted lover or a cuckolded husband on the scene, it wasn't obvious. Schultz considered Rebecca Singer, who had worked closely with the man for years. She was thirty-nine years old, divorced many years ago, freeing herself from a teenage marriage. There seemed to be no love interest in her life, but perhaps there was love that wasn't returned. Could she have been the person Washburn let into the gallery that night? He tried to picture Singer shooting the man she loved in the back and then yanking the phone cord out of the wall as he crawled toward the desk. PJ would pounce on him for sexist thinking, but he just couldn't see Singer doing that.

On the other hand, love and hate had a lot in common besides being four-letter words, and flipping from one to the other was plausible.

Power as a motive didn't gel. There was a certain amount of prestige involved in owning the gallery, but if power was involved, it would have to be on an intimate basis: power over an individual's life. One of Washburn's sons was oblivious to power, at least of an earthly nature, and the other son hadn't been under Daddy's thumb. James's lifestyle clearly showed that he was left alone to pursue whatever he wished.

He wondered what Rebecca Singer and James Washburn were doing a year after the killing. He felt this was a case that could benefit from a second look. If he stretched things a bit, he could even claim that CHIP should be involved to re-create the crime a year after the fact. He rationalized that his reasons were objective, and not at all related to the fact that the victim looked like himself.

He spun around in PJ's chair, trying to find something

to focus his gaze on besides the eyes of the big cats in her nature prints. He ended up staring at her computer screen, which had multi-colored dots moving rapidly in spirals.

Trace the money, then. Schultz closed his eyes, took a deep breath, and decided to follow his nose. So often, easy wealth smelled of arrogance and blood.

CHAPTER

3

The killing had been clumsy and bloody, like a lion cub taking its first prey.

Columbus hid his clothes and sneakers, and the hammer, in his room until the next day, when his parents were at work. Then he took a long bike ride to a vacant lot where homeless people sometimes built cooking fires. He built a small fire with a can of Sterno and some wet tree branches that sizzled in protest. He burned his clothes, mixing the ashes in with those of other recent fires. The sneakers, with bloody soles and a couple of holes burned by splashed acid, went into a trash bin in the back of a grocery store, buried under rotting produce. He didn't think they would burn completely. When it came to getting rid of the hammer, Columbus found that he couldn't part with it. He knew he shouldn't keep it. He'd seen enough cop shows on TV. He took it back home and put it in an old toy chest in his closet, among the stuffed animals and outgrown action figures.

Since it was spring break at the school, he wasn't sure when the body would be discovered. It turned out he had to wait until Sunday evening, when every news station in the city carried the story. Each station implied that their reporters had been first on the scene, and probably had actually been there when the murder was committed but weren't at liberty to admit it.

It was thrilling to see the news on the set in his room, and then listen to the Cow and the Turd rant about how terrible it was and how they hoped the killer would be caught right away. That was when it really sank in. Columbus had taken a life, not a small insignificant life, but a human life, and gotten away with it. There weren't any cops knocking on his door, and there wouldn't be. Who would suspect a twelve-year-old honor student? There was speculation on TV that the teacher was involved in drug dealing and had stiffed someone important. It didn't matter that anyone who knew Mr. Mitchell wouldn't believe that for a second. The reporters latched on to it, and the story grew from one telling to the next. That would make a good journal entry later, when he wrote down the events of the day. Many ironies were recorded in his journal, which he had kept for the last year, putting down in precise cursive the most important occurrence of each day.

The journal was a daily diary that the Cow had given him for his last birthday. It was apparent to him that she wished he was a girl, since it wasn't the type of present usually given to sons. He had set it aside in favor of the new computer games he also got as presents. But a few weeks later, he had come across the diary on his cluttered desktop and, as a whim, made a sarcastic entry in it. He had written in it again the next day, although he couldn't say why, and since then it had become a habit. He had dignified it by calling it a journal instead of a diary. He would never admit to enjoying it, at least not in the same way he enjoyed having control over the things around him.

Columbus had attained a new level of power, he was certain of that. He could play with people's lives and no one would stop him. Could stop him.

His parents didn't even catch on that it was Columbus's school that was involved. Columbus wasn't sure they even knew the name of his school.

Since the move to St. Louis two years ago, Norm and Vicky Wade rarely saw their son. The move was tied to a major career step for Norm. They chose a pretentious three-story home in south St. Louis, fully rehabbed with all the amenities. Nanny had been left behind in Nashville, and Columbus was deemed responsible enough to stay by himself after school. When there weren't any bad repercussions from that, he was allowed to stay home during summer vacation. It wasn't the money. The Wades didn't scrimp where their son was concerned; it was simply the path of least involvement.

Columbus lived physically on the third floor of his parents' home on Magnolia Boulevard, which had originally been the maid's quarters, but he spent his time in virtual reality worlds he designed. Specialized programs on his computer, which was a far more powerful model than the first one he had gotten seven years ago, allowed him to set up three-dimensional environments which he could "walk" through by clicking on different parts of the screen. He didn't have a head-mounted display, or HMD, which would have projected a pair of screens a few inches from his eyes. The screens blocked out all other visual input and gave the wearer the sensation that he was actually in the scene. Columbus wanted a real HMD, but didn't know how to go about getting one. Even his parents, who were liberal with money and asked few questions, would balk at the cost of a good setup, which was about the same as their latest sports utility vehicle.

His first effort at virtual reality was modeled after a wax museum he had gone through, eyes wide at the sensational and gory exhibits. His effort wasn't very good, but it did re-create the feel of the place, and he spent many hours visiting its displays even though they were only three inches high on the screen. When he was in a simulation, he didn't have to deal with his parents. He didn't have to deal with emotions, which was good because it required such effort on his part to analyze the situation and pick an appropriate response from his repertoire.

Eventually he set aside the wax museum simulation. It seemed rather childish, and Columbus didn't like thinking of himself as a child.

Last September, at the start of the first semester of seventh grade, Columbus had gotten involved in role-playing games. There was a group that met at the house of a kid down the block after school. The group, five boys and one girl, would play Magic or Dungeons and Dragons, taking the parts of fantasy characters and playing out adventures. At first Columbus was intrigued with the colorful playing cards and the pewter game pieces styled as wizards, fanciful beasts, or warriors. After some intensive sessions over Christmas vacation, when the participants barely surfaced long enough to scarf down the snowman cookies provided by the host's mother, Columbus wearied of the games. Too tame. Too much fantasy and not enough reality.

He broke from the group and began playing graphic computer games instead. Cop shootouts, martial arts battles, alien invasions, everything he could get his hands on that had blood and guts. The Cow and the Turd were oblivious to all, simply giving him money for the games, which apparently they envisioned as Pong and Pac Man.

It wasn't long before the violent games lost their appeal, too. One afternoon, while casually ripping the head off a creature he had backed into a blind alley on his computer screen, Columbus imagined that the creature was Mrs. Barry, the principal of his school. She had hassled him that day for being out in the hall after the late bell.

Much better.

Blood gushed from Mrs. Barry's torso as he held her severed head aloft, and satisfaction coursed hotly through Columbus as he gave the ruined body a disdainful kick.

He was definitely on to something.

Ignoring his science homework, which was usually his favorite, he resurrected the wax museum and modified it. A few hours later, he had a passable simulation of Deaver Junior High, complete with classrooms, cafeteria, gym, and playing fields.

By midnight, after he pretended to go to sleep, he had figured out how he could populate the school with real people. He had gotten a scanner as a Christmas present, a high-profit item suggested by the clerk at the computer store when the Cow went shopping. It was still in the box, buried in his closet under an avalanche of clothes, odds and ends of computer equipment, and used paper plates and plastic forks from the times when he was able to avoid eating dinner with his parents.

The photos came from the school yearbook he checked out of the library the next day. It was last year's, since the new books didn't come out until April. No matter. A few teachers had left, but the majority were there, grinning insipidly at him in black and white. When he got the photos scanned in and crudely pasted over the heads of his standard simulation characters, the results weren't great. The heads looked glued on and weren't responsive to subtle movements. In fact, they sometimes became detached and floated around the classroom like benevolent balloons, smiling down on the students. But the whole effect was good enough, as long as he used his ample imagination.

It had taken him two whole weeks to develop a custom subroutine to handle the blood spatters.

Besides the school, he created other real-life scenarios. The grocery store. The movie theater. The mall. It became a game to collect photos of people he could put into the mini-worlds. Newspapers were handy, especially neighborhood journals which relied on large, grainy photos to fill the space in their columns.

Once he had a photo, he owned the person.

The VR worlds Columbus created were immensely satisfying to him because he could do whatever he wanted to do with no consequences. He could even kill the simulated people who inhabited his worlds. If a teacher gave him a bad time, or a fellow student criticized him, Columbus would play out the scene again that very night. It would have a different ending, though. He had tied Mr. Gregor, the P.E. teacher, to a soccer goal and bombarded him with soccer balls, then with hockey pucks, then with circular saw blades flipped like Frisbees. Harry Trent was an obnoxious lump of an eighth grader who always called him Brain. Harry got suspended upside-down above a toilet and dunked repeatedly, ruining his great hair, until Columbus got tired of playing with him and just kept his head underwater a little too long. Then there was Patty Remen, rhymes with semen, who had teased him in front of a group of girls when he came out of the john one time with his zipper down. She got the dissection table in the biology lab.

With the killing of Mr. Mitchell at the school, Columbus

had crossed the line, carrying his murderous inclinations into reality. He had as much power in the real world as he did in his virtual ones.

Sunday night, after hearing the news broadcast, he spent a lot of time in his VR school. He reenacted the experience over and over, breaking in through the delivery door, navigating the hallways, lifting out the heavy bottle, swinging the hammer. He chuckled when he thought that, sooner or later, every kid has a fantasy of wiping out a teacher. But the other kids were satisfied with those wimpy computer programs where someone else, the creator of the program, called the shots. Columbus would never go back to that. He had to be in charge. The power was his, and it felt good to wield it.

He hadn't actually hated Mitchell. The man just got in the way. On the other hand, there was Mrs. Eddington, the science teacher he had last semester, the one who played favorites in class, and he wasn't one of the favorites. He remembered exactly who they were, too. That Gray kid and the nerd he hung around with, the one with the name that sounded like cigarettes.

Columbus needed photos of Winston Lakeland and Thomas Gray.

He felt a little nagging displeasure that he hadn't obtained the acid, but if that was the price of this new level of power, it was worth it.

CHAPTER

4

PJ and Thomas drove home Sunday afternoon. The weather had turned tauntingly gorgeous again and the park was full of springtime promise. It would have been fun to be spontaneous and stay a few more days, and if PJ hadn't been working at her new job for less than a year, she would have done so. But PJ was still proving herself, and she didn't want to give Schultz or her boss Lieutenant Howard Wall the impression that she was flighty. Heaven forbid a professional woman should appear flighty. That was number two on the list of forbidden behaviors, right after crying in a meeting.

Every mile of the trip north, it seemed as though winter had a tighter grip on the countryside. Thomas had started out chatty, but near the end of the trip they both sat in silence, watching the miles go by. With about an hour to go, PJ talked about Ed Mitchell. She didn't want Thomas to be surprised the next morning at school. He was disbelieving at first, then angry at the senselessness of it. There was little she could do but reach across the seat and hold his hand.

By the time she got back to St. Louis, the city appeared dismal, with traces of street-soiled snow at the curbs and buds still locked tightly on the trees. While she unpacked, Thomas went over to Mrs. Brodsky's house. Their next-door neighbor had taken in the mail while they were gone.

The two of them sat at the kitchen table sorting through the mail. In her stack, PJ found a large yellow envelope, greeting-card size with extra postage, addressed to Thomas. She recognized her ex-husband's writing. She had a momentary urge to hide it and open it later by herself. Before she could do that, Thomas noticed it and relieved her of the envelope and the decision.

"It looks like a card," he said. "What gives? It's not my birthday or anything."

"Sometimes people send cards for no reason but to show that they love someone." She watched him tear open the yellow envelope.

"Yeah, like Dad would do anything like that," Thomas said.

PJ remembered that there had been a time when Steven did all kinds of silly things to show his love for her. And she had done them, too, all the romantic gestures. Putting little notes in his briefcase. Greeting him at the door wearing a negligée. Sweeping him off for surprise getaway weekends at places with whirlpools for two. Heart-shaped boxes of candy on Valentine's Day. But it was no wonder that Thomas didn't remember them. By the time he was old enough to be aware of such things, she and Steven had both given up working on the marriage. It had taken her months to see past the anger she had experienced when Steven left her for a younger woman. She knew now that there was blame on both sides, but hers was more of omission, whereas his was definitely of commission.

Thomas pulled the card out of the envelope, and several photographs spilled out onto the table. They were five-by-sevens, which accounted for the large envelope. Her son looked at the card first, then handed it to her. It was a smarmy "miss you" type, with little teddy bears and hearts on the front. Evidently Steven's new wife Carla did the shopping for greeting cards, as it certainly didn't look like a card he would pick out. Inside was a note from Steven, inviting Thomas to come to Denver to meet his new half-brother and enjoy the summer in the mountains. There was a strong hint that he'd be welcome to stay when the school year rolled around, too. PJ practically gagged when she got to the line about Thomas staying in his old room and everything being like old times.

The pictures were even worse: a smiling couple, the woman holding her four-month-old baby in her arms, posed in familiar surroundings. The baby looked wonderful, like one of those impossibly beautiful ones in magazines. Ernest, his name was, and at least the name wasn't as beautiful as the face.

Thomas gathered the photos and card and ripped them all in half. His mouth was twisted, and his eyes looked hot.

"He's doing this on purpose. He's trying to hurt us, get back at me 'cause I wouldn't come out to Denver to visit. That part about staying in my old room! What a creep he is. He knew you'd see the pictures, too. Mom, I hate him!"

His words stabbed at PJ. She had tried to keep Thomas's relationship with his father afloat, but Steven seemed determined to sink it. PJ stood up and went around to his side of the table. She held out her arms to him as he sat slumped in his chair, and, for once, his twelve-year-old pride didn't get between them. He hugged her tightly, pressing his face against her midsection.

PJ saw the uncharted territory of single parenthood stretching out in front of her. She felt as though she were navigating unknown waters, and everywhere she looked on her faded, crinkled map was the legend "Here there be dragons." She only hoped that love and common sense would get both of them through it.

They had Chinese food delivered for dinner. Their cat Megabite spurned all offerings of chicken, even after Thomas washed off the sauce for her. The cat was aloof all evening, evidently punishing them for leaving her alone for a week with no one but an undoubtedly taciturn Schultz as a visitor. PJ thought the cat's actions were perfectly appropriate.

After Thomas went to bed that night, she retrieved the photos from the trashcan and taped them back together. Perhaps in the future, they might mean something to him.

Monday morning, after seeing Thomas off to school with an extra hug, PJ had to work hard to put on her professional attitude. She was in her office, rooting through the pile of papers that had accumulated on her desk in her absence. She felt like skipping out on it all, browsing in a software store, picking up some fun new program, and having a chocolate shake at Millie's for lunch. It was her version of the classic female escape of shopping for new clothes.

Schultz pushed open the office door, which she had only partially closed. He had a bulky folder under his arm and what passed for a smile on his face.

"Nice vacation, Doc?"

"Not long enough to make me miss you." She said it with a straight face.

"Good line. I'll put that one in the hopper," he said as he lowered himself onto one of her two folding metal guest chairs. He swept a place clean on her desk and put his own folder in front of her. In spite of her bad mood, her curiosity was engaged.

They talked for a few minutes about the lack of progress in catching the teacher's murderer. Schultz was his usual scornful self when talking about Detective Barnesworth.

"What have you got against that guy?" PJ said.

"Aside from the fact that he's an incompetent asshole, not a thing."

"Somebody must have confidence in him, since he's working on such a high profile case."

"Did it occur to you that someone doesn't want that case solved?"

"Really, Detective. You have a twisted mind."

"It's come in handy over the years. Aren't you ever going to ask about the folder I put on your desk?"

"Okay, I'm asking."

He gave her a summary of the Washburn case. She found herself drawn into the story, particularly when he got to the part about the alarm system being turned off from inside the art gallery. It was much easier to lose herself in a tale of theft and murder in the art world, something removed from her daily life, than to think about blood spattered on the walls of her son's school.

"You think it would be okay with Wall if we looked into this one?" PJ said.

"Of course. Technically, we're supposed to be working on all homicide investigations all the time."

"Gosh, now I feel guilty if I take time to read the newspaper at lunch."

To her surprise, Schultz didn't pick up on the banter. His eyes narrowed and his lips pinched together.

"What?" PJ said. "Did I say something unflattering to the Department? I still need coaching on this cop mystique." Since PJ was a civilian employee, she found that her subordinates closed her out of some aspects of their lives. It was a sensitive point with her.

"Every folder like this means there's some creep out there who got away with it," Schultz said, tapping the folder with his forefinger. "That bothers the shit out of me, each and every one of these. It should bother you, too."

PJ opened her mouth to retort, then thought better of it.

"You're right, Leo. It's nothing to joke about," PJ said. She ran her fingers through her hair and firmly put aside thoughts of her personal life. "I suggest we visit James Washburn and Rebecca Singer and see what they're doing a year later."

"My thoughts exactly."

CHAPTER

5

Schultz wanted to go straight to the gallery. They took his car, a red Pacer which had faded to orange and pulled to the right as though it was trying to crawl up on the sidewalk. He had gotten the Pacer from Vehicles when he was first assigned to CHIP, and somehow he managed to keep it, even though he wasn't doing field work one hundred percent of every day. Most likely Vehicles was glad to have palmed it off on someone, and wasn't eager to get it back.

At this time of the year, the fact that the Pacer didn't have air conditioning didn't bother PJ. Schultz had gotten used to the pulling effect on the steering, and automatically compensated for it without even swearing. She had originally been embarrassed by the orange color, but had long since figured out that there were plenty of cars in the St. Louis area that looked worse.

Her embarrassment returned when she noticed that none of those worse-looking cars were to be found on the private street where James Washburn lived. Schultz had called the gallery and asked to speak to James. He was told that the owner rarely came in, and would he like to speak to the manager instead? He had gotten off the phone quickly, leaving no identification.

They knew from the files that James Washburn lived in the home his father had purchased and renovated. A few blocks from Forest Park, it was a gracious mansion from another era. It was U-shaped, on a large, extensively landscaped lot. As Schultz pulled slowly down the street and approached the house, PJ got a glimpse of the caretaker's home in the rear. It put her own rental house to shame. There was a driveway leading to a four-car garage, but it was blocked by a massive gate. The whole property was surrounded by an ironwork fence at least eight feet high. Schultz pulled up to the curb and got out. PJ rolled her window down—it stuck halfway—so that she could hear what happened. Schultz punched a button on an intercom next to the gate.

"Two to see James Washburn, please," Schultz said. She thought that was extraordinarily polite of him. It sounded as though he were requesting seating in a restaurant. A moment later, a voice responded.

"Sorry, Mr. Washburn isn't seeing visitors today. If you're here on gallery business, please contact the manager, Yolanda Elkins."

Schultz pressed the button again. "Mr. Washburn is seeing these visitors. Detective Leo Schultz, St. Louis Police Department, Homicide. Open the gate." He released the button with a flourish.

A moment later, the gate slid open. Schultz got back into the car and pulled through. "I love doing that," he said. "Makes up for taking a lot of crap otherwise."

PJ nodded her agreement. Some days she felt exactly the same way.

At the door they were greeted by a young man who didn't fit PJ's preconceptions of a houseman or butler. He was in his mid-twenties, muscular, and casually dressed in jeans and a cut-off T-shirt that said "Show Me . . . I'm From Missouri" in big letters. In small print under the first phrase was the single word "Pity." PJ wondered if the man was a bodyguard rather than a house servant. He inspected Schultz's badge and PJ's ID card, then had them wait in the expansive lobby while Mr. Washburn was fetched. PJ thought that given the size of the place, that could be a major task.

"The last time I saw so much marble, I was in the State Capitol Building," Schultz said.

"It is impressive," PJ answered. It was hard to keep from whispering.

"Detective Schultz? Dr. Gray?" They both turned to the sound of James Washburn's silky voice. He was still twenty feet away from them. PJ would have started toward him, but Schultz's body language told her to hold still and let James come to them. He did so, after hesitating slightly. *Round one for the good guys,* PJ thought. James shook both of their hands. He had an aggressive grip that clashed with his voice.

"The garden room is pleasant at this time of day," he said. "Why don't we have our visit there? Some tea for our guests."

The last portion was evidently not directed at them, and PJ spotted Mr. Pity hovering at the edge of the foyer. James set off at a good pace; she and Schultz hurried to catch up. The garden room turned out to be a large lean-to greenhouse with tile floors, flourishing plants, and an ornate ironwork table with four padded chairs. There were vents open at the top of the glass walls, and there must have been a circulating fan somewhere, although PJ didn't see it. Large leaves swayed gently, and PJ felt fresh air on her face. It was a delightful place, and it almost made her forget why they were here.

Schultz scowled as he sat down in one of the chairs. It was a tight fit. He appeared uncomfortable to her for more than one reason: not only the chair clamped on his posterior, but the entire ambiance of wealth. Mr. Pity arrived with a tray containing a crystal pitcher and several tall glasses. Schultz declined, but she accepted iced tea, sipped it, and found it delicious.

Smiling up at Mr. Pity and savoring her tea, she decided he wouldn't be so bad to have around after all. She caught herself responding to his casual physicality, and shifted her attention to their host.

PJ sat across the table from James Washburn and studied him for a minute, as he was doing to them. He was in his early thirties, which meant that Patrick Washburn had married young and fathered his two sons right away. He was tall and trim, and his face was full of sharp angles— there wasn't a comfortable place to rest her eyes on it without sliding down one slope or another. His hair was light brown like his father's, and his eyes were washed-out blue. PJ decided to make the opening bid.

"Detective Schultz and I are looking into your father's death. Could you answer a few questions for us?"

"Certainly. But I thought that investigation was closed months ago. Unfortunately, the killer was never caught."

"The investigation was never closed, Mr. Washburn," Schultz inserted. PJ could hear the attitude in his voice, and hoped it wasn't as obvious to James. "It's just that the police had a few other things to do for a while, and now we've come back around to this case."

"I see. Well, we all want to see justice done. Perhaps you'll have more success than the original detectives. Fire away."

"I understand you're the owner of the gallery now," PJ said.

"Yes, I'm Father's only heir."

"Oh, so your brother Henry is recently deceased?"

PJ saw James momentarily clench his jaws. "No, Henry is still very much alive, if you call that kind of existence living. A correction, then. He and I share my father's estate equally. I'm the trustee for his half." James picked up his iced tea glass and made a show of sipping slowly. "I care for my kid brother. He'll get the best treatment available for as long as he needs it."

"So who's running the business if you're sitting around drinking tea?" Schultz said.

"You two certainly are . . . direct. I have an office in this home fully equipped for doing business, including international video conferencing, if necessary. All my stores—New York, San Francisco, Paris, Hong Kong, and, of course, St. Louis—are on the Internet. The managers chat every day. If my presence is needed, to authorize an auction bid for instance, I'm not hard to find. You did so easily."

"Patrick Washburn went to his place of business frequently. He was killed there, working late in the back of the store," PJ said.

"My father was a person who lived in the past. He liked to shuffle papers, feel the fabric, stroke the wood. I don't."

"You have a new manager, Yolanda Elkins. When you took over the business, why didn't Rebecca Singer stay on? Were you dissatisfied with her?" PJ noticed that James consistently addressed her, and gestured in her direction, even if Schultz had asked the question. Either he found her less threatening or he was flirting with her. Either way, she had the urge to reach out and slap the guy.

"The polite way to put it is that Miss Singer and I didn't have the same vision for the galleries. I wanted to bring the business into the computer age, and she wanted to carry on as my father had."

"So you fired her."

"No, no, she left voluntarily. There weren't any ill feelings, just a difference in style. We haven't kept in touch. I wonder what she's up to these days. Do you know if she still lives in the area?"

PJ, who had been resting one hand on the table while holding the glass with the other, suddenly found her hand trapped by his on the table. James had put his glass down, and was leaning toward her across the small table.

PJ extracted her hand, picked up her pen, and made some notes. The tips of her ears were burning. She imagined what Schultz was thinking, and it wasn't pleasant.

"She does. We plan to talk to her next. Did your father have any enemies?" PJ asked. It was lame, but she gave herself a B+ for recovery.

"Of course he did," James said. "He was both a businessman and an art lover. A few decades spent as either of those, and you're bound to have stepped on someone's toes. But someone who hated him enough to kill? I don't think so."

PJ thought of the phone cord ripped out of the wall, the dying man's only means of helping himself. It was a very personal crime, she thought. A crime with a lot of hate in it.

"What's your theory, then?" Schultz asked.

"A thief, of course. Paintings were taken. I think Father was unlucky enough to be there when the gallery was robbed."

"Then how do you explain the alarm system that was turned off from the inside?"

James shrugged. "I think the police made too much of that the first time around. Father had just forgotten to turn it on, that's all. When he got stressed, he got careless. He was working on his taxes, and I suppose he was preoccupied."

A young woman walked into the greenhouse. She was wearing a two-piece swimming suit that made it clear that body toning needn't be on her list of New Year's resolutions. The suit was covered by a filmy shirt that ended at mid-thigh. PJ almost laughed aloud when she saw Schultz reflexively sit up straight and suck in his gut.

"Jimmy," she said, "will you be long? I don't know whether to go to the pool or get my tanning done first."

What a dilemma, PJ thought. Somehow the twenty extra pounds that had taken up residence on her hips felt as though each and every one were clamoring for attention. As for a two-piece swimming suit, there were still some issues with her figure left over from childbearing.

James stood up. "If there are no more questions . . ."

Schultz and PJ rose, PJ fumbling the pad back into her briefcase. She had written nothing on her pad, but had doodled the beginnings of a nice floral border.

"Feel free to call on me again," he said. PJ thought she saw James wink at her, but she wasn't sure. Mr. Pity materialized and led them back to the front door.

Back in the car, Schultz started laughing. "Christ, that guy couldn't act more guilty if he tried! I thought he was trying out for a part on *Columbo*."

"He did come across like a crook, almost theatrically so." PJ wasn't going to mention the flirting business unless Schultz did.

"Did you see the way he was coming on to you?"

Too late.

"The fucker was getting a hard-on just stroking your hand. Then Miss Tan 'n Tits comes in."

"Let's keep this professional, Detective."

"If I hadn't been on the scene, I think he would have suggested you three manage a triage."

PJ blinked. "I think that's menage à trois. In fact, I'm sure of it." Schultz seemed to be veering into territory she would rather not explore with him. "This case is fascinating," she said with a little more enthusiasm than was called for. "An opportunity to study the dynamics of how a murder affects the lives of the survivors, too. Tomorrow we'll visit the gallery. I'd like to do a VR simulation of the murder."

Schultz looked at her, an amused look that lasted so long she began to worry about his driving.

"Keep your eyes on the road," she said.

"I can always tell when something's getting under your skin. You get this big grin on your face and start spouting that shrink talk. I saw you making eyes at that muscle-bound houseboy, too. What's the matter, your Lover-boy no good in the sack?"

PJ bristled. "I haven't bugged you about striking out with Nurse Helen, have I? Why don't you just lay off the sex talk?"

Schultz clammed up. His fingers were white on the steering wheel, and she was sure it didn't require that much pressure to correct the crab-wise motion of the car. She knew she should apologize, both for her tone of voice and for throwing Helen in his face, but the words just wouldn't come.

CHAPTER

6

The next morning, PJ and Schultz were in her office finishing up morning cups of coffee. They were just about to leave to interview Rebecca Singer, and PJ was looking forward to it. She had read the Washburn case folder the night before, including the previous interviews with Singer. The two of them also planned to stop by the gallery, to get the detailed measurements and descriptions that PJ needed for her VR simulation. It would be a challenge, because the crime scene was a year old, and the business had been active during that time. It would be the first case in which she had to work from a scene so removed in time.

That prospect opened whole new scenarios to her concerning her job: going back and working on unsolved crimes, seeing if her computerized approach would provide some new perspectives where conventional investigative techniques had failed. Old murder cases were being reexamined in the light of new techniques such as DNA analysis. Why not computer simulation? If she could double or triple her budget, she could have multiple teams working current and past crimes. Even as the thought occurred to her, she knew it was unlikely to happen. She couldn't even get funding for the conference room she had requested months ago, a place for the CHIP team to gather and discuss business.

The phone on her desk rang just as they were at the door. Schultz waved her on with him, but PJ couldn't ignore a ringing phone. She punched the speaker phone button sharply with her finger, imagining that it was James Washburn's nose.

"Gray, CHIP," she said. It had become her customary way of answering the phone, even though it was cryptic enough to leave some callers wondering whether their calls had gone astray.

"PJ, it's Wilma. I've got some old fart down here at the desk wants to see you. He won't tell me why, but he's carrying a newspaper article about you all the way back from that decapitation case. He ain't no newspaperman, I can tell you that. Whaddya think?"

PJ felt her plans deflating as though the phone receiver was a giant thumbtack. She glanced at Schultz. He motioned her on impatiently. She knew what he would do in the same circumstance. She sighed.

"Send him down, Wilma."

Schultz was shaking his head as she ended the call. "You have to be more discriminating," he said. "You have to assert yourself. Nut cases can waste a lot of your time."

"I'm a psychologist. I'm used to nut cases."

"Suit yourself. Don't expect me to wait around for you." He took off down the hall, closing the door behind him.

PJ put on a fresh pot of coffee. She had time to straighten

the top of her desk and comb her hair by the time there was a knock at the door. It was followed by a commotion of shuffling feet, a bump, and a voice protesting something. PJ went to the door and opened it.

In the hallway stood a young officer doing her best to escort an elderly man, trying to keep her hand under his elbow for support. He was pushing her away.

"That's quite enough, young lady. I think I can manage from here."

The officer shrugged and left the man standing at PJ's door.

"Come in, please," PJ said.

Before we have to call the medics.

The man inched his way into the room using a three-footed cane. If it wasn't for the cane, PJ would have sworn Santa Claus had come for a visit. A folder of papers was tucked under his free arm. He was dressed in a suit and vest that had seen better days but were clean and pressed. His shoes looked freshly shined. A visitor's pass was pinned crookedly to his lapel. He was rotund, and a neatly trimmed white beard accentuated the Santa look. PJ resisted the urge to take the man's elbow as the officer had done. Instead, she went to the coffeepot.

"Coffee?"

"No thanks. Makes me jittery. People think I've got the DT's."

PJ, who was turned away from him, smiled and took her time. She poured herself a cup and fiddled with the cream and sugar, allowing him to make his own way. She managed to get back to her desk just as the man settled himself into a chair across from her. He plopped the folder on the desk between them. She studied his face. His receding hairline left his eyebrows stranded, like islands in a peach-colored ocean, but his eyes were bright with intelligence and spirit.

"What can I do for you, Mr. . . ."

"Harquest. Emory Harquest. I know you from your picture in the paper. You're that shrink who solved the Ballet Butcher case."

"I worked on that case, yes."

Hard-edged images moved in PJ's mind like fractures in the ice on a lake, one leading to another, spreading out from a point of impact, shrieking and popping in the cold, still air.

Shaking her head, PJ regretted not going with Schultz. Most likely he had Rebecca Singer confessing to a sordid plot by now. Some days sordid was good.

"What brings you in today, Mr. Harquest?"

"I have some information about that teacher's murder. Terrible thing, isn't it? You see"—he lowered his voice so that PJ leaned forward—"I live right across the street from the school."

"If you have anything that might help solve the crime, you need to speak to the investigator on the case. That's Detective Barnesworth. I'll give him a call for you."

His hand shot out with surprising speed as PJ reached for the phone. He pushed her fingers away.

"No, no, if I'd wanted to talk to that idiot, I would have said something when he knocked on the door of my home. You're an educated woman, Dr. Gray. I wanted to talk to someone intelligent and with a jot of decency. From what I've read about you, you're the one I want. You're the one who will catch the killer, no doubt about it."

PJ's first reaction was amusement, but then a shiver went down her spine. He spoke with such conviction that his words had the force of precognition. He continued speaking while her thoughts strayed.

". . . used to teach at Deaver," he said, thumping his chest. "Forty-three years, until I had to make way for some young snot right out of college. That's why I want this vile criminal caught. No one should do that to a teacher."

"All right, let's hear what you've got."

"I saw someone go into the school that night," he said. "I couldn't sleep, can't get to sleep before the wee hours since I started that new medication that makes me pee like a horse. I was sitting at my desk in the den doing crossword puzzles. Close to the bathroom, you know. The curtains were drawn, but the window was open a few inches. I like a cool house at night." He paused and ran his hands over the folder in front of him. PJ had to restrain herself from snatching the folder away and spreading the contents on her desk. It was taking him a long time to get to the point.

"I heard a loud car in the street. I'm sure it was the McCarney brothers. I've called their parents, but they don't do anything about it. I stepped over to the window to look out, but by then the car was too far down the street. It was about eleven-fifteen. I remember because I looked at my clock and thought those two boys should be in bed. How are they going to improve their schoolwork if they're out gallivanting all night?"

PJ sat up a bit straighter. This wasn't in Barnesworth's reports. She jotted a note on her desk pad: *McCarney brothers*.

"You didn't tell this to the detective who came to your home?"

"Of course not. I already told you he was an idiot. Besides, those two boys are troublemakers, but they haven't got the balls between them to bash a teacher over the head. Pardon my language, young lady. No, I saw someone else, right near the front door of the school."

PJ's hopes soared. She might be sitting across from an

eyewitness who could break the homicide case. Already she was evaluating him as potential courtroom material. The outlook wasn't promising. He'd need a new suit for starters.

"I couldn't see very well."

Ouch. The jury doesn't need to hear that.

"It was dark," he continued, "and the light over the school door's been burned out for weeks. But I saw a woman there. She got on a bicycle and rode off down the street. I'm sure of it. I even took pictures. There was a full moon that night so my camera caught everything. I've had that camera since 1976. Took it to the Grand Canyon and almost dropped it in." He dramatically dumped a handful of three-by-five photos from the folder.

"Double prints. K-Mart special," he said.

She picked up one of the photos and eagerly scanned it. It was underexposed, very dark and grainy, with a bright spot in the middle. Off to the side there was a vague shape.

PJ cleared her throat. "Uh, Mr. Harquest, I think this is a tree."

"No, no, next to the tree. Ignore that bright area—that's just the flash bouncing off the window. Don't pay any attention to my reflection in the window, either. Can't you make out that woman standing there? She turned around right then, so I only got her back."

PJ shuffled through the rest of the photos, trying to keep the disappointment from her face and voice. "I appreciate your bringing these to me," she said. "I'll make sure they're put to the best possible use. Now I'd like to call an officer to take an official statement from you. Name, address, what you saw, that kind of thing."

PJ tapped in Anita's extension and was gratified to find her subordinate at her desk. Anita Collings was a competent, insightful, and patient officer, although PJ found her distant at times. She was just the person to take Mr. Harquest off her hands without offending him.

"Thank you for bringing these to my attention," PJ said as she handed him off to Anita.

Once her office door was closed again, PJ got a magnifying glass out of her desk and studied the photos. In one or two, she was sure she could make out a shape next to the tree. Perhaps with computerized image enhancement, it wasn't hopeless after all. Since there were two copies of each print, she decided to keep one set and send the other along to Barnesworth. Feeling that Schultz was ethereally present and applauding her deviousness, she opened her desk drawer and slipped the photos inside.

Detective Barnesworth wasn't at his desk, sparing her the personal delivery. Instead, she put the photos in a paper evidence envelope, filled it out, and took it to the Evidence Room. She left the detective a voice mail message telling him about Mr. Harquest's visit and directing him to Anita for the statement taken. She felt sorry for the old man. Barnesworth would surely descend upon him as soon as he got the news. Any crumb would do for a starving man.

When she got back to her office, she was surprised to see Schultz there, leaning back in one of her chairs. He let it thump down to the floor when she came in.

"I never got to talk to Singer," he said, preempting her question. "She skipped out on the appointment."

"How disappointing for you," PJ said smugly.

Furrows appeared in Schultz's broad forehead as the smugness registered on him. "What gives? Something come of that nut case?"

"He wasn't a nut case, and I wish you'd stop disparaging anyone who doesn't fit your narrow definition of an acceptable human being." Every word that Schultz said, and the tone of voice he said them in, moved the importance of her find up a notch. Another few sentences and she'd be personally bringing the murderer in as headlines screamed CRIME-SOLVING SHRINK SCOOPS POLICE.

"Christ, she's dragging out the big words," Schultz said. "Now I know something's up. The Great Lady Detective strikes again. Tell." He crossed his arms and planted a serious look on his face.

PJ slid open her desk drawer and removed the photos. She dealt them out like a hand of cards for his inspection. His eyes scanned the glossy rectangles, apparently seeing all he needed to see in one quick glance.

"This one's got a blurry tree in it," he said, tapping one with a meaty finger. "Plus the nut case did a pretty good job of taking his own picture in these two. See that reflection in the window? Shithead used a flash up close to the glass."

PJ felt that she was somehow responsible for the quality of the photos, and leapt to their defense.

"Take a look at this one with the magnifying glass," she said, pushing the lens at him. "There's definitely a person next to the tree."

He reached for the magnifying glass and held it to his eye with a flourish. "I didn't know you were into this Sherlock stuff, Doc. You bring the deerstalker and I'll bring the handcuffs. Might make for an interesting evening."

PJ was annoyed, but her curiosity won out. "What's a deerstalker?"

"It's that hat that Sherlock Holmes wore. At least in the movies."

"Oh. I don't think Holmes had any handcuffs. He wasn't a cop."

"Wouldn't be a hot evening without handcuffs."

"Leo."

"Yeah, yeah, okay." He picked up the photo she had

indicated and studied it. "There's someone there, all right. It could probably be brought out a lot better. What am I looking at?"

PJ folded her hands in front of her on her desk, then realized that made her look like she was lecturing. She picked up a pencil and tapped one of the photos with it instead.

"These were taken by a man who lives right across the street from Deaver." She paused for emphasis. "On the night of the murder."

"You're saying that this is supposed to be the creep who whacked the teacher?" A spark of interest flared in Schultz's eyes, but his voice was still on the edge of sarcasm.

"That's what Emory Harquest believes. He's a retired teacher. Very credible." She regretted handing the man off to Anita. She would have liked to wave his statement at Schultz. The detective could be so infuriating.

"Tell me everything. First tell me if Barnesworth knows about this."

"I delivered a set of photos to the Evidence Room and left him a voice mail message."

"Shit."

"I kept the extra copies. He doesn't know about them."

"You take his statement, this Mr. Harquest?"

"I turned him over to Anita."

"Excellent."

"Mr. Harquest seemed so certain," PJ said. She had started out defending the man because of her own ego, but that had changed. "He deserves to be taken seriously. We should at least check out these photos, see if anything can be done," PJ said. She thought about what the man had said: *You're the one who will catch the killer . . .*

Schultz was disturbingly quiet, with an odd look on his face. He looked like he was about to steal cotton candy from a child. She wouldn't put it past him, especially if he thought it would bring a criminal to justice. "What exactly are you thinking, Detective?"

"I'm thinking"—he leaned forward conspiratorially—"that if there's anything to this, we can ace out Barnesworth. I could check the photos out of the Evidence Room. There would be a record of it, of course, but he wouldn't know to ask about it. Too bad about that voice mail. Any way we can erase it?"

"What?" PJ's voice rose and squeaked a little. "Shouldn't you show any concern for proper police procedures? Aren't we all on the same team here, trying to solve a homicide?" She conveniently forgot that moments ago she was ready to claim the glory for solving the case herself.

"Get off the high ground, Doc. It's just you and the angels up there, and they don't know how to throw a good party."

PJ thought about it for a minute. She didn't like Barnesworth because he stepped on others' feelings to make himself look good, even the feelings of crime victims and their families. He brought to mind James Washburn, the gallery owner who had come on to her in front of Schultz. She had a feeling that what Barnesworth did openly—climb on others' shoulders to get ahead—Washburn did quietly and insidiously. She couldn't strike back at Washburn, but Barnesworth was a tantalizing target. And when she looked at it objectively, there wasn't much chance of this evidence amounting to anything. She had been ready to dismiss it herself until Schultz had pulled her chain. If anything did result, she'd make sure it was passed along to Barnesworth.

Besides, she hadn't done anything petty in quite a while. She was due for it.

"I think I might be able to do something about that voice mail," she said. "But you'd owe me one."

"I'll be your sex slave," Schultz said.

"I was thinking more of lunch at Millie's tomorrow," PJ said, suppressing a smile. "But I'll keep your suggestion on file."

When Schultz left with the photos to search out Anita, PJ phoned Louie Bertram, the audio/visual tech she had spoken to several times. Pleased with her attention, and the fact that she treated him as a human being rather than an extension of his equipment as others did, he had offered to help her whenever she needed something.

"Louie, it's PJ."

"PJ? Dr. Gray? What . . ." There was a clanging noise. Louie had dropped the handset. It wasn't something she expected from him; he was usually meticulous in his handling of all types of equipment. She pictured him with sticky tape wrapped around the ends of his fingers.

PJ wondered how Louie would retrieve the handset from the floor because he was in a wheelchair. Then she remembered the nifty long-handled grabber that he carried strapped to the back of the chair. All he had to do was reach over his shoulder, pull the grabber out of its leather loop like an arrow from a quiver, and squeeze the trigger to operate the metal fingers. As a shorter-than-average woman, she noticed things that could extend her reach. That gadget would come in handy. She wrote *grabber* on her desk pad, right under *McCarney brothers*.

"Sorry," his voice came back a moment later. "What can I do for you?"

She explained the situation. Louie had no qualms about cooperating. The voice mail system wasn't his area, but he knew enough about it to get the job done. He volunteered to erase all of Barnesworth's messages for the day.

"It'll be easier that way," he said. "I won't have to worry if I got the right one."

"I'd prefer to have just my message wiped out. Can you do that instead?" After all, PJ reasoned, it was conceivable that the jerk did have something important waiting for him.

"Yep. But it would be a lot more fun to dump 'em all."

"I know just what you mean. Do you handle computer enhancement of photos?"

"Nope. Edith does that. She's real backed up right now, but if you've got something, I could probably get it speeded up. She owes me a favor. I kept her snakes for her when she went to Guatemala."

PJ decided to let that one slither by. "Tell her Schultz will be up with a couple of photos she should find interesting. A challenge, if nothing else." She thanked him and asked Louie if he'd be in his office for the next half hour. Perplexed, he said yes. She walked outside the Headquarters Building, glad to be out of her windowless basement office even though the temperature was around freezing and the sky was overcast. She made her way through the lunchtime crowd—diminished due to the depressing weather—to the Flower of China restaurant where she frequently ate lunch. Instead of hogging one of the four tables in the tiny eating area, as she usually did, she got her order to go. Louie was surprised but delighted when she pushed aside the electronic clutter on his bench and set out the food. She found that his skill with chopsticks put hers to shame and that he blushed when his fortune cookie said: "Stop looking for love and let it find you."

CHAPTER

7

Columbus usually brought his lunch to school. If possible, he ate outside on one of the long, low benches lining the soccer fields. It minimized contact with other kids and especially with the overly cheerful lunchroom staff, and that suited him. He normally packed a brown bag the night before, a cheese sandwich, pretzels, and an apple most of the time. He didn't pay much attention to food, with two exceptions. He craved granola bars and ice cream. If the Cow had troubled herself to go to the grocery store recently, there would be a couple of boxes of chocolate chip granola bars in the pantry. He would take the boxes up to his room, although he didn't think anyone else in the house ate them except him, and immediately stick a note on the refrigerator asking for more. Not that the Cow ever made a special trip for him. He had to wait until the freezer and pantry were practically empty.

He looked forward to lunch whenever there was a granola bar in his bag. Otherwise, it was just a distraction from class work.

Columbus hadn't packed his lunch because he had been up late working on a new subroutine. When the alarm went off, he uncharacteristically slapped it off and rolled over for a few more minutes of sleep. By the time he dragged himself into the bathroom for a shower, he barely had enough time to get to school. It wasn't that he minded being late, but he didn't want to do anything to call attention to himself at school. He had done a good job on his "stunned student" act after Mitchell's murder. No sense inviting extra scrutiny.

Columbus scanned the tables in the lunchroom for his targets. As long as he had to eat with others, he might as well accomplish something else, too. He had stopped at the bathroom before going to lunch to ensure that Thomas Gray and Winston Lakeland would make their way through the line ahead of him and choose their seats. He spotted them sitting together near the end of a long table. There was enough room next to them for him. He went through the lunch line, impatient with the girl in front of him who hesitated whenever a choice was to be made. What did it matter whether she took applesauce or corn? He was about to give her a rude nudge in the rear when she finally completed her selections and went to the cashier. Columbus took whatever dish was closest at each serving area, paid, and sauntered over to the table where the two boys were hunched over their trays, talking quietly to each other.

"Anybody sitting here?" He had watched carefully; he knew no one was using the chairs next to Thomas and Winston, but it was polite to ask. Politeness was something he slipped into or out of like a Halloween costume.

Two faces turned toward him, surprise in their eyes,

words of their private conversation still hanging like a suspension bridge between them. Usually no one wanted to sit with them. Winston was one of those kids who was always on the outside. The word nerd had been coined for him. When Thomas started school last fall, fresh from out of town, he took up with Winston right away. Columbus had noted it at the time, as he observed everything that impinged on his world, but it had seemed inconsequential. Columbus expected Thomas to drop the nerd after he got his bearings, after he felt his way around the intricate social webs that seventh graders spun. Instead the two boys seemed to have become good friends and they still hung out with each other a lot. That alone merited study.

Thomas waved him to the chair next to Winston.

"Your name's Columbus, isn't it? As in discovering America?" Winston said.

"Yeah. Pilgrims and all that shit. I suppose my parents thought I'd live up to the name."

Winston snorted. "Jeez, I hope my parents don't expect me to live up to mine."

Thomas and Columbus both gave him a puzzled look.

"It's a joke, guys, don't you get it? Winston? Cigarettes? Live up to being a coffin nail?"

Thomas sneered. "Yeah, I get it. You're a real stand-up, Win."

"Better stick to computers," Columbus inserted smoothly. "Comedy isn't your field." He unwrapped his sandwich and took a big bite.

Winston was eager to move to new territory. "You interested in computers?" he said.

Columbus thumped his chest. When he was in chameleon mode, wearing the emotions he had studied, he was very good. Indistinguishable from a normal twelve-year-old, he liked to think. "Hey, man, I'm the best."

Thomas was watching him intently. "Best at what?"

"You name it, I've aced it."

Thomas puffed up for a moment, as if he was going to try to top that statement somehow. Then he deflated, his shoulders sagging. "There's a lot of games my mom won't let me have," he said.

"Yeah? Like what?" Columbus asked, feigning actual interest.

"Blood Warriors."

"Got it."

"HyperStrike."

"Got it."

"Adam Smasher."

"Got it. I can lend them to you if you'd like to try them out. I can even get you through Novice level fast so you can get to the good stuff."

"I don't know. Mom would probably have a fit if she found out."

"I didn't think you were such a mama's boy, Tommy," he said, allowing his voice to dip into sarcasm. "Does Mama keep your balls in a jar on her dresser?"

Thomas reddened but said nothing.

"How about you, Winston? You a mama's boy, too?" Columbus knew perfectly well that Winston lived with his father, and that his mother was in a halfway house struggling with multiple addictions. Winston's father may or may not have restricted his access to the gory games Columbus had mentioned, but one thing was certain: the Lakeland family couldn't afford the games and the high-powered computer needed to play them in the first place.

"Shit, no," Winston said. "You can skip that Novice crap entirely, though. I'm sure I can handle Expert. Let's get together tonight."

Columbus allowed the corners of his mouth to turn up.

The encounter was moving in the right direction, and fast. "Yeah, tonight's good. My parents are out of the house every Thursday. We'll have the place to ourselves. Coming, Tommy?"

"You bet. And I don't like to be called Tommy."

Columbus took a bite of his apple and chewed it noisily. The smells of the lunchroom were bothering him. They washed over the savory aromas of defiance and guilt coming from Thomas and the scent of adulation from Winston. He didn't appreciate anything that watered down his experiences. He finished his apple, keeping eye contact with Thomas the whole time. Let the kid wait.

"Yeah, whatever," Columbus said when he had finished the apple and tossed the core over Winston's head into a trash can. "See you guys tonight. Magnolia and Elm, three houses down from the corner. The one with the big front porch. Seven o'clock. That's not too late, is it? I mean, you do get to stay up past eight?"

"We'll be there," Thomas said.

"Yeah," Winston chimed in. "We might just whip your ass."

Columbus nodded, struggling to keep a straight face. "See you," he said. He stood up and picked up his tray. Most of the food remained, but that wasn't unusual. Lots of kids didn't finish their cafeteria lunches. He put the tray on the conveyor belt and watched his food march around a bend and out of sight into the kitchen.

The rest of the afternoon, Columbus found it difficult to concentrate on his schoolwork. His mind danced ahead, galloped down what-if corridors and leaped over no-can-do canyons.

There would be plenty to write in his journal that night. Project Morph was underway, and the outlook was promising.

CHAPTER

8

When Thomas got home that afternoon, he hurried through his homework, cleaned the downstairs bathroom, and filled Megabite's food and water dishes. He considered doing the laundry but decided that would look suspicious as too much of a good thing. By the time his mother got home, he was waiting at the kitchen table. She came in the back door, looking tired. Tired was much better than he had hoped for, which was simply that she was in a good mood. Since she was tired, there wouldn't be any Mom-and-son activities to get through.

"Hey, Mom, what's for dinner?"

PJ plopped down on one of the kitchen chairs, put her elbow on the table, and rested her chin on her palm. She gave him a fierce look.

"Ever heard of 'Hi, how was your day?' or 'Glad to see you,' something like that?" she said.

"Oh, yeah. Well, glad to see you. How was your day?"

"I don't want to talk about it."

"See?" He slammed his palm to the table in fake consternation. "That's why I never ask."

She stood up and came around to his chair.

"Your menu, sir," she said, placing an imaginary menu in front of him with a flourish. He opened it and pretended to study the numerous items.

"The soup's especially good tonight," she prompted.

"Ah, I'll have the soup. How about a sandwich to go with it?"

"Grilled cheese is the specialty of the house."

He snapped the menu closed and handed it back to her. "Make it so."

They burst out laughing. Mom had a great belly laugh. Lately he hadn't heard enough of it. They seemed to be snapping at each other constantly, over things that were important to him but dismissed as trivial by her. Then she would infuriate him further by blaming it all on teenage hormones. Jeez, he wasn't even a teenager yet. Couldn't she accept that sometimes she was to blame?

He shoved those thoughts aside. If things were going to go his way, he needed to have all the right answers for the next few minutes. The time when Mom got home from work always seemed to be crucial to whether they spent the evening glaring at each other and slamming doors—well, he was the one who slammed doors—or whether they could have a decent time.

"Get out the sandwich stuff," she said. "I'll open the soup after I change clothes."

PJ headed upstairs. Thomas busied himself getting out cheese, bread, and plates. She was back a few minutes later, wearing her old flannel pajamas and a thin flannel robe with a rip at the left elbow. Anytime Mom put those on before nine o'clock, he knew that he'd be on his own for the evening.

She put the soup into the microwave and buttered the bread. She slapped four pieces of bread, butter side down, onto the warm griddle and he put two slices of cheese on top of each piece. He moved over to the table and poured glasses of milk as she covered the cheese with another piece of bread. They had done it many times before, and the familiarity of it was comforting.

She asked him how he was feeling about the death of Mr. Mitchell. It still bothered him a lot. Mostly he was mad that someone could do that and get away with it. No one had been arrested, and his mother was close-mouthed about the investigation. That had caused him some problems at school, since a few kids expected him to know inside information about the crime and had bugged him a lot. The chem lab was closed for the time being, and there were some flowers outside the door. He felt bad whenever he walked down the hall and saw the flowers. Some of the kids were a lot worse off than he was. A few were so upset they hadn't been back to school since the body was discovered. His mom reassured him that both his response and theirs were normal, and that people reacted and grieved in different ways.

"Some kids don't seem affected at all," Thomas said. He was thinking of Columbus.

"That's okay," PJ said. "Really, they are, but it's just on the inside. Some people don't show their feelings very much." Her eyes narrowed, and she touched her upper lip with the tip of her tongue. She did that when she was starting to get worried about something. He knew she wasn't one of those people who kept everything on the inside. Sometimes when she was being a shrink instead of a mom she was unreadable. He wondered what thought had been running around in her mind, and then he saw her glance down at the thin white scar on her forearm. He still found it hard to think about it, that day when Mom almost died. He pushed the memories away, sat down at the table, and downed his glass of milk. He went to the refrigerator for a refill.

"I finished all my homework," he said.

She nodded.

"I fed Megabite and cleaned the bathroom."

She nodded again as she flipped the cheese sandwiches over in the pan to let the other sides brown.

"I'd like to go over to a guy's house." The microwave binged and she headed for it with pot holders in hand.

"On a school night? I don't think that's such a good idea. Can't it wait until the weekend?"

"I'll be home by ten," he continued as if she hadn't said anything. "You don't even have to drive me. It's close. I can take my bike."

She frowned. He knew she was running through all the Mom stuff, boy out at night, going who knows where, probably buying drugs on the corner.

"I've got the phone number where I'll be," he said. Fortunately the Wade family was in the phone book. "Winston's coming, too."

"Who's your new friend?"

"His name is Columbus Wade. He's a neat guy. I'm sure you'd like him." Thomas tried to keep his voice from sounding too eager. He was looking forward to the evening of computer games, and the fact that his mom disapproved of those games added a thrill. He'd blow everything if she picked up the scent of wrongdoing.

"Columbus, like the explorer?" she said.

He saw the decision in her face before she announced it.

"Yeah, but don't mention it. He's a little touchy about it."

"Okay, I guess it's all right. Ten o'clock. Sharp."

CHAPTER

9

The phone rang Friday just as PJ was brushing her teeth after breakfast. She thought it might be the parents of Thomas's new friend. She had done that a few times in the past, called the parents after Thomas said he was visiting a friend. She'd stopped after he complained that she was sneakily checking up on him, which she was. Now if she had any doubts, she was up front about it and called in advance, with Thomas right in the room with her. She worried that he and his friends would each tell their parents they had gone to the other's house and then go somewhere else altogether, someplace that wouldn't have been approved had the parents known. It was a trick she had played on her own parents more than once, at just Thomas's age.

It baffled her that kids forgot that their parents had once been twelve. Didn't they know that parents knew all the tricks?

She assumed that everything had gone well last night. Thomas had arrived home exactly on time and slunk into his room with barely a whispered goodnight. Not atypical behavior after the twelfth birthday, but it triggered just a little worry somewhere in the back of her mind, the part that went on silent alert whenever Thomas was out of her sight. It had taken a lot of willpower to keep from dialing the Wades' number last night. She was making a deliberate effort to loosen up a bit, and congratulated herself on a good start. She told herself that if it turned out to be more than a one-time thing with Columbus, she'd call his parents and introduce herself, perhaps come up with some excuse to go over and check out their house and make sure it wasn't an arsenal or a den of prostitution.

It wasn't Columbus's parents on the phone. It was Schultz.

She could get him to drive by the Wades' house and at least look at the outside. Knowing him, he'd probably take a peek in the windows, too.

"It's eight o'clock already, Doc. You gonna sleep the whole day?" he said.

"I'm just getting ready to leave, not that it's any of your business. I'm the boss, remember?" She cradled the phone against her shoulder, brushed damp hair out of her eyes, and sat down on the edge of the bed to put her shoes on. These days, unless she had some meeting to go to, she wore loose-fitting slacks, a simple shirt, and comfortable walking shoes. On meeting days she substituted a silk blouse. PJ had given up trying to impress anyone with the power wardrobe that seemed so important in her previous job in marketing research. Since she had gained about twenty pounds during the divorce and the move to St. Louis, most of her business clothes didn't fit very well anyway. It had taken her nearly a year to admit it.

"I read someplace that only insecure people have to keep reminding everybody that they're in charge," he said.

"Does this call have a purpose other than to make me even later than I already am?"

"I've got another appointment with Rebecca Singer. She promised not to skip out on me again. She works at a gallery in Clayton that doesn't open until ten. She gets there at nine, so we'll have plenty of time for a private little talk. I thought you might want to go directly to the gallery instead of coming downtown first."

"That's thoughtful," she said. "What's gotten into you?"

He ignored the barb. "In fact, why don't I just drop by and pick you up? I can be there in about half an hour."

After getting off the phone, PJ rummaged in her closet for a clean blouse that was dressier than the one she was already wearing, which was a white cotton with daisies embroidered around the buttonholes. She found one still in the wrapper from the dry cleaner's, and settled on it by default. She slipped the V-necked red silk shell with cap sleeves over her head, and added a gold chain that rested lightly across her collarbones. Her auburn hair brushed her shoulders just the way she liked it to, and she thought she fully deserved Schultz's appreciative whistle when she answered his knock on the back door. It had been more than an hour since he called her, but he offered no explanation for his lateness. They weren't going to have much time for chatting before the gallery opened after all.

She knew something was up when he held the car door open for her, but she figured he'd get around to it in his own good time. He drove in silence. It occurred to her that he was one of the few people she had met who were truly comfortable with silence.

As they moved from south St. Louis toward the affluent suburb of Clayton, the neighborhoods changed character.

No more statues of Mary, concrete toadstools, or pink flamingoes on the lawns. Instead, the houses had more green space around them and were set back further from the street. Two stories with ivy-covered brick predominated. Landscaping was more imaginative than one evergreen bush under each front window. The automobiles gradually changed from pickups and older full-size cars to Mercedes and BMW's. The Clayton business district was a financial center, mirroring downtown St. Louis on a smaller, more intimate scale. Shopping tended to be pricey and quirky: boutiques, import shops, and, of course, art galleries. Parking was always difficult to find, and arriving in the area at nine o'clock had given the business people a head start. Shoppers who were arriving in the area were vicious and refused to make eye contact when there was a convenient parking spot at stake.

The gallery had a small storefront with a green awning imprinted in gold script with the simple name Art World. There was a tiny off-street parking area next to it, with numerous signs threatening everything short of decapitation for unauthorized parking. The three spots were conspicuously labeled PROPRIETOR, STAFF, and GUEST. Apparently one customer at a time was the norm. A pale-blue Toyota Corolla was already in the STAFF position; Rebecca Singer's car, no doubt. The other two were empty. Schultz unhesitatingly pulled into the PROPRIETOR spot and turned the key to shut off the Pacer's engine. The engine ran on for a few seconds and gave out a hearty belch before stopping. PJ felt she should apologize for the car's rudeness. She looked over at Schultz and found him grinning, whether from the car's noise or from his blatant usurpation of the parking spot, she couldn't tell.

She opened her car door and got out before he could puff his way around the front and open the door for her.

He tried to retaliate by moving in front of her to open the gallery door. She wondered what sort of game they were playing. Apparently only Schultz knew the rules of today's game.

"After you, ma'am," he said, his hand on the ornate brass doorknob.

The door was locked. The gallery didn't open until ten o'clock, and Rebecca apparently did her preparation work locked in with the treasures.

"Just testing," Schultz said, trying to recover.

PJ nodded, filing it away in case she needed to trot out some embarrassing moment later on. The commotion at the front door attracted Rebecca's attention, and she opened the door from the inside after disabling the alarm system. PJ stepped inside, with Schultz so close on her heels that he practically stepped on them.

After setting the alarm again, Rebecca led them through the narrow main aisle of the shop, which was lined with brazen statuary that was not to PJ's liking.

Where are those fig leaves when you need them?

The paintings on the walls were large canvases of brilliant colors. None of them were recognizable from her college art appreciation course, but she did react to the emotions radiating at her. It would be too much of a good thing to be around them all the time. She thought that a single one of the paintings would overwhelm her small home, and she'd have to sneak glances at it from odd angles and around corners to avoid emotional overload. She wondered how Schultz was taking it all, but when she looked at him, she saw that he had gone into his blank cop stare. A convenient all-purpose defense, just like the nonjudgmental face she could summon up as a practicing psychologist.

Rebecca took them to a small office at the rear of the

store. There was a worn desk, a wooden swivel chair, and director's chair with bright orange fabric inserts. The place was so tiny that the three of them were practically bumping elbows. PJ wondered what it was like to work day after day in this cubbyhole with PROPRIETOR. She hoped, for Rebecca's sake, that she spent most of her time on the sales floor. Unless, of course, PROPRIETOR was a Harrison Ford clone.

Rebecca gestured for PJ and Schultz to sit. PJ took the swivel chair, leaving Schultz the orange director's chair. He shrugged and plopped into it. It was touch and go for a moment, but it held.

Rebecca leaned against the desk, crossing her legs at the ankles. She was doing a good job of trying to look relaxed, but PJ knew that she was agitated. The air around her practically hummed.

PJ studied the woman. She was shorter than average, about PJ's height, and a few years older. She was built like a sparrow, with delicate hands that waved and fluttered as she spoke. Her pale face was angular, accented by hair pulled back tightly and worn in a waist-length single braid down her back. She wore a long-sleeved white turtleneck tucked securely into a sky-blue skirt splattered with yellow suns. The skirt came down to her ankles, which were covered by leather lace-up ankle boots. Very little actual skin showed, and PJ thought that perhaps the woman had some disfigurement, perhaps an old burn scar. Both the woman and the clothing gave the impression that she was hiding something.

"I'd offer you some coffee, but Mrs. Trent doesn't drink it, so we don't have a coffee maker. I can fix some tea, if you'd like," Rebecca said.

"No, thank you, Miss Singer," PJ said. She was certain

Schultz would wait for her lead in this situation. "It is Miss, isn't it?"

PJ surprised herself with the question, thinking that some of Schultz's brusque manner must have rubbed off on her. That wasn't the sort of question she normally asked within two minutes of meeting someone.

"Yes. I've never married. I suppose that makes me an old maid."

"I prefer to think of it as a woman who won't settle for anything less than the best," PJ said, "and is still looking."

That got a snort from Schultz and a brittle laugh from Rebecca. PJ let the moment stretch out, hoping Rebecca would speak, rushing in to fill the vacuum. She had found that a useful way of extracting information, but in this case it didn't work.

"Detective Schultz and I are going over the Washburn case, interviewing all those who were involved in any way, hoping to get a fresh perspective," PJ said. "Could you answer a few questions for us?"

"The detective explained all that on the phone. I can certainly try to answer all your questions, but what happened to stir up interest in Mr. Washburn's death? I thought the police had written it off to a burglar surprised in the act."

"There's no such thing as writing off a case, Miss Singer," Schultz injected. "The killer's gotten away with it for a year, and we'd like to see justice done."

"Justice. Yes. Go ahead with your questions."

"You're the one who discovered the body. Can you tell us what occurred?" PJ said.

"I've been over this . . ." Hands fluttered briefly, then rested against her thighs, ready to take flight again. She nodded. "Fresh perspective. All right. Mr. Washburn gave me a small package to ship to London just as I was leaving.

It was about five o'clock, my usual quitting time. He asked me to wait just a moment while he addressed the package."

"What was in it?"

"A crystal bud vase which a client had requested. It had taken Mr. Washburn about a month to locate the exact one the client wanted. It was paid for in advance. Routine. Mr. Washburn handed me the package at the door, then turned on the alarm system as soon as I left."

"How do you know that?" Schultz said.

"The system beeped when you did certain functions. Activating it had a particular series of four beeps. I could hear it from outside."

"How did you spend the evening?" PJ said.

"It was too late to ship the package, so I went directly home. I fixed dinner and read for a couple of hours. Then I went out for a walk before showering and going to bed."

Flutter.

"Anyone see you on this walk?" Schultz asked.

"No. Usually I see a couple of neighbors walking, too, but that night it was chilly and drizzling. I was the only one out. The next morning, I got to the gallery a few minutes late because I stopped on my way to ship the vase. Are you sure you wouldn't like some tea?"

"No, thank you. Take your time, Miss Singer. I know this must be hard for you. What happened when you got to the gallery?"

"The front door was closed, but the alarm system was turned off. I was surprised about that, because I was usually the first one to arrive in the morning and I had to deactivate the alarm myself. Even if one of us was working inside, the alarm stayed on until the shop opened at ten. Just like here at Art World."

"So you suspected something was wrong?"

"I didn't just suspect it, I knew it. I had a terrible feeling.

I went straight to Mr. Washburn's office. The door was standing open, which it usually wasn't. I saw blood on the floor. A trail of blood. It was horrible."

She paused for so long that PJ thought she'd have to prompt for more. Then one of Rebecca's hands flew up and landed gently at her throat.

"I saw him. Patrick . . . Mr. Washburn. First I saw his shoes. Then I went further into the office and saw . . . the rest of him. There was so much blood. I ran back out and called the police from the wall phone near the front door. Then I went to the bathroom and threw up."

"We're sorry to have to put you through this again," PJ said. There was a grunt of agreement from Schultz.

"The galleries were closed for a week. There are five of them, you know. Then James took over. I left a couple of weeks later. It took me almost six months to find a new job. I like Art World."

It sounded as though she was trying to convince herself of that. PJ couldn't shake the feeling that Rebecca was covering something up. Maybe it was the way the corner of her eye twitched a little when she talked about James.

"Tell us about James," PJ said. "I gather you two didn't see eye-to-eye about running the galleries?"

Rebecca hesitated before answering. "His ideas were very different from mine. For example, he wanted to computerize the business right away, and I'm old-fashioned. Mr. Washburn kept all the records by hand. In fact, that's what he was doing in his office that night, getting tax information ready for the accountant as he had done for years."

Schultz stood up abruptly. "I'm sure we don't need any more of your time, Miss Singer," he said.

PJ was slow in responding, but got to her feet.

"I'll see you out, then," Rebecca said. "It's almost time

to open up the shop anyway. Mrs. Trent will be here in a few minutes."

Schultz was just backing the car out when Mrs. Trent arrived. She glared at them for having taken her parking spot. The two cars did an awkward dance, since neither had much room to back up. Eventually Schultz pulled out in traffic, waving cheerfully. He was rewarded with a scowl.

"Christ, I think her face froze like that a few decades ago," he said. "So what do you think?"

PJ knew he wasn't talking about Mrs. Trent's face. "I'd have a hard time putting her in that bloody scene with a gun in her hand," PJ said. "But I do have the strong feeling she was hiding something. I'm not sure what it was, but I think she didn't want people to know she was in love with him. He had a long-term faithful marriage and was caught up in his memories after his wife died. Rebecca did say she was old-fashioned. She's probably used to concealing her feelings for Washburn."

"Score one for you. She didn't do it."

"Just like that, you're sure?"

"As sure as I can be of anything in this business. The thing is, she didn't expect to find him on the floor. It was a terrible discovery. You can see that on her face when she relives it."

"Speaking of reliving it, I've got a computer simulation ready. We can run through it when we get back."

"I think you should put something together on the teacher's murder," Schultz said. "Anything come of those photos?"

"Nothing yet. I can make a simulation based on Barnesworth's reports, but I'll have to do it on my own time. We're not officially on that case."

"Do it. I have a feeling that case is going to come knocking."

PJ's first response was a flare of anger. She was the boss, after all. Schultz didn't give her assignments.

"I'll take care of my own schedule, Detective," she said. She poked him in the arm for emphasis.

"Simmer down, Doc. I just think it's more up your alley than Barnesworth's."

"What makes you say that?"

"Because of the way it was done. Overkill. Anybody has that much pent-up shit inside, it's going to spew out again. You should be profiling this creep. Looking at him up, down, and sideways on the computer."

"You think there will be another killing." PJ had felt that way all along, and in a morbid way she was pleased to hear a confirmation from Schultz. He turned toward her, letting the car fend for itself in traffic. For a moment his eyes were tunnels straight into his soul, the soul of a man who had killed in the cause of justice and who might have to do it again someday.

"Damn straight. Things are going to get worse before we catch the creep."

He returned his attention to his driving, but she noticed that his hands gripped the steering wheel tighter than necessary.

You're the one who will catch the killer . . .

PJ shuddered. She had known the teacher, Ed Mitchell. This was the second time in her brief career with the St. Louis Police Department that someone she knew had turned up as a murder victim. In the forty years of her life before joining CHIP, she had come up against death. Her father had died of a heart attack, an older brother of a childhood friend had gone to Vietnam and never returned, a colleague had been killed in a small plane crash. But violent crime hadn't cupped her heart in its icy fingers the way it did now.

She thought about Bill Lakeland, Winston's father. Perhaps he was better off not getting to know her.

She wondered how Schultz stood it, year after year.

"Doc?"

"Sorry. I'll get on it this weekend."

"Speaking of this weekend, you got any plans? We could get together."

"No, I . . ." PJ stopped as what Schultz was saying sank in. She was about to find out why he had been being so solicitous all day. "Leo, are you asking me out?"

"Shit, no. Not that a good-looking woman like you shouldn't be dating. I could introduce you to some of the guys in the department. You shouldn't be wasting your time on limp dicks with crazy wives."

PJ was stung by his reference to her friend Bill Lakeland, and irrationally disappointed that he wasn't asking her out, even though she wasn't sure she'd have said yes. Then she recognized the defensive, nervous tone in his voice, and knew that meant only one thing.

"Does this involve Nurse Helen?"

CHAPTER

10

They were stopped at a traffic light, and Schultz studied his outside mirror, avoiding any chance of eye contact with PJ.

"I thought it might be a good idea to go slow with her," Schultz said.

"Slow? You've known her for nearly six months, and in all that time she hasn't shown the slightest interest in you. That's not just slow, it's glacial."

Helen Boxwood was a nursing supervisor Schultz had met during a previous case. He knew he had gotten off to a bad start with her by using the sarcasm that others who knew him on the job had learned to deflect. He had asked PJ to intervene on his behalf, to learn more about Helen. In talking with her, PJ had learned that Helen had an abusive husband who was serving time in jail for murdering a man in a bar fight. With her husband out of the picture, Helen had taken years to build up her self-respect. She had her grown daughters and her job, and no inclination to begin a relationship with another man. Any man, including Schultz, who wouldn't accept the situation. He couldn't accept it.

He was in love.

It wasn't as if he was some pimply-faced kid who confused love with a quick grope in the backseat. Fifty-four years old was old enough to know his own mind, he reasoned. He had parted with Julia, his wife of thirty years, and the divorce was nearly final. The two of them had grown apart, and realized that they were two strangers sharing living quarters, with nothing in common but a smart aleck son who embarrassed his cop father by selling drugs to kids in front of a school. Rick was in prison, and Schultz hoped that he could help his son turn his life around when the jail sentence was over. It wasn't going to be easy, since Rick was lazy and irresponsible.

Schultz had once been madly in love with Julia, and that was the way he felt about Helen now. He wasn't about to let a little thing like her total indifference stop him.

"I'm not going to let that comment get to me, Doc, because I razz you about your men friends and you pretty much take it. We can talk to each other about these things." He glanced at PJ's face and found one corner of her mouth upturned. He took that for a smile and a signal that he should continue.

"I figure we could all go out together, you know, like a double date."

"You and Helen and me and one of the limp dicks."

"Yeah, I suppose I could put up with one of them for the evening. Make it Lakeland. He's almost okay, even if he's not good enough for you."

A short, sharp laugh burst from PJ, even though her hand had moved up to her mouth to stifle it.

"You're not my father, Detective. You don't have to approve of the men I'm seeing."

"It's not like you're really seeing them. The way I read it, neither of them has made a play for you yet."

"Just where do you hear things like this?" PJ fairly sputtered. "Is this department gossip?"

"The walls have ears," he said. "The corn, too."

"I'd like to know just what . . ."

"Look, we're getting sidetracked here," Schultz said. "You want to go out or not? Dinner and a movie. Saturday night. We don't even have to see a shoot-'em-up. The women get to choose the flick."

PJ appeared to be considering the proposition, so he pressed his advantage. "Late dessert. You know, someplace romantic with tablecloths and candles."

He turned into the Headquarters lot, pulled into a parking spot, and killed the Pacer's engine. This time there was no belching from the car's dubious digestive system. A quick look at PJ revealed that the lines between her eyes looked like a miniature Grand Canyon. Doubt. Suspicion.

The jig was up.

"Have you asked Helen yet?" she said, using her Boss Woman voice that could peel paint from metal. The Pacer had probably just increased its ugly quotient a hundred-fold.

"I thought maybe you could do that," he said. Best to play it straight, as if PJ maintaining his social calendar was the expected thing. She shook her head.

"Hey, don't I at least get some points for thinking of it?" he said. "Maybe she'd go for it. It's not the same as me asking her out, which I've already found out doesn't work."

"I've told you that you should give up. It's a lost cause."

"Maybe she just needs some positive relationships in her life, as you shrinks would say. How about it, Doc?"

To his surprise, PJ looked thoughtful. He wasn't down and out yet.

"It would be nice for Helen to get out for an evening," she said.

His heart flip-flopped.

"She doesn't have any social network, with her daughters away at college. I'll bet she hasn't seen a movie in years. No romantic late-night desserts and candles, though," she said sternly. "You'd have to keep this on a friendly basis."

"I can be friendly."

"And no pressure."

Schultz raised both palms in a placating gesture. "Do I look like the kind of guy to pressure anybody?"

"All I can do is ask," she said.

Schultz rubbed his upraised palms together, then opened the door to get out of the car. "Should I bring flowers or candy? Or both?"

PJ sighed and got out of the car. He made no effort to open the door for her.

CHAPTER

11

Schultz trailed after PJ as she headed back to her office. He stopped in the men's room across the hallway from her office door. Too much coffee had passed his lips as he had sat at home, fortifying himself before picking up PJ. He had built up his nerve to ask her about the four of them going out to dinner, and he was pleased with the result.

When he entered PJ's office, she offered to make coffee. He declined, inwardly wincing at the thought of more caffeine. As she seated herself at the wooden desk that had probably been present at more briefings than he had, he saw her slip on her law-enforcement demeanor. It was like watching a doctor come in off the golf course and put on the white coat. Ready for business. He accepted that about her.

The two of them were alike in many ways, but that was

the biggest difference. He wore his white coat all the time. Slept in it, in fact.

She pressed a few keys on the computer keyboard, getting ready to run the simulation of the gallery murder.

"Want to try it out?" she said. She held the helmet out to him.

He took the contraption from her. It looked like an upside-down colander with wires sticking out. Whenever he used it, he half expected spaghetti to fall out. An HMD, she called it, for Head-Mounted Display. She had told him it was not one of the commercial versions. The grant money that had purchased the high-powered work station in PJ's office didn't stretch to include sleek add-ons. She had wormed the helmet and some fancy mesh gloves out of Dr. Mike Wolf, a researcher at Washington University.

For a while, Mike had seemed a promising match for PJ. He was smart, earned good money, and was into the same computer stuff as she was. But the guy had turned out to be an emotional basket case. PJ told him the story one day over milkshakes at Millie's Diner. Mike's druggie wife had tried to commit suicide with a gunshot to the head and only gotten the job partway done. She ended up in a home somewhere, with the smarts of a two-year-old, or maybe not even that. Mike acted like he pulled the trigger, and the poor guy just couldn't get on with his life. Basically he wanted a shoulder to cry on, while it was apparent to all that PJ needed to be laid.

Bill Lakeland had possibilities, but he was also tied to the past. His wife didn't try to blow her head off, but she was also struggling with drug addictions. The woman lived in a supervised halfway house, and Bill claimed she'd make it back to his loving arms "one of these days." He didn't know what it was about PJ, but she seemed to attract the guys with so much emotional baggage they could travel around the world.

Except for himself, of course. He would have been good for PJ, would've taught her a thing or two in bed, too, but his heart belonged to Helen.

Although, he mused as she helped him with the data gloves, there was nothing wrong with a little straightforward lust, and men and women their age didn't need to be coy about it.

PJ was a very attractive woman, when you got past that shrink attitude. She reminded him of that chocolate sauce you poured onto ice cream that hardened into a thin shell. Once you broke through the shell with a spoon, the ice cream was at your mercy.

In all the years of his marriage to Julia, he had never cheated on her. He just had no urge to. There were a lot of nights away from the house, and he'd had plenty of offers from women who liked a man in a uniform with broad shoulders, a flat stomach, and a trim ass. He treated women with respect, and even more important, had a full head of hair then. Oh, sure, he had a good fantasy life, those lovely, understanding women who sprang to life in his mind at that point in his marriage when he began waking up with more hard-ons than Julia appreciated. He imagined most married men had their fantasies. But the cords that tied one heart to another, one life to another, had been severed, and Schultz was adrift.

Everything seemed up for grabs, and if PJ got close enough, he might just grab her. Chuckling, he flexed his fingers, bending the fine mesh gloves.

"What are you laughing at?" PJ said. "I thought you always took these reenactments very seriously."

"I do. I was just picturing you and me doing it on the

desk, with the computer going wild. Input. Too much input.''

He couldn't see her face because the helmet blocked his view, but he knew that it had grown a nasty frown, and that the tips of her ears were red. Whatever else his boss was, she was fun to tweak.

"I'm starting you outside the gallery," she said, as if he hadn't said anything. "The whole thing runs about three minutes. You'll be an FOTW this time through."

Fly On The Wall. An observer of events, unable to affect the course of the simulation. Kind of like the last five years of his marriage to Julia.

His eyes were greeted by the two blue rectangles which were actually two small monitors. The HMD blocked other sources of light, so that the monitors became his visual world. His mind would interpret the images on them as life-size and 3D. He was about to enter a world that existed only in a computer's memory. Actually, PJ had explained to him that the memory of the workstation wasn't large enough to contain the entire complicated set of images that the brain processed regularly as "reality." The real world, the one he lived in and could see without the helmet, surrounded him and went on even outside the room he was in. In the computer's world, the only thing that appeared were images in the direction in which he was looking. If he turned his head, a different set of images were rapidly swapped out from the computer's storage to active memory. If it was done rapidly and smoothly enough, it appeared as though he was in one continuous world. Virtual reality fooled the mind into thinking it was much larger than it actually was.

He thought about the implications for porno films.

"Ready?"

"Ready," he said. It took his eyes a moment to adjust.

He was standing in the showroom of the Washburn Gallery, which he recognized from the crime scene photos taken a year ago. PJ had visited the gallery, pretending to be a customer, to see what had changed. She had refused to take him along because he didn't look like the typical customer, and she wanted her visit to be unremarkable. That was true, that part about the typical customer, but he'd given her a hard time about it. PJ had reported that the layout was basically the same as in the photos. Only the items on display had changed over the course of the year.

The entire showroom was about twenty-by-twenty. He immediately got the sense of having things crowded around him, which was the way the gallery had come across in the crime scene photos. The statuary, pottery, and even the paintings and woven hangings on the wall seemed to press in upon him. He pushed out with his elbows as if to define a cylinder of space around himself. He didn't like to have his own space infringed upon, even though he used that tactic frequently on other people. He could see the front door, and, twisting his head slightly to the right, the door to the rear office, which was standing open.

There was a knock at the front door—the HMD had built-in speakers—and Patrick Washburn walked into the showroom, coming from the rear office. The likeness was remarkable. PJ had taken a photo of Washburn and scanned it into the computer. Then her program had taken the image, filled in the parts that were missing in the photo, and set the whole apparition in motion. She called it scanimation. He thought of it as raising the dead.

Washburn approached him and passed, paying no attention to Schultz, who remembered that he was an FOTW. The man looked out the peephole on the door, frowned, and punched keys on the alarm console next to the door.

The console beeped its compliance and the door swung open. A man shoved his way inside, one of her generic male creations she called a Genman. He was wearing a nondescript jacket, jeans, and leather gloves, and his face was that of the classic man in the crowd. Washburn and the Genman began to have a vocal argument, but the words weren't clear.

Schultz used the data gloves to move forward by tapping his left palm with the fingers of his right hand. He moved into the scene one step for each tap. That had taken some getting used to when he had first immersed, as PJ called it. At least he didn't thrash around quite as much now.

Up close, he still couldn't hear the argument distinctly. It sounded like crowd noise at the ballpark. He figured that was a good substitute, since PJ didn't know what the people actually said. Or, for that matter, if there was an argument at all. She was using the computer to extrapolate from known circumstances.

"I see you're not going for the straight burglary scenario," Schultz said, talking to a PJ he couldn't see but knew was there.

"I thought we threw that out a long time ago," PJ responded. Her disembodied voice seemed to come from the statue of Venus in the corner of the showroom.

"That's what I ..." Schultz nodded vigorously, and immediately regretted it. The virtual world bobbed wildly as it tried to adjust to his rapid head movement. Objects and people alike blurred into gray streaks. He felt dizzy as his inner ears told him he was spinning off balance even though his body sense told him he was standing still.

He felt PJ's hand on his arm, a steadying influence.

"Close your eyes," she said. He complied, and the spinning lessened.

He felt the warmth of her hand, the slight electricity of

her touch. The hairs on his arm rose. She lifted her palm, but kept her fingers in contact with his skin and slid them down his arm, lingering slightly on the back of his hand. He took a deep breath, drawing in her clean scent. If he hadn't been wearing the HMD, she would have seen his frank interest.

Christ, what's going on here?

"What you're feeling is what happens to some people every time they try VR," PJ said. There was something odd about her voice, something controlled.

Did she feel it, too?

"You'll be okay in a minute, Leo. It was just that quick head motion."

He liked the way she said that, called him Leo.

He opened his eyes, and the scene was back to normal. The simulation clock had kept running while he was out of commission. When he refocused on what was happening, he was just in time to see Genman pull a gun from beneath his jacket. The scene was so real and the action so sudden that Schultz lurched forward in an attempt to intervene, to disarm the man and prevent what was about to happen. The motion caused some blurring of what he was seeing, and he bumped hard into PJ, but it wasn't enough to miss what happened next. Washburn turned around and ran toward the office, evidently seeing it as a safe haven, maybe a place he could call the police. He didn't quite get there.

The first bullet caught up with him and hit him low in the back, about where his right kidney was. Washburn's body shook, but he was still on his feet, still moving. Still looking for that safe haven. The second shot, fired in quick succession, punched him a little higher and ripped through his liver, as the autopsy had shown.

Schultz was breathing fast, caught up in things, exhaling

hard through his nose. Washburn toppled like a drunken man, hitting the floor hard and lying still. Schultz's own experience supplied the smells that were missing, the blood, urine, and fear, and the sense of a life slipping through his fingers, seeping out onto the floor.

The hair on his arms rose again, this time with the chill of encroaching death.

Genman moved closer, standing right next to Schultz, looking down at the fallen man. Washburn groaned and began to crawl across the office floor, trying to reach the telephone on the desk, trying not to give up and lie there and die. Blood formed a wide path behind him, and his hands, as they clenched and slipped on the vinyl floor, left patterns that looked like the kind of stylized flowers children drew. Genman stepped across the crawling man and plucked the phone cord from the wall jack, then disconnected it from the phone. He balled up the cord and stuffed it in the pocket of his jeans.

With Washburn still futilely crawling, Genman began removing paintings from the walls of the showroom, stuffing them quickly into zippered portfolio carriers he pulled from a cabinet in the corner of the office. When he had as many paintings as he could carry, he left without a backward glance at the man on the floor, who had now stopped moving.

Schultz pulled the helmet off. "Christ. That was one mean son-of-a-bitch."

"He was an SOB who knew something about art, too. Did you notice from the report that he took only the most valuable pieces?"

"If it was a burglar, he would have cased the place ahead of time. He would know exactly what would bring the best price. Those guys are no dummies. It's not the same as knocking off a liquor store." Schultz stripped off the gloves. "Was the office door closed when you visited the gallery?"

"Yes, it was. Why?"

"I figured it would be closed when customers were wandering around. It was probably in the case file but didn't stand out like it did when I saw it in the simulation. Sometimes this computer shit actually does some good."

"What stood out?"

"Even if our burglar checked the place out in advance, posing as a customer like you, how did he know to make a beeline for that cabinet with the big envelopes in it? Guy's got X-ray vision?"

"So maybe he was a former customer. Customers might have been taken into the office."

"Weak. There were a couple of chairs and a table out in the showroom where crass things like the handling of money took place."

"So you're thinking only an employee would know where to look for the portfolios."

"Or a family member," Schultz said. He could think of nothing more delightful at the moment than slapping handcuffs on Washburn's obnoxious son James.

"There are five galleries worldwide. Each has a manager and at least two assistants. Assuming the stores all use the same distinctive wrapping to protect valuable purchases, that means a lot of employees would know. Fifteen, by my arithmetic."

"Spoilsport."

She looked down her nose at him. "It seems to have fallen to me to point out the inadequacies of your logic."

"Bullshitting intellectual."

"Really, Detective. Did you speak to your former boss like that?"

"Hell, yes. That's why he's former. Have you been through this?" He gestured at the helmet.

PJ sometimes shied away from her own virtual reality creations, especially from taking the role of the killer. The intimacy of it made her feel as though she was committing the crime herself. Schultz didn't understand that attitude and put it down to the difference between a civilian and a member of the Department. He didn't have any problem with the simulations, even though he tended to get caught up in them. To him, they were a tool, nothing more.

He had re-created crimes in the real world countless times, using other willing cops as killers and corpses, playing out scenes in slow motion, trying to understand. Trying out angles of attack, arcs of weapons, where bodies would fall. Always trying to get that edge, that one thing that would allow him to catch the creep. Sometimes, during one of those re-creations, things would snap into place for him, and he'd find himself staring, mentally at least, into the killer's face.

He was a little embarrassed that he had lunged forward when Genman pulled the gun, trying to stop the killing. If PJ realized what he had done, she had the grace not to mention it, in spite of his provocation.

"Yes, I've been through it. Several times," she said, turning her eyes away momentarily. "I wanted to grab the gun away and arrest Genman on the spot."

"I'd do a lot more than arrest him," Schultz said.

"Now that you mention it, I might have stomped on his toes."

The two locked gazes for a moment, both trying to keep straight faces. Schultz was the first to give. His laughter bounced off the walls of the office, and it was joined shortly by hers.

"So can you see Rebecca Singer doing that?" she asked when things had settled down.

"Probably not."

"What's this probably business? In the car you said you were sure she hadn't done it."

He shrugged. "I reconsidered. I decided all women are capable of the vilest acts under the sun."

He made a quick exit as she pelted him with paper clips.

CHAPTER

12

On her way home from work, PJ stopped at a grocery store to load up for the weekend. She started out bouncy, steering her cart with the enthusiasm of a 1950's housewife. After a few aisles, she was lagging and tossing whatever looked even slightly appealing into the cart. She knew that later on she would have to justify how three different types of cookies, a couple of cinnamon rolls, and a box of frozen jalapeño poppers somehow made it into her grocery bags. She headed for her car, pushing the cart, and found herself standing and staring at the green Ford Escort. She just couldn't get used to it. She missed her VW Rabbit convertible, which had been reduced to a sorry-looking charred frame the last time she saw it. With a sigh, she walked around to the back of the Escort and popped open the trunk lid.

Loading in four gallons of milk, she reflected on how fast her son was growing. His bones practically lengthened in front of her eyes. It seemed that his skin couldn't possibly grow fast enough to keep up. And as far as attitude was concerned, he was twelve going on sixteen. Defiance was popping out all over, like other kids grew pimples.

She had been riding a tidal wave of change in her life for the last couple of years, and she didn't expect to reach smooth sailing with Thomas for another ten years or so. During the divorce, he had blamed her for concentrating too much on her career and not spending enough time with the family. In his mind, that was the reason Dad sought out another woman. Thomas had a more balanced view now, but PJ had come to realize that she hadn't worked as hard at keeping the marriage going as she could have.

Her career as a psychologist involved in marketing studies had seemed compelling to her then, a magnet drawing her away from family life. She had enjoyed using her profiling skills and computer simulations to develop VR grocery stores. Consumers had paced the virtual aisles, plucking products from the shelves, as she had just finished doing in the real world. Showing a customer a drawing of a new packaging idea wasn't in the same league as allowing the customer to pick the product up off the shelf, examine it, and make that mysterious decision to toss it in the shopping cart or put it back. Packaging and products that were flops could be weeded out before they reached the expensive stages of manufacture and distribution. Research subjects practically beat down her door to be included in a study. It was a lot more fun than standing in a shopping mall answering survey questions.

After months of self-examination, she knew that she wouldn't have been an iron filing to the career magnet if there hadn't already been something deeply wrong in her relationship with Steven. There had been a kind of hollowness, like a jack-o'-lantern whose flesh sank in on itself after Halloween, until there was nothing left but an orange pancake and a few dried seeds.

It was an unfortunate mental image of her current love life.

At least the Escort, with its vinyl upholstery and Spartan dash, had a good heater. Warm air dispelled the cold fear that she had traded one type of hollowness for another.

She replayed in her mind what she was already calling "the incident" with Schultz, what had happened during the brief unsteadiness he had experienced during the computer simulation.

Wanting to reach out and rest her hand on his thigh.

Her hand on his arm, leaning close, letting her fingers run the length of his arm, reluctant to lift them.

Her fingers stroking him.

His nostrils flaring, chest rising and falling with her scent inside him. If he hadn't been wearing the HMD, he would have seen the heat in her eyes.

What on earth is going on? I've got to get a life, or at least a man.

An hour and a half later, she was back in the Escort with Thomas, on the way to talk with his science teacher. It was the first year he had decided to enter the Science Fair, and Mrs. Eddington had suggested a conference so that she could offer suggestions and talk over the rules. PJ would rather have settled down with a book, a cinnamon roll, and some hot cocoa, but she was driving to school instead. She had even phoned Mrs. Eddington at the school right after dinner to confirm the appointment, hoping that the woman would announce "I'd rather go home and take a hot bath, if you don't mind. Let's make it some other time." No such luck.

The night had a wild feel to it, with fog dimming the

outlines of cars and houses, making it seem as though the street was a canyon, the familiar houses on either side transformed into forbidding walls. Rainwater coursed along the canyon floor, toiling at its work of carving the chasm down from the level of the rooftops.

The rain, which had briefly stopped, picked up volume just as she pulled into the school's parking lot. She had been hoping the lull would last long enough so that they could stay dry on their way into the building. The lot was about half full. There was an event going on in the gymnasium, a music recital by eighth graders. Rectangles of light from the windows should have provided a warm welcome on the damp, chilly night, but instead they reminded PJ of the cold chemical glow of lightning bugs.

PJ didn't like umbrellas, so she decided to make the dash to the door. Thomas was out of the car and waiting for her, rain dripping from the hood of his jacket as she dragged her tired, and now wet, self into the shelter of the overhang above the door.

If she had still been with Steven, she could have bribed him into coming tonight. Single parenting was hard, and it wasn't going to get any easier. There was only herself to rely upon. Steven was far away in Denver, and involved with his new wife and son. She gave herself ten seconds of feeling overwhelmed, then lifted her chin and stepped up to the door.

She was a little ashamed of thinking about bribing someone, even Thomas's father, to take the boy to a teacher's conference. PJ pulled the door open and said, a little heartier than necessary, "I'm glad Mrs. Eddington could find time for this."

"Yeah, Mom, I'm wet and tired, too. Let's go see what the old broad has to say."

She raised her eyebrows at his language but didn't pursue it. As far as she could remember, Mrs. Eddington was about PJ's age. It was nice to know that her own son probably thought of his mom as an old broad.

As they made their way through the halls, they could hear noise coming from the gym. It sounded as though a lot of determined students were stomping their feet. Any accompanying music was drowned out. PJ gave silent thanks that Thomas wasn't in the eighth grade, or she'd have a headache on top of her other miseries.

Mrs. Eddington's room was on the first floor. The hallways were brightly lit due to the evening activity at the school, and looked oddly empty. There should be kids swarming between classes, lockers banging shut, called-out plans for getting together after school. She looked at the papers tacked up on the walls as she made her way down the hall. There were reports on ecology, drawings of dinosaurs and the first American flag, and various renditions of the Bill of Rights, some of which came out more like the Ten Commandments.

Thomas lagged behind at a drinking fountain, so PJ got to the door first. It was closed, which PJ thought was strange if the woman was expecting someone. Thinking that it was probably closed to block out the noise from the gym, she reached for the handle. She stopped, her hand frozen a couple of inches away.

CHAPTER

13

There was blood on the handle, and as soon as she saw it, she could smell it. It was fresh. Another smell registered, something she had run across before and hoped never to encounter again: human butchery. An image came of the ground beef she had bought at the grocery store, sitting in its Styrofoam tray with just a few drops of blood collected underneath. Plunging her hands into it, shaping it. She closed her eyes and squeezed the thought away.

There was a window in the door, but it was covered from the inside with a poster of some kind as effectively as if the poster were a window shade. Light filtered through from inside the room, but she couldn't see in.

She looked at Thomas, who was down the hall bent over the drinking fountain. She wanted to shout at him to run, but was afraid that whoever had left the blood there might still be in the building. Shouting might bring unwanted attention.

If anyone was going to attract attention, it was going to be her. Like a bird flopping around with a fake broken wing to protect her babies, PJ wanted to draw whoever had left the blood on the doorknob to her. She reached for the knob and turned. It felt slippery under her palm. She pushed the door open and took one step inside.

Her eyes skittered up and came to rest on a hornet's nest on a branch, mounted in the far corner of the room. She didn't want to see the torso propped up in Mrs. Eddington's chair.

Thomas would be coming soon, so she forced herself to look at the blood on the floor. On the blackboard the spatters looked maroon. The torso looked bleak and inhuman, but she noticed that only the hands, feet, and head were missing. The arms and legs were intact.

The missing parts were on the children's desks. Mrs. Eddington's head was turned toward the door, ready to say hello to her visitors. Except that her mouth was taped shut.

The room was empty of the living, although there was such a strong sense of the killer at work that PJ's skin crawled. She stifled a scream. She backed out, closing the door behind her, and bumped into Thomas.

"Mom?" He was reading the horror on her face.

She had enough presence of mind to tuck her bloody right hand out of sight behind her back. She put her other hand on his shoulder and turned him around. Looking both ways in the hallway, she saw that no one else was in this wing of the building besides the two of them. The three of them, rather, if she counted Mrs. Eddington.

Unless someone was hiding in one of the other classrooms.

"We're going back out to the car," she said, her voice barely under control. "Walk quietly and keep looking straight ahead."

His eyes were round as marbles, but he moved to do as she said. She felt his shoulder trembling under her hand, a rabbit under the fox's paw.

The hallway seemed menacing, with doors that might spring open at any moment, revealing an attacker. The stomping from the gymnasium stopped abruptly, and PJ heard the thudding of her heart and the quick rasp of her breathing. She took a deep, deliberate breath and nudged Thomas forward.

The hallway was at least ten times longer than it had been coming in. She moved steadily down it, keeping Thomas slightly behind her so that she faced the unknown first. She couldn't bring herself to think that the killer might be behind her.

The two reached the outside door, then stood under the overhang. She could see the Escort parked a couple of rows away.

Go for it, in the dark? What if the killer was waiting in the parking lot? Turn back into the hallway, find the gym, find a phone? Thomas made the decision for her. He took her hand and ran into the parking lot, tugging her with him. At the car, she fumbled with her keys. When the door opened and the ceiling light came on, her eyes swept the interior of the car before she would let Thomas enter. He threw himself across the backseat. She locked the doors. They were both breathing rapidly, shivering from much more than the cold. She started the engine, moved the car a block away, and pulled over to the curb.

PJ flipped open her cellular phone. She knew she should call 911, but her fingers tapped out Schultz's number.

It seemed only a few moments later that a flashlight shone through the driver's window, startling her.

"It's Schultz. Open up."

She explained briefly, aware that Thomas was soaking up every word, and said only that Mrs. Eddington was dead. She told Schultz that she had spoken to the victim on the phone no more than an hour ago.

A few minutes later, a number of uniformed officers searched the building, finding no intruders. They quietly pulled the principal from the assembly in the gymnasium and explained the situation to her.

PJ, waiting in her car, wanted to blurt out that the woman's blue eyes had pleaded to her, and that if the tape were yanked off her mouth, her trapped screams could still be heard.

Schultz came back over. "You see anyone leave the building?"

"No."

"You left the scene unsecured, with a murderer inside with a bunch of kids," he said flatly.

"I wanted to get Thomas out. I don't know if the murderer was there or not. What are you saying?"

"You should have called from inside. Watched the exits."

"What are you saying?" PJ repeated, her voice getting shrill. "I should have searched the halls and captured the killer? Held him at bay with a piece of chalk? Are you nuts?" She pounded the steering wheel with her fists. "I had my son with me. There was nothing else I could do!"

Schultz put both hands on his hips, bent over, and stuck his face into the car window. "At the least you should have alerted the people inside," he said. "He could have killed again, or taken a child hostage. You had a chance here and you blew it."

"You leave my mom alone!" Thomas yelled from the backseat. "You don't have any right to say things like that. Go fuck yourself!"

"I think you should move away from the car, Detective," PJ said. "We'll talk about this later."

She could see the anger leaving Schultz. His shoulders fell. It was almost as though the light, steady rain outside the car melted him.

"Sorry," he said. "You're right. Under the circumstances, you did the best thing. I'm just pissed, that's all. He was practically in our laps, and now all we can do is mop up."

"Under the circumstances!" she fired back, not ready to let him off the hook so easily. "Don't ever forget I'm a mother first. Catching killers is a distant second for me."

"You're right," he said contritely. He leaned into the window again, speaking to Thomas. "Sorry, son."

He looked so crestfallen that she couldn't stay angry. She knew that he was thinking of a time when he had been close to a killer, had practically felt the motion of the air as the man walked past, but someone died anyway. She sat in silence, wondering if she would feel the same guilt as he did now, going over and over the night's happenings in her own mind, questioning her actions. If she had left home earlier she might have interrupted the killer at work. Mrs. Eddington might still be alive.

Or she and Thomas could be dead.

Anita Collings, one of CHIP's junior team members, took Thomas home, after he had gotten hugs and reassurance from PJ that things were under control. Thomas had still glowered at Schultz, and her heart swelled at her son's protectiveness, even when he must be hurting badly himself.

With Schultz, she went back into the building. He

opened the door to Mrs. Eddington's classroom with a gloved hand and peered around inside. Then he went to the gymnasium while PJ and Dave Whitmore, another CHIP member, waited in front of the science-room door. The program in the gym was nearly over, and it had been decided that an orderly finish was best. Schultz was planning to pull the principal aside again and talk to her. He wanted her to make a brief announcement at the end of the program that the police would be at all doors, collecting and identifying information from everyone who had attended.

PJ could imagine how that was going to go over with the parents, but it was possible that an attendee at the recital was the killer. If so, the person would have had to dispose of bloody clothing and the cutting tool before returning to the gym.

In a short time, Schultz was back. The crime scene technicians had been called, but most of them were asked to wait outside until the parents and students left the building. Uniformed officers blocked both ends of the hallway, securing the crime scene from the curious. The ME's office had been notified earlier, and an assistant was due to arrive soon. The assistant and photographer could work behind the closed classroom door without drawing too much attention, and by the time they were finished, the building would be cleared. Neither Schultz nor PJ wanted to make a big scene in front of the children.

There was a commotion at one end of the hallway that led to a door which opened onto the schoolyard. The cop stationed at that position, charged with controlling access, was talking to someone. It was Barnesworth, who had picked up the scent and arrived with a couple of his detectives to stake their claim.

Schultz looked like he could make good use of a stake.

He had found a better target for his outbursts than PJ, a target that she was sure Schultz wouldn't be apologizing to anytime soon. Schultz hustled down the hall, belligerently shoving himself into Barnesworth's face. They were practically belly to belly.

"This is my case, Schultz. Get the fuck out of my way," Barnesworth said.

"Oh? I thought I was the first detective on the scene. You were probably out dicking around with that slut of yours, the one with the red hair. Your wife know about that piece?"

"Where I was is none of your fucking business. I'm here now, and you gotta leave."

"Says who?" Schultz poked Barnesworth's chest with a rigid finger.

"You shithead. You know this is the same killer. This is my case."

"Same killer? Let's see now. Bashing in the head versus dismemberment. Male victim versus female. Nope. Doesn't sound like the same killer to me."

"How about two teachers whacked in the same school? That give you any thoughts, or is that head of yours too thick?"

Schultz pulled himself up. He radiated so much hostility that PJ thought she might be burned at twenty paces.

"Different killer. My case." He crossed his arms over his chest, an impassable object. Barnesworth's glare bounced right off him.

"Just wait until I talk to Lieutenant Wall. He'll have your balls for breakfast," Barnesworth said. He spun and headed for the door.

"Tattletale, tattletale," Schultz said in a singsong voice, loud enough for both PJ and Barnesworth to hear. The man clenched his fists but kept walking.

Schultz strutted back to PJ like a victorious cock who had chased the intruder from the henhouse.

"I'm probably in for a chewing-out in the morning, but that was worth it," he said. He gestured in the direction of the classroom. "Does all this mean we'll have to postpone our date?"

"How can you—"

"Think of things like that with severed body parts in the vicinity? Life goes on, Doc."

The recital was over, and parents, some carrying sleeping toddlers in their arms, were beginning to trickle out of the gym. Most looked nervously toward PJ and Schultz. The parents were met by uniformed officers, who kept a log but didn't detain any of them.

It was nearly two A.M. by the time PJ got home. She found Anita still there, reading at the kitchen table. Anita reported that Thomas had gotten to sleep with difficulty, eventually giving in about midnight when exhaustion won out over fear, anger, and anxiety.

After saying goodnight to Anita, PJ wearily climbed the stairs to her bedroom. She went to check on Thomas and found him sleeping nearly sideways on the bed, with his feet hanging off. She roused him enough to get his legs back under the blanket, tucked him in, and lightly kissed him, keeping her face near his to feel his breath warm her cheek. Megabite jumped up on the bed and began kneading on Thomas's pillow. Satisfied with her nest-making, the cat settled herself next to him.

PJ remembered the worn-out toddlers she had seen at the school, arms cast around parental necks, hair mussed, heads heavy against trustworthy shoulders. It seemed like such a short time since she had carried Thomas like that, nuzzling into his hair, picking bits of Play-Doh out of it, and breathing in baby shampoo. Such a short time, and the rate at which he was growing up had skyrocketed since he turned twelve.

"Goodnight," she whispered, "and don't let the bed-bugs bite."

CHAPTER

14

"Could we get down to work here?" PJ said. She was in her office Saturday morning, with Schultz, Anita, and Dave crowded in. Schultz had been regaling the others with his treatment of Barnesworth the night before.

"I am working, Doc," he said. "Best thing I could do for this case was keep Barnesworth from walking all over the evidence. Any reason to think this killer's got something personal to say to you?"

PJ was shaken by his abrupt implication. "You think this was a message for me?"

"You did have an appointment with the victim. The killer might have known about that, knew you would find the body."

PJ forced herself to think objectively. "The head was situated so that it was ... staring at me. But that would have been the case for anyone who opened the door." She pictured kids arriving, bustling in the halls, slamming locker doors, turning the doorknob. "No, I can't see that this had anything to do with me."

"What about someone else in the building last night?" Dave asked. "Someone attending the music recital?"

"I doubt it. What reason would the killer have to think that someone attending the recital would leave the gym and come to the science room?" PJ said. "The display of the body would have been a waste. No, I don't think there's a message for anyone in particular. I think it's an acting out of something important to the killer."

"Okay, important in what way?"

PJ considered. "Dismemberment is a huge topic. It can be done in a rage or in a cold manner. Before or after death. Planned or spontaneous. I'll have to spend a lot more time going over the scene and getting some forensic results before I have much to say about that. One thing that stands out is that the tape on the mouth could have meaning for the killer besides preventing the victim's screams from being heard."

PJ didn't want to put Mrs. Eddington's name in that sentence. She understood why homicide investigators used impersonal labels.

"Don't dance around, Doc. What kind of meaning?" Schultz asked. His question was followed by a loud slurp from his coffee cup, which everyone ignored.

"It might be a personal grudge, something the teacher had said to offend the killer, something that the killer thinks should never have been said."

"So the killer probably knew the victim," Schultz said. "That means we should look at her personal and professional life, maybe going back for years. That could amount to thousands of people. A disgruntled student, maybe, grown up and coming back to get all the teachers who gave him poor grades."

"A parent who blames the teacher years later for little Joey not getting into a prestigious college," Anita said. "I've read that parents are fiercely competitive about things like that. Maybe someone felt that there were lost opportunities for a child."

"Don't forget the earlier murder. We should look at where the two victims' lives intersect," PJ said.

"The other teacher's death could have been a stranger murder. Interrupted robbery in the lab," Schultz said it convincingly, but his expression told her he didn't believe it.

"I don't think so. I think it was more personal than that, just like the art gallery murder," PJ said.

Schultz tilted his head and looked at her for a moment in silence. "What makes you come to that conclusion?"

Several answers to that went through PJ's head about the psychological nature of the crimes, but her conclusions seemed to be based more on feelings than on science. "I don't know. Intuition, I guess."

Schultz nodded. "I respect that. You're starting to grow some instincts."

The phone rang, and PJ picked it up on the first ring. It was a short conversation.

"Lieutenant Wall wants to talk to me," she told the group when she replaced the handset. She pinned Schultz with a knowing look.

Schultz rolled his eyes to the ceiling. "Haven't the faintest."

"Good luck, boss," Dave said.

He stood to make room for her to pass in the cramped quarters, and Anita winked at her.

"Give him hell," Schultz said as she made her way into the hall. Then he closed the door behind her, leaving the three of them in her office and leaving her to face the music alone.

When she got to Wall's office, Louie Bertram, the A/V specialist, was on his way out. He nodded at her but avoided her eyes and tried to maneuver his wheelchair to get past her in the hallway. She put a hand on his shoulder to stop him.

"Louie, did I get you in trouble?" PJ was regretting that she had asked him to erase Barnesworth's voice mail messages. In retrospect, it seemed inexcusable. Involving another person in some petty revenge just wasn't her way. It wasn't professional, and as a civilian and a psychologist she had enough of an image problem in the Department already.

"It's okay," he said. "I've been in trouble before. It all blows over in a couple of days."

"I'm sorry. I shouldn't have asked."

"Don't worry about it." He shrugged, loosening her hand from his shoulder. He didn't come out and say it, but she felt that he had enjoyed his role as saboteur. The gleam in his eyes confirmed her feeling. She gave him a thumbs-up and moved toward Wall's door.

"Watch yourself in there," Louie said over his shoulder as he rolled effortlessly down the hallway. "He's mad."

She rapped on the door and went in without waiting for Wall to invite her. Best to take the initiative, although she didn't have the slightest idea what she was going to say in her own defense.

Wall had his back to her, fiddling with something on the battered credenza that spanned nearly the entire rear wall of his office. He let her stew for a minute or two, and even though she knew what he was doing, she found it hard not to spill some words into the space between them.

He spun around in his chair and placed his hands on the desk in front of him, steepling his fingers.

"Was it your idea or Schultz's?" he asked.

She wasn't sure whether he meant deleting the voice mail message or chasing Barnesworth out of the school the night before. But there was no question in her mind where the responsibility was. The boss is responsible for the team members. Best to get it over with.

"Mine. It wasn't the right thing to do, and it'll never happen again."

"A pretty speech. Which offense are you apologizing for?"

"Whichever one you have in mind."

His eyes widened in mock innocence. "Are there more than I know about?"

"Which ones . . . Wait a minute, let's stop playing games here," she said. "I'm talking about running Barnesworth off the scene last night."

"I couldn't care less if Barnesworth got his feathers ruffled at the school. The first detective on the scene establishes the case file until a review shows that the two homicides are clearly connected. Schultz was within his rights at the school, although he could have been nicer about it."

"He didn't start it," she said, coming to her man's defense.

"You'd never know that to listen to the other side."

PJ crossed her arms over her chest. She was getting riled and losing sight of her original intention to be apologetic. Wall hadn't been there, hadn't gotten blood on his hand and stared into the accusing eyes of the dead. From what Schultz had told her, he wasn't cut out for it. He had a reputation for squeamishness. Somehow she felt that put her a step above Wall on the crime-solving ladder even though he outranked her. She visited crime scenes in order to be able to more accurately re-create them in the computer. Her mind sidestepped the fact that sometimes she left the full 3D immersion in the computer simulation to Schultz.

And she was sure Wall was getting a skewed version of the incident from Barnesworth. The man seemed bent on advancing himself at the cost of hampering the investigation. Schultz's actions seemed more and more reasonable as the conversation went on.

Wall put the subject away with a wave of his hand. "That's old stuff between the two of them. Think no more about it."

"Well, then." She started to rise from her chair.

"Then there's the matter of the photographic evidence," he said. She sat back down, waiting for the blast. It wasn't long in coming.

"What the hell do you think you were doing, lady? Your actions can be construed as concealing evidence, making you an accessory to murder. At the very least, you have impeded a lawful investigation."

"I didn't actually conceal anything," PJ said. "I took the photos to the evidence room and logged them in with the proper case number."

"All of the photos?"

It was obvious that Barnesworth had seen the strange entry in his own case log, checked it out, and felt that the photos had considerable significance. He must have talked with the witness, Emory Harquest. Otherwise, the duplicate photos wouldn't be an issue.

"Well, no. But I didn't think it did any harm to keep the duplicates."

"For what purpose?"

PJ reddened. Her answer wasn't going to sound good. "I thought I might look into the case on the side."

"This is a professional law-enforcement agency engaged in homicide investigations, Dr. Gray, not your personal leisure entertainment. This is not Mystery Dinner Theater."

The whip cracked, and PJ felt the stripe across her back.

"If the investigating officer had gotten access to all available evidence in a timely fashion, perhaps there wouldn't even be a second victim. We can't rule that out."

Salt in the wound.

"What's done is done," Wall said. "Let's hope that your actions won't be a problem when this case comes to trial. There are two things you're going to do now."

PJ fidgeted in her chair. She had thought this man was a soft touch, even though others in the Department had told her otherwise. It was just that she'd never run afoul of him before.

"First, you're going to educate yourself on police procedures. We'll write this episode off to ignorance rather than ill intent. I won't have any trouble persuading my superiors about the ignorance part." He tossed a heavy handbook across the desk in her direction. It was the item he had retrieved from his credenza. It was dog-eared and coffee-stained. "Read it. Memorize it."

"Yes, I—"

He cut her off. "The second thing you're going to do is give Barnesworth your full cooperation. CHIP is on this case effective immediately, working under him. Any questions?"

PJ shook her head. Words failed her.

"Dismissed. Tell Schultz I want to see him."

On her way back to her office, lugging the heavy procedural handbook, PJ squeezed back tears. Tough as her session with Wall had been, she had the feeling he had been holding back with her, the way people don't really get too mad at a puppy who messes the carpet before it's learned to whine at the door. That made her even more upset, thinking that Wall was shielding her. It was clear that she was still an outsider.

She took a moment to compose herself before opening her office door. All eyes turned toward her as she entered, and conversation stopped. She imagined they could see her shredded blouse, blood from the lash dripping onto the linoleum.

"You're next," she said to Schultz.

CHAPTER

15

"Good thing Wall doesn't have high blood pressure," Schultz said as they walked into Millie's Diner. "He'd have popped an artery today."

The diner was crowded. Schultz assessed the situation and headed for the counter. There were two stools available, but one of them was the wobbly one that all the regulars avoided. He claimed the sturdy one and let PJ have the other. She seated herself cautiously, knowing what to expect. She wasn't exactly a stranger to the diner, but Schultz had been coming there for many years.

When the front door of the diner closed behind him, it shut out not only the weather but the pull of time. The floor still boasted black-and-white linoleum and the counter still had those little inlaid gold flecks. The chrome stools with their black leatherette tops looked like mushrooms, the kind that picked themselves up and danced in Fantasia. There was a large cutout in the wall between the serving area and the kitchen where food was passed through, and from where Schultz was seated he could see the cloud of grease droplets suspended over the grill. When someone opened the loading door in the back to take out the trash, the cloud blew out and settled on every surface. The plates and coffee mugs were heavy and white and didn't say Taiwan on the back, and there was always a Daily Special.

He rapped his knuckles a couple of times on the counter. "Service!"

The proprietress, a formidable woman who could fry eggs on a grill with one hand and refill coffee cups with the other, approached the two of them. She pointedly ignored Schultz, but reached out and patted PJ's hand.

"Nice to see you, dearie. We've got a wonderful three-cheese soup today. You sure you want to sit next to this guy? I always got to wipe the stool with disinfectant after he leaves." She beamed at PJ.

"The floor, too," the two women said in unison. It was a familiar ritual.

"I'll have the soup and a side salad. Lemon slices, if you have them."

"Of course I do. This is a high-class joint." As Millie turned toward Schultz for his order, her chin lifted and her lips compressed and practically disappeared into her face.

Schultz ordered his usual burger and fries. Millie went off without a word.

"So how did it go with Wall?" PJ asked.

Schultz shook his head. "It's a wonder I can sit down on what's left of my ass. Most of it's in large, bloody chunks on the floor of Wall's office."

PJ winced. "Bad, huh?"

"Not the most pleasant fifteen minutes I've ever spent.

How're we going to work this crap about reporting to Barnesworth?"

"I guess we play it straight," PJ said. "It would probably work better if I did the talking to him and you kept your mouth shut."

She looked as though she was expecting an argument on the issue, but Schultz nodded in agreement. He had taken the entire episode very well, and he could see that it annoyed PJ that she hadn't done the same.

"You haven't said a lot about your own meeting with Wall," Schultz said. "Want to talk about it?"

Schultz was giving her a chance to blow off steam. She pursed her lips and considered. Stalling, she reached for the sugar dispenser on the counter and aligned it with the napkin holder, put the salt shaker on one end and the pepper shaker on the other, then added the ketchup and mustard containers, making a neat row.

"Very nice," Schultz observed. "If I need my condiments rearranged, I know who to call."

It appeared that PJ hadn't even heard him. She was too wrapped up in her inner dialogue.

"I wasn't going to talk about it, but since you twisted my arm, here it is," PJ said. "I'm embarrassed that I let these things happen. I'm even more upset that Wall slapped me down like a naughty child. To him, I'm a know-nothing civilian. Obviously I haven't proven myself, and now I've got even further to go."

Schultz didn't answer right away. He could see that PJ regretted having spilled her emotions like a sack of marbles on the counter. They had skittered away from her, and she couldn't grab them all fast enough and stuff them back in the sack. Her eyes glistened with tears held in check. She probably hadn't cried in front of Wall, or at least he hoped she hadn't, and she certainly wasn't going to do it in front of him. Or Millie, who was hovering at the end of the counter doing an excellent job of looking busy while eavesdropping.

"He throw the handbook at you?" Schultz said.

"Well, he didn't exactly throw it, but yes."

"He make you feel guilty, like the second victim would still be alive if you hadn't screwed up?"

"Yes."

"Well, then, you didn't get any special treatment," Schultz said. "And you've proven yourself to me."

He felt his heart leap out to her, and he wanted to make everything better.

She reached out and placed her hand over his, drawing on his compassion. The contact brought something more, something he wasn't willing to explore. As if she shared his sudden emotional surge, she drew her hand back.

"I'm going to work on that handbook," she said, "and you're going to give me pop quizzes. I don't want Wall sending me to some camp where I have to do a hundred pushups before breakfast."

"If you can do a hundred pushups, I'll swallow my knife and fork," Schultz said. "Sideways." His voice was gruff with emotion, but he showed only practiced neutrality. From the look on her face, PJ had decided it was time to get on more neutral ground.

"I'm going to take Barnesworth through the art gallery VR simulation this afternoon," PJ said. "It should familiarize him with the techniques. I've got something worked up on the Mitchell case, but it's rough. I'll try to polish it up tonight."

"Give me a call when you get finished," Schultz said. "I'd like to see it before Barnesworth gets his paws on it."

Millie materialized with PJ's salad and a cup of coffee for him. He raised his cup and let the industrial-strength steam fill his nose, blocking out the smell of the lemon slices that PJ squeezed onto her salad. Lemons reminded him of a chore he'd always done at his Aunt Lydia's house, where he had gone to live at the age of nine. Every Saturday morning, he had scrubbed the bathrooms with a lemon-scented household cleaner. His younger brother George had gotten off easier. All George'd had to do was dust.

Leo and George Schultz had moved in with their aunt after a fire destroyed their family's farmhouse. Schultz's parents and two sisters had been killed in the fire, which started when lightning struck a nearby tree. The hollow old oak had split, and a large, fiery branch collapsed onto the roof of the house. Nine-year-old Leo and his little brother, three years younger, had been out messing around in the woods. They came out of it with their lives and the clothes on their backs. Aunt Lydia had taken the two country boys into her home and done her best to raise them as city folk like herself. The transformation had worked on George, who now lived in New York and felt at home in a crowd. For Schultz, city life was a veneer, and underneath there was a little boy who longed to run barefoot and splash in the creek when the spring rains filled it.

PJ seemed lost in thought as she speared forkfuls of her salad and raised them to her mouth.

"How's family life these days?" Schultz said.

"What?"

Her fork paused in mid-air. She probably thought he was going to go on again about the men in her life, if that was the correct word for them. He sniffed and said, "You know, family. That short person who lives in your house."

"Oh, you mean Thomas. He's torn up by some shenanigans his father is pulling, but he's handling it well. It looks like Steven wants him to come out to Denver and join the happy trio. He said Thomas could have his old room back. He knows just what buttons to press," she said. She poked a radish with more vehemence than it deserved. "He should have some sort of relationship with his father. I've tried not to be too judgmental."

"Thomas is a bright kid. He knows an asshole when he smells one."

PJ wrinkled her nose. "I guess that's not your special province, then. The loss of two teachers at his school is big news, of course. He says the kids have hardly talked about anything else since Mitchell died, and there's the murder last night on top of that. I wouldn't be surprised if some parents keep their kids home for a while. I know some are requesting transfers to other schools. Mrs. Barry, the principal, brought in counselors who have had both group and individual sessions, and I'm sure they'll have their hands full next week. The school's doing all it can."

"How's Thomas holding up?"

"Well, I think. He's sensitive, but tough as a tank underneath. He's really angry about it, which is right on target. What all the kids need to see is the killer caught."

"Kids shouldn't have to cope with shit like this," Schultz said.

"At least Thomas should be able to get his mind off the murders today. He's spending the day with his new friend Columbus. They're taking in a matinee and then going back to Columbus's house to play computer games. Winston's going along, too."

"Columbus as in the explorer?"

"Yes. I'm sure he's heard that a million times."

Millie delivered the rest of the food. PJ's cheese soup didn't smell half bad. PJ snatched a French fry from Schultz's plate as Millie set it down in front of him.

"Watch it, dearie—"

"Ouch."

"—those are hot," Millie said. "Love to stay and talk, but the place is hoppin' like a frog on the Interstate."

Schultz grabbed the hot sauce and liberally doused his fries before PJ could take any more. The woman had no scruples. He plucked the little flag on a toothpick out of the bun of his hamburger. It was Millie's trademark, that toothpick flag. If he'd collected them since he first started coming to the diner, he'd have enough to decorate Arlington National Cemetery on Veteran's Day by now.

"Why does Millie seem to be giving you the cold shoulder lately?" PJ asked.

"That sounds too straight up for shrink talk. Shouldn't you say she's displaying repressed anger or something?"

She looked down her nose at him. "Don't get huffy. I asked a simple question."

"I forgot to leave a tip a couple of weeks ago," he said.

"Oh. Have you tried making it up?"

"No, and I don't plan to, either. She'll have to live with it." He didn't mention that not only was Millie not speaking to him, she was skimping on his burger toppings, too. His onion slices were so thin they could pass for onionskin paper.

"Anyway, I'm glad to see Thomas broadening his horizons," she said. "Not that I don't like Winston. It's just that boys his age usually travel in packs. I'll have to meet Columbus's parents soon. I've been meaning to ask you . . ."

"Yeah?" Schultz said around a mouthful of hamburger.

"Never mind. I'll take care of it. What's new on the Washburn case?" PJ emptied a pack of oyster crackers into her soup and drowned them with her spoon.

"I thought we should meet James's younger brother."

"The one who's incapacitated? Surely you don't suspect him."

"Something's bothering me about what James said. 'I am Father's only heir.' Sounds like he's rushing his kid brother to the grave. I just think we should get Henry's side of the story."

"The way I understand it, Henry's not going to be able to tell us anything about his father's death," PJ said. "I'm not sure he's even aware of it."

"I've been wondering if there was something fishy about that plane crash," Schultz said.

"So now you've got James knocking off his whole family," PJ said.

Schultz shrugged. "Bad is bad. People get caught up in these things."

CHAPTER

16

"Jeez," Winston said, throwing his arms up to his face, "what's with the flash, man?"

Winston was the first one through the front door of Columbus's house. Thomas, following close behind his friend, moved aside to avoid Winston as the boy stepped back and nearly trod on his toes. Then the flash went off in Thomas's face. "What gives?" Thomas said irritably.

"It's nothing," Columbus said as he collected the two Polaroid shots. "Just a little project of mine. Kind of my own school yearbook."

"Yeah, well, warn us next time," Thomas said. "I don't like being blinded and stepped on."

"Sorry. I didn't think it would bother you this much." The camera and pictures, which were just starting to develop, disappeared into a storage compartment under the seat of a hall tree. "Let's go check out the movie listings," Columbus said.

Columbus led the two boys into the kitchen, where he had spread the entertainment section of the *Post-Dispatch* on the table in advance. As he had predicted, they were immediately distracted, discussing whether or not they could get in to see the latest R-rated action movie. Simpletons. He couldn't understand why Mrs. Eddington had favored them last semester. He should have asked her, but by the time he thought of it, it was too late.

"Where're your mom and dad?" Winston asked when he stopped panting over the movies.

"Out," Columbus said. "Mom left us some sandwiches, though."

Yes, everything is normal in the Wade household, he thought. *I should have made an apple pie.*

Columbus had made the sandwiches himself. The Cow was making the rounds of garage sales and the Turd was playing golf with a business associate. Neither had given a thought to leaving Columbus on his own for the entire Saturday. It was such a relief to them, he was sure, that they didn't have to be cooped up with him.

Columbus served the food. He didn't share any of his chocolate chip granola bars or cookie dough ice cream, though. It was one thing to try to make a good impression and another to actually sacrifice something that mattered to him. His two guests ate like pigs at the trough, especially Winston. He pictured the boy hung up as a skinned and gutted pig, his thighs as pink hams, his calves thick chops. He rolled the idea around in his mind, savoring it. Perhaps he should try a VR simulation of a slaughterhouse.

He ate lightly, content with his images.

Settling into the theater seat an hour later, he watched the faces of his companions as they took in the movie. They had been all bluster and bravado, but when it came down to putting their balls on the line, the group had ended up at a PG-13 comedy. Columbus had simply followed along. He was in chameleon mode, and concentrated on not laughing at an inappropriate point. As soon as he caught the gist of the ridiculous movie plot, he could operate on automatic, and was free to think about other things.

Everything had gone according to plan last night. Well, almost everything. He'd had to improvise when the Turd suggested some wimpy father-son thing at the library. Imagine the man thinking that Columbus would be interested in holing up in a corner and alternately reading aloud chapters of Mark Twain. The place probably had bean-bag cushions, too.

Claiming that he was coming down with a cold, Columbus had begged off. It bugged him to see the obvious relief in the Turd's face. Clearly it had only been an obligation. It did open a new channel for irritating the man, though. He'd have to find some really obnoxious activity and tweak the Turd into taking him. A dog show came to mind. The Turd claimed to be allergic to dogs, and so Columbus had never had one. Too bad. There were a lot of interesting things a boy could do with his dog.

Once in his room, it had been easy to get out of the house. Since his bedroom was on the second floor, he had asked for a collapsible safety ladder. Said he'd learned about it in fire safety class at school and all the kids had them. What did they know anyway? Kids might as well be aliens as far as they were concerned.

The ladder was stored under his bed, and it was a simple matter to unfold it and attach it to the windowsill. After all, it was meant to be used in emergencies. "So simple even a child could do it!" exclaimed the packaging. His window faced the rear yard, and there were trees next to the house, so neighbors wouldn't be curious about a ladder dangling from the second-story window. The last thing he wanted was some nosy shithead calling the cops.

He wasn't worried about his parents discovering the ladder. He knew that as soon as he went to his room, they would veg out in front of the TV. About nine o'clock, they'd yell upstairs and ask if he wanted them to fix any extra popcorn for him. When he didn't answer, they'd just assume the answer was no.

He knew that's what would happen because he had trained them that way. It came in handy.

Mrs. Eddington had been surprised to see him, but not threatened. Adults just weren't threatened by a kid with scrawny legs and flyaway hair. Too bad he didn't have freckles. That would have been the icing on the cake.

Moving behind Mrs. Eddington, making small talk about the Science Fair, he had slipped the length of duct tape over her head and tightly around her throat, slapping the ends onto the back of her chair. Her hands had jumped to her throat, just as he predicted. He had come prepared with several lengths of the tape stuck loosely inside his jacket. He had to move fast. He knew he had only a few seconds before she recovered enough to angrily unpeel the tape. He dove for the floor and fastened a piece around each ankle, anchoring her to the chair. She started screaming, but the door was closed and the music program in the gym was gearing up. The next piece of tape went across her mouth. Not only did that shut her up, but it increased her panic, which played right into his hands. Hands. Her hands were the most difficult to deal with. That was the tricky part. Unfortunately, adults were stronger than he was. He had anticipated that, and brought out the hacksaw.

A quick slice across her right forearm brought sudden tears to her eyes, and she pulled her right arm protectively up next to her body, pressing her left hand over the wound to stop the blood. He slashed her left forearm. Reflexively she balled her fists, and he went for her right wrist, wrapping the duct tape around it and then around the obliging arm of the chair. She fought him with the other hand, but it was her left arm and so not as strong. He had counted on that, checked that she was right-handed, figured every detail, and played it out on the computer ahead of time, reserving every advantage for himself. He was proud of his plan. He'd only had three days to work out the murder, since he'd only learned from Thomas about the appointment during lunch on Tuesday.

When she was immobilized, he brought out the roll of duct tape, doubled up on all the fastenings, and added some higher up on her arms and legs, leaving a gap of pink skin. He needed room to work at the joints, after all.

When he was done, he changed clothes, stuffing his old ones into a trash bag and then into his duffel bag. He had brought along a package of Baby Wipes, which he used to clean his hands and face, collecting the bloody ones in a plastic bag.

He was finished and out of the room ten minutes before Thomas and his mother were expected. He put his duffel bag in his locker and strolled down the hallway to the gymnasium. He opened the door and went inside, unnoticed in the crowd of people with their eyes and ears fastened on the stage. He sat on a folding chair at the back of the room and gradually maneuvered his chair close to a family group which had four kids. He watched the others and took on the mannerisms of the child who was closest to him in age. After a few minutes, a casual observer would have thought the family had five kids. In fact, they did. One of the kids was on stage.

When it was time to leave, and police officers were at the door of the gym, he walked out with the family. The officer duly recorded Carol and Drew Brendt and paid no notice to the herd of kids. For the most part, kids were invisible anyway.

When Columbus was out of the building, he let the night sweep him away.

He went home and recorded his success in his journal. He was finding that writing in the journal was almost as good as reliving the event in a VR simulation. Almost.

The duffel bag containing the bloody clothes, the roll of duct tape, and the hacksaw remained in his locker. On Monday he would remove it and dispose of it. He had sealed the plastic bags tightly so that the smell wouldn't be any worse than a typical seventh-grade boy's locker.

When the movie was over, the credits finished, and the obligatory rehashing of the best one-liners was done, Thomas needed to use the restroom. Columbus and Winston waited outside. Columbus moved close to the other boy and spoke softly enough that Winston had to lean toward him to hear.

"I probably shouldn't be telling you this," Columbus said, "but I hate to see a nice guy like you made out to be a total prick."

Winston shoved his hands in his pockets. "What're you talking about, man?"

Columbus shrugged. Every gesture was rehearsed, every word planned.

"A guy hears things. You know, in the halls or the bathroom."

"You hearing something about me? Something you figure I should know?"

"I'm just telling you this so you know, because I feel bad about it. It's not what I think."

"Yeah, let's hear it."

"Some of the guys are saying that your mom's a crackhead and your dad's a fag. That your brain's fried and your ass has been reamed, man."

Columbus watched the words strike Winston like a shower of needles.

"That's not true," Winston said. "None of it. My dad's no fag. My mom's OK now, and she never did crack. No way. I never did any of that crap, either. You tell me who's been saying that and I'll beat the shit out of him."

Columbus was pleased to see the boy's face redden and his hands ball into fists. He watched dispassionately. *Pull this string, get this jerk. Jerk.*

"C'mon, man, tell me who's saying that about me."

The timing was just about right . . . There. Thomas came out of the restroom. Columbus nodded toward Thomas. It had the desired effect. Winston turned toward Thomas, eyes widening in disbelief.

"Couldn't be," Winston said. His voice was low and raspy with anger.

"Just thought you should know," Columbus said as Thomas rejoined the group.

"Know what?" Thomas said. "I miss something?"

Columbus saw Thomas's brows push together and his eyes narrow as he searched first Columbus's face and then Winston's. Apparently he didn't like what he saw in Winston's face. "What's eating you, Winnie? The movie wasn't that bad."

"Don't call me Winnie."

"Sure. Okay. What's the deal?"

Columbus stepped in, literally and verbally. "Hey, guys, let's get a move on. We've only got a couple of hours before my parents get home. I've got a new game I want to show you." He steered the two boys toward the exit.

The group bicycled back to Columbus's house, and by

the time they got there, the incident was shelved but certainly not forgotten. The rest of the afternoon, Winston displayed an emotional state Columbus was intimately familiar with: detachment. It was rewarding, as always, for Columbus to watch his plans come to life. Or death.

CHAPTER

17

PJ watched apprehensively as Samuel Oliver Barnesworth donned the HMD for the second time. The first time he had put on the device, about half an hour ago, he had decorated her desktop with a half-digested Chicago-style jumbo hot dog. She was expecting his dessert to follow, but to his credit the man clamped his lips together and kept his stomach under control.

Barnesworth was one of those who had to work at the immersion experience. The sensation of movement caused by the shifting displays on the monitors in front of his eyes didn't jive with what his inner ear was firmly telling him, which was that he was standing still. His eyes and his inner ear resolved their differences on the battleground of his digestive system. PJ knew it was a documented response to VR simulations, but she hadn't seen it in action until today. Fortune had it that she and her team were not afflicted.

Schultz would be delighted when she told him.

When the simulation was over, she helped Barnesworth remove the helmet and data gloves. She got the feeling he was prolonging the removal in a disgusting attempt to hit on her. He'd probably try an ass pinch next.

It was unpleasant to be so close to him. He apparently thought that liberal applications of scented deodorant and after-shave cologne compensated for infrequent showering. His clothing hadn't had the benefit of a trip through the washing machine in quite a while. The smell of tobacco permeated his skin, and his teeth and first two fingers of his right hand showed the yellow stains of a passionate smoker. He was a large man to begin with, and his multiple odors and rings of sweat on the shirt under his arms made his presence seem even more overwhelming. The zone around the man merited monitoring by the air quality people.

"Whew!" he said. "What a fucking trip. You could sell this shit. Teenagers would fucking love it."

She narrowed her eyes at him. "This isn't entertainment, and I'd appreciate it if you'd clean up your language."

"Yes, ma'am. Didn't think you shrinks were prudes, what with listening to everybody's wet dreams."

She smiled sweetly. "Why, Detective, I've heard things that would make even your short hairs curlier. That doesn't mean I like to wallow in it like some people."

He snapped his mouth shut and glared at her, sizing up the opposition. All he knew about her so far was that she worked with Schultz and lacked the equipment to join the Good Ole Boys Club. She was determined that he would leave her office with a much clearer impression. He tried a different tack.

"Seeing as how you report to me on this case, Miz Gray, I—"

"That's Dr. Gray."

"All right, Dr. Gray. Let's get the fuck—let's get the ground rules clear. You can sit around and play your computer games all you want, but I need Schultz, Collings, and Whitmore out there in the field, doing things my way."

PJ took a deep breath and decided to ignore the brush-off. It was clear he didn't respect her pilot project on the computer, and he didn't even want or need her input.

Schultz, Collings, and Whitmore. What am I supposed to do, fetch the coffee?

It wasn't in her nature to let a challenge like that slip away. It was hard, but she kept her voice under control. "What exactly is your way?"

"Getting answers. Getting people to talk without being namby-pamby about it. Following practical leads and doing the footwork."

While you sit at your desk, no doubt, PJ thought. Then her mind got stuck trying to picture any of her teammates being namby-pamby, especially Schultz.

"I can see where this stuff"—he gestured at the helmet—"might be useful after the fact, in the courtroom after we've got the bastard. You know, show the jury how things went down."

She recognized his statement as a feeble effort at appeasement.

"You could probably charge admission, too," he continued. "I personally know a couple reporters who would cream their pants to see this shit."

Apparently the language cleanup involved only the F word. PJ was beginning to understand the antipathy between this man and Schultz, and she knew which side she was on. Compared to Barnesworth, Schultz was the embodiment of justice and virtue, with a little apple pie on the side.

"I'm sure Schultz and the others would be glad to do meaningful field work," she said icily. "If you've got any to be done."

"Oh, it's meaningful, all right. We've got to go over the whole neighborhood again, door to door, now that we've got photos of the suspect. True, they're only from the back, but the jacket has that distinctive design."

He opened the folder which he had brought to her office. It contained eight-by-ten enlargements, cropped and enhanced, of the best image of the batch taken by Emory Harquest. The computerized enhancement had helped, but the result was still a grainy, dark image, no matter how optimistic the viewer.

In the photo, a slim figure stood next to an angular frame that reflected in the moonlight, a shape easily recognizable as a bicycle. It was believed to be an adult twenty-six-inch bike, but it wasn't distinctive enough so that a brand could be determined. There was a bulky cube behind the seat of the bike, a piece of luggage or a box strapped on, but that portion was in shadow and it wasn't possible to make out anything beyond the fact that something was attached.

Comparing the presumed measurements of the bike to the figure next to it led the pathologist to describe the person as five feet tall, weighing about eighty-five pounds or a little less. The length of the arms and ratio of torso length to leg length pointed toward a woman, but certainly not conclusively. Whoever it was, the person was riding a bicycle with a wheel size that was too large. No one that height could straddle the center bar and place his feet securely on the ground.

The jacket, which was oversized, hid the waist and hips, so nothing could be seen of the roundness of hips or narrowness of waist. The weight estimate could be off depending upon what that jacket concealed.

The jacket itself was the most tantalizing part of the photo. With a fair amount of squinting and a lot of imagination, there appeared to be glints of moonlight forming a pattern on the back, as if reflected from silver studs. A western-style jacket had immediately been suggested. Both PJ and Schultz thought the pattern and the idea of the studs were highly speculative. There just wasn't enough in the photo to go on.

There had already been an attempt to restage and duplicate the photo, using an assortment of bicycles paired with various members of the Department. Samples were shot with the same type of camera from the same distance, but investigators would have to wait for another full moon to roll around and hope that the weather conditions were similar. The photographer had tried lighting the scene artificially to simulate the moonlight. It had been quite a show for the people living near the school. Several had turned off their evening TV programs, brought out lawn chairs and light stadium blankets for the evening chill, and watched the proceedings with great interest.

PJ had her own idea of what she was going to do to recreate that scene, but despite Wall's warning about full cooperation, she hadn't spoken up about it. After all, Wall hadn't said that her cooperation had to be timely.

It had turned out that the closest approximation of the actual photo was achieved using a thirty-year-old petite Asian woman, the wife of one of the Vice detectives. Barnesworth had glommed on to that tenuous bit of information like an octopus fastening on to its prey.

"You're reading a lot into some blurry snapshots taken at night from across the street," PJ said. "Even if you were to find the person in the photos, that alone doesn't establish any link with the murders."

"You're right there, Dr. Gray," he said, accenting her title as though to reinforce her outsider status. "But once I get my hands on that woman, we'll have a confession in no time."

The body odor alone would wring a confession out of most people, PJ thought. "You're sure it's a woman?" she asked.

"I'm not sure of anything except that I'm going to break this case," he said, "but there aren't a whole lot of men that weight and height. Fucking jockeys, maybe. If it's an Asian woman, that should narrow things down right there."

Evidently Barnesworth could only clean up his language for a limited period of time. PJ thought back to the pictures she had examined. "Your Asian woman rides a man's-style bicycle."

"A lot of women do. I checked around at bicycle shops. Gotcha, Dr. Gray."

"See if you can stretch your mind a little," PJ said. She was going to have to watch it with this man. She was starting to get into a Schultz frame of mind. "Have you considered a teenage boy?"

"Considered and discarded. Doesn't fit the profile which you have so kindly provided us, and which I checked out with the FBI, incidentally."

The profile which PJ had developed called for the killer to be a thirty- to thirty-five-year-old male. The profile covered only the second murder. There was no common signature between the two killings: one was clearly unplanned and the other was a brutal execution. Everyone involved with the murders felt that there was a connection, but purely in terms of psychological analysis there wasn't enough to link them. Schultz was somehow certain it was the same killer. Two teachers murdered at the same school within a short time naturally evoked efforts to tie them together. PJ had to continually remind herself that there was still the possibility that no connection existed.

She decided to ignore the barb about double-checking her work.

"The killer being a woman doesn't fit the profile, either," PJ said. "Anyway, a profile should only be used as a general guide. It should be factored in without becoming the complete focus of the investigation. It just might turn you away from the perpetrator. It's especially dangerous to rely on portions of a profile out of context."

Barnesworth shrugged. "I don't hold too much with that shrink shit anyway. You gotta go with your instincts, something you get after years on the job."

Something you don't have was his unspoken put-down.

"Wait a minute," PJ said. "A minute ago you used the profile to support your assumption about the age of the killer. Now you're downplaying it because it doesn't point you in the direction you've already decided to gallop."

Barnesworth tapped his forehead with a thick finger. "Instinct."

Exasperated, PJ drummed her fingers on the desk. It was better than picking up a letter opener and going after the man.

"A man can't be ruled out," she said. "A jacket like that could be worn by either sex."

"You're determined to make this killer male," he said, "in spite of the fucking evidence." With that, he picked up his folder and left her office.

PJ tapped a pencil on her desk. Barnesworth's bluster faded as rapidly in her mind as his bulky, sweating body had retreated down the hall. PJ stared at the wall, seeing

Mrs. Eddington's eyes, trying to read the message she was sure was there behind the agony of the last few minutes of her life. Were they the eyes of someone who knew her killer?

CHAPTER

18

Sunday morning PJ awakened early. After tossing in her bed for a half hour, she gave up the prospect of getting a little more sleep. She pulled on her robe and went downstairs to start a pot of coffee. As the familiar aroma filled the kitchen, she stood at the window over the sink and watched Mother Nature turn up the brightness knob, spreading the early-morning light into her backyard. She was renting her home on Magnolia in south St. Louis, but she hoped to buy the place. She'd known from the moment she'd first stepped inside, last year when she was fleeing Denver and the aftermath of divorce, that she wanted to make a new start for herself and Thomas in this house.

It was a story and a half, brick to the eaves. Inside, wood floors gleamed and stained-glass windows caught the light on either side of a fireplace that had seen a lot of use over the winter. The kitchen was modern, with white cabinets, a gray countertop, and a striking white porcelain sink. It was large enough for a table and four chairs, which allowed PJ to convert the dining room to a study. Upstairs there were two large bedrooms, each with a generous walk-in closet. Inside each closet was an access door to the attic space under the eaves, so there was no shortage of storage space. She hadn't brought that much with her from Denver anyway. As soon as she had rented the house, she'd had to go out and buy an entire house full of modest furniture.

The upstairs bath had a marvelous claw-foot bathtub where PJ relaxed and tried to float her troubles away, mentally launching them on little rafts and sending them down river.

The backyard was small, but very pleasant and private. It was bordered with perennials, and there was an annual bed in the middle which, PJ could see in the growing light, needed a lot of work. She hadn't done a proper fall cleanup. Under the sweet gum tree in the corner, crocuses were showing, clumps of blue and white opening to the sunshine. The driveway—she was lucky enough to have off-street parking—ended in a turn-around circle in the backyard, and it was lined with early daffodils with heavy, drooping buds that would burst open any day. It was the first week of April, and nature was clearing away the evidence of winter and moving on with things.

It seemed ages ago that she and Thomas had roasted hot dogs and marshmallows in southern Missouri.

PJ resolved that she would call first thing on Monday morning to find out if the owner of the house was willing to part with it. After nearly a year in St. Louis, it was time to claim the city as her new home.

Megabite rubbed against her leg and asked what was for breakfast. PJ poured the cat a bowl of milk, promising her something more substantial when Thomas got up.

PJ took her coffee into the study. At her computer, she dialed in to a private service that offered a few secure chat rooms. The rooms were all free this early on Sunday morning. She entered one and typed a nonsense phrase about comets. She imagined her voice echoing in an empty room. She didn't have long to wait before she was joined by her longtime friend and on-line mentor, Merlin.

What's the buzz, Keypunch?

PJ considered how she was going to begin this conversation. Nothing was casual to Merlin, and she knew that he could read meaning into a punctuation mark.

Although she had known him since her college days, she had never met Merlin in person. It seemed that whenever she wanted to talk with him, he was available for her on-line, and would come to her as soon as she entered one of the private chat rooms the two of them utilized. She could remember only one time when Merlin hadn't joined her. He had explained the next time they talked that he'd had the flu, but she had always thought it must have been something a lot more serious to keep Merlin away from his computers.

Merlin started every one of their sessions in the same way, with the nickname she'd acquired by being the fastest keypuncher in her class. When PJ was in college, information and programs were entered into computers through card readers. Programmers typed their instructions on a special machine which punched patterns of holes into cards. In those days, back strain from lugging around boxes of punched cards was a real job hazard.

It's been a long time since we talked, PJ typed on her keyboard. *I hardly know where to begin.*

Tell me everything, especially the juicy parts.

Megabite came in from the kitchen and jumped up onto the desk, where she cleaned her face and whiskers until there was no possibility of any milk remaining. Then she arranged herself like a sphinx on a pile of PJ's income tax papers, folded her front paws under, and closed her eyes. She looked like a statue, but PJ knew it was a ruse. The cat was alert and waiting for sounds of food preparation in the kitchen.

PJ started with the murders of the teachers, because it was not only a case she was now officially working on but something that had struck close to her heart. She had known Ed Mitchell and Clara Eddington, she had discovered one of the bodies, and most worrisome of all, Thomas had been exposed to the violent deaths of two people he knew and liked. PJ felt an urgency about the events, as though the two victims had grabbed her arms and were pulling her forward.

She began typing, telling him everything.

This sure is a lot more interesting than when you were designing shampoo bottles, Merlin said after she had poured her thoughts and feelings out.

Don't be flippant. If I want flippant I can turn on a radio talk show.

But you wouldn't get my keen observations.

Such as?

The bike. Who do you see on bikes too big for them?

PJ thought about it for a moment. Why would an adult buy a bike that was too large? It wasn't as though legs would somehow lengthen and the bike would be the right size in a year or so. Unless the bike was stolen by a short adult, it had to belong to a child.

Kids whose parents don't want to have to buy a new bike every year, she typed.

Bingo.

You think a kid did these horrible things?

Merlin didn't answer. PJ reviewed what she knew about

crimes by the young and tried to fit it into the facts of the homicides.

Kids kill with guns, she typed. *Or sometimes in knife fights or beatings by a gang. I have a hard time picturing a child with the organizational ability to do this. Especially Mrs. Eddington's death.*

Stretch your mind.

It was exactly what PJ had told Barnesworth. Was she, too, guilty of taking the well-traveled road and overlooking the barely discernible path? She'd have to give it a lot more thought, and it struck her that other areas of her life could benefit from a little mental exercise too.

I'd like to talk about another case, she typed. *You have a few more minutes?*

For you, all the time in the world.

PJ told him in detail about the art gallery murder.

I have a friend in the art world, Merlin responded. *I could ask about the paintings. Whether they've surfaced.*

That would be a big help. I'm assuming that you mean a connection to the black market.

Well, I wouldn't be that blunt about it.

If the paintings are found, we could work backward from there to the killer.

I'll see what I can do. How's Thomas holding up in all this?

Good, generally. I'm worried about his relationship with Winston. I talked to Bill Lakeland last night, and it seems that the boys had some kind of falling out. Looks like Thomas has a new friend to fill the gap, though.

Shifting sands. Surely you remember your social life at that age.

Megabite threw herself into action, diving off the desk and racing for the kitchen.

Gotta go now. I hear Thomas stirring. PJ was ready to sign off, but she waited for his response. She didn't have long to wait for one of his ubiquitous lists.

CHAMELEON

Don't stay away so long, and don't think you're going to get away without your list, he said. *A short one today.*

1. *Children can be vicious. Just ask one of them.*
2. *Juicy gossip should never be taken lightly. You never know when your source will dry up.*
3. *Ditto for juicy sex.*
4. *If you need first aid, don't ask a judge. I speak from experience.*
5. *The word for the day is "juicy".*

Take care, Keypunch.

CHAPTER

19

During breakfast with her son, PJ found herself observing him as if he was a patient in her private practice, looking for signs of stress. Thomas had bad things pressing in on all sides, things that an adult would have difficulty coping with, yet he seemed to be handling it well. A little too well. Her son had a tendency to govern his emotions until they burst out in intense episodes, a thunderstorm over and done rather than a long, soaking rain. When the events of the past couple of weeks surfaced, there would be a mighty tempest in the Gray household.

"What's the plan, man?" she asked as they cleared the breakfast dishes.

"I've got some homework to do, and then Columbus is coming over this afternoon. If that's okay. He's bringing a game to install."

"What kind of game?" It seemed to PJ that her concern for Thomas always came out sounding like the Inquisition.

She could only hope that he realized it was done out of love.

"Actually, it's not much of a game. It's morphing software. He said he's got pictures of some of the guys loaded and it would be fun to morph them."

PJ knew that morphing was a computer technique which transformed one object, or person, into another, smoothly and believably, on the monitor. The name was taken from metamorphosis, the process that turned caterpillars into butterflies.

"Sounds like fun," PJ said. "Maybe you can go over it with me tonight. I'd like to see what you look like as the Wolfman. Better yet, as a girl."

Thomas made a face.

"It's not a death sentence, you know. There are some advantages."

"Like what?"

Like being a mother. "Like being able to do this." She captured him, gave him a hug, and planted a kiss on his forehead. The child in him held still for it for a few seconds, then the almost-teen squirmed and pulled away.

"Don't do that in front of any of my friends, okay?"

"Wouldn't dream of it."

"It makes me look like a little kid."

"Can't have that, can we?"

He rolled his eyes and turned back to the table for the last of the dishes. PJ stood at the sink, the wet dishcloth in her hand. It was too good to pass up. She twirled the dishcloth, then snapped it, connecting with his rear.

"Ouch! No fair! I wasn't looking!"

"If you were looking, I couldn't have gotten away with it."

"Sheesh, Mom, when will you grow up?"

* * *

When Thomas was upstairs doing his homework, PJ picked up the phone to call Schultz. She wanted to bounce her ideas off him. She'd been thinking about a child taking a hammer and smashing someone on the back of the head, maybe when the man was bent over. About a child approaching Mrs. Eddington, getting close enough to slap on that first piece of restraining tape, about her dismissing it at first as some sort of student prank and realizing too late that it wasn't. PJ wouldn't admit to Schultz who had sparked the idea in her mind, though. Schultz had come around quite a bit on the use of computers in homicide investigations, but she didn't think he was ready for Merlin yet.

CHAPTER

20

Schultz ignored the first few rings of the phone, hoping it would stop. He was naked, fresh from a long, steamy shower, and lying on his bed. Casey straddled him, bent low over him so that her breath, coming in soft pants now, warmed his cheek. Her abundant breasts brushed his chest in rhythm with his thrusts. His hands were on her hips, and he moved them up her back, losing them in the tumble of blond hair that he had loosened from the waist-length braids she wore.

The phone kept up its insistent noise. When he couldn't shut it out any longer, he sat up, his erection hard between his legs. Casey was banished to the fantasy realm where she resided between visits to Schultz's bed. His disappointed penis was rapidly losing tumescence as he fumbled for the phone.

"What?" he growled.

There was a pause on the other end. "Did I catch you at a bad time?" PJ said.

"Of course not," he said. "I have no private life. I'm at your beck and call twenty-four hours a day."

PJ responded defensively. "We're working on a murder case, after all. Two of them, in fact."

"Forget it."

"You did tell me to call," PJ said.

"As I recall, I said to call me when you had something on the computer for the Mitchell murder," he said.

"Oh. You know, you're taking all the fun out of this."

Schultz glanced down and sighed. "Get on with it, Doc."

She filled him in on Barnesworth's introduction to VR, omitting no disgusting detail of content or splash pattern, which made the interruption of Casey's ministrations almost worthwhile.

"I do have a simulation I'd like to go over with you today. Grab Dave and Anita, too, if they're available."

"Of course they are. It's my business to make sure they have no private life."

She didn't get the irony of it. Perhaps she had forgotten the beginning of their conversation. He lamented the fact that good humor was often wasted on shrinks, particularly of the female type. Then PJ launched into her new theory about the oversize bicycle and what it revealed about the figure in the photo.

"I think you've got something there," he said. He could feel her beaming at him through the phone, and figured it was a good time for a question of his own. Ride the wave, that was his motto. "By the way, have you set things up with Helen yet?"

"No. But I will. Did any of you have any luck showing those photos in the neighborhood around the school?"

Schultz was disappointed that PJ hadn't talked to Helen,

and even worse, had dismissed what was so important to him with four little words. He kept his voice neutral. "No. Dave and Anita weren't too happy about canceling their Saturday night plans, either."

There had been grumbling when he had called them and told them to haul their asses in, especially from Dave. Dave actually had some pretense of an outside life. He'd been dating a graduate student from Washington University, and things seemed to be getting serious. If Schultz was reading the modern dating scene correctly, moving in with someone was still considered serious. But he knew that when called upon, both of the team members would put their professional lives ahead of their personal ones. Just like he did, with the possible exception of his date with Helen.

He knew he was being irrational about the date. First of all, PJ might not be successful in getting Helen to go along. Secondly, how could he hope to break through the wall Helen had built around her heart during dinner and a movie, with PJ and Limp Dick tagging along?

"I thought that was a good way to get off on the right foot with Barnesworth," PJ said. "Show that CHIP is cooperating and all that."

"You're about twenty years too late for that. He gave up appreciating any favors long ago. He give you the story about the Asian woman?"

"Yes," PJ said. "I think he's way off base there, but I don't see how it could do any harm to take the photos around."

"No, it's worth a try. Hey, Doc, I just thought of something. How come you never have to knock on any doors and shove pictures in people's faces?"

" 'Cause they're payin' me the big bucks," she said, and hung up.

Schultz briefly considered inviting Casey back for a second attempt, but duty beckoned. He contacted Anita first. She was awake and ready to go. Dave sounded like a sleepy bear. Schultz heard a voice in the background that he could have sworn said "Get that thing off me, you big oaf." Go, Dave.

He went downstairs to the kitchen in search of something to eat before leaving. He lived in a three-story rehabbed home in the Lafayette Park neighborhood of St. Louis. He and Julia had bought it when its owner was transferred to Oregon. The rehab hadn't been complete, which meant the price was attractive, but Schultz had no idea what he was getting into. Julia reveled in the chaos of a gut rehab while Schultz simply breathed dust, ate takeout food, and tolerated workmen in the bathroom at seven A.M. After his wife left, Schultz thought he should sell the place because it was so large and everything seemed to be one flight of stairs away. He lived in only a few rooms, the kitchen and living room on the main floor, a bedroom and bath on the second. The high ceilings and oak staircase seemed impractical for his lifestyle, as if his life had any style. The third floor, for lack of anything else to do with it, had been finished as an apartment with a kitchen, bath, and bedroom, but Schultz wasn't the type to take in roomers. Besides, there was no separate entrance, which meant anyone living up there would be prancing through Schultz's living quarters at all hours of the day and night. The basement had always intrigued him, since the house had been a funeral home at one time in its century of history. The basement had a low ceiling, only six feet high, and was divided into small rooms, a couple of which had ominous gutters and drains in the floor. There was a large coal bin which he had never gotten around to sweeping out.

The refrigerator didn't have a lot to offer in the way of nonmoldy food. The grocery shopping was supposed to have been done a few days ago, but things kept coming up. He chuckled, thinking he'd have to use that line on Casey. One thing about fantasy women was that they laughed at his jokes.

He decided to stop off at a convenience store and pick up a bag of chips to eat in the car. Might as well go for a couple of sodas, an apple, and some cheese and bread, too. A package of Oreos wouldn't be unwelcome. If he didn't watch it, he'd turn into a walking Food Pyramid.

The obvious thing to do was to sell the house and move into an apartment. A bachelor pad. But he couldn't seem to do it, even though the house fit him like an overcoat that was three sizes too big.

Lately he had been thinking that Helen might want to redecorate.

CHAPTER

21

PJ looked around her office and thought about how fortunate she was. The people gathered there, Schultz, Dave, and Anita, were competent—more than competent—and easy to work with, if she didn't count Schultz's occasional gruffness. Her boss, she was learning, was tough but fair. There was nothing that he had said to her that time in his office that didn't deserve saying. By the luck of the draw, she could have ended up working with or for a man like Barnesworth. Then she'd be looking for another job, and most likely would have missed out on the tremendous rewards of her work in law enforcement.

Anita Collings reminded PJ of Tinkerbell. She was petite, had wispy blond hair, and PJ could imagine her leaving a trail of pixie dust. The woman wasn't flighty, though. She was serious about her work, and was taking night courses in criminal justice. Dave Whitmore was over six feet tall, pleasantly rounded in both his body and the features of his face, and soft-spoken. Black hair tumbled over his forehead and shirt collar. Dave was good with details, and Anita was the intuitive spark. Together they made a good investigative team, when Schultz let them off the short leash he had a tendency to use.

Having all three of them in her office at the same time strained the tiny space to its limits. She had put in a requisition for a conference room for the CHIP team months ago, but it was probably buried on Lieutenant Wall's desk. Other items she had requested, such as the pager she wore at her waist, she had eventually gone out and acquired out of her own pocket. A conference room, though, was a little more than she could swing. In the meantime, the group would have to make do. It occurred to her that she was the only one who seemed to be bothered by the situation. The others seemed comfortable with the confinement, although they guarded their own personal space. There was as much distance separating them as the walls allowed.

"The photos were a bust," Anita said. "At least around the school. We've got Yantz and Estavez talking to gang members about that jacket. They might get lucky, though they were skeptical. Not enough to go on."

"You could say that about this whole case," Dave said. "Especially the first murder, which is the one loosely tied, and I do mean loosely, to the photos. Anybody else thinking we got two perps here?"

Dave was the only person PJ had run across in the Department who used the word perp. She didn't watch TV shows, so she hadn't been familiar with the term. The first time she heard it, she thought Dave had said "herp," for herpetologist, a person who studies reptiles. It had taken her on an interesting tangent during their discussion.

"I think we might be premature," PJ said. She decided to play devil's advocate and see where the conversation went. "The profile I've written covers only the second victim, and assumes the first murder was committed during a burglary or a drug deal. That was the speculation at first, wasn't it? That Mitchell was dealing drugs and something went wrong."

"Gimme a break," Schultz said. "Mitchell shines like Mr. Clean's toilet. Or used to anyway. He wasn't into drugs, using or selling. And who'd steal from a school lab? All they had was baby stuff."

"Not so babyish," PJ said. "Perhaps the criminal was looking for components of designer drugs."

"Christ, Doc. You need to live in the real world and not get your information from some woman's magazine. You spout off like that to Barnesworth and even he will tear you to shreds."

"The school is a powerful connection," Anita said, ignoring the issue of whether there was one killer or two. "Dave and I have been looking at the records. Eddington started there nineteen years ago, straight out of college. Mitchell had been teaching there for eight years. Each teacher works with roughly a hundred students a year, so that's almost two thousand students for Eddington and eight hundred for Mitchell. The records are computerized but don't allow a search on a combination of two teachers, so we've got to work on it by hand. So far we've got about two hundred fifty kids who had both teachers."

"Yeah," Dave said, "and that's not taking into consideration extracurricular activities like the science club. These kids currently range from eleven to twenty years old, so some of them aren't kids anymore. Probably a lot of them don't even live around here."

"That wouldn't prevent a determined person from coming back," PJ said.

"We can't ignore staff members, either," Schultz said.

"Regardless of what Barnesworth thinks, we shouldn't channel the whole investigation into looking for someone who fits that photo. We don't even know if the old fart across the street took that photo on the night of Eddington's murder. We're taking his word for it, but he could be mistaken or lying. Maybe he's got a whole basement full of bloody hammers and saws himself. Anybody search his place?"

Heads shook all around. Schultz looked smug.

"Are you saying he's a suspect?" PJ said. "You haven't even met the man."

"Oh, and I suppose the fact that he flattered you automatically makes him innocent."

"What do you mean, flattered me?" PJ said indignantly.

"I mean he picked the person on this team with the least law-enforcement experience to come to with his story. Why would he do that if he's serious about catching the killer?"

You're the one who will catch the killer. Emory Harquest's words echoed in PJ's mind. "Some people just don't like you, Detective."

"Hold on, boss," Anita interjected. "He's got a point. Sometimes a person who comes forward like that wants to misdirect the investigation so that it won't focus too close to home."

PJ subsided. Anita was right, of course. She just didn't like the way Schultz had put it.

"Okay, I shouldn't have put it quite like that," Schultz conceded. "That's water under the dam. Let's get on to the computer stuff."

"Bridge," PJ and Anita said in unison.

"The women are after me," he said.

"You can go first," PJ said, holding out the HMD to

Schultz. "The simulation is rudimentary. It's only a few minutes long. We'll talk again after we've all been in it."

Anita and Dave wandered off, assuming they could have a ten minute break before their turn. PJ figured they just didn't want to see Schultz waltzing around the room with an upside-down colander on his head. Not quite as exciting as Tom Cruise playing air guitar in his underwear.

PJ pressed the keys on her keyboard to start up the simulation and then made an overdue trip to the restroom. By the time she got back, Schultz had removed the equipment. He looked grim.

He handed her the HMD, which she slipped over her head. The monitors inside the helmet glowed blue in front of her eyes as she slipped on the data gloves. "Press F10 and start a fresh pot of coffee, will you?" PJ said.

CHAPTER

22

She closed her eyes before the display popped onto the monitors, then opened them to a dark scene. It took a few seconds for her eyes to adjust.

She was across the street from the school. Moonlight lay at her feet, flowing across the concrete and up the side of the building. Trees and bushes were indistinct shapes, but as her eyes adapted, she began to make out branches and even individual leaves. There were streetlights about a hundred feet on either side of the door, which leaned back into the darkness like the mouth of a cave.

She had only been waiting a short time when the bicyclist arrived and dismounted. PJ moved forward in the simulation, crossing the street and approaching the figure.

As she did so, the person turned so that the moonlight fell full on the back of the jacket, and PJ could make out the design. It was a snake, twisting from the left shoulder to the right hip, and it was fashioned of rhinestones. The computer's extrapolation capability had filled in the skimpy information from the photo with a best guess.

The person unstrapped a bag from the luggage carrier of the bike, and then stowed the bike behind some bushes near the front door, where it would be unseen from across the street. PJ took a few steps, placing herself in the figure's path.

She faced an adolescent boy, a Genman with the age adjusted downward from the standard adult model. PJ had developed models of generic males, females, and children—Genman, Genfem, and Genkid—for the computer to use when no specific person was identified. For any known individuals, she used her scanimation technique to make the model as lifelike as possible. In this case, she had gone with the former student scenario that Dave and Anita were investigating, making the killer about sixteen years old and small for his age. A late developer.

The boy approached her and passed right through her. She was a ghost in the virtual world.

She followed him into the school. The science lab was dark around the perimeter, but a pool of light from a single ceiling panel provided enough light to work. The boy took off his jacket and put it on the counter, either to have more freedom of movement or to ensure that no chemicals spilled on it. He rummaged through his pack and came up with a hammer, which he used to whack the padlock off the chemicals locker.

PJ looked at his hands. He was wearing gloves.

The killer pulled a metal flashlight from his pack and shone it into the back of the locker, searching for the right chemical, reading the labels. A police inventory of the locker taken the night of the murder had not revealed anything sinister, but perhaps the killer expected something else to be there besides the jars of common acids and bases used for demonstrations. Still shining the flashlight into the locker, he used his left hand to pick up one of the jars because it was blocking his view.

At that moment, Mitchell came dashing from the dimly lighted portion of the room. PJ was startled and stepped quickly out of his way, even though that wasn't necessary. Without saying a word, Mitchell tackled the killer, planning to subdue first and question later. The killer was knocked sideways, sending the jar of sulfuric acid he was holding crashing to the floor. Mitchell rolled and started to rise, but the killer got to his feet first. He turned on Mitchell and, using the heavy metal flashlight he was still holding, struck the teacher with it.

Mitchell, who had only gotten to his knees by then, took the blow on his right temple. He swayed and nearly toppled, giving the killer time to retrieve the hammer from the countertop nearby.

The first blow splattered blood in PJ's direction. It passed through her and struck the wall behind her. She closed her eyes, preferring not to witness the next few moments, and when she opened them, the scene had changed. The killer was already outside.

A light flashed across the street. It was Emory Harquest, the retired teacher guarding his beloved school, taking pictures through his window. There were several more pinpoint flashes. The killer didn't notice them. PJ stood in the empty street, the school with its dark burden behind her, watching until the darkness blanketed him.

CHAPTER

23

The four of them didn't feel much like talking about it after they'd all watched Mitchell die. PJ made a few halfhearted comments about the gloves, asking about prints at the scene. Schultz told her that the prime piece of fingerprint evidence was the shattered jar of acid. A number of prints had been found on the large shards, but most were smeared and ill-defined. The spilled acid had eaten away some of the prints. Of those that were identifiable, all had been traced to people who normally had access to the chemical locker. That turned out to be Mitchell and two others, student lab assistants.

PJ perked up momentarily when she heard that one of the assistants was Columbus Wade, Thomas's new friend. Barnesworth hadn't questioned either of the students, both of whom were male. As far as he was concerned, their suspect was a woman.

Anita wondered if the killer had seen the flashes from

Harquest's camera. They should have been visible from where the mystery bicyclist was standing. If so, the man might be in danger. Schultz said that if the killer had seen the flashes that night and known photographs were taken, the old man would already be dead and the police wouldn't have the pictures. There would have been a double murder. There were nods of agreement all around.

PJ made a copy of the lab simulation to take home. The computer she used at home wasn't powerful enough for a smooth, full VR experience, but she could display simulations on the screen like jerky video games. If she studied it at home, running through it a few more times, perhaps something significant would jump out at her.

PJ called Barnesworth, updated him on CHIP's activities, and told him where she could be reached for the rest of the day. Then the team went their separate ways. It was late Sunday afternoon, and PJ was anxious to spend some time with her son. She needed to connect with him and sound out how he really felt about all the things that were going on. She was looking forward to a quiet evening together.

She brought home Chinese takeout, chicken with mushrooms for herself and a double order of fried rice for Thomas. She came in the back door and was greeted by Megabite, who forgave her for the lengthy absence as soon as she caught the scent of food.

"I'm home, T-man," PJ said, bending down to pet Megabite. She got a raspy lick and a flick of the cat's tail, telling her all was right with the world, at least from a cat's point of view.

She kicked her shoes off and sighed. The house wrapped itself around her, offering comfort, conversation with the most important male in her life, and the prospect of a hot bath.

She was reminded of the warmth and welcome of the home she grew up in, the farmhouse with the U-shaped porch on the edge of Newton, Iowa, where her mom still lived. It was hard to believe Dad had been dead for almost twenty years.

Thomas came out of the den. "Hi, Mom. Whatcha got in the bags?"

"Chinese."

"Cool. I hope there's enough for Columbus, too."

PJ's heart plummeted. She had wanted some old-fashioned quality time with her son. She managed to conceal her disappointment. "He's still here?"

"Yeah. It got so late I invited him to stay for dinner. I hope that's okay."

"Of course," PJ said. "What have you boys been doing?"

She saw something flicker across Thomas's face. She could have sworn it was fear.

"Stuff," he said.

"What kind of stuff?"

"Computer stuff. That morphing program I told you about this morning."

PJ brought up her hand and rubbed her temples. He had told her about that. It seemed so long ago, but it was only a few hours. She put the bags of food on the counter and shrugged out of her jacket.

"We'll just divide everything I brought," she said. "I'm sure there'll be enough. I only have two fortune cookies, though. We'll have to fight for them." She finished with a weak smile, trying to lighten her mood. A few minutes ago she had been looking forward to the evening. Now it seemed like something to plow through before she could drop into bed. Normally she enjoyed the friends Thomas brought home, especially Winston. That thought brought a stab of worry. What was wrong between the two boys?

Preteen tiffs didn't last more than a few days, at least not the kind she remembered.

She just didn't feel like meeting anyone new tonight, even if he was only twelve years old.

PJ headed for the closet to hang up her jacket, and suddenly there was the boy, leaning against the doorjamb. He seemed to be studying her intently. She wondered how long he had been there, and whether he had gotten the idea from her tone of voice that he wasn't welcome.

He stiffened slightly, as though he had been caught at something he wasn't supposed to be doing, but recovered quickly and moved toward her. He seemed to be approaching too closely, like he was going to hug her, when he abruptly stopped and thrust out his skinny arm. It was as though he didn't quite understand the concept of personal space. She edged back, restoring the social distance.

"Nice to meet you, Dr. Gray," he said.

She responded to his gesture unthinkingly, and found herself solemnly shaking hands.

"Good to meet you, too, Columbus. You can call me PJ. Whenever someone says Dr. Gray, I look around for somebody with a white coat and a stethoscope."

There was a slight pause, followed by a laugh that didn't sound natural. Something about it . . . She pictured Columbus in front of a mirror, practicing how to laugh and not quite getting it right. It was like the way she had practiced her smile when she was a high school freshman trying to catch the eye of the most popular guy in class.

"Well," she said, trying to sound cheerful, "I hope you like Chinese food. Thomas, how about something to drink for our guest?"

Thomas took the hint and came up with three glasses of lemonade over ice. The three of them sat at the kitchen table. The food was still hot and tasted wonderful to PJ, whose lunch had been a low-fat strawberry breakfast bar from the box she kept in her desk drawer. Thomas ate with his usual fervor. Columbus was quiet during the meal, looking from one to the other of them as she and Thomas caught each other up on their days. She was careful, as always, not to talk about her work in much detail. She wanted to explore how Thomas felt a few days after the second murder, but it was inappropriate to do it in front of his friend. She kept the conversation neutral.

PJ cleaned up after dinner, and Columbus didn't offer to help, as though he was used to being waited upon. Thomas didn't spring to it, either, but she thought that he was just imitating his friend, trying not to look uncool. Peer pressure at its finest. She let him get away with it.

The boys disappeared back into the den. PJ had been hoping the visitor would leave right after dinner so that she could at least salvage the evening. She didn't want to make a fuss about it, so she changed into sweats, and, although it was the last thing on her mind, forced herself to do some housecleaning. She chased dust bunnies across the wood floor in the living room, much to the amusement of Megabite. Then she cleaned both bathrooms and sorted through a stack of mail that had accumulated for the past week. It was solidly dark and beginning to rain by the time Columbus was ready to leave, and she insisted on driving him home. She had an ulterior motive. She wanted to see his house, at least from the outside.

She loaded Columbus's bike in the trunk of the Escort. It was too big to fit entirely inside, so the trunk lid rode up a little over the handlebars. The two boys sat in the backseat. PJ was accustomed to being the Invisible Driver, not intruding on the interactions between Thomas and his friends. At his age, he still needed good ole Mom but didn't like having his face rubbed in it, and she respected that. In a few short years, she would have to fight him for the car keys.

The rain began in earnest, and there was lightning in the western sky. She turned the windshield wipers on high speed. After a minute or two, she noticed that it was quiet in the car except for the thump-thump of the wipers, not like the last time she had driven Thomas and Winston somewhere. No whispered confidences, no shoving, no assortment of belches and farts. Was her son growing up that fast? Had the recent events depressed him? Or was there something about Columbus's company that discouraged fooling around?

It wasn't more than twenty blocks to Columbus's house, an easy bike ride or walk under better circumstances. At his direction, she pulled up in front of a grand three-story brick with landscaping that put her little flower garden to shame. All the windows were dark except one. The drapes were drawn back on the window, leaving the task of privacy to the sheers underneath. The blue light of a TV flickered through them.

Columbus politely said goodnight to both of them, breaking the Invisible Driver rule—didn't he know about it?—then got out to unload his bike. On impulse, PJ hopped out, too. She was going to walk him to the door and introduce herself to his parents.

Columbus seemed puzzled to see her standing in the cold rain. Thomas's face peered through the steamed-up rear window, but he made no effort to join the two of them. PJ expected Columbus to go around the back, since she and Thomas customarily used the back door at their house. The front door was for company. Any small town girl knew that, and PJ's habits were set by her childhood in Iowa.

Schultz always used the back door.

The thought of him sent an unexpected shiver down her spine which had nothing to do with the cold, rainy weather.

Instead of heading for the back door, Columbus rolled the bike up the front walk and then struggled to get it up onto the covered porch where it was dry. PJ could have lifted the bike's rear wheel, but she sensed that he didn't want any help. He dug into the pocket of his jeans and produced a door key. He opened the door and the two of them stepped into the entry hall. There was no welcoming call.

She realized her hair was plastered to her cheeks and she was dripping on the floor. Not a good way to make a first impression. Columbus was wearing a yellow raincoat with a hood. Evidently he had anticipated the turn in the weather. He slipped off his raincoat and hung it on a polished brass coat tree in the foyer. Water pooled on the marble floor beneath it. He ignored it with the assurance of someone who wouldn't think of getting a towel and wiping it up himself.

"Mom, Dad, we've got company," Columbus said, raising his voice so that it could be heard over the TV.

A minute later, a woman appeared in the doorway. She was even shorter than PJ. Her red hair was several shades brighter than her son's, probably with the help of hair coloring. She was slightly built and looked very much like Columbus morphed into a woman and aged thirty-plus years. Her eyes had the unfocused look of someone awakened from sleep, and there were wrinkles on the side of her face from lying on something like a corduroy toss pillow. Most likely she had fallen asleep in front of the TV, even though it was only eight P.M.

"Hello, Mrs. Wade," PJ said, trying to make the best of

the situation. "I thought I'd introduce myself, since the boys have been spending time together. I'm PJ Gray, Thomas's mom."

"Oh. Nice to meet you. You didn't have to do that, though. Columbus is a big boy. He can get himself home." She didn't leave the doorway. "Norm's gone to bed already. He's got the sniffles."

"Well, say hello to him for me. I hope I didn't get Columbus home too late. He didn't say what time he needed to be home."

"He pretty much comes and goes as he pleases," she said tersely. It was obvious that the subject wasn't one of normal parental concern for her. "He's got a key."

On the edge of her vision, PJ caught a glimpse of Columbus. His eyes were narrowed and his lips pressed together. He seemed to be concentrating intently. He looked like he was willing his mother to shut up.

"I'd better be going. Perhaps we can get together sometime, when your husband is feeling better," PJ said.

"Yes, we'll do that. Goodnight." With that, she turned and went back into the TV room, leaving the two of them standing there.

Was she drunk? Antisocial? Concealing a wild party in the family room? PJ had the odd feeling that the woman was nervous dealing with her own son. Nervous, or perhaps frightened.

"Thanks for the ride home, Dr. Gray. I mean, PJ."

She hated to leave the boy there. It seemed like such a cold home, and she didn't mean the temperature. She wondered when Columbus had last gotten a hug. Wet clothes and all, she reached out and wrapped her arms around him.

"Come anytime, Columbus. You're always welcome at our house."

He was taken by surprise, and she thought he might bolt. But he stayed within the circle of her arms until she released him. Then he launched himself up the stairway of his home without a word, but paused and looked back at her when he got to the landing.

She let herself out.

She was too tired when she got home to do more than sit on the couch next to Thomas while they watched a *Star Trek* episode she had on tape. Thomas leaned against her and Megabite curled up on her lap, and she was grateful for their company.

Late that night, Thomas tossed in his bed, unable to sleep. Images paraded through his mind, a succession of horrible faces and mutilated bodies. Columbus's morphing program was like none Thomas had ever heard about. They had started with simple things, like turning the principal, Mrs. Barry, into a gorilla. Her face had gradually changed shape, her eyebrows jutting forward, her shoulders hunched up, and then she got very, very, hairy. Thomas had laughed, and Columbus had watched him laugh.

Then Columbus had selected a knife-shaped tool with the cursor and slashed the gorilla's face with it, moving it down in a quick, practiced stroke. Blood dripped out and ran down the fur. It was disturbing, because the picture had started as someone Thomas knew, but the action was cartoonish enough to offset the discomfort he felt. And, besides, Thomas was a big boy now, a teenager in a couple of months, and it would have been babyish to be afraid.

More teachers, more transformations, and the mutilations became more grotesque each time. Columbus acted impassive about it, but his breathing was fast and he was totally absorbed in the agonies of the creatures on the screen. At least he didn't start with the knives until the familiar faces had been morphed into something else, some animal or a fictional character like Frankenstein's monster. But the thing about morphing was that the resulting face retained some of the characteristics of the original. Not much, but just enough to suggest the human underneath.

Thomas felt that it wasn't right, what Columbus was doing, yet on some level he was fascinated with it, and with the sensations it created in him. He thought that these were the sensations adults sought out when they went to violent movies, and Thomas was eager to experience adult privileges.

His mother wouldn't approve. She would be shocked, and that was part of the lure. Only part of it, though— the rest came from some sick feelings inside himself, like watching some kid squish a bug and secretly enjoying it. He wondered if all adults had those sick feelings, and if so, how they dealt with them. It wasn't the kind of thing he could ask his mom, any more than he wanted to talk to her about the way he couldn't concentrate on anything but Hailey's tits when he was near the girl, or the ejaculations he sometimes had at night. Besides, Mom was a psychologist, and that would just get her started. He'd be getting weird looks for months.

And then Columbus had offered him the knife . . .

CHAPTER

24

Monday morning was bright and clear, a jewel of a spring day. PJ was up early and drawn to the outdoors. The fresh air with the cold bite to it delighted her, and she drew it in selfishly, not wanting to share it with her neighbors, who were beginning to stir and make household noises. Sunshine rested softly on her shoulders and warmed the top of her head as she took a leisurely tour of her backyard, comfortable inside her sweat suit, steaming coffee mug in hand. She let the morning work its magic, and for a few minutes pushed aside all her concerns.

Later, as she drove to work, she thought about how Thomas had remained in his room, skipped breakfast, and then made a dash for the door when it was time to meet the boys he walked to school with. Obviously he was avoiding her, and she intuitively connected it with the odd look she had seen on his face when she came home last night. She turned the moment over in her mind, and was certain that her son had been afraid of something. Of his father's pushy, intrusive behavior? Of the killings at school, and the threat of more until the murderer was caught? Of Columbus? Thomas's new friend seemed a bit socially inept, and given the brief glimpse of his home life she had gotten, that might be understandable. But frightening? Surely not.

The incident wouldn't let go of her, and by the time she got to work she had determined that she shouldn't let go of *it*. She'd have to find a way to talk to Thomas and help him get his feelings out in the open. Then, no matter what it was, she was confident that the two of them could deal with it together.

Maybe I'm catching on to this single parent stuff, she thought.

The first order of business was a phone call to the realtor PJ had worked with when she first moved to St. Louis. She couldn't reach the woman, but left a voice mail message requesting that she find out if the rental house was for sale and, if so, the terms offered. Scratching that off her mental list, she next called Bill Lakeland, Winston's father. He picked up on the second ring.

"Bill, PJ here. Have you got a few minutes?" She knew that Bill, who was a lab technician at a hospital, sometimes had rush jobs and didn't have a spare moment to talk.

"Sure. What's up?"

"You told me earlier that Thomas and Winston had some kind of falling out. Do you know anything more about it than that?"

"I've been meaning to ask you the same thing. Winston's really down about it. The most I can get out of him is that he thinks Thomas said some nasty things about him at school. The other kids there have been giving Win a hard time, you know, pointing, stuff said behind his back."

PJ was appalled that Thomas would do such a thing to his best friend. "What kind of things?"

"I don't know. Rumors, I guess, probably about his mom."

"I'm really sorry if that's what's happened. I'll talk to Thomas about it," PJ said.

"That'd probably just make it worse. The kids have to work these things out themselves. It'll blow over."

"You're probably right," PJ admitted. She would have resented her parents interfering in something like this. Then something else popped into her mind. "How did Win know that Thomas was the source of the rumors?"

"Columbus told him. You met that boy yet?"

"Yes." PJ was going to say more, then decided to see how Bill felt first. His revelation that it was Columbus who had directly caused the rift made her uncomfortable. What if it had been Columbus who started the rumors in the first place and then blamed Thomas? What reason could he have for doing that? And was she just letting her suspicious mind get the best of her?

"I'm not sure he did Win a favor by telling him," Bill said. "Things like that are better left to die on their own. I probably shouldn't be saying it, but that kid strikes me as a little weird. What do you think of him?"

"He seems nice enough. His home situation might be a little screwy," PJ said, thinking of the interaction the night before with Columbus's mother. "I can't think of any reason why he'd want to drive the boys apart, though. I thought they made a good threesome, with their interest in computers."

Bill was silent on the other end of the phone long enough that PJ thought they might have gotten disconnected.

"I didn't say anything about driving the boys apart," Bill finally said. "But you've got me thinking about it now."

"I don't mean to make you suspicious," PJ said. *Or did I?* "We should just keep an eye on things."

"Yeah."

"I'm going to change the subject completely and ask for a favor," PJ said. She explained about the double date with Helen and Schultz. Bill was already familiar with the basics, so she only had to tell him the latest chapter. He seemed amused by the whole arrangement, but he agreed to go along if PJ set it up.

"Does that mean we'll be on a real date?" Bill asked.

PJ laughed. "I think we'll mostly be refereeing the two of them. Better bring along a whistle and some protective gear."

"Oh? Which one do you think is gonna kick me in the balls, Leo or Helen?"

"Might be me, after a couple of hours. Thanks for doing this, Bill."

"Hey, maybe we can go out ourselves sometime, without the Dogs of War."

A warm flush went through PJ, starting at the top of her head and ending somewhere south of her belly button. "I'd like that. Whenever you're ready, that is." She quietly kicked herself for the lame ending.

After she got off the phone, she realized that she had propositioned a married man, and it hadn't bothered her one bit.

Schultz rapped on his boss's office door and then pushed it open before she had a chance to respond. She had an undeniably goofy look on her face, and he was never one to let such an occurrence slip by.

"You auditioning for a Disney cartoon?" he said.

"What? Oh, Schultz. Come in."

"Is that just small talk or a heartfelt invitation?"

She caught on. "Men are despicable," she said with good humor. "Have a seat. Let's talk murder and mayhem."

What's wrong with her this morning?

He sat down and studied her. She fiddled with some papers on her desk and started humming.

Christ, the woman's been laid. Or expects to be.

The thought stirred feelings that he quickly put aside. "If you can tear yourself away from your important paperwork," he said, "we need to make a trip to Tall Oaks SNF. That's Skilled Nursing Facility, as I have been informed in triplicate. They're expecting us at ten."

"And we're going there because . . ."

"Because that's where James Washburn's brother Henry lives. Can't you keep these things straight? I'm not your personal secretary, you know."

When she didn't take the bait, he started to wonder if she was sick. When he got the flu, he had a hard time thinking straight. Maybe she ought to be home in bed, and not with a companion.

"You okay, Doc?"

"Of course I am. Tall Oaks. Henry Washburn. You drive."

And so he did. Tall Oaks was in Eureka, a western suburb of St. Louis. Eureka had been a small town with an independent spirit and its own shopping district, feed store, post office, and homey cafes. Then a major amusement park was built nearby, and there was an influx of fast food restaurants and other businesses that catered to the day crowd. Still, the town held on to its character, and the old and new had a truce.

The latest challenge was the spread of housing developments. Those who fled the city had previously settled in the western suburbs of Manchester, Ballwin, Chesterfield, and Ellisville. As those areas became more fully developed and started to look like cities themselves, urban flight moved out a tier and spotted the wooded hillsides and pristine views around Eureka. Served by Interstate 44, which made commuting tolerable, the area was experiencing explosive growth. Schools were bursting at the seams and the town struggled with new attitudes and goals. Residents who had lived their lives in the town looked about and wondered where it would all end.

It was a beautiful day for the trip, and as he admired the scenery, Schultz found himself wondering if there would come a time in his life when he would return to his country roots. Tall Oaks was set away from the busy strip that fronted I-44, on about twenty acres of woods, oak interspersed with cedar. A winding drive brought them to a small parking lot. There was also a covered pull-through at the lobby of the building. It reminded Schultz of a hotel, but there was no doorman. He drove up and stopped the car directly in front of the door.

"Shouldn't we use the parking lot?" PJ asked.

He shrugged. "So give me a ticket." He opened the door and got out, prompting her to do the same. "Besides, it doesn't exactly look like Grand Central Station here. We're not in anyone's way."

She gave him a frown that said there was a lecture in the offing. He turned away and studied the building, not giving her the opportunity to talk about setting an example as law-enforcement professionals.

The building was tastefully designed, a red brick crown for the hillside, with large expanses of glass to take in the views.

There was no one in sight outdoors. He headed for

the lobby, PJ trailing behind. Inside there was a generous reception area with vaulted ceilings and an imposing stone fireplace. Logs were blazing away, filling the space with the welcoming scent that stirred memories of snowy evenings and watching his dad split firewood. There were half a dozen people in chairs, soaking up the heat of the fire like cats on the hearth rug. A couple of them had fallen asleep.

Schultz tried to picture himself dozing in front of the fire, his life's work behind him, waiting for his body to give out. There would be no visitors, Helen having turned down his advances, his ex-wife having built a new life for herself with her CPA dreamboat, and his shit-for-brains son six feet under, having played the drug dealing game and lost. In spite of the warmth of the room, Schultz felt chilled.

He shook off the feeling and went to the reception counter. A couple of minutes later, the director of Tall Oaks came out of his office and headed toward them. More like slid out, like an oyster down Schultz's throat.

"Dr. Dyson, Albert Dyson," the man said, thrusting out his hand. "Pleasure to meet you. Hope you had a lovely drive out. Beautiful day, yes?"

Schultz wondered if the man could pack any more trite observations in one burst of speech. He knew from long experience that people spoke that way when they didn't want to say anything of substance. Or because they lacked substance entirely. He wondered which was true in Dr. Dyson's case.

Schultz stepped forward and shook the man's hand. The contact gave him a bad feeling, one that he had encountered before. In the few seconds since the doctor's office door had opened, Schultz had formed an opinion of him:

he wasn't just a slippery oyster, he was slime on the bottom of the sea.

Schultz had an ability to evaluate people that he never questioned. Physical contact, even as brief as a handshake, told him a lot about a person, whether he or she was basically good or bad, hiding something, genuinely distressed over the death of a spouse, whatever was appropriate. It was one of the tools he used in his investigations, as concrete to him as a crime scene report. When he talked about it, which was rarely, he called it instinct or playing a hunch.

There was another tool, one he would never dream of acknowledging. He was able to connect with a killer, feel a link between them which he visualized as a slender golden thread. Gradually, as he acquired more facts during an investigation, the thread became a cord anchored firmly in the killer. Schultz could visualize himself sliding along the cord as unerringly as a spider moving toward its prey in the web. The other end of the cord was always the same: it was buried in evil, in a black heart born that way or made that way by the sad and violent circumstances of life.

Schultz closed his eyes briefly and cast about, searching for the thread. There was a glimmer, but no sudden inexplicable certainty that he was in the presence of a killer. Or possibly, he just didn't have enough information yet for things to fall into place.

Schultz watched as PJ moved up and introduced herself. She didn't often mention her title, but she used it this time.

"A medical doctor, yes?" Dyson said. He seemed nervous. Schultz hadn't told him that he was bringing company. It had seemed like a good idea to spring his boss on Dyson, and, seeing the reaction, he knew he'd guessed right. This guy didn't want scrutiny, at least not by anyone with a jumble of letters after their name.

"A psychologist. Are you the Washburns' family physician?"

"No. I have no connection to the family other than through this facility. Mr. Washburn—James, that is—called upon me because of the superior care we offer at Tall Oaks. He wanted the best for his brother."

"By called upon you mean he just looked you up in the Yellow Pages?" Schultz asked. The doctor took the question seriously, which told him a little more about Dyson's frame of mind.

"Many of our clients do. We have a large ad. It helps people focus under stressful conditions, and most situations we are called upon to deal with are stressful to the family. Let your fingers do the walking, yes?" Dyson put out his hand and made walking movements with the fingers. Then he gestured down the hallway. "If we could move on . . ."

Schultz and PJ obligingly followed the man into the east wing of the building. Walking behind him, Schultz noticed that the doctor had a bald spot on the back of his head, about where it would contact the headrest of an automobile seat. Schultz wore his own bald spot up front. Seeing that he had something in common with Dyson humanized the guy a little, as did the small stain on the left side of the doctor's pants, just at the point where his slender cheek brushed lightly against the fabric. PJ leaned close and whispered in Schultz's ear: "Chocolate."

Schultz was still wondering how the man could get a chocolate stain on his butt when the three of them arrived outside Henry's room.

"You understand I can't discuss Mr. Washburn's medical condition, yes?" Dyson said. "I don't have the family's

---

186

consent, and Mr. Washburn is in no condition to give informed consent himself." He looked at PJ, hoping for corroboration, one professional to another. She kept her mouth shut. Her tightened lips appeared to be holding back some cutting remark.

Dyson pushed open the door and started to lead the way inside. Schultz moved in front of him. "We'd like to talk to Henry alone," he said. No need to be subtle.

"Of course," Dyson said, backing off. "Let me know when you're done. Perhaps you'd like a tour of the facility, yes?"

"This isn't a social call," PJ said. "We're here as part of a murder investigation."

Damn straight.

"Surely you don't suspect Henry Washburn? He was transferred here from another facility just a year ago, but he's been in continuous care for ten years."

PJ was getting tired of the pest. "We'll draw our own conclusions, thank you. Now, if you'll excuse us." She turned her back on the man and strode into Henry's room. Schultz was left in the hall with Dyson, a situation he quickly remedied.

The room was bright and cheerful, in contrast to the occupant. The head of the bed was inclined so that Henry was sitting up. He was covered up to his neck with a blindingly white blanket. The shape beneath the blanket was pitifully small, and there was no movement, not even a rustling of the sheets, as they entered the room. Although Schultz had known that the man was paralyzed from his airplane accident, somehow he wasn't prepared for what he saw.

Henry Washburn looked like a wax doll.

PJ walked up to the bed without hesitation. Schultz gazed out the window as he marshaled his emotions. He realized that just a few minutes earlier, out in the lobby, he had been feeling sorry for himself because of his lonely circumstances. But if he had to live like the man in the bed, he would plead with someone to put him out of his misery.

Then he realized that the man didn't even have a way to plead.

PJ was bending over the figure. "Mr. Washburn, can you hear me? Can you respond in any way?"

Then she did something odd. She reached out and tapped him on the nose.

"What are you doing?" Schultz asked. She turned around and, without any warning, snapped her arm out and tapped Schultz on the nose as she had done to Henry.

"See the difference?"

"Ah, no."

"You blinked. He didn't."

"So? I've always had good reflexes."

"Most people in a normal state of awareness will blink when something comes at their face unexpectedly. I don't think Henry's really here in the room with us. Take a good look, Schultz. He won't bite."

Schultz, who had avoided approaching the bed until forced to do so, bent over and inspected Henry's face. He saw good muscle tone, slightly parted lips, and eyes that looked in his direction but saw nothing. The eyelids slid down and up in a languorous way, working on automatic to keep the eyes moist.

"Asleep?" Schultz asked. "Painkillers? Head injury?"

She shook her head. "I don't think any of those. He's dissociated. I've seen it before in the severely mentally ill."

"As far as we know, Henry doesn't have any history of mental illness." Schultz sat down in a visitor's chair conveniently placed near the head of the bed. "Unless this place drove him batty."

"I wonder if there's been a neurological consult," PJ said.

"I'm thinking that we should get an independent doctor in here," Schultz said.

PJ was gazing out the window, deep in thought.

"Doc?" No answer. "Great. Now I'm in a room with two people who really aren't here with me."

"It's not funny, Detective," came the retort. "I think I've heard about this before. It could be ketamine."

"Now you've really lost me."

"It's also called the date rape drug. It's not used with people anymore, but it's still in common use by vets. It's been in the news because rapists have gotten hold of it and used it on their victims. It makes a person compliant—immobilized, actually—and there's no conscious memory of what happened."

"Yeah, I've heard about that. I still don't have the connection with Henry. You're not telling me somebody here is raping him, are you? Christ, the poor guy's already quadriplegic."

"I doubt if it's anything to do with sex. I think someone wants to make sure Henry doesn't talk to anyone."

Schultz nodded. "Because he knows something about the murder. Now that makes sense."

"Does it? Why not just kill him and be done with it?"

Schultz rubbed the arms of the visitor's chair he was sitting in. "Because then he wouldn't make a very good audience."

Schultz and PJ walked out of the room. They could see Dr. Dyson hovering at the end of the hall, pacing back and forth, obviously unhappy to leave his charge alone with two investigators.

"That looks like a man with something to say," PJ said.

"Yeah, he just doesn't know it yet," Schultz said. "Say,

Doc, how about waiting in the car for me for a few minutes? I gotta use the john.'' He winked at her.

It wasn't until Wednesday that PJ made it back out to Tall Oaks to talk to Henry. Barnesworth had kept her occupied with busywork.

There had been one good development in the meantime. The inquiry about her rented house had turned out even better than she'd hoped for. The owner was already living in Florida. She had been spending summers in St. Louis and winters in a manufactured home in Florida, but had decided to relocate permanently. A short negotiation had led to an acceptable price and a surprise offer of owner financing. PJ was on her way to becoming a St. Louis homeowner.

An interesting story had come tumbling out of Dr. Dyson after Schultz had spoken to him privately at the end of their last visit.

Dr. Dyson had, at James Washburn's request, kept Henry drugged with ketamine for days or weeks at a time. Periodically James would call and schedule a visit, and the doctor would bring Henry out of his stupor so that he was alert when James arrived. There was no need for restraints; the paralysis was real. The brothers were together for a couple of hours, then Henry would be drugged again before James even left the room. For his compliance Dr. Dyson had been paid generously, enough to purchase the yacht he had always wanted.

Dr. Dyson swore he was the only one at Tall Oaks who was involved in the scheme. The nursing staff had been told that Henry was receiving an experimental painkiller. James had visited only a few days ago. He wasn't expected for at least a couple of weeks, according to the pattern he'd been following lately. The investigators had a grace period before James found out about their activities.

Schultz chatted genially with the officer outside Henry's room. He was being watched over so that there would be no "accidents." PJ pushed open the door, as she had done a couple of days ago. She was pleased to see that Henry was sitting up in bed looking out the window. He turned toward her and smiled. The plane crash had taken away movement below the shoulders, but his eyes were clear, intelligent, and very blue. She hadn't noticed the color before.

"You must be Dr. Gray," he said. "Thank you for all you've done for me."

She moved the chair down toward the foot of the bed so that he could see her without having to turn his head sharply. "I didn't do it all myself. I had some help," she said, thinking of Schultz's satisfied look when he had finally come out to the car the day of their first visit. "I'm delighted that you're feeling so much better."

"It's hard to believe an entire year has gone by," Henry said. "To me, it's only been a few days since Pop died. Since James killed him."

"You've only had a few days of alertness," she said. "But it really has been a year." She heard the door close as Schultz slipped into the room. She turned her head just enough to see him leaning against the wall, and she understood that he meant for her to go on with the interview herself.

"Tell me what you remember about James's visits."

Henry's face darkened. "James always said Pop favored me. But that wasn't true. Pop loved us both. When Pop tried to tell him there was more to life than girls and fast cars, James would just get mad and scream at Pop. He got in trouble with the law a few times, too. That broke Pop's heart, but James couldn't see that. Finally Pop had enough. He told James he was cutting him out of everything unless he shaped up."

Henry's gaze flicked to the bedside table, where there was a pitcher of water. PJ poured him some and held the cup so that he could sip through the straw. He was calmer by the time he finished.

"He killed Pop. He told me all about it while I was lying here. I had to listen to him tell over and over how he shot Pop and watched him crawl across the floor."

Henry's eyes closed. PJ thought he was going to cry, but when he opened them, they were dry and hot.

"I hate my brother. I never thought I'd say anything like that in my life. I knew he was a troublemaker, but I figured he'd grow out of it. I hate him. For what he did to Pop, and for making me listen. You've got to arrest him for murder. Nothing would make me happier than seeing him in jail for the rest of his life."

Schultz cleared his throat and stepped closer. "That's going to be tough, Mr. Washburn. We've only got your word for what happened, and you're not even an eyewitness. There isn't any physical evidence tying your brother to the murder."

"Wait a minute!" PJ said. "How did James know that part about crawling across the floor if he wasn't there?"

Schultz squashed her elation immediately. "James was at the crime scene. He had to do the inventory of the gallery so the police knew what was stolen. He would have seen the blood trail on the floor."

PJ nodded. She didn't like the look on Henry's face, but Schultz was telling it like it was. "Think hard, Henry," she said. "Did he ever tell you the location of the stolen paintings?"

"Paintings? He never said anything about stolen paintings."

PJ felt deflated. If they could recover the paintings from James's possession, they would have the link they needed.

"If he had taken paintings," Henry said bitterly, "he would have sold them at the first opportunity. He didn't care about art or antiques at all."

"That's what we were afraid of," Schultz said.

They assured Henry that they would do everything possible to bring his father's killer to justice. Schultz left the room. PJ talked quietly to Henry for a few minutes about therapy, mental and physical, and about the latest developments in computer-assisted mobility. Tall Oaks, under a new director, was scheduling an aggressive program of therapy for him.

On her way out of the building to join Schultz, the futility of it descended on her like a piano from the sixteenth floor. It looked like James Washburn was going to get away with murder.

CHAPTER

25

PJ sat across from Helen Boxwood and studied the woman as she emptied packs of artificial sweetener into her coffee. PJ had lost track at about six, focusing instead on the delicate manner in which Helen tore open the packs and stirred the coffee after each one. Her small hands, accentuated by long red fingernails, looked as though they had been grafted on to her otherwise blocky shape. She was older than PJ but probably a few years younger than Schultz, and looked about as approachable as PJ's old professor of comparative anatomy.

It was hard to imagine the woman across from her as a battered wife.

Helen had put that part of her life behind her, but in doing so she had fashioned walls around herself. Not just walls, but a fortress with cannons.

They had already eaten lunch together in the hospital's restaurant, not the staff cafeteria but the rooftop establishment where hospital execs entertained their visitors. PJ had worried that Helen would feel out of place there, but the woman had accepted the invitation and chatted comfortably and at length, even though her nurse's uniform stood out in the crowd of dark suits and dresses. Steaming cups of coffee and thin slices of cheesecake topped with fresh raspberries followed a delicious meal.

PJ had to get down to business now that the dessert had arrived.

Helen sipped her drink. "Schultz put you up to this, didn't he?"

PJ nodded, wondering where to go from there. Years of training and clinical experience, and she was tonguetied.

"I thought so," Helen said. "He tried a few phone calls. Even found out when my birthday was and sent me flowers. Now he's sending in the troops."

"An evening out won't do any harm, especially with me and my friend along. Take a chance, Helen. You never know where it could lead."

"I'm a married woman," Helen said.

"You're just hiding behind that marriage certificate," PJ said. "You should have divorced Jack long ago. He's a murderer, for God's sake!"

That had just popped out. PJ didn't want to embarrass Helen. For all she knew, no one at work was aware of Helen's circumstances. PJ glanced around, noting that the restaurant had nearly emptied out and no one was seated nearby. The only reason PJ knew about Jack was that Helen herself had told her. The two women had gotten to know each other well enough that PJ had even talked about her own reasons for divorce.

She realized that Helen was the closest thing she had to a confidante. It wasn't fair to talk about how she felt about Steven with her son. She didn't want to bias him against his dad, and anyway he was only twelve. It wasn't appropriate to burden him with the pain she had felt about Steven's infidelity.

There was Merlin, whom she told everything. But she had never had a face-to-face conversation with him, and sometimes she suspected he wasn't even flesh and blood.

Helen picked up the spoon and stirred her coffee, sloshing some out on the table. Her usually precise movements had given way to nervous jerks. She used a napkin to blot up the spill.

"Men can be such bastards," PJ said. She was thinking about Steven's latest incursion, trying to get Thomas to move back into his old room.

"You're right."

PJ wasn't sure she if she was talking about divorcing Jack or men being bastards.

"I'll go," Helen said.

PJ blinked. Had she won the woman over so easily?

"But only if Schultz keeps his hands to himself." A smile formed on Helen's face. PJ thought it might have been the first time she had seen her smile. It looked good on her.

"I think that can be arranged. After all, I am his boss," PJ said, keeping her voice and face straight. "I'll just make it an order."

The two women settled on a week from Friday. Helen had to work over the coming weekend.

On the drive back to Headquarters, PJ used her cellular phone to call Schultz and give him the news. He was unabashedly delighted, which made all the trouble she was going through worthwhile. After an uneventful and unproductive afternoon in the office, she skipped out early and arrived home just as Thomas was getting home from school.

Columbus was with him.

It was Thursday evening. Generally Thomas didn't have company on school nights, but she didn't want to rock the boat. It wasn't a coincidence that Thomas brought home his friend. She'd tried to have a talk with him the night before, and it hadn't gone well. Thomas had clammed up immediately and none of her usual tactics had worked. They had ended the evening by retreating into busywork. Today the two of them needed some emotional distance from each other. Having company was Thomas's way of avoiding more talk.

She was certain there was a problem he didn't want to discuss. She would have bet her Mom's license on it. If she pressed too hard he would bury it deeper. In spite of her urge to help, she had decided to back off and hope he would come to her.

She served pancakes for dinner, because it was quick and easy. Columbus seemed surprised to have pancakes at that time of day; evidently, no one turned things topsy-turvy at his house. After dinner, she excused the boys to use the computer while she cleaned up.

Columbus left early, about eight P.M., and assured her he could ride home on his bike with no problem. Thomas hardly said a word to her before bedtime.

Cold ripples were running through her relationship with her son, and it made her sad.

The phone woke her a half hour before the alarm had a chance to do its dirty work. It was Schultz, and the news wasn't good.

Emory Harquest, whose blurry photographs provided the only clue to the identity of the killer, was dead.

CHAPTER

26

It was the newspaper boy who had found Harquest's body. When PJ got to the scene, Dave and Schultz met her with the story.

"Kid's eleven years old. He's got a bike route and rides partway up each driveway, tosses the paper, and circles back out," Schultz said. "He has it down great, and gets home in time for breakfast before school."

"So this morning he finds a body?" PJ said.

"Not exactly. He rode his bike through the dried blood before noticing what it was," Dave said, pointing. "He could see that the blood was heavier near the bushes by the porch. He was scared and didn't approach, which probably spares him a lot of nightmares. He waited for the patrol car he knew would be along in a few minutes. Every morning he waved to the officers, but this time he flagged the car down. Told them about the blood, and that he thought a large animal had been hit in the street and dragged itself into the bushes. A deer, maybe. Sometimes deer get into city neighborhoods and the results usually aren't good for the deer."

"Sensible kid," PJ said.

"Yeah. Anyway, the kid must have seen the look on the officer's face, because by the time I got here he was crying and insisting that he had to deliver Mr. Harquest's paper. I went along with it and tossed the paper up on the porch. That seemed to calm him down. He's over there in my car. Either of you want to talk with him?" Dave asked.

Schultz shook his head.

"I don't think so," PJ said. "Just get his name and take him home. Be sure to tell his parents what happened. He's going to need to talk about this."

Schultz mumbled something about kids being exposed to too much violence as the two of them carefully made their way up the driveway. PJ looked around at the onlookers gathered behind the crime scene tape, their faces rapt. They were hoping for a glimpse of death, as long as it was on someone else's lawn.

The body was concealed, although not very well, under the forsythia bushes near the porch. The bushes, oblivious to the grisly work of mankind, were responding to nature's cycle with yellow blossoms and new green leaves.

The first thing PJ saw when she approached the bushes was Harquest's cane. It was bloody and as callously discarded as his life had been. She wanted to wipe it clean and hand it back to the round little man who looked like Santa Claus. She remembered how he hadn't wanted to be helped by the officer who brought him to her office. He'd wanted the dignity of making it on his own.

There was a lot of knife work on Harquest's body. PJ turned away after getting the general idea. Schultz went over to the medical examiner kneeling next to the body and exchanged a few words.

"Looks like there was a blow to the head, although probably not a fatal one," he said when he returned to her. "Won't know any of this for sure until after the autopsy. There are a lot of superficial cuts and a few deeper ones. It looks like efforts were made to carve out the heart. He's got the duct tape over his mouth. ME says the cutting's amateurish and was done before Harquest died. The cause of death might be one of the deeper stabs in the area of the heart."

"Time of death?" PJ asked.

"Sometime last night. Christ, Doc, you know the ME doesn't like to be pinned down on this stuff while the body's still in the field."

PJ shifted gears. "No blood in the house?"

"No. Shit. That's a real puzzle here. The blood trail starts on the lower steps of the front porch. It's like the killer lured the guy out here."

"Why would the killer risk being seen?" PJ said. "Even if he lured Harquest out, why not drag him back inside after knocking him unconscious?"

The answer came to them both simultaneously. "Because Harquest was too heavy," Schultz said as PJ nodded. "Our suspect is either a short woman or a teenager."

The contrast between the smiling man sitting in her office doing his part for justice and the sad remains under the bushes suddenly smacked into her. It was too much to take. She turned her head away and struggled to keep the tears from flowing. Schultz put a hand on her shoulder.

"Go on back to the car, I'll join you in a minute."

You're the one who will catch the killer.

"No," PJ said. "That's not going to do Emory Harquest any good. This is my job, Schultz, as much as it is yours."

She pulled a small notebook out of her coat pocket and began making notes as the evidence techs measured and photographed. Schultz left her alone. A few minutes later, she called him over again.

"How about breakfast at Millie's?"

"You're talking my language, boss. Give me a few more minutes. They're about ready to move the body."

The fresh-squeezed orange juice was tart and had a lot of pulp, just the way PJ liked it. There was an apple cinnamon muffin on her plate that was practically as big as the plate. She didn't have much of an appetite after the morning's events but was making a valiant effort to eat. Schultz had just loaded up his first forkful of fried eggs. She hated it that he always had the yolks runny, and that at the end he would sop up the yellow chick juice with a piece of toast.

No wonder his wife left him.

"Do you have to get eggs for breakfast all the time?" she said.

"Huh?"

"Never mind. I've been thinking about Clara Eddington."

He nodded with his mouth full.

"I have a feeling that I almost tripped over the killer that time. When I was walking down the hall to her classroom, I should have met him coming out. He either had to come toward me or go the other way into the gymnasium. There weren't any exits where he could have ducked out."

"The gymnasium has doors to the outside. He could have gone out that way."

"None of the people there saw a door open. There would have been a rush of cold air and probably some rain blown in, too. Someone would have noticed."

"Good point. The rest of the rooms were searched. You're saying we should look at the families in the gym."

"I saw lists being made at the door. Has every person been accounted for?"

"I see what you're getting at. We focused on the adults in the room. We should take a closer look at the kids."

PJ had to admit that the muffin was delicious. She would never have suspected that she'd get the best muffin she had ever tasted at Millie's Diner. "Exactly. It was an eighth-grade event, but parents could have brought their older children along for the evening."

"I don't know about that. When I was in high school, I wouldn't have set foot in that gym with a bunch of thirteen-year-olds. Besides, there's something you haven't thought of. You're not thinking like a person who just chopped up a teacher."

"Well, thank goodness."

"There's the problem of disposing of the weapon. And what about the messy clothes? Our guy couldn't just sashay into the gym with blood on his clothes."

"He could have brought a change of clothes with him and hidden the bloody ones and the weapon somewhere in the school."

"Where, exactly? A team searched the place thoroughly."

PJ was stymied. She buttered the second half of her muffin and broke off a big piece. "Thomas has a combination lock for his locker."

"Yeah, so?"

"Did they open all the lockers with locks on them?"

"I doubt it. Shit."

"I'll bet the search team just assumed those belonged to little kids and there wouldn't be anything inside except smelly sneakers," PJ said.

"So the killer packed all the incriminating things in a backpack and stuffed it inside a locker," Schultz said, pausing in the ravishment of his breakfast. "He picked out a vacant locker and put a lock on it so we'd think it belonged to one of the school kids. He must have come back the next day when the police were gone from the building and removed it. Doc, you're brilliant."

"Thanks. I'll keep that one in my pocket and drag it out when I need it. There are a couple of other possibilities you haven't considered."

"Which are?"

"The killer is the older brother of a student, and knew the combination for one of the in-use lockers. Or the last one: the killer put the bag in his own locker. He's a student at Deaver."

Schultz was quiet for a time, predictably sopping with his last bite of toast. "Can you picture Thomas chopping off someone's head," he said, "or trying to cut out a living heart?"

"Of course not. But that doesn't mean there isn't such a thing as a child sociopath. Where do you think adult sociopaths come from? That they suddenly spring into being at age thirty?"

"I'll get Anita and Dave to go over that list, talk to everybody again, including all the kids who were there."

"Good. I'll talk to Barnesworth about it, although I can imagine what he'll say. We shouldn't blindside him, even though the thought appeals."

Schultz grunted in agreement. "Something else," he said. "Do you still have that extra set of pictures Harquest gave you?"

"No, I turned them over to Barnesworth."

"Good. If the killer's going to go after anyone else, I'd rather it was that SOB than you."

"What do you mean?"

"Well, there was no reason to go after Harquest unless the killer saw the flashes of light and knew photos were taken. We haven't released anything about them to the press."

"Agreed, although I can't figure out why he waited so long. Harquest came in almost two weeks ago."

"Maybe the killer goes by the phases of the moon, or some shit like that. We don't have the slightest idea yet what motivates him. Has it occurred to you that the killer asked Harquest about where the pictures went, maybe tortured him to get information? That he's following the trail those pictures have taken?"

"No. Damn it, Schultz, now I'm worried."

"We should leak to the press that Barnesworth has a photo of the killer and he's keeping it secret from everybody else so he can claim all the glory himself."

"You're kidding," PJ said. "That would be . . . You are kidding, aren't you?"

"You going to finish that muffin?"

Dave was the one who struck pay dirt. He and Anita had been on the phone checking out each of the entries on the logs recorded by the officers at the Eddington murder. The Brendt family, Drew and Carol, had five kids. They were on the list as leaving the gym with all five, but one of their children had been up on stage during the performance. Those children had left by the stage door and been individually accounted for, along with the teachers who were serving as stage crew and musicians. Jeremy Brendt was on the stage door list. Who, then, was the fifth child who left with the Brendts?

The oldest girl, Sarah, remembered a kid crowding in

behind her as they were going through the exit. She remembered him because he stepped on her heel. He apologized quickly, and she didn't even turn around. She thought it was a boy because the voice didn't sound like a girl's, but she couldn't say for certain. Bottom line: there was an extra boy in the gym that night, but no one could say what he looked like or even how old he was.

PJ was gratified to have her theory pan out, but in practical terms they were no closer than before. Schultz requested a universal locker search, with every child opening his or her locker in front of Mrs. Barry, the principal. PJ suggested that the searchers be on the lookout for a jacket with a rhinestone snake on the back.

The search turned up nothing except a little grass and a few porno pictures, duly dealt with, and some angry parents who felt their children's rights had been violated.

A forensic technician had followed Mrs. Barry around, shining a UV light into the open lockers in the hopes of bloodstains showing up. The ALS, or Alternate Light Source, caused even minute amounts of blood to be visible. There was a momentary fuss when a skirt in a girl's locker revealed a barely there stain. The embarrassed girl admitted that she had stained the skirt during her period, changed into some jeans she kept in her locker for just that reason, and washed the skirt out in the restroom. Several of her friends vouched for her story.

"It was a long shot anyway," Anita told PJ when she and Schultz informed her of the results of the search. PJ had met the two of them at the school. "We figured any bloody items would have been in plastic, and then put inside a backpack or duffel."

"What do you suppose the killer did with the weapon and clothes once they were safely away from the scene?" PJ asked.

"If it was me," Anita said, "I'd burn the clothes and chuck the weapon in a river."

"The burning part sounds right. But sociopaths sometimes keep the weapon because it has significance to them. There doesn't seem to be anything missing from the victims themselves—no lock of hair, no fingertip, no jewelry, things like that."

"Could be he takes pictures, and that's how he savors the killing over and over," Schultz said.

"Or he replays everything just by getting the weapon out and handling it."

"You're giving me the creeps, boss," Anita said. "If we're looking for a teenager, presumably living at home, wouldn't his parents notice a box of bloody weapons sitting around his room?"

"Not if it's as messy as most teens' rooms. Seriously, teenagers can be privacy freaks. They guard their rooms, and Mom and Dad may not notice anything unusual about that. This kind of kid probably has a long history of alienation from his parents anyway, so there may not be a lot of interaction. Or there may be an unhealthy interaction going on."

PJ thought of the way Mrs. Wade had acted the night she had taken Columbus home. There were certainly signs of both alienation and an unhealthy relationship there. But there were degrees of unhealthy. She resolved to get to know the Wades better.

It had been a long day, beginning with a corpse at dawn. When she got home, somehow PJ wasn't surprised to find Columbus sitting at her kitchen table, with Thomas rummaging through the cabinets looking for snacks. She set out some milk and sliced fruit for the boys and went upstairs for a bath, figuring she'd order a pizza later. As she settled into the steaming tub, she tried to figure out just what it was she liked about her job.

Schultz stopped on the way home for a sack of tacos. He chided himself for living out of fast food bags. He never seemed to have time to go to the grocery store, much less cook himself a meal. He figured all that would change when Helen moved in. He needed a woman to take him in hand. And that gave him an idea.

He doused the tacos liberally with hot sauce and ate in front of the TV. He skipped through the channels with the remote the way Julia had always hated. There were some advantages to living alone. He wondered if Helen was more tolerant. If not, he would have to change. He wasn't going to blow the chance for romance, not to mention a little companionship.

After a couple of hours, he acted on his earlier idea. Helen would never know about Casey, and he figured it wasn't really infidelity anyway.

CHAPTER

27

When Columbus got home that night, he found the house dark except for twin slivers of light from beneath the door of the Turd's office and the master bedroom. His mother must have had one of her spells of depression that sent her to her room as soon as she got home from work. What could be so bad about working as a legal secretary anyway?

Thomas's mother sliced pears and apples, arranged them in a circle on a plate, and mounded raisins in the center. Most of the time the Cow didn't even know when Columbus came home from school.

Thomas's mother came down from upstairs smelling like flowers and ordered pizza delivered. Then she sat at the table with them and talked about their day at school. The Cow said she had a headache and went off to read a romance novel, propped up in bed with pillows.

When Columbus was ready for bed, he'd brush his teeth,

flip off the light, and crawl under the covers without so much as a goodnight from down the hall. Most likely, Thomas got tucked in and kissed on the cheek.

The Cow would sleep late on Saturday morning, drag herself out of bed, and not speak to anyone until she had a few cups of coffee and read the morning paper. Thomas's mother was probably up an hour early to bake cinnamon rolls for breakfast.

It was the first time Columbus had gotten an intimate view of what another kid's family life was like, and he didn't like the way his own stacked up. He could live like Thomas, he knew he could. He was The Chameleon, after all, and he could fit himself into any situation after a little bit of study. He had watched how Thomas and his mother got along, how affection practically clogged the air between the two of them.

He could do that. And why shouldn't he? Why shouldn't he have what Thomas took for granted?

Thomas lived only with his mother. Perhaps that was the problem. His own family was marred by the Turd. If he made his family more like Thomas's, he would be wrapped in the same circle of warmth.

He wondered if that was desirable. Why not just leave things the way they were? He had freedom and money for the things he wanted.

Lying in his bed that night, after making a cryptic journal entry that avoided the whole issue, Columbus shook with an emotion he couldn't identify at first. Emotions were a tricky thing with him. Most of the time they were absent. When he did experience emotion, he was often out of sync with those around him and had to correct himself immediately, fitting himself in, taking on the facial expressions and body language of others. It took him a long time to sort through stories he had read, comparing how he felt with how the characters in the stories felt.

Before he drifted off to sleep, he had a name for it: jealousy.

CHAPTER

28

On Saturday morning, the blue sky drew PJ out into her backyard. That phrase had new meaning—her backyard—since she had signed the home loan papers yesterday.

It was too early in the year to work in the flower beds. They were too muddy, and that was perfect justification for sitting in the lawn chair relaxing and soaking up the sunshine. Her dark-blue sweatshirt kept the wind off her arms but didn't reflect any of the sun's warmth. Heat built up until she felt that Millie might be along any minute to fry an egg on her belly.

In spite of all the death she was dealing with, her spirits rose like a submerged balloon bobbing to the surface.

She decided to take Thomas to the science museum. She had a brochure about it but just hadn't had time to make it there. It would be wonderful to get away for a few hours. She went inside and found her son at the kitchen table. He was just pushing the bowl of milk left over from his Cheerios toward Megabite, who was up on the table.

"Caught you red-handed," she said. Megabite wasn't supposed to get people food.

"Oh, c'mon, Mom, you do this all the time."

"Never."

He stared at her.

"Well, once or twice. What's the plan for the day?"

"Don't know. Just kicking back, I guess. I've got some homework, but I can get it done tomorrow."

"How about a trip to the science museum? Pizza, souvenirs, the works."

"Sounds great, Mom. They have a life-size T-rex that roars that I'd like to see. Winston said it was really neat."

It was nice to know that her son was still interested in places like the science museum. In a few years, going someplace like that with his mom would be too boring for words. "So you and Winston are talking again?"

"Nah. That was before Christmas when we talked about it."

"How about giving him a call? He can come with us. It'd be fun."

For a moment, a promising smile lit up her son's face. Then it faded. "I don't think so. I'm kind of mad at the way he's treating me."

"T-man, one of you has to take the first step. That's how things like this get resolved."

"Why don't we just invite Columbus instead?"

PJ found herself backpedaling. "I think it would be fun with just the two of us."

"But you said I could invite someone along."

That's not exactly what I said, PJ thought. "Give him a call. Tell him to make sure it's all right with his parents."

A few minutes later, he was back, and said that things

were all set. Mr. and Mrs. Wade didn't mind, and Columbus would be over in about forty-five minutes. "And Mom, don't buy us kids' meals, okay? That would be embarrassing."

"I wouldn't think of it. I might get myself one, though. I hear they come in little buckets with cute animals on them."

"That's at the zoo," he said. He sneered at her and hurried off to get ready.

She took the easy way out with Barnesworth and left him a voice mail message saying she'd be out for a few hours and he could page her if necessary. Then she thought of something else she could accomplish, and dialed Schultz's number. She expected him to be sleeping in, but he answered on the second ring and sounded uncharacteristically perky.

"Detective, how about getting a charge out of static electricity today? Or feeling an earthquake under your feet?"

"What the hell are you talking about?"

"I'm taking Thomas and a friend to the science museum. I thought you might enjoy a few hours away from the job." She could hear him frowning. "Even homicide detectives have to take a sanity break. Doctor's orders. Besides, I want to stop at Art World in Clayton and have a talk with Rebecca Singer."

"Now that's more to my liking. You got any doughnuts for breakfast?"

"No, but I'll get some, if that's what it takes to get you over here."

By the time he arrived, PJ had two sugared jellies in a bag and a travel mug filled with coffee for him.

"The royal treatment, eh?" Schultz said. "That fucked-up ex-husband of yours doesn't know what he's missing."

"Sshh. Watch your language. I have enough trouble without you setting a bad example."

"You think your son never heard anybody say fucked up?"

PJ put both hands on her hips. "That's not the point."

Schultz mirrored her stance. "Enlighten me."

"Thomas has a list of words he's not allowed to use. Three lists, actually, the A, B, and C list. Using a C word costs Thomas a dime, a B word costs a quarter, and an A word costs a dollar."

"No wonder my kid's in the slammer. We didn't have swearing lists."

They were interrupted by a knock at the rear door. Columbus had arrived and parked his bike around back. Schultz opened the door. He clapped his hand on Columbus's shoulder and dragged him in. The boy was startled, and his mouth froze in an O.

"I'm Schultz. Nice to meet you, kid."

Ambivalence flashed onto Schultz's face, and PJ wondered if he realized that his brash approach wasn't suited to the child's personality. Columbus just didn't seem the roughhousing type to her. She saw Schultz abruptly release his hold on the boy's shoulder as though he had gotten a mild electric shock.

Schultz wanted to drive, so she sat next to him in the front seat of the Pacer, with the two boys in the back. The drive to Clayton was silent except for the noise of Schultz alternately downing his coffee and his doughnuts. He managed pretty well for a man keeping the car from climbing the curb and having breakfast at the same time. When they got to Art World, he smoothly pulled into the vacant PROPRIETOR parking spot. PJ gave him a thumbs-up.

Thomas asked to come inside the gallery, and since she didn't really want to leave the boys alone in the parked car, she said yes. Schultz warned them to keep their hands to themselves or they'd be paying for some broken Chinese vase out of their allowances for the rest of their lives.

Inside, PJ was reminded of the statues that needed fig leaves. She shook her head as the boys immediately noticed—how could they not—and began pointing and comparing. Schultz thought it was funny, and regained some of the good mood that had seeped away after meeting Columbus. She needed to get Schultz alone and ask him about that.

Rebecca, alerted to the entrance of visitors by the bell over the door, came out of the back room. She was about to shush the boys, politely of course, since she didn't know the situation yet. They could be spoiled brats of high-paying customers, which called for a different approach than if they were ordinary hooligans. She spotted PJ and Schultz, and the warning died on her lips.

They went into the back office to talk, even though Rebecca was clearly nervous about leaving the boys in the gallery unattended.

"They'll be okay," Schultz said blandly. "What harm can they do? They're only kids."

He's got a cruel streak, PJ thought. *Wish I'd thought of that first.*

"We'd like to talk to you again about the Washburn investigation," PJ said. "How well did you know Patrick Washburn's younger son?"

"Henry? Surely you don't suspect him?"

"We have a suspect," Schultz said, "and I can tell you that it isn't Henry."

PJ watched Rebecca closely. The woman took a deep breath and seemed to be having some kind of internal struggle.

"I'm glad to know that," she said. Her voice was controlled. "It's about time someone paid for that crime. Henry, now. Henry was a good son. Mr. Washburn adored him, and hoped that someday he would take over the business. James didn't seem to have any interest along those lines, except for whatever money he could squeeze out of it. But Henry would have done it for the love of art. I liked Henry very much. Then there was the accident."

Rebecca leaned to the right, trying to see around Schultz into the showroom. The boys were suspiciously quiet. Schultz shifted to block her view.

"Mr. Washburn tried to convince his son that life could go on, that he could run the business from a wheelchair. Many people do manage very well, you know, and it isn't like this is the Olympics." She spread her arms to indicate her working conditions. "But Henry was depressed and couldn't see that. Mr. Washburn should have tried to help more, should have insisted on the right kind of therapy, but he was mourning for his wife. Sometimes I think he never really accepted that she was gone."

"Did you know that Henry was moved to a new care facility soon after his father's death?"

"Yes, of course. James told me about it. He said he wanted Henry to have the best care possible, and the new place had an excellent program. I thought Henry might start living again instead of wasting his time dwelling on the past."

"Did you ever visit him?"

"I called once to arrange a visit, but the director, Dr. Bison, something like that, told me that Henry had taken a turn for the worse. He wouldn't be able to recognize me, the doctor said, and discouraged visiting until Henry was better." She looked from one to the other, and her hand flew up to her mouth. "You're not here to tell me Henry's dead, are you? Are you?"

"No."

"Oh, thank goodness. Mr. Washburn loved him so, and it . . . pleased me that at least one of the sons made his father happy."

"What do you know about the stolen paintings?" PJ asked, abruptly changing the subject. There was a short pause, and PJ thought that she'd hit on something Rebecca didn't want to talk about.

"As far as I know, they were insured, like everything in the gallery, and the insurance company settled some time ago. Why? Did any of them turn up?"

"We were hoping you could tell us that," PJ said. "With your connections in the art world, have you heard of any of them being acquired by collectors, for instance?"

Rebecca shook her head. "Really, Dr. Gray, I'm not as connected as you must think. I don't deal with the black market at all."

"I was just thinking that if the paintings were to be found in our suspect's possession, we'd finally have enough physical evidence to go to trial." Schultz gave her an odd look, but PJ charged on. "That's the real key to this investigation, the location of the stolen paintings."

"I'm sorry, but I can't help you there," Rebecca said. She moved sideways too fast for Schultz to counter, and got a good look into the display area.

The two boys were sitting on the floor hunched over a pocket video game. All three adults breathed a sigh of relief.

Schultz had never been to the science museum. He was surprised at the quality and variety of the displays. It occurred to him that on casual glance, he, PJ, and the two boys looked like any of the other families visiting on a

Saturday morning. Well, maybe he was a little older than most of the dads. He reached up and smoothed the strands of hair that thinly covered his bald spot. A family of four. A family.

Schultz and PJ trailed behind the kids as they went from display to display in the museum. Lunch had been in the Albert Einstein cafe, on a balcony overlooking the exhibits. The T-rex roared relentlessly in the background. Schultz had insisted on paying for lunch, and no kid's meals were purchased. He had to admit he was enjoying himself.

"What was that all about with Singer?" Schultz said.

"You mean about the location of the stolen paintings?"

"Yeah. You were really dumping that on. Talk about subtle."

Schultz watched PJ's cheeks redden. They were a nice contrast to the dark-blue sweatshirt she had on. He looked at her appraisingly. Her hair shone in the sunlight from the expansive windows, the gray she probably fretted about transmuted to silver framing her face. The top of her head came only to his shoulders, and she was pleasantly rounded in the hips, the way he liked his women. He wanted to protect her. He had an urge to slip his arm around her waist, and wondered what she would do if he did.

"I was acting on a hunch," she said. "You do that all the time."

"What hunch?"

"I think Rebecca knows a lot more than she's telling us. She might have been involved with the homicide."

"She was in on it? Shit, why would she do that? I think she was in love with the old geezer."

"Maybe it's James she's in love with."

Schultz gave her an incredulous look. "She's mighty tolerant of his bimbos, then."

PJ shrugged. "Don't assume everyone else has your standards for a love relationship. Maybe she thought she could change him, and now he's scorned her.''

Schultz turned that over in his mind, but he just couldn't see the two of them as a couple. "You're not serious, are you?"

PJ sighed. "No. But I mentioned it to point out that you need to keep an open mind on these things. Love does funny things to people."

He didn't bother to correct her about his open mind. The years he'd spent investigating homicides had taught him what a powerfully destructive force love could be. Or what people thought was love. "I don't get it about the paintings," he said.

"I just wanted to make it clear to her that she could still get back at James. After what we've heard from Henry, and if the paintings were to be found in James's possession . . ."

"Christ, you're devious. I love it." He punched her in the arm lightly. She punched back. They walked on in silence for a time.

"How well do you know Thomas's new friend?" Schultz asked. They were on an enclosed walkway that crossed Highway 40. It led to the planetarium, another portion of the complex which predated the museum. The boys were fascinated with the clear inserts in the floor where they could see the cars whizzing by underneath. There were radar guns set up which could be aimed at the traffic below to show whether or not the cars were speeding. Most of them were.

"What do you mean?" PJ asked.

The fact that she was defensive wasn't good. It meant there was something to the feeling he'd gotten when he first met the boy.

"Ticket," Schultz said, watching the speeds of the

oncoming cars flash on the display. "Ticket. Big ticket. Why isn't Traffic on top of this? They could make a mint from up here." He turned toward PJ. "I thought the question was clear enough."

"He's been over to the house several times," she said. "I've met his mother."

"And?"

"And truthfully, I'm a little worried. Right about the time Columbus came into the picture, Thomas stopped seeing Winston. Those two have been friends ever since we moved to St. Louis."

"Seems a little too convenient, doesn't it?"

"I've thought the same thing. That maybe Columbus wanted to be friends with Thomas and he somehow engineered the breakup."

"So he could have Thomas all to himself."

"Jeez, it sounds sinister when you put it that way. I think it's more that Columbus wants to get away from his home environment. It doesn't exactly seem like love is in the air over there."

"I get a bad feeling about that kid," Schultz said. He'd decided to be blunt. What he didn't say was that when he had grabbed Columbus's shoulder, what he'd felt was a cold void. Like putting his hand in a freezer. Even visiting the museum, when the boys should have been having a lot of fun, letting loose, doing silly stuff, he felt that Columbus was guarded. When the kid laughed, he was a beat behind everyone else, like he had to plan it first.

Schultz closed his eyes, blocked out the traffic noise, and searched inside for the golden thread. It came to life and sparked in his mind, coiling sinuously. But the other end wasn't anchored yet. Close, but no cigar.

PJ was looking at him with concern. "Bad in what way?"

"Just bad. Like he's not what he seems to be."

They didn't speak any more of it. He could see that PJ had her own reservations, and he thought he'd just let them perk along on their own. She was a psychologist and a fiercely protective mother. It wasn't likely she'd let Columbus be a bad influence on her son.

He looked up and saw that the two boys had gotten tired of the floor "windows," and that Columbus was staring at him disapprovingly, as if Schultz's thoughts had been written in a little balloon over his head.

CHAPTER

29

What's up, Keypunch?

Thomas was in bed, and finally asleep. PJ had fixed herself some hot cocoa with a liberal handful of miniature marshmallows and dialed up the private bulletin board she used to converse with her mentor.

I'm worried, Merlin, she typed without preamble. *Thomas is hiding something from me. I don't know how to handle it. I do better with outright hostility.*

Don't doubt yourself. You're the best mother I know. Didn't you ever hide anything from your parents when you were young?

Yes. I remember I tried smoking and got caught because I accidentally started a fire in a trash can in the basement. And sometimes I would go out with a boy when I said I was with a girlfriend.

There you go.

This is different. It feels way different, in a whole other league. PJ typed. *He's jittery, scared maybe. Having trouble sleeping, and that's not like him at all.* She closed her eyes and pictured Thomas and Columbus together. Thomas was bigger physically, but somehow Columbus seemed to dominate her son. Thomas was looking to him, taking cues from him.

Drugs.

What?

You heard me, you just don't want to think about it.

Oh, God, Merlin, do you think it could be drugs?

Maybe his new friend introduced him to more than some new software.

Not Thomas. No way. He's smarter than that.

That's what all the other parents said, the ones who have to pick out the flowers for the funeral.

All right. You've beaten me over the head with it. I'll look into it. I should talk to Winston, too, and find out what is really going on. Those two boys were close.

Or it could be some kind of cult thing. Don't cult leaders alienate their followers from family and friends?

You're really cheering me up, Merlin.

Here to serve.

A smart aleck, too. I should have known what I'd get from you.

I'm the one constant in your life. Off the subject, I didn't turn up anything about the paintings from the Washburn gallery. If they've been sold on the black market, my contact doesn't know it. And he's in a position to know. Here's today's list:

1. Sex, drugs, and rock and roll. Self-explanatory.
2. Don't panic. Millions of other parents have been there ahead of you.
3. It is impossible to shelter a child from all evil. The best you can do is give him a self-contained evil detector and hope for the best.
4. Okay, panic a little.

5. *The word for the day is* self, *as in* self-doubt. *A little goes a long way.*

Take care, Keypunch.

PJ drank the dregs of her cocoa and sat in front of her computer, thinking. Deciding. She rinsed her cup in the sink and walked upstairs. Checking on Thomas, she found him spread-eagled on the bed, outside the covers. She worked his legs back under the top sheet and blanket, wondering how many times she had done that before, starting from those times when she knew he was warm inside his footed pajamas but longed for a last touch before her own bedtime. Turning from his crib and seeing Steven in the doorway, watching the two of them, sharing a secret smile with her, neither of them quite believing what they had brought into the world. She still had that feeling, but there was no man in the doorway to share it with.

Thomas snorted gently, his lips fluttering. She got to work, her decision made. She shoved the ethics aside and let her concern for Thomas override his privacy.

She searched the room thoroughly, even getting a flashlight from her nightstand and looking behind his bed and in the corners of his closet where odd and endearing things were piled. Half an hour later she was convinced there were no drugs in the room. If he was using them, his stash was elsewhere. She thought about Mrs. Wade's casual attitude about her son's whereabouts. She was sure that woman never searched her son's room. She probably wasn't even sure which room in the big house her son had claimed as his bedroom.

Thomas was restless, and he flung his arm over his head and groaned. She froze, her hand under the socks in his bureau drawer. What would she say if she was caught? She waited until he resumed his deep, regular breathing before she continued her search.

She could forbid Thomas from seeing Columbus. She was, after all, the parent, and she had taken firm stands before. But that might drive Thomas into seeing the boy secretly, and she would have lost her ability to keep tabs on things. Besides, in spite of the alarms clanging in her head about Columbus, he had just enough of the injured bird in him to appeal to PJ's protective instincts. She knew from her studies, and from experience, that a single adult reaching out to a troubled child might be enough to keep that child from destructive ways. If there was a chance she was that person for Columbus, how could she turn away?

Bending over to kiss her son, PJ had one last thought about a hiding place. She slipped her hand underneath the mattress. Nothing. She was about to remove it when impulsively she kneeled by the bed and pushed further, past Thomas's hips toward the wall. He shifted, his legs moving briefly as if he were running.

Her fingers connected with something hard. Slowly she drew it out. It was a computer disk.

Clearly it wasn't drugs, so now she was in an even grayer area of privacy. It could be a diary. It could be love letters to a girlfriend. It could be what her own mom would call naughty pictures. Whatever it was, it was almost certainly none of her business.

She took the disk downstairs to her computer and made a copy of it. She put the copy in her desk, locked the drawer, and carefully replaced the original under the mattress. She would examine the disk later on if it seemed necessary. She'd had enough sneakiness for one night.

CHAPTER

30

Columbus felt the pressure building inside him. He was like a tea kettle and the heat was turned up high. Outwardly, though, he was just a kid with a bowl of buttered popcorn about to sit down with his mom and watch a piece-of-fluff movie on cable.

He didn't like having things out of his direct control, but he wanted to make sure there could be no possible connection between himself and the evening's events. The target was so close to him that additional precautions were warranted. Besides, he wanted to be right in the room to see the Cow's face.

It would be a masterpiece, if it worked. Something for the record books. Something to put in his scrapbook to show the grandkids.

As if he would consider having kids. They'd probably turn out to be traitorous little shits like himself, and he could never turn his back on them.

Starting the rumor had been delicate work, since the rumor was about himself. He'd had to study the currents, pick the time, and wade in. Get it—Wade in. The word was out that Norm Wade wasn't exactly the boring chief financial officer he appeared to be. Oh, sure, he was that—but he also supplied drugs to his company's very special clients.

Columbus had known that the rumor had taken root and flourished when he started getting odd looks in the hallway between classes. Awed looks was more like it. In some circles, having a father who handed out drugs enhanced a kid's reputation, not that he worried much about what other kids thought of him. His world was an inner one. Other people and things were necessary only in that they gave him an opportunity to exercise the power that was rightfully his.

It was a new extension of his power over people's lives, this rumor business. It had worked to get Winston out of the picture, and it would work for him to get the Turd killed.

Columbus knew that kids talked to kids outside the school, and some of those talked to older kids, and some of those older kids knew brutal people. People who would kill for a few dollars, much less the tens of thousands of dollars of drugs that Norm Wade was supposedly transporting in his Buick Riviera, metallic blue, with leather seats and luxury accessory package.

If Columbus was lucky, if the rumor had reached the right people, there would be a vicious carjacking in St. Louis tonight. An upstanding citizen, the CFO of a respected corporation returning home from a business meeting, would be dragged from his late-model Buick, shot, and dumped in the gutter. The carjackers would tear away in their prize, which would either be broken down into parts within a few hours or be several states away by morning, or both. It would make the news. The police would say they're doing all they can, and the well-to-do men and women of the city would lock their car doors and maybe buy another gun for the glove compartment. In a few days, it would be ancient history.

The 'jackers would find no drugs, and assume the motherfucker had already made his drop. Shit happens.

Columbus had high hopes for the Cow. Once his father was removed from the scene, he expected her to blossom into a clone of Dr. Gray, transforming his life, remaking it into a duplicate of Thomas's. And they all lived happily ever after.

Project Fairy Tale was underway, and the prospects were indeterminate so far.

He could use a big success after Harquest. It had always seemed so easy to rip a person's heart out in video games. In real life, he'd had to admit that he had done a sloppy job. He hadn't anticipated that Harquest would come all the way down the steps. The guy had a cane, for Pete's sake. Columbus was supposed to ring the doorbell, Harquest would open the door, and Columbus would tackle him low, knocking him back inside. Whack! The head blow. Zip! The duct tape, everywhere. Instead, the old fart had come down the front steps as soon as Columbus pulled into the driveway on his bike. He must have been watching out the window. Didn't he ever sleep? The camera was the last straw. Flash! That's when Columbus decided to do the heart thing before the old man died instead of right after. He got Harquest down on the ground, all right, smashed him with his own camera. But then he was too heavy to be dragged up the steps by Columbus. And that idiot dog down the block had cut short his working time by barking.

He wondered if the police realized that the camera was missing from the house.

He was on his third bowl of popcorn and second insipid movie—how could she watch that stuff—when the doorbell rang. A thrill went through him. He licked his fingers and hopped up.

"I'll get it," he said. She didn't budge off the sofa, even though she must have realized that it was too late for someone selling Girl Scout cookies.

He was back a minute later. "Mom, it's the police. They want to talk to you." It was hard to keep the excitement out of his voice, hard to get that proper tone of concerned-but-letting-the-adults-handle-it.

Showtime.

She turned the TV sound on mute and levered herself up from the sofa. There was a look on her face halfway between worry and irritation. Probably thinking she had been caught on camera, running a red light, wondering why they didn't just mail the ticket.

The officers—a man and a woman—introduced themselves and asked to speak to her alone. He hadn't counted on that.

"Columbus, wait in the kitchen," the Cow said. Her anxiety had been tweaked up a little, but she didn't seem to be anticipating the bad news.

Didn't the woman know about cop shows? Didn't she know the routine?

He went into the kitchen and closed the door, then eased it open a crack. Not ideal, but it would have to do. Anything else might make the officers suspicious.

"Mrs. Wade," the lady cop said, "your husband was the victim of a crime about nine P.M. this evening."

Here it comes! Unfortunately, the Cow had her back to him.

"I'm sorry to have to inform you that your husband Norman Wade died at the scene of an apparent carjacking."

There was no response. No scream. No hysterical crying. She just stood there.

"Mrs. Wade, do you understand what I just told you?"

The Cow sank to the floor. She had fainted.

Shit. He had been hoping for something a little more dramatic.

CHAPTER

31

Tuesday afternoon PJ had a meeting with Rebecca Singer. The woman had called and asked to meet with her and specifically without Schultz. It was even more mysterious because Rebecca wanted to meet at a coffee-house, not at the gallery where she worked. It must have been her day off.

The coffeehouse was on Euclid Avenue in the Central West End, an eclectic collection of shops and restaurants bounded by a city park appropriately named Forest Park, a large multi-hospital medical campus, and a residential area with houses ranging from humble duplexes to large mansions on private drives, like the Washburn family home. In years past, the shopping area had been not far from Gaslight Square, the center of St. Louis night life, with jazz floating from the open doors of clubs, cobble-stone streets, and genuine gas lights. Some of the streets were still cobblestone, but the clubs were gone.

The coffeehouse turned out to be a delightful place. There was outdoor seating, but it was too cool and windy to be enjoyable, so she took a table near the window. PJ had misjudged the amount of time it would take her to get there, so she arrived about twenty minutes early.

The door was propped open and a stream of fresh air came her way. It must have circulated into the kitchen first, because it carried scents of cinnamon rolls, croissants, and fresh-brewed coffee. The windows were huge and sparkling and the pedestrian activity on the street was interesting to watch.

PJ decided to have tea, since she'd already had her quota of coffee at Millie's. When the waiter approached, she asked what kind of teas were available and was given a list of about twenty, including her favorite, Constant Comment. The waiter brought her a tray with a large basket of tea bags, sugar, honey, and a steaming teapot with a flowered cozy. She poured, set a bag steeping, and inhaled. The aroma lifted her spirits, as it had done many times before.

When Rebecca arrived, she didn't seem like the same hesitant woman PJ had met earlier. Gone were the nervous fluttering of hands and the clothing that concealed both her body and her thoughts. Rebecca couldn't hide behind the plain blue shirtdress she was wearing. Even her straightforward gold ball earrings promised decisions made with no looking back. PJ waited while the woman sniffed at the tea and ordered more of the same, and requested a cinnamon roll, no icing, and two plates. Evidently, she'd been to the place before.

"Thank you for coming," she said. "I've been thinking about what you said the last time we talked. About the stolen paintings."

PJ sat up straighter. She hadn't known what to expect from this meeting, but Rebecca had just gotten PJ's full attention. "You have some information on that? Henry doesn't know anything about them. He wasn't even aware that anything was missing from the gallery."

"James is the one who did the inventory of the gallery for the police, to determine if anything was stolen. After you talked to me, I called the insurance company and got a copy of the inventory he filed. I'm sure they wouldn't give it out to just anyone, but I was their main contact for years. I went over it very carefully, Dr. Gray."

"Please call me PJ. If we're sharing a cinnamon roll, we should be on a first-name basis."

Rebecca smiled for the first time that PJ could remember, and it did wonders for her appearance.

"You've got a lovely smile. You should do it more often," PJ said.

The waiter brought a mountain of a cinnamon roll which had been neatly divided and placed on two heavy white plates. It smelled heavenly. The queasiness she had felt earlier at Millie's had vanished, leaving her ravenous.

"Thank you. Patrick always said it was my best feature. Puts the clients at ease."

So now it's Patrick, not Mr. Washburn. PJ picked up her fork and planned her assault on the roll.

"About the inventory," Rebecca said. "James listed the contents of the office safe. Nothing was taken from there."

PJ nodded, wondering where she was being led. The roll not only smelled heavenly, it tasted heavenly. She had to stop herself from picking it up with both hands and wolfing it down.

"He didn't mention anything about the floor safe."

"There were two safes? Why?"

"The office safe was for show. It made customers feel

important if their items went directly into the safe, or if Patrick had to get something out of the safe to display to them. Some customers insisted on watching him remove or place objects in the safe. It actually boosted the prices."

PJ raised her eyebrows.

"It was a business, PJ. A competitive one, at that. Patrick loved art and antiques, but he also made a good living. Part of what he sold was the perception of value."

PJ wished she had brought along a tape recorder. She had a feeling things were going to get even more interesting than the revelation of a hidden safe in the gallery.

She waved the waiter over and ordered a slice of Chocolate Decadence pie. "Skipped breakfast," she explained. He nodded as if he'd heard it all before.

"The floor safe was the serious one, and it was secret. The insurance company didn't even know about it. Only four people knew."

"Patrick, James, Henry, and you," PJ said. Alarms were ringing in her head. The insurance company didn't know?

"It was kind of a family secret, but I was as trusted as a family member."

"Rebecca, forgive me for asking this if I'm off base. Was that safe used for anything shady?"

Rebecca looked down at her plate and pushed a crumb around with her fork. "Patrick had a worldwide reputation for being able to find what clients wanted. A select group of clients paid very well for things that were especially difficult to find."

Oh for that tape recorder.

"You said earlier you had no black market connections."

"Strictly speaking, I didn't and still don't. Patrick handled that aspect of the business himself."

"Why are you telling me all this?" PJ said. "It's in the past, isn't it? Or has James continued the family tradition?"

She snorted derisively. "The kind of business I'm talking about is built on trust. Patrick's special clients wouldn't trust James to buy a pound of butter for them. They've gone elsewhere. Remember, I said it was competitive. The galleries are still profitable, though. Don't get me wrong. There were plenty of legitimate sales."

"Back to the safe."

"Yes. I have a feeling that if the police were to search the floor safe, they would find the missing paintings."

PJ sat back, stunned. The paintings were literally under their feet all the time? The waiter came over with the pie and brought a fresh pot of hot water. PJ appreciated the time to collect her thoughts.

"How exactly do you know that?" PJ said.

"I don't suppose you'll just take it as an anonymous tip?"

"If that's what you wanted, you could have phoned it in to the police," PJ said. She put down her fork and leaned forward earnestly. "Rebecca, you've come this far. Isn't there more you want to tell me?"

There was a long hesitation. "More. Yes, I suppose so. I don't want to go through the rest of my life like this." She sighed. "James is blackmailing me. We planned it together. He's got a letter I foolishly wrote with an outline of the robbery."

"So the motive was theft after all."

"It was more than that."

PJ let the woman have all the time she wanted. She shouldn't be interested in food at a time like this, but the pie was fabulous, and she gave it her attention while Rebecca firmed up her resolve.

"I'll talk to you, PJ, because I think you can understand what I'm about to say, and God knows I could use a little understanding. So here goes. I loved Patrick Washburn and had for many years, even though he was devoted to his wife and family. Even after his wife's death, it was as though she was still at his side. He didn't want to move on. More than once, I overheard him talking to her in his office."

"Many people have trouble letting go," PJ said. "It's fairly common to feel the physical presence of a spouse after death, especially when doing long-familiar activities."

Rebecca nodded. "I know. I never faulted him for it. It was hard working with him knowing that he thought of me as a loyal and knowledgeable employee, but nothing more. I wasn't trying to steal him from his wife, you understand. That wouldn't have been fair, even if it had been possible. But I wanted him to see me in a new light. Just once, I wanted him to appreciate me, to know that I shared his deep love of art and that we had something in common besides the day's receipts."

Once Rebecca started talking, her words came in a rush. PJ struggled to keep up with her. She nodded encouragement. The wrong response would shut off the flow like a faucet.

"I came up with the idea of a burglary. Valuable paintings would be stolen, everyone would be desolate, and I would rush in and solve the crime."

"And Patrick would open his eyes and see what a treasure he had in you," PJ said.

PJ had run into it before. A firefighter starts the fires he then heroically combats. A teacher plants a bomb at the school and then gets all the kids out safely. A customer poisons over-the-counter medications and then "discovers" the tampering in time to save others. It was a desperate bid for attention.

Rebecca sagged in her chair. "Silly, isn't it? How I have regretted the day I came up with that. I'm not the sort of person to do frivolous things. Of course, Patrick wasn't supposed to be killed." Her voice trailed off.

"How did the plans go wrong?"

"I approached James with the idea. I offered to pay him, because I knew about the debts he had run up. I paid him twenty-five thousand dollars to do the actual breaking in. I didn't think I could do it myself. It was one thing to talk about it and quite another to sneak into the gallery and do it. We planned everything, and he insisted on keeping the written plan we made. It specifically said no violence, and the break-in was supposed to happen when the gallery was empty."

"He betrayed you, didn't he?" PJ said. "He had his own agenda. His father was about to cut him off. With good old Dad out of the way, James was free to exploit the business."

"I didn't know about that," Rebecca said. "He turned my plan into cold-blooded murder. And afterward, he had to make sure his brother Henry was in no condition to fight for ownership of the galleries. I've only recently found out about that, thanks to you and Detective Schultz."

PJ knew that the woman's pinched lips were just the smallest outward sign of the bitterness she felt. Her bid for attention had backfired in the worst possible way. She had lost her secret love. Adding to her grief, James had been blackmailing her, keeping her from going to the police because of her own involvement. No doubt she feared she'd be put away for murder.

"That's why I'm doing this," Rebecca continued. "Because of Henry. My life is ruined, but when I found out what that bastard had done to Henry, I knew I couldn't let him get away with it.''

"Are you sure the paintings are in the floor safe? What if James has removed them? It's been a year," PJ said.

"He doesn't know about it. I put them there myself last night."

Rebecca had managed to surprise her again.

"I've had the paintings ever since that terrible night. James gave them to me to hide. He planned to try to sell them eventually, but he'd filed an insurance claim and he wanted to make sure the fraud investigator wouldn't get wind of the sale. They've been at a summer cottage I own in the Ozarks."

No wonder PJ's mentor Merlin hadn't been able to turn up anything with his contacts in the art world. The paintings hadn't surfaced yet.

"How did you get them back into the gallery?" PJ asked. "What about the security system?"

"I didn't know if I'd be able to get in or not, but James had left the alarm system set up with the same password. The numbers were his birthday, so I guess he didn't want to change it. He did change the combination of the floor safe, though, and I thought that was the end of my mission. Patrick had always kept the combination written down in the file cabinet, concealed in the customer mailing list. There was a fake customer in the list, and the customer's phone number was the combination. I checked there, and stupid James had written in the new combination."

The waiter wandered by and asked in a knowing voice if there would be anything else. PJ resented his implication that she would order a third dessert. Truthfully, she had been considering it, but there was no way she'd give in after the way he acted. She told him to bring the check and shooed him away.

"You're the one who planted the idea about finding the paintings," Rebecca said. "You couldn't have been more obvious if you'd rented a billboard. I thought you had already figured out the story."

PJ shook her head. "I had a hunch you were involved in some way, but I had no idea it was like this. Rebecca, I'm so sorry things have turned out the way they did for you. I'm not condoning your original plan, but I understand it."

Rebecca's composure slipped. She closed her eyes briefly and turned away. "It means a great deal to me to hear you say that," she said.

That was the final thing PJ needed to take Rebecca's story as the truth. It had occurred to her that Henry and Rebecca were conspiring against James, and the two of them were framing him for the murder. PJ needed to see that flash of sincerity—and vulnerability—in Rebecca.

"If the police come with a warrant to search the floor safe," PJ said, "James will know it had to be either you or Henry who told them about it. When the paintings show up there, he'll know it was you who set him up. And he's already proven himself a vicious killer."

"I know. I've made my decision, and I'm going through with this."

PJ nodded. "If you'll excuse me for a few minutes, I'd like to make a phone call. I need to find out where to go from here."

She walked outside and sat at one of the tables to use her cellular phone. Schultz answered, and she told him what she had learned.

"Chalk up one for you, Detective Gray," he said. There was glee in his voice. "James is on the operating table with his balls exposed, and you've just given me the scalpel."

"Um, does Rebecca have to be involved in this?"

"You mean go the anonymous route?" He thought

about it for a minute. "We can get a search warrant that way. I'm sure we can. The paintings were worth two million bucks, which the insurance company has already forked over. Those guys tend to take fraud very seriously, leaving out the fact that murder's involved. I'm sure that between me and the insurance investigator we can come up with a willing judge."

"What about the letter she says James has? The one he's blackmailing her with?"

"Did she sign it?"

"I don't know. I didn't think to ask."

"Okay. If she didn't sign it, then if James tries to use it against her, she can claim he made it all up. Who's to say he didn't? If she did sign it, she'll have to go for forgery. A good lawyer can handle that. Her plan's for theft, not murder, which probably gets her out of conspiracy to commit. There's a lot there to work with. And there's one more thing."

She waited.

"Evidence sometimes gets lost before a trial."

"Schultz!"

"Hey, I'm not saying it would get lost. Only that it's been known to happen."

"I'd have to give that a lot of thought," she said, amazed at herself that she hadn't summarily rejected the idea. PJ felt her principles swaying and creaking like a dam about to break.

It had certainly been a lot easier to be moral in her previous job in marketing research.

"I'll get working on the warrant," Schultz said. "I can hardly wait to see the look on that son-of-a-bitch's face."

PJ told Rebecca that things were moving. She didn't tell her anything else she and Schultz had discussed, because she didn't want to give the woman hope if there was none.

Rebecca left with her head high, certain that she was doing the right thing. PJ wished she could say the same for herself.

CHAPTER

32

"Ready?" Schultz asked. He was feeling good, looking good, and smelling good. In honor of the date with Helen on Friday, he had visited the health and beauty section at Walgreens and purchased some shampoo. For years, he had simply run a soapy hand over his head in the shower. What little hair he had was freshly lathered, a trial run for tomorrow night. Rinse and repeat. He had bought a fresh deodorant stick, too, so he wouldn't have to use the one with hairs stuck on it.

"This isn't going to be violent, is it?" PJ zipped up her jacket. "If it is, I'd just as soon wait in the car."

"Christ, Doc, this isn't a drug raid. This artsy stuff is all very civilized."

"They're looking out the window at us," Dave said. "We better get in there, or we won't have anything to confiscate."

It was ten A.M., opening time for the Washburn Gallery, on a splendid Thursday in April. There had been rain overnight, but it ended a little before sunrise. The clouds had sped away on a brisk wind, the sky was an amazing blue, and the air had a freshly laundered smell. It made Schultz long for the country home where he'd spent his early boyhood. On a day like today, he would have skipped school, grabbed his little brother, and gone out into the woods. The creeks would be running. They'd look for tadpoles. Probably too early in the year for them, but the search was ninety percent of the enjoyment. No matter how long Schultz lived in the city, he'd never lose touch with the rhythms of nature. He was amazed at how many of his fellow cops never looked up at the sky, day or night.

As if reading his mind, PJ looked over at him and asked, "Did you notice the beautiful moon this morning, Leo? I saw it from my backyard."

He nodded, puzzled, wondering why she was talking about it on the sidewalk outside the gallery. He knew that PJ had grown up in corn country in Iowa. Maybe she was pulled to the outdoors the same way he was.

"When I was in the cabin in Big Springs with Thomas, it had been raining most of the evening, but the clouds parted and I saw the moon, big and round and bright as a searchlight."

"That was the night Mitchell was killed," Schultz said. Her eyes met and held his, both of them feeling the pressure of a killer on the loose. So far there had been one death roughly every week. Their time was measured in the phases of the moon, and they knew more blood would be spilled before the next full moon.

Unless they got lucky or the killer made a serious mistake.

"Let's go wrap this one up," she said, laying her hand on his arm.

"Boss, we've got backup and we're ready to go in," Dave said. He pointed at the patrol car pulling up to the curb. "If you're done yacking about the moon, that is."

PJ yanked her hand back.

Schultz headed for the gallery. He saw a face peeking nervously at him from a curtained window, but it was quickly withdrawn as he neared the door. The door opened before he got there, and a tall, willowy woman stood with arms crossed, trying to block the way like a patch of ornamental grass in front of a charging rhino.

"May I help you?"

PJ had given him descriptions of the staff from her covert visit to the gallery earlier, so he recognized the person standing in front of him as Yolanda Elkins, the manager who'd taken Rebecca Singer's place. He showed his ID and displayed the warrant, which specifically authorized a search for the stolen paintings in the floor safe. Schultz did all the talking, but he was aware of PJ at his back. This one was for her, too.

"I really can't deal with this," Elkins said. "I don't know anything about a safe in the floor. You'll have to wait until I contact the owner."

"You go right ahead. Get him down here. He'll be answering his share of questions in a few minutes."

Elkins scurried off to the back room, no doubt to make a frantic phone call. Schultz motioned the others into the gallery.

The officers they had been waiting for at the curb had brought a metal detector. It took only a few minutes to locate the metal safe under the wooden floor, even less time to move aside the chair and antique rug which covered it. It was a little trickier to find the set of concealed latches that allowed a section of the floor to be lifted away, revealing the door of the safe. If Rebecca hadn't given good instructions, they'd have been crawling around on the floor for quite some time.

At that point, Schultz decided to wait until James arrived. It didn't take long. He must have broken every traffic law on his way.

James bustled in with a good indignant act. His face was pale, and tight with some emotion Schultz couldn't pin down. It might have been fear or hatred or just plain arrogant superiority.

"Detective ... Doctor," he said, nodding to each in turn. "What's going on here? Yolanda says you want to do some kind of search."

Schultz waved the warrant. James took it and read it. Schultz wouldn't have thought it possible for him to get any paler, but he did.

"We've already found the safe without your help," Schultz said. "And now I'm going to open it in front of witnesses. Your former manager Rebecca Singer has provided me with the combination."

It was a bit of grandstanding that Schultz had come up with. As far as James knew, the combination that Rebecca had provided was the old one. It wasn't going to open the safe. James wiped his brow and stood back. He was beginning to recover some of his bluster.

Sure enough, the combination didn't work. Schultz stood back, consternation plastered on his mug. He was going to win an Oscar for this one.

"Let me try," PJ said. She was horning in on his act, but she was, after all, the boss.

When she, too, was unsuccessful, Schultz indicated they'd have to drill the lock open. "It'll take a while, but I'm sure we can get it eventually."

James stepped forward, eager to be gracious. "That won't be necessary," he said. "I think I can save you a lot of time and trouble." He dialed the combination and pulled the door up.

To no one's surprise but James's, there was a bundle inside, wrapped with the distinctive packaging of Washburn Galleries.

"Step back, Mr. Washburn," Schultz intoned in the most threatening tone he could manage, "I'll take it from here."

James spun around. His face was no longer pale. He looked like an apple on a stick, and he did the one thing that Schultz wasn't expecting. James launched himself into a flying tackle and hit Schultz at the knees, knocking his feet out from under him. He fell forward on his belly. Schultz's breath whooshed out of his lungs and he cracked his chin. Groaning, he rolled over, only to be leapt on by James. Schultz found himself looking up at the ceiling, being pummeled in the stomach.

"Will somebody get this bastard off me before I break his neck?" he bellowed.

Dave and one of the officers pulled James back and restrained him. The man was sputtering and cursing. Schultz got to his feet, and just as he did, James broke free. He swung his fist wildly at Schultz and connected. Schultz heard his nose break as his head snapped to one side. As his head twisted, he saw PJ frozen in place, eyebrows raised and her mouth a little O.

James was wrestled to the ground and handcuffed.

Schultz stood glaring at the man and wondered if it was worth the extra paperwork to go over and kick the shit out of him.

PJ came up and held out a handkerchief. "You're bleeding."

"Goddamn it, I know I'm bleeding. My goddamn nose is broken."

"You said there wasn't going to be any violence."

"Well, I was goddamned wrong."

A female customer opened the door of the gallery, took one look at Schultz and the man squirming on the floor, and hastily left.

"Oh, Christ," Schultz said, hanging his head.

"What is it?" PJ moved closer. "Does it hurt?"

"That's not it. My date with Helen is tomorrow, and I'm going to look like shit."

Friday morning, James did the predictable thing and, via his attorney, trotted out the letter which purported to make Rebecca responsible for everything. When Schultz got a look at the letter, he laughed, then regretted it because it made his nose hurt more. It turned out to be an unsigned, sketchy timetable which bore little resemblance to the actual crime. James had changed almost everything about her plan. He had been blackmailing a grieving woman more by force of will than with actual evidence. It would be up to the lawyers to hash it out, and by mid-morning, Rebecca's had fired the first volley. The letter, the lawyer said, was merely a plot outline for a novel Rebecca was working on. Rebecca had casually given it to James for his suggestions on improving it.

It was brilliant. It was believable.

As a crowning touch, Rebecca also stated that she had given the same letter to Henry, and, of course, he supported her claim. Schultz had no doubt that by dinnertime, an actual rough draft of a novel based on Rebecca's plan would turn up and be entered as evidence.

He wished he could see the son-of-a-bitch's face when he got that little surprise.

CHAPTER

33

PJ was running late Friday evening, the day of the big date. Barnesworth hadn't made many demands on her time during the week, which was good because she had been involved in the Washburn case. In the evenings, she had spent the time developing computer simulations of Eddington and Harquest's murders, but hadn't immersed herself in them yet.

Columbus's father had been killed the past Monday, and she had hardly seen the boy all week. Evidently he wanted to be home with his mother.

Maybe that was a good sign.

She had taken Thomas out of school that afternoon to attend the funeral. He wanted to go, though she suspected there was some morbid curiosity mixed in with the desire to stand by his friend. He had never been to a funeral before, but knew generally what to expect from TV and movies.

Mrs. Wade had been very detached. PJ thought that the purpose of funerals was to give the bereaved public permission to begin the grieving process. Mrs. Wade apparently had a long way to go before she acknowledged that the proceedings had anything to do with her. Columbus was at her elbow, unusually solicitous, guiding her about, his natural solemnity more in keeping with the surroundings than with places like school or the science museum.

Neither of them shed a tear.

Thomas had been planning to go home with Columbus afterward, but the boy didn't want company. Columbus seemed eager to get home with his mother. Or more precisely, to get her alone. PJ wrote it off to clinginess after the loss of a parent.

Thomas had work to do on a social studies report, and he told PJ he'd spend the evening on it to get it out of the way for the weekend. PJ thought that was very mature of him, not waiting until the last minute to get his project done. A couple of years ago, he would have been frantic on Sunday night, working on something due Monday.

PJ wasn't in the mood for the evening's festivities, but she didn't want to disappoint Schultz and the others. She would make the best of it and reward herself at bedtime by reading a few chapters of the Dean Koontz book she had picked up. Surely that would take her mind off her own worries. It didn't guarantee a good night's sleep, though.

She was standing in front of her closet pondering what to wear when the phone rang.

"Gray, CHIP. No, wait, that's from work. Um, hello."

"Sounds like you need to get away more often." It was Bill Lakeland. His warm voice poured into her ear, and she realized how much she was looking forward to seeing him. She had another agenda for the evening, too. She planned to corner Bill and get more out of him about the dispute the boys were having.

If we both had daughters, she thought, *everything would be out in the open. They might tear each other's hair out, but at least there'd be no skulking around.*

"How can you tell?" PJ said, and they both laughed. "I'm trying to decide if I should be sultry or sensible tonight."

"You're not going to like this," Bill said, "but I have to cancel out. Winston's got the flu. He feels terrible. I don't think I should leave him alone."

"Can't you get a sitter?" PJ regretted the words as soon as she said them. If Thomas was really sick, she'd want to be home with him. "Sorry, I didn't mean that. Of course you should stay with him."

"Some other time then. Sorry."

PJ immediately dialed Helen's phone number. No answer, and no answering machine. The woman had already left, and was on her way over. The foursome had arranged to meet at PJ's house.

PJ would feel awkward going out with Helen and Schultz, but Helen hadn't agreed to go out with Schultz alone and she didn't want to put the woman in that position unfairly. So PJ would have to tag along as the third person. She turned back to her closet. At least that made the clothing selection easy. She didn't have to impress Bill, so she would go with sensible. That meant no pantyhose. Dark gray wool trousers, a loosely fitted black sweater, long-sleeved with a jewel neckline. A chain with a gold heart locket. Black leather flats. Lipstick and a quick dab of powder.

Ta-dah. The woman emerges from beneath the drab exterior.

The doorbell rang and she practically skipped downstairs to answer it. Then she remembered she wasn't a teenager going on a date.

It was Schultz. He was carrying flowers and a wrapped

but unmistakable box of candy. His nose was bandaged. She hadn't seen him since the confrontation in the gallery. It didn't look too bad. Helen would understand. She was a nurse, after all.

"Is she here yet?"

"No," PJ said. "Come on in, I've got some news. Does that hurt?"

"What do you think?" he said. Then his face hardened slightly. "News about the case?"

"It's Bill. He won't be able to make it tonight."

Schultz showed no reaction at first, then a smile spread over his face.

"Try to contain your disappointment, Detective."

"Three is good. Three gets me even closer to an actual date."

"Hardly. Three is even more . . ."

The phone rang. With trepidation, PJ went to answer it. She was back a couple of minutes later.

"We're down to two," she said.

"It's okay, Doc, if you have to be somewhere else."

PJ sighed. Schultz was still clutching the bouquet. Daffodils bobbed among the green stuff that florists used to fill in the spaces. It was hard to keep her eyes off the big white patch in the middle of his face.

"Helen has to work tonight," PJ said. "A couple of her staff are out with the flu. She tried to call in a favor with one of the other nursing supervisors, but couldn't swing it."

His face fell. Even the bandages seemed to droop.

"Go ahead, Schultz, I give you permission to slam the door on your way out."

"Who says I'm leaving?"

"Huh?"

"These flowers would go to waste, and if I take this candy

home I'll just eat the whole box. Besides, you're all dressed up. Don't tell Dave or Anita, though. I wouldn't want them to think I was brown-nosing.''

PJ considered it. Go out with Schultz? Earlier she would have relished the idea of having the evening to herself. Something about funerals did that to her. She was going to decline.

"That's a . . ."

She changed her mind halfway through.

". . . great idea."

"Here, put these in some water," he said. "I'll go tell the squirt we're leaving."

He came down a few minutes later, slightly red-faced. "Took some grief from that kid. Thinks I'm Casanova or something."

"Is that a new shirt?"

"Yeah. I even had it ironed at a laundry."

Schultz took her to Cunetto's, an Italian restaurant not far from her home. They had cannelloni and wine, and didn't talk about work. The food was delicious. The waiter treated them like a couple out on the town. PJ felt like a person with a life of her own, even though it was Schultz sitting across the table from her.

Back at her house, they unwrapped the box of candy. It turned out to be a Whitman's Sampler, a two-pounder. The two of them sat at her kitchen table looking at the chart on the inside of the lid and picking out their favorites.

It was after one A.M., when Schultz left. PJ checked her answering machine before going to bed, and was surprised to find four messages. She had turned the ringer off on the phone so that Thomas wouldn't be disturbed. It was Barnesworth all four times. He wanted to let her know he was calling a task force meeting for Saturday morning at seven. Increasingly irritated that he couldn't reach her, he stopped just short of calling her a slut because she was out on Friday night, or at least not picking up her phone. Obviously he pictured an orgy going on in the Gray household. She wasn't quite sure if he was offended because her son might witness the debauchery, or because he wasn't invited.

Impulsively she dialed his number and was delighted to awaken him.

"My pager number's 555-8765," she said, not giving him a chance to wake up fully. "I've told you that before, and if you can't remember it, it isn't my fault." She slammed down the receiver with satisfying force.

She was already in bed when she realized that Barnesworth might not have called the rest of the CHIP team. It would be just like him, hoping to have them not show up, embarrassing PJ. So she called Schultz. He answered on the first ring, and she told him to deliver the bad news to the others.

Just before dawn she woke up to screams. Thomas'd had a nightmare, a bad one that left him covered in sweat and shaking. She held him and rocked him, wrapping her arms tightly around him until finally he pushed away and slumped to the floor at her feet. The front of her pajama top was damp with his sweat and tears, and glistened where he had wiped his nose.

Her son was in trouble and she ached to help him. He didn't want to talk about it, so she let it go. By then the new day was under way, so there was no point in the two of them going back to sleep. They went downstairs in their pajamas and ate chocolates for breakfast.

CHAPTER

34

The task force meeting was held in the large open room where Schultz had his desk. He had arrived early to make sure nobody took over his space, such as it was, and to get first pick of the doughnuts.

There weren't any doughnuts, and he was pissed about that.

One wall of the room had a large green chalkboard that was filled with Barnesworth's sloppy printing. It was divided into three columns, one for each of the victims. Before and after pictures of the victims were taped up next to each name. To the side was a large poster of the key photograph taken by Emory Harquest, the one that showed the bicyclist from the back. Schultz wondered for the hundredth time if it wasn't just some kid sneaking home from a friend's house or somebody getting a little exercise after the evening shift.

The room got noisier as the task force, which now numbered about fourteen, filed in. Nobody grumbled about the hour or the fact that it was Saturday. Barnesworth came in and shot the breeze with his cronies. A few minutes before seven, Lieutenant Howard Wall slipped into the room. He pulled one of the chairs away from a desk, positioning it against the back wall, and took a seat. His presence was acknowledged with nods. Wall wasn't much of a buddy-buddy type.

A few minutes after the hour the meeting got under way, with one conspicuous absence. PJ hadn't shown up yet.

Barnesworth stood in front of the chalkboard with a wooden pointer—Schultz closed his eyes and heard the smack of the pointer against the teacher's desk all the way from the fifth grade—and went through the particulars.

Edward Mitchell	Clara Eddington	Emory Harquest
Thursday	Friday (8 days)	Thursday (6 days)
approx. 10pm– 1am	approx. 6pm– 7:30pm	approx. 8pm–11pm
chem lab	classroom	front porch
blunt instr.	hacksaw?	mult. stab wounds
no tape	duct tape	duct tape
teacher	teacher	former teacher
mult. blows	post-mort dismem.	ante-mort excise heart
black male, 36 yrs	white female, 46 yrs	white male, 72 yrs
motive: robbery?	motive: ??	motive: poss. witness
bike/jacket photos		

POSS. SUSPECT ASIAN FEMALE MID-THIRTIES

It looked like a game of Clue. Schultz was surprised the man actually knew the word "excise." Everybody yawned. There wasn't anything new on the board.

When PJ came in, he saw lines of tension around her mouth and eyes. He hoped it didn't have anything to do with the night before. She quietly said good morning to Wall. She was the only one in the room to have spoken to him.

When Barnesworth was done and asked for input, PJ stood up. Schultz winced. Barnesworth hadn't meant he wanted anything substantive, certainly not contradictory, in front of his whole team. But PJ had read the situation like the civilian that she was. She reminded everyone that although it seemed likely that the murders were connected, they should keep an open mind about the possibility of two killers because of the lack of a consistent signature. Barnesworth tossed it back in her face that the killer, singular, showed a pattern of escalating violence from panicked overkill to mutilation after death to deliberate torture.

She went on to discredit the suspect as an Asian woman and said that the focus should be on a young person, a student or former student of the school. Her repeated suggestion that the school be closed and the teachers given temporary leaves, with the strong recommendation that they get out of town, was not well received. It was the third or fourth time she had brought that up. Personally, Schultz thought it was a good idea, but he didn't want to take on the Chief about it. That's who would have to deal with the school board, and take the flack about not being able to find his ass in a bathtub, much less a killer targeting teachers.

When the two of them got into motives, things really got hairy. Schultz tuned out and let PJ dig herself in deeper. When she finally sat down in a huff, everyone in the room except the two combatants silently cheered. It was time to get on with business, which for most people meant searching for something edible. The meeting broke up and the others drifted out, including Wall and the object of PJ's wrath.

She came over to his desk. "That . . . that bastard! What a waste of time. He's running this investigation like he's on a big ego trip!"

"Is that your professional opinion, Doc?"

That brought a tentative smile. "I suppose it is. Want to skip out for breakfast?"

"Only if I can eat my eggs the way I like them and not have to listen to complaints."

All through breakfast he debated whether he should point out her blunder. He knew that it was a sore point with her, being an outsider in the Department. Whenever she conducted a meeting, she expected a genuine exchange of ideas and contributions by all present. She hadn't grasped yet that, particularly with Barnesworth, new ideas were best presented in private. Then, if the ideas had any merit, or any chance of being lucky guesses, they'd be taken over and put on the table as his own.

When they finished their meal at Millie's, she left an extra quarter next to his plate when she thought he wasn't looking. Millie probably wouldn't fall for it, but he thought it was nice that PJ wanted to smooth things over for him.

PJ spent most of the day at home with her son. At least she had been in the same house with him. He holed up in his room and she saw him only at lunchtime, when he shared a bowl of macaroni and cheese with Megabite. She was there if he wanted to talk, but she didn't want to be pushy about it.

On Saturday night, PJ was drawn back to her office. There was something she wanted to try out on the newly developed simulation of the Eddington murder.

She turned on the Artificial Intelligence, or AI, portion of her program. PJ's experimental software combined straight virtual reality techniques, in which the user controlled the action and determined the outcome, with AI. Under the AI feature, the program examined all of the elements that had been provided about a situation and extrapolated from there, calling upon a huge database of possible actions. In other words, it used its imagination.

The blue monitors in the HMD flickered a couple of times, and then PJ found herself in the hallway outside Mrs. Eddington's classroom. Since she had been there in real life, the virtual reality simulation took on an enhanced sense of presence for her.

She had no desire to join the killer as he immobilized and dismembered Clara Eddington. Perhaps some other time she would enter the classroom, but not today. She waited outside in the hall.

The door opened and a face appeared, checking both directions in the hallway. The figure was in the shadows as it—he, there was a definite maleness to it, slight as the shape was—leaned against the doorjamb and stripped off its socks. Socks? She peered at the feet and saw that he was wearing sneakers but had pulled on heavy woolen socks over them, like the socks worn inside boots for outdoor work. The socks were bloody. That accounted for the lack of footprints inside the room. The police had been hoping for identifiable prints on the blood-splashed floor which would provide information such as shoe size and type, and if luck was smiling on them as it had not on Mrs. Eddington, the sole print of a brand-name shoe. Only smears had been found on the floor.

Still in the doorway, still checking the hall up and down, he pulled off his outer clothes, which were a lightweight wind breaker and matching pants, the kind runners used in inclement weather. Water-resistant enough for a brief rain shower, they had kept the bloody mess off him. He stuffed them into some small bag or case that he had placed on the floor—the clean floor—of the hallway. Rubber gloves, the kind from the grocery store that are used for household cleaning, were peeled off his hands and dropped into the bag. They were followed by plastic safety goggles and a ski mask. Everything was carefully planned to make sure the killer could walk into a group of people without dealing with those embarrassing blood spatters.

Ring around the collar popped into PJ's mind. She tried to squelch the inane tune. *Ring around the collar.*

The killer stepped out into the bright hallway and PJ gasped.

She was face-to-face with Thomas.

CHAPTER

35

Schultz had to ring the bell half a dozen times before anyone came to the door. He had just decided to go around the back and knock when the door opened and Vicky Wade stood there. She was wearing a housecoat and looked as though she hadn't bathed in quite a while. She held a TV remote control loosely in one hand, and Schultz got the feeling that if she could, she'd click him off.

Reminding himself not to be judgmental about the way other people handled grief, he went into his spiel.

"Mrs. Wade, I'm Detective Leo Schultz, St. Louis PD, Homicide," he said. The badge was up and out. She nodded without really seeing it. "I want to express my sympathy on the loss of your husband. I'm sure the Department is doing everything it can to find the person or persons responsible." Christ, that sounded lame even to him.

She nodded again. He wondered if he should have been more specific. "Loss of your husband" sounded like she'd just misplaced him. The door started to close. Schultz scooted forward with his practiced foot-in-the-door move. "I was wondering if I could talk to you about your son."

Her pinched eyebrows indicated puzzlement.

"I'll only take a minute of your time." *And, besides, you'll have to break my foot to get that door closed.*

She opened the door wider and motioned him in with a vague wave of her hand. He wondered if she was on tranquilizers. Sometimes physicians prescribed a little something to get the widow through the first few days.

"More accurately, talk *to* your son," he said once the door was safely closed behind him.

"Why?" she said. It was a milestone—her first word. His own son's first word had been "pizza."

"You probably know about the teachers who were killed at the school Columbus attends."

Another pinched look. "That was at Columbus's school?"

Yes, ma'am, and little green men have landed on the roof.

"Yes, ma'am. I'd like to talk to Columbus, if I could."

"Why?" There was a tinge of suspicion now. Schultz arranged his face so that he looked slightly put-upon but still the dutiful public servant.

"One of the murders took place at the school on the night of a music recital," he said. "We're interviewing students who might have attended."

"I don't remember any music recital. I'm sure Columbus didn't go."

"Could I talk with him for just a few minutes, ma'am? He may know some of the other students who were there." It was flimsy but backed up by two hundred and twenty pounds of cop, and after all she had invited him in.

She led him further into the entry hall. At the base of

the stairs, she called up to Columbus. Twice, three times. There was no response.

"I don't think he can hear you," Schultz said. They were standing at the door to the living room, and he pointed at the TV, which was chattering loudly to no one. She didn't move to turn off the TV, as he had expected. She led him up the stairs, as he had hoped.

The TV noise was muted in the upstairs hallway. It was a large house, and there were several doors leading off the hall, all of them closed but one, the bathroom door. Mrs. Wade hesitated as though she wasn't quite sure which one was her son's bedroom. After a few seconds, she went to the second door on the right and knocked.

No answer. She knocked again, then tried the knob. The door was locked. Just as she called out the boy's name in a loud voice, the door opened. The name hung in the air, and she seemed embarrassed, like a person speaking loudly in a crowded room when there's a sudden lull in the conversation.

Columbus stood there in a T-shirt and boxer shorts. His face was pale and he was sweaty. The shirt was damp and stuck to his chest in one spot. He tented it with his fingers, then let it go so that it wouldn't cling.

"Sorry," he said, "I'm not feeling very good. I was lying down, and I guess I fell asleep."

"You don't look so good," his mother said.

"I think I have the flu."

"There's a lot of that going around," Schultz said. The three of them stood there awkwardly. "Do you feel well enough that I could ask you a few questions?" He'd gotten in the door, he might as well press the advantage.

"Okay, I guess," Columbus said. He was still blocking the door.

"Mind if I come in?"

Columbus stood aside, and Schultz pushed past him into the room. It was large for a kid's room, and very cluttered. Evidently Columbus didn't have a chore chart.

The blankets were mussed, but something about the bed looked wrong. Schultz couldn't pin it down.

"Were you at school on the evening of Friday, April third?"

"No, sir." That little catch on the "sir," a lilt of sarcasm. Well, Schultz had once been twelve. He was pretty sure he hadn't answered any questions with even that degree of civility when he was between twelve and eighteen. Come to think of it, he still didn't.

"You want me to get some Tylenol?" Mrs. Wade asked.

"Do you know what happened that evening?" Schultz continued, ignoring her. Columbus ignored her, too, as if he was accustomed to it.

"Of course. Everybody's talking about it. Mrs. Eddington got killed. There was a recital, and while everybody was in the gym, she got attacked. All the kids who were there thought it was creepy that it was done while they were just down the hall."

"All what kids?"

Columbus shrugged. "Just kids. I don't hang out with the eighth graders."

Schultz coasted around the room, taking everything in. He didn't really expect to find the box of bloody weapons Anita had mentioned, but stranger things had happened. Columbus trailed after him. Mrs. Wade was still in the doorway.

Schultz fingered some Hot Wheels cars on top of a bookcase. They were shiny and looked nearly new, yet Columbus was probably too old for that kind of toy. Most likely they were unwanted presents, rolled once across the floor and then put up.

There was a walk-in closet. Boldly Schultz walked in and pulled the string dangling from the ceiling light to turn it on. It was too narrow for Columbus to follow, so the boy hovered at the door.

"We think there was a kid there that night that we can't account for," Schultz said. His back was to Columbus, and his voice was muffled by the clothing in the closet, some of which was on hangers. "Maybe someone who went with a friend's family. You hear anything about that?"

"No" came the answer from behind him. The *sir* had gotten lost.

There was a musty smell in the closet, something old and rotten, but there were piles of clothing and some fast food containers, plates, and napkins on the floor which more than justified the smell. His attention was caught by a toy chest in the corner. He lifted the lid and found a large collection of action figures and a few stuffed animals, all of them years old and worn, unlike the Hot Wheels. The kid was certainly hard on his toys, especially the stuffed animals, most of which were missing appendages. He bent over, picked up a Superman figure, and turned around to face Columbus.

"I didn't know they still made these. I had Superman when I was a kid."

The boy's face was a shade paler, and he seemed nervous. No, *a lot more* nervous.

"Isn't he dead?" Schultz said.

"What?"

"Superman. Didn't he get killed off?"

Columbus shrugged.

Schultz tossed the toy back into the chest and pulled the chain to turn off the light in the closet. "Mrs. Wade, do you know where your son was that night?"

She had her arms crossed on her chest and a disapproving look on her face. Apparently it had sunk in that her son's room was being casually searched.

"Of course I do. He was home, here with me. He does his schoolwork in his room every night after dinner. In fact, sometimes he eats dinner in his room."

"And how do . . ." Schultz began.

"No more questions. Don't you need a warrant or something? I think you should leave now."

He had finally gotten a flash of anger from her. Time for a quick escape.

"See you around sometime, Columbus," he said.

"Yeah."

Driving home in a fine example of April showers, he realized what was wrong with the bed. The covers were rumpled, but the pillow had been plumped up. There was no impression of a sleeping head. Columbus hadn't been sleeping right before the knock on his door. The kid was hiding something.

But maybe it was a *Penthouse* magazine under his pillow.

A niggling doubt remained, like a tiny ache centered in his chest where the golden cord spun out into the world. But most likely it had been a wasted trip.

Columbus sat down on the bed and let the air whoosh out of him. He was rattled, and that was a new feeling, one he couldn't immediately put away on the shelf where he kept his stock of emotions. This wasn't supposed to happen. Had his power slipped away?

He went out into the hall. The Cow had gone back downstairs without a word. She was well trained, and he rather liked the way she had come to his defense. Actually, it wasn't his defense, but defense of herself as a mother. The result was the same.

However, he had to admit that Project Fairy Tale was pretty much a flop. His mother had not instantly transformed into a clone of Thomas's mom. No aromas of cinnamon rolls greeted him in the morning, no plates of sliced fruit were delivered, no stories were shared at the kitchen table. Well, some projects just didn't hack it. He smiled at the image.

In the hall bathroom, he splashed water on his face. His hands finally stopped trembling. He hoped the detective hadn't noticed, or at least had put it down to the flu. That was quick thinking, at least.

He took a towel back to his room, locking the door behind him. Digging around in a bureau drawer, he uncovered the flashlight he was searching for. The batteries weren't very old. He had used the flashlight not long ago, when he had gone out hunting bats at night. Unfortunately for him, and fortunately for the bats, he couldn't find any in his neighborhood. He pushed the switch and was rewarded by a strong beam.

He opened the window in his room and used the towel to wipe the wet windowsill. Leaning out slightly into the night, he shone the flashlight down toward the ground. The bushes beneath his window had more than a few new leaves on their branches. Draped across them was the emergency ladder he had used to climb down from his window and go on a little field trip. He laughed silently at the thought. Field trip. Perhaps he should write up a trip report and turn it in for extra credit at school.

That he could laugh about it was a good sign. He hadn't lost his power. Everything was still all right, and the detective suspected nothing. He snapped off the flashlight, although he didn't think his neighbors would be watching their backyards on a rainy night. Even old Mrs. Grillman wouldn't let her wretched poodle out until later, when the rain had stopped. The dog could cross its legs and whine pitifully—he had heard it on summer nights—but she wouldn't let it out if she thought it would track in mud. With old lady logic, she apparently thought the mud vanished as soon as the rain stopped. Of course she would whack the hell out of the dog if it peed in the house. He had heard that, too. He ought to consider putting the poor thing out of its misery. The poodle, not Mrs. Grillman. Or maybe both of them.

Later that night, after the Cow was snoring away down the hall, he'd go out and get the ladder. He'd have to bring it in the back door, along with the pack that held his bloody clothes. It had been too wet to go somewhere and burn them, so he'd come home with more baggage than usual. He would have to be careful of the mud, just like Mrs. Grillman's dog. He didn't want any questions from the Cow in the morning.

When Columbus had rounded the corner on his bike earlier, he had been astonished to see Detective Schultz's car just three doors down, in front of his house. There was a streetlight outside his house, and there was no mistaking the Pacer crouched beneath it, its right front tire mashed into the curb. He remembered the car from the trip to the science museum.

Schultz was out of the car and on his way up the front walk. In a few seconds he'd be at the door. Columbus's mind raced. He wasn't paying a social call on the new widow. Either he was there about the carjacking or something was wrong, wrong, wrong with the killings.

Holy shit, he had to do something. The contents of the pack on the back of his bicycle were enough to send him up for life, or get him executed or something. Did they do that to kids? He had heard of sixteen-year-olds being tried as adults, but what about preteens?

Nonsense. No one would suspect him. Columbus shut his mouth, which had been hanging open since he came around the corner, and started pedaling slowly, keeping as much in the shadows as he could. When he got near the light cast by the streetlamp, he got off and walked the bike across the lawn and around the back of the house. He could hear the doorbell ringing. With any luck, the Cow wouldn't answer it. Of course, then the detective might come around back and knock.

The doorbell stopped ringing.

The ladder was right where he'd left it. He took the pack off the back of his bike, parked the bike, and shoved the pack under the bushes. He climbed the ladder faster than he ever had in his life and got into his room. A quick check, and he saw that the bike wheels had kicked up a little mud onto the legs of his jeans. He slipped them off and put them under some other clothes on the floor of his closet, along with the Chameleon jacket he'd been wearing.

A knock at his door sent him flying for the window. There was no time to stow the ladder, so he lifted the hooks that held it to the windowsill, leaned out, and dropped it into the bushes. His shirt got wet when he leaned against the sill, but there was no time to change.

The knob turned.

Luckily he had locked the door. He started toward it, heart thumping in his chest. He checked himself in the mirror over the bureau as he approached the door. Okay, he was pale, the rain on his skin could pass as sweat, the wet spot on his shirt wasn't too big, and there was a cap on his head.

A cap! He'd worn a cap because of the rain. He spun and tucked the cap under his pillow, and plumped the pillow on top of it. Nothing showed.

Schultz had walked around his room, had used those eyes of his like floodlights slithering across every surface. He'd gone in the closet, making Columbus's knees weak and his heart rate go up another notch.

Superman. He'd picked up Superman. Inches below in that toy chest were a hammer and a hacksaw, a knife and a camera. Lethal weapons with the bloodstains to prove it, and a camera with an undeveloped picture inside that showed him rushing at Harquest.

At that moment, Columbus wasn't thinking about power. He wasn't thinking about schemes, masterpieces, or Project Fairy Tale. He was a scared kid.

That unpleasantness was past, and now he was himself again. The threat was gone, and everything was under control. He had another two or three hours before the Cow went to bed, so he dug out a box of chocolate chip granola bars from his nightstand and unwrapped one. At the computer, he called up the Loring simulation and began modifying it. He had managed to stay pretty close to the scenario he had practiced, but there were little things—trivial ones—that didn't go according to plan. Afterward, he always went back in and made the adjustments. He thought of it as fine tuning.

Jerry Loring was a social studies teacher at Deaver. His hobby was rocketry, and he shared his enthusiasm with the students by conducting after-school sessions during which kids got to build, paint, and fire neat rockets. He had also organized the Rocket Ready Club. The club was open to anyone, but the sessions were eight weeks long and had a waiting list. Columbus had signed up near the beginning of the school year, but the final session had started three weeks ago, and the cutoff on the list was the kid right above Columbus. The other kids, including

Thomas, had started their rockets, but Columbus was going to have to wait until next fall.

It wasn't right that Mr. Loring should have power like that.

Columbus had begun work on the Loring scenario right away, but other things had gotten in the way, namely Harquest and the Turd. He had set Loring aside, but earlier he'd had some fun getting Thomas to work on it with him.

He wondered what Thomas would do when he found out that the horrible acts the two of them played out in virtual reality were being brought to life.

Thomas was coming along nicely. The boy was both drawn to and repulsed by the violent games Columbus had introduced him to, particularly the ones involving recognizable people from their lives. Columbus understood that fascination and tapped into it, manipulating carefully, pulling the strings, and always, always, upping the stakes. Thomas couldn't stop. He had to see what was around the next corner, and he'd never tell his mom about it. What was he going to say? *Hey, Mom, guess what? Torture is cool.*

There were new arrivals at Mr. Loring's house, twin baby boys. He had brought in pictures and proudly put them up on the bulletin board in his classroom. Twins meant a lot of expenses, so Mr. Loring had taken a second job a few evenings a week as an auto mechanic.

Columbus had never actually operated a winch before, but he caught on fast.

CHAPTER

36

Thomas the virtual killer passed PJ in the hall and moved down toward the gymnasium. She stood for a moment, stunned, forgetting to breathe, then she gulped air and hurried after him when he rounded a corner and disappeared from sight.

Breathing hard, as though she really was rushing down the hall instead of standing in her office, she caught up just in time to see him spin open a combination lock and dump his bag into one of the lockers that lined the hallway. Seen from the back, the figure didn't look quite like Thomas, even though he was wearing the sweatshirt Steven had given him the Christmas before last. Then it came to her. There was no scar on the back of the boy's head.

When he was five, her son had tried on his Halloween costume, which was Spiderman. He'd tried to cling to the wall, and the result was a trip to the Emergency Room, PJ holding a sanitary napkin tightly to the back of his bloody head. She'd held his hand and tried to calm him as he got six staples put in. Getting them taken out a couple of weeks later was nearly as traumatic for him. The damage to the hair roots was permanent, so Thomas had an inch-long stripe down the back of his scalp where no hair grew.

Calmer now, she reached out her hand to ruffle the hair on the back of the figure's head, double-checking for the stripe. Her hand passed through, as she was doing FOTW.

It's not Thomas. Not.

As she followed the boy from the locker to the gymnasium, she figured out what had happened. The AI was speculating that a student at the school was the killer. It had replaced the Genman with the closest approximation available in its database, which was a picture of Thomas she had scanned in months ago. The picture showed Thomas only from the front. The AI didn't know about the scar.

The boy went to the gym. He had entered through a back door, and the stage was in front of him. PJ's computer system couldn't handle animating an entire crowd, so only a small number of people near the boy showed any movement. The rest looked like a painted backdrop, including those up on stage. It was actually the first time she'd used her crowd subroutine, and she was pleased it was doing its thing.

The noise inside the HMD had jumped up in volume when the killer opened the door. Even though a performance was going on—of what, PJ couldn't tell—there was considerable movement among those who represented the crowd. Little kids popped up to go to the bathroom, parents switched seats, letting Dad sit between Joe and Roger so the two kids didn't bean each other, Mom fumbled under the seat for the diaper bag or her purse with the antacids in it, Granny changed seats with Gramps so she could get a better angle for a picture. Cameras flashed. Grownups stood along the edges with their camcorders. It was amazing that anyone actually listened to those up on stage, or that the performers could concentrate. In other words, it was a typical grade-school recital. PJ could see that it would be easy for the killer to move among the attendees and attach himself to a family group. If she wasn't an FOTW, she could do it herself, and she wasn't even a student.

One of the figures on the stage came to life. It was the announcement by Mrs. Barry. When she was able to bring the room to silence, she made her brief statement. There was a huge buzz of conversation the moment she stopped, and people made for the door in a disorganized way, all trying to get their kids away from the site of a murder, or at least not get caught in the traffic jam in the parking lot.

She watched the killer leave with a family of two adults and four children, all chatting among themselves. His body language suggested that he was participating in the conversations, although he didn't say anything. He was an expert at blending into the situation, a natural chameleon. He accidentally stepped on the oldest girl's heel, a flaw in an otherwise perfect performance. The parents talked to the officers at the door, and the little group left. The monitors went dark.

When PJ took off the HMD, she was surprised to find Lieutenant Wall sitting in her office.

"Quite a show, even viewed from the outside," he said.

She was several feet from the computer, as far as the connecting cables would let her go. She tended to travel during simulations, even though it wasn't necessary. She hoped that the HMD had concealed her reaction when she saw Thomas as the killer. She remembered herself gasping and breathing hard. Maybe Wall hadn't come into the room by then.

She said the first thing that came to mind. "It isn't a snake on the jacket. I think it's a chameleon."

He looked puzzled for a moment, then caught on. "Good insight," he said. "Be sure to pass that along."

She nodded.

"The Chief's been in touch with the school board. I talked to him this afternoon about your suggestion, for the second time, I might add. Deaver's closing until this situation is resolved. The word went out this evening to the teachers, all of them who could be reached anyway. They're on temporary leave. Those who are able to get away for a while will go. The students will be bussed to other schools where there will be classrooms set up in trailers or in the cafeterias and gymnasiums. Obviously not ideal. No one likes to admit that we've gotten to this point."

"No," PJ said. "But it's safer for everyone. Probably a lot of parents will keep their kids home anyway." Left unspoken was *It's about time someone listened to me.*

"You're going somewhere with this case. You're coming up with ideas. Barnesworth isn't. The Chief wants results, and needless to say, I do, too. I'm springing you from Barnesworth's team."

A grin leaped onto PJ's face. She tried to moderate it into a polite smile. "That's good news."

"That doesn't mean I approve of your earlier actions."

"Yes, sir, I understand."

"As soon as this case winds up, I have a test for you. You have been studying, haven't you?"

PJ's eyes went wide. "Sort of."

Actually she had been using the thick handbook he'd given her to prop open her window at night. She liked sleeping in a cool room, and her window wouldn't stay at the height she wanted. It had two adjustments: closed and all the way up.

"Is Schultz still around?" Wall said. "There's something I need to talk to him about."

"No, he left an hour ago," she said, eager to change the subject. "He had an appointment with somebody named Casey. I think she's an informer or something."

As soon as the door closed behind Wall, she dialed Schultz. He was slow to answer, and his voice sounded rough.

"Help!" she said. "Wall's going to give me some kind of test. You've got to help me study."

"Oh, shit," Schultz said. "Not again."

CHAPTER

37

"You really don't want to go in there," Dave said. PJ could see that Dave was sincere. His face was pale and off-color, if not exactly green. The restraining palm he laid on her forearm was sweaty.

"What's the situation?" PJ said. "Wall just gave me the address." It was Sunday morning. The rain of the previous evening had washed the world clean. A weather pattern had developed of gentle showers almost every night which cleared by morning and left everything sparkling, including the grass. Death shouldn't intrude when there were rainbows underfoot.

PJ was tempted to drop everything, grab Thomas, and run off. She longed to make things right between the two of them. It seemed like his withdrawal had been going on forever, although she knew it had been less than a month.

"When Loring didn't come home by dawn, his wife asked her mother to come over and stay with her kids.

Twin boys, just four weeks old," Dave said. "Sometimes he'd work all night on a rush job, but he'd come home by breakfast. When he didn't show up, she went to the repair shop to see how much longer he'd be."

"And she found her husband dead."

Dave wiped his brow. "God, I hate to think of her walking in on that."

PJ looked around. There were officers aplenty, but she didn't see anyone who looked as upset as she imagined Amanda Loring would be. "Where is she now?"

"Hospital. She got hysterical. I imagine they'll get her drugged up enough so she can go home later today. Her mom's still with the kids."

She opened the door to the repair shop. There was a service counter which held a cash register and a display rack with a few sorry-looking bags of potato chips. Half a dozen narrow chairs with worn upholstered arms clustered around a small, old TV set with rabbit ears and dials. A brand-new soda vending machine dominated the waiting room. There was no clear indication of where to go, so she chose the door that had a sign saying "Authorized Personnel Only" taped crookedly to it.

The smell of death was strong, and mingled with grease and oil to make a nauseating combination. There were several loci of activity in the room, little whirlwinds around body parts, connected by streams of blood.

Connect the dots.

Schultz was at the center of activity, doing absolutely nothing, like the eye of the storm. She headed for him, stepping carefully.

He nodded at her. "Looks like we should have gotten the teachers out of town a little sooner," he said.

"He's a teacher?" PJ said. "No one told me that."

"Social sciences at Deaver."

"I just assumed that since he wasn't at the school, he wasn't . . ."

"I keep picturing this guy," Schultz said. "Picturing him in one piece, that is, loading those babies and his wife into the car and heading out for Texas or North Dakota or someplace. Anyplace but here. One day. Christ. Only one day too late."

"Oh, God, how are we going to stop this?"

For once Schultz had nothing to say. PJ took out her notebook and forced herself to begin making notes.

Later that morning, they took their seats at the counter in Millie's Diner. Millie took one look at them, skipped her usual wisecracking routine, poured cups of coffee, and left them alone.

Schultz tried to pay attention to what PJ was saying as she caught him up on the latest developments with Wall. It was hard to concentrate. His mind kept slipping back into the repair shop.

"It's clear to me he's throwing Barnesworth to the wolves," PJ said. "The Big B's talking with the FBI this afternoon, and the media's freaking out. We've got reporters pouring in from all over the country. Probably all over the world. It's unprecedented, closing the school like that."

"Wolves are too good for that man. Should be hungry lions."

"Piranhas."

"Sharks."

"Pit of snakes."

"Pit of lawyers."

"Flesh-eating bacteria, starting below the waist."

"You gonna order," Millie said, "or just take up space in this fine establishment?"

PJ ordered a waffle with strawberry topping and Schultz had his usual breakfast. He had no idea the diner had all those things on the menu. It'd been a real eye-opener since PJ had been tagging along. Come to think of it, he didn't think he'd ever seen a menu.

He looked over at PJ. She seemed to have regained her composure, and he could see Determination written all over her face, with a capital D.

"I want to take a close look at all the kids in that school, or ones who have recently graduated from it. Did Anita and Dave ever finish that search they were doing? I remember they had over two hundred kids who'd had both teachers in class. If we do the search on kids who had Loring, too, that's got to cut down the number."

"I'll check up on that right after we leave here."

The food arrived and he dug in. Somehow gore didn't seem to affect his appetite. He had that cop's habit of eating whenever food was available because he never knew when he'd end up working thirty-six hours without a break. PJ, though, was picking at her waffle with her fork like it was road kill. The strawberry topping probably didn't help.

After a few minutes, he couldn't stand it anymore.

"What's bugging you, Doc?"

She knew he wasn't talking about their recent visit to the auto shop, which was more like a medieval torture chamber. "Thomas is bothering me. Schultz, I'm practically out of my mind with worry. There's something seriously wrong, and with the pressure of this case I haven't done justice to it. He's withdrawn. He's having nightmares, at least one really bad one I know about. Those few hours we spent in the science museum were the best he's had lately. And all of this has happened in less than a month."

"Drugs can do that," he said. He pictured his son Rick selling drugs to kids Thomas's age. Rick would be out of prison in a few months, and he was going to make damn sure that scuzball found some useful employment. He looked sideways at PJ. He must have hit on something, because she hadn't jumped all over him the way he'd thought she would.

"You're the second one I've talked to who mentioned that," PJ said. Little dots of emotion blossomed on her cheeks, but she said nothing further.

"Tell," Schultz said.

"I searched his room. I, Penelope Jennifer Gray, Ph.D., clinical psychology, and fight-to-the-death proponent of a child's right to privacy, stooped to searching every inch of his room while he was asleep."

That convinced Schultz that he didn't want to tell PJ about his own search of Columbus's room. Schultz personally had no qualms about what he had done, and figured that any kid living at home had only whatever privacy he could get behind the bathroom door, and sometimes not even that. His search hadn't turned up anything worth laying out on the table anyway. "And?"

"Nada," she said. "And before you ask, yes, I know what to look for."

"Maybe he keeps his stash elsewhere."

She shrugged and picked a little more at her waffle. "I want to know why that day in the museum you said that you had a bad feeling about Columbus."

Like dipping a hand into the cold blackness of space.

Schultz searched for a way to express himself that wouldn't sound too weird. "I've got a really good people sense," he said. "Actually, it goes beyond that. Sometimes when I make contact with people, shake hands, rub shoulders, I get feelings about them."

Christ, what am I doing? I've never told that to anybody, not even Julia.

She was waiting expectantly, head tilted, fork still, eyes measuring. He plunged on. "Whether they're . . ."

"Good or evil?"

He nodded.

"Isn't that what everybody calls 'cop sense'?" PJ said. "What I've been reminded time and time again I don't have?"

"Cop sense is more like knowing when you're in a bad situation. Knowing when somebody is jerking you around. This is deeper than that."

"A seventh sense?"

"Didn't you skip one?"

"There's the usual five," PJ said, "plus I count awareness of the position of parts of the body. When you close your eyes, you still know how your arms and legs are oriented. That's what I call the sixth sense."

"I guess that's what I'm saying, then, a seventh sense." He was only halfway out on the limb. He'd have to talk about the golden thread business to get all the way out.

PJ held up her hands and wiggled her fingers like a child being a ghost. "Whooooooo . . ."

His cheeks burned. So she didn't have an open mind.

"I'm just kidding, Schultz," she said. "I take what you're saying seriously."

The sincere look on her face convinced him that she did. He had talked about it and she was comfortable with it. He couldn't imagine doing that with Wall, say, or Anita.

"And I notice that you haven't answered my question yet. How do you feel about Columbus?"

"I think he's evil and does a fantastic job of covering it up."

PJ blinked. Probably she'd been expecting something more moderate.

Millie came over and left their checks. "Something wrong with the waffle, dearie?"

PJ shook her head. It seemed to Schultz that she was shaking her thoughts around inside rather than answering Millie's question.

"You wanna doggie bag? You should eat that tonight for dinner. Put some flesh on those bones of yours."

Another shake of the head.

Schultz tried to picture what a waffle topped with strawberries would look like after it had been jostled around in a bag for a few hours. For such a practical woman, Millie dispensed rotten advice.

"Wouldn't hurt you to speak a word or two to your friends, you know. I'm not a serving girl." Millie went off in a huff. It was the first time Schultz had seen her unhappy with PJ.

"Most likely you're going to start getting poor service," Schultz said. Raising his voice, he added, "As if the service around here was good to start with."

"I was thinking about the fingerprints," PJ said as though she had missed the whole episode. "The ones on the acid jar. You said there were three sets of identifiable prints. One of them was Columbus's."

"Actually, the ID's on those prints were all pretty shaky. Not enough clear points. To keep print matching as objective as possible, there have to be matches on unique features, like a broken loop. Each unique feature counts as a point. The standards are different, but seven points is about the minimum you can get away with in any court."

"Columbus's were . . ."

"Five points. Christ, Doc, would you stop jumping ahead of me? Let a mere mortal tell the story."

She ignored his gripe. "What about the other prints besides the victim's?"

"Belong to a kid named Terrance Kelly. He was in Europe with his parents at the time of the murder, and he won't be back until the end of April. The whole family probably had a collective heart attack when Interpol showed up at the hotel to take the kid's prints. His father had an extended business trip and decided to take the family along to yokel at each other in the Swiss Alps."

"That's yodel, not yokel."

He didn't answer. Digging into his wallet, he counted out enough money to cover his bill plus his usual twenty-five cent tip. PJ was on her own.

"I think the design on the jacket is a chameleon," she said. "Not a snake like we originally thought."

"That fits," said Schultz.

There was more that PJ wanted to tell, but a certain heaviness in her heart kept her from doing it. The thought had crystallized as she talked to Schultz. She was worried that if Columbus was involved in the murders, so was Thomas. Directly, indirectly, she couldn't say. There was only one of the four interwoven murders in which she could be assured that Thomas wasn't involved. He had been right down the hall from her when she had put her hand on the bloody doorknob of Clara Eddington's classroom. When the other murders had occurred, he'd been out of her sight.

It had been suggested that the position of Clara's head had been a message of some type for her. She hadn't thought so at the time. To her it had been something meaningful to the murderer, more like talking to himself than giving a message. The more she thought about it, the less certain she was.

There was a message there, but maybe she wasn't the intended recipient. It could have been another round of a game Columbus and Thomas were playing.

She was going to have a look at that computer disk she had copied, the one she had pulled from beneath her sleeping son's restless body, privacy be damned.

CHAPTER

38

PJ went back to her office, though she couldn't seem to accomplish anything. Her thoughts raced but got nowhere. Her inner eye peered into dark corners that as a psychologist she knew existed in everyone, but as a parent she would prefer to think weren't in her son's makeup.

Most killers went to their executions with their mothers proclaiming that they were good boys.

Barnesworth came in and wanted to chat about the latest killing, and, as he put it, pick her mind about it. It was obvious that he was besieged and looking for hints, anything he could use to fend off the press and the Chief.

He had chosen the wrong time to mess with PJ. She informed him that her mind was not a peach or an orange to be picked at will, and that he could get his sleazy fingers off it.

She was beginning to understand the rewards of Schultz's attitude.

Preoccupied, she missed the first few rings of the phone, and picked it up just as her voice mail recording came on. It didn't automatically kick off, so she and the person on the other end of the line both waited for the beep.

"Sorry," she said. "I'm usually a little faster on the draw. Gray here, in person, not the recording. How can I help you?"

"This is Dr. Penelope Gray?" The voice was female, authoritative, and unknown to her. Who would be tracking her down at work on a Sunday afternoon? Had something happened to Thomas?

"Yes, that's me."

"Dr. Gray, I'm calling from Westchester Hospital. I have a boy here named Columbus Wade who requested that I contact you. His mother has had an accident at home. She fell down a flight of stairs and is suffering from back pain. She needs some tests and won't be able to go home for a few days."

"I'm sorry to hear that. She's a recent widow. It's terrible that something like this happened to add to her troubles."

PJ was wondering what the situation had to do with her. She heard a child crying in the background, a high-pitched, reedy sound, the type of cry that came from gangly twelve-year-old boys with legs as thin as chicken bones and permanently mussed hair.

Oh, no, don't ask me. Don't put me in this situation.

"I'm from the St. Louis division of Family Services, Dr. Gray. We can't let Columbus go home to an empty house for an uncertain number of days, and his mother tells me there are no relatives with whom the boy can stay. Although I've assured him we can find a good emergency care home for him, he insisted that you be asked. His mother has given her permission for him to stay with you until she gets out of the hospital."

No. Absolutely not.

"Yes, he can stay with me. I'll be at the hospital in an hour. Westchester, you said?"

One single adult reaching out to a troubled child. That's all she was doing. It was time to get her imagination under control and act like a grownup. She called Schultz at his desk, hoping for some reassurance.

"You're nuts," he said, after she explained. "Completely nuts. That boy's a suspect. More than that. I've already got him pegged. I just need to round up some proof."

She sighed. "Don't you see, Schultz? What if we're way off base? How can I turn away from that kid? He's lost his father, his mother's hurt, and now some witch is threatening to put him in a home."

"When did a social worker become a witch? I thought you shrinks had some kind of noninterference pact with them."

"Very funny. Do you have any sleeping bags?"

"Huh?"

"You know, like for camping. I don't have an extra bedroom. Columbus is going to have to sleep on the floor."

"It just so happens I do. But I think you should be looking for a straitjacket instead. Have you thought about the fact that you're endangering Thomas?"

PJ bristled. "Of course I have. But the victims so far have all been adults. Anyway, if he's in danger already, I don't see how he's in any more danger by having Columbus in the house. If the boy wanted to find Thomas, he'd find him. At least this way I can keep an eye on both of them."

PJ phoned Thomas at home. He reacted with near indifference, which reinforced her decision. If there was something wrong, wouldn't Thomas refuse to have Columbus in the house?

By the time she brought Columbus home from the hospital, Schultz had arrived with the sleeping bag. He was parked in front of her house waiting for her.

Schultz looked daggers at Columbus, but the boy acted like a frightened child grateful for a haven. He had a little bag of clothing, a couple of books, and a pitiful expression.

"He's a good actor," Schultz hissed to her when he handed over the sleeping bag. "Don't let him out of your sight."

She agreed that she would watch him closely, and she meant it.

It wasn't until Monday afternoon that she got a chance to examine the disk. She left the office early. PJ and Columbus were being bussed to another school, one of several where the regular teachers plus a group of substitutes had absorbed the sudden influx of students. She didn't expect the boys home until about four-thirty. That gave her a couple of hours in the house before they arrived.

There was only one file on the disk. It was password protected, but she got the password on the third try by going through her son's favorite characters. It was SKY-WALKER.

There was a program on the disk, several files she took to be subroutines used by the program, and one data file. Clicking on the program, she found herself looking at a rudimentary VR composing screen, complete with a toolpad that contained some tools she wasn't familiar with.

It looked as though Thomas had taken an interest in VR and was generating his own simulations. Nothing wrong with that. Most people would be pleased to find their offspring following in the parental footprints, and she was no exception. She resolved that when—not if—the case she was working on broke, she'd take Thomas to work for a more elaborate VR demonstration. She had several appropriate scenarios, rated G, that she had developed to show off her software, and she thought he'd probably go wild over the HMD and data gloves.

She assumed the boys were working on this as a joint project, and it was what accounted for all those hours spent at the computer with the study door closed. Presumably when Thomas went to Columbus's house, they used his computer for the same thing.

Curious to see how sophisticated the program was, and aware that she had slipped from righteous searching to prying, she brought up the simulation file that was stored on the disk.

Her first impression was that it wasn't very good. There was a strong gamelike quality to the hard-edged surfaces and the saturated colors.

Two figures strolled down the street, or would have been strolling if they had better control of their limbs. They looked more like puppets on the move. Her earliest simulations had been very like these. She wondered why the boys hadn't asked for her help, then remembered how independent—and obstinate—she was at their age.

Faces floated above the figures' shoulders, and she recognized with a start that she was looking at Thomas and Columbus. There was no smooth integration, as in her scanimation process, but it wasn't bad. The faces were frozen in one expression and weren't responsive. Still, the program was more sophisticated than she originally thought.

There didn't seem to be any way to change the course of events, no way to control the characters. The simulation didn't respond to her attempts at input through the keyboard or mouse. That meant that everything in it was hard coded once created by the design tools.

CHAMELEON

Each boy carried a baseball glove in one hand and a wooden bat in the other, resting the bat lightly on his shoulder. They appeared to be just two kids going to baseball practice. She wondered if she was about to see a simulated baseball game, in which Thomas and Columbus participated with famous players. Sports VR was becoming more and more feasible. Those serious fans who weren't up to pro status could pit themselves against well-known stars, even those of the past. Pitch to Babe Ruth or Mickey Mantle or Roger Maris, or take a few swings at Dizzy Dean's fast ball. If that's where the simulation was headed, she was curious to see how the program handled the teams. Could it animate a multitude of characters? If so, maybe she could actually get some pointers from the boys. Then she remembered that she was snooping. She couldn't discuss the simulation with them without confessing how she got hold of it.

Instead of heading for a baseball diamond, the boys stopped in front of a nondescript-looking building and went inside. Columbus opened the door, but it failed to remain open for Thomas, who simply passed through the closed door. Minor problem.

They were in a room with a waist-high counter. On one end was a cash register and on the other end something that looked like a small Christmas tree with oddly shaped ornaments. Beyond the counter to the right she could see chairs in a semicircle around a low table. On the table was a box she recognized as a TV because of the dials and antenna. In the corner was a large upright shape that looked like a refrigerator, but with flashing lights. An arcade video game, perhaps.

The perspective changed as the boys moved further into the room and headed for a door. PJ's first view of the door took her breath away and nearly stopped her heart. There was a sign on the door that said "Authorized Personnel Only."

The boys were in the auto repair shop where Jerry Loring had died the kind of death that brought to mind the Spanish Inquisition, not twentieth-century middle America.

PJ sprang out of her chair and paced around the room. Her mind was running away from what it saw on that monitor, and her body followed suit. After a couple of minutes, she was thinking more clearly, and directed herself back to the computer. She had to see how the rest of the situation played out.

The boys went into the work area of the shop that was off-limits to customers. A creeper, the rolling cart mechanics lie on when working underneath autos, suddenly backed out from under a sketchy-looking green car that wasn't recognizable as any particular make or model. The man who'd been using it stood up. He didn't look anything like Jerry Loring, or any of the other teachers, but given the setting of the repair shop there was no doubt in PJ's mind that he was supposed to represent Loring. The man approached the two boys, smiling. A cartoon voice bubble appeared over his head, and words formed. "Hello, boys. What are you up to?"

It dawned on PJ that there was no sound capability. Everything that had happened so far had been completely silent.

A bubble appeared over Columbus's head. "How about a little batting practice?"

Megabite jumped up on the desk and walked in front of PJ, delicately making her way across the keyboard. PJ ducked down to look between the cat's legs. She was compelled to see and couldn't miss a moment, even the amount of time it took for the cat to cross in front of her.

Columbus swung the bat, impacting Loring sharply on his left arm.

A balloon appeared above the point of impact, saying "Whack!"

The man crumpled toward that side and Columbus swung again, hitting him in the left leg.

"Smack!"

Loring dropped to his knees. Thomas stepped forward. PJ held her eyes open by force of will. Thomas raised the bat over his head and brought it down on the man's head.

"Crack!"

Columbus drew something flat from his pocket and spread it across the man's face. It was supposed to be duct tape, she was certain. They tugged the limp body over to one of the support columns of a hydraulic lift and wrapped both legs around it. Columbus picked up a piece of towing chain and snaked it repeatedly around the waist and then around the ankles, forming an S shape with the chain. Loring's body was arched backward like a bow. Thomas attached the heavy hook from the winch's cable to the chain.

The man regained consciousness and shook his head with an exaggerated motion. If the duct tape hadn't been there, he would have been screaming, balloon style. His arms were free and he started to use them to work at the chain.

It's not happening. It didn't happen. Not my boy, in this room.

Columbus fiddled with the controls of the winch. The cable retracted sharply, bending Loring around the hydraulic lift's shaft. Bending him too much. Columbus released the winch's pull. Loring, his spine broken, sagged in his chains. Thomas approached and repositioned the winch cable, fastening it securely around Loring's upper arm.

PJ looked away. She knew what was coming. At the end of the simulation, she glanced back briefly to verify that the simulated Loring had met the same fate as the living one.

Dazed, not thinking clearly, she wondered exactly how specific the news coverage of the murder had been. She hadn't talked to them about it. Could the boys have picked this up on TV?

No. The police had withheld crucial details of the crime, such as the use of the winch, hadn't they? The injuries to the left arm, leg, and the head reported in the autopsy were consistent with what she had just seen, and she didn't think that had appeared in the media, either.

The fog in her brain lifted, and she remembered that she had searched Thomas's room and copied the disk a full week *before* the murder.

She had just seen a rehearsal. And, dear God, her son had not only been present but had swung the bat and then fastened the cable that pulled a man to pieces.

A scene came back to her vividly, the one in her own simulation when she confronted Clara Eddington's killer in the hallway of the school and the killer had been her son. Had the computer been eerily accurate?

There had to be some other explanation, something other than the one that was ricocheting around inside her head, refusing to come to rest, refusing to be examined. She looked at the clock. The boys would be home in a few minutes.

Her fingers operating on automatic, she exited the program and locked the disk back in her desk drawer. She reached for the phone to call Schultz. She had to talk to him right away and get some help. Advice. Something.

PJ stopped before picking up the handset. The disk was very incriminating. Taken at face value, it meant a premeditated murder charge. If Thomas was involved in anything beyond the planning stage, should she let him face the consequences? Could she possibly condemn her own son?

It wasn't a decision she could make in the few minutes before Thomas and his evil companion came in through the back door. Or did she have that backward? What if Thomas was the instigator and Columbus the follower? She couldn't bear the thought. She got up and got moving, away from the computer.

Upstairs, she hesitated in front of her son's bedroom door. It was closed. She turned the knob and went in. The sleeping bag was on the floor, but from the unmade bed, it looked as though Columbus hadn't slept on the floor last night. Thomas always made the bed. Evidently Thomas had been persuaded or had volunteered to sleep on the floor. Clothes were strewn across the bed, and the dresser top was uncharacteristically messy. The sleeping bag was neatly laid out in one corner, and all of Thomas's clothes were either hung up or in the hamper.

PJ walked quickly over to the bed and slipped her hand between the mattress and the box spring. The original disk was gone. Her hand fell on Columbus's jeans that were lying on top of the bed. A vague plan formed in her mind, and she reached into the pocket of the jeans.

The key was there. The key to the Wade house, the one that Columbus had used to open the front door the night she drove him home.

The night she had hugged him and told him he was welcome in her house anytime.

Schultz was right. She was the one who had thought she could help the boy. She had been blind to Schultz's certainty, and after what he had told her in that rare moment of openness about his ability to judge people, that seemed both arrogant and stubborn.

PJ had let a killer into her house, had blithely served him cookies and milk at the table, and, before that, had let him into Thomas's life. She—an adult, an experienced parent, and a psychologist—had been duped by the boy's chameleonlike behavior. How much easier had it been for her son to fall under Columbus's influence? Was Columbus a cult leader with a following of one?

She heard voices in the kitchen downstairs. She had been too preoccupied to hear the back door open, but the boys were already in the house. She escaped from the room, key in hand, hurried down the hall into her own room, and locked the door behind her. A couple of minutes later there was a knock at the door.

"Mom, you in there?"

Of course they had seen her car parked around the back of the house. They knew she was home.

She cleared her throat. "Yes." It came out sounding strangled.

"You don't sound good. Is something wrong?"

Inspiration struck. "I came home early from work," she said, trying to give a nasal sound to her voice. "I think I'm catching the flu. You guys get your own dinner tonight, all right?"

"Sure. Take it easy." It was Columbus's voice, high-pitched, solicitous. Just like it had been at his father's funeral, as he guided his mother around, arm in arm.

His father was dead, suddenly, a victim of a random crime in the midst of a month of murder, a month of pent-up violence released. Could a twelve-year-old boy arrange a carjacking? And his mother, the last person PJ had heard him treating in a solicitous manner, was in the hospital.

You're the one who will catch the killer . . .

An inch and a half of wooden door separated her from the killer, or, if her worst fears were true, the killers. There was a phone in her room. She should call. Press 911. The disk was locked in the desk drawer, and it could take her son away from her.

"You sure you're okay? Can I get you something?" It was Thomas's voice, close on the other side of the door, almost as though he were whispering intimately in her ear. She didn't answer, couldn't answer. "Take care of yourself, then."

Swing the bat, crack!

The bat! She remembered that Thomas had broken his bat at the end of the last season, and she had promised him a new one in the spring. He didn't have it yet. He didn't have a bat. Hope flooded in, and she was a willing receptacle.

The hope was short-lived. It would have been easy for him to obtain a baseball bat, easy to break it up and stick it down a sewer. The fact that there was no bat in his room meant nothing.

She threw herself on the bed, muffling the noise of her sobs with her pillow. An hour later, dry-eyed, having concocted and rejected a dozen reasons why she hadn't seen what she'd seen, and having irrationally blamed Steven for everything, she was ready to act. But she had to wait until tomorrow, and it was going to be a long night.

Columbus was irritated at having to fix his own dinner. It wasn't what he'd had in mind. On top of that, Thomas had told him that his mom expected clothes picked up, the dishes done, and the bathroom cleaned once a week. Project Fairy Tale looked like it was going downhill in a hurry. *And they all lived happily ever after, except for cleaning toilets.*

There was also the matter of the cat. It put fur on things, and last night had actually jumped up on his bed, undoubtedly thinking it was going to curl up on Thomas. He aimed a kick at the cat, who had come to beg food at the table. It scooted away and glared at him from the doorway of the kitchen.

"You're toast, furball," he muttered.

"What?" Thomas said. He had his back to Columbus and was stirring an omelet at the stove.

"I said, I'll make the toast."

CHAPTER

39

The next morning, PJ didn't have to pretend that she felt bad. She had slept fitfully and her eyes were puffy from crying. One glance in the mirror showed her that she didn't need any artifice to look like a woman who needed a day off work.

PJ made a brief appearance at breakfast. She thought it would appear suspicious if she didn't. Thomas was agitated, as though he had gotten some bad news. He didn't seem at all like the boy who had whispered "Take care" outside her bedroom door. That time it had really been her son talking. Thomas acted as though he wanted to speak with her privately, but Columbus never left the two of them alone for a moment. Was it her imagination that Thomas was frightened of the other boy?

She didn't worry about sending them off to school. Nothing would happen during the day's classes. That didn't fit the pattern. As explosive as Columbus seemed to her, she didn't think he'd blow up surrounded by other students, with the routine of the classroom serving as a safety valve on the pressure cooker.

She waved the boys off on the bus, saying that she was going to go lie down.

Her stomach churned. She felt deeply alone.

The first thing she did was unplug the phones in her house and turn off her cellular phone. If Schultz called her now, she would blurt something out. Then PJ went to the desk and removed the incriminating copy of the disk from the drawer.

She erased it, deleting all the files and then reformating it. She slipped it into the pocket of her jeans.

She drove to a hardware store in Ballwin, where no one recognized her, and had the key to Columbus's house duplicated. She had plenty of time to think, on the drive there and back.

She was convinced that Columbus was the killer, and that he had somehow coerced her son into helping to plan at least one of the killings. But plan was all he had done, she was certain.

Most killers went to their executions with their mothers proclaiming that they were good boys.

Over and over, she tested her belief. Was she deluding herself? No, she couldn't be that wrong. Her son had gotten in trouble somehow and needed her help, that was all.

She was going to go to Columbus's house and search for the proof she was sure must be there, the proof that he alone committed the murders. She was also going to search for the original disk of the Loring simulation. She had already destroyed evidence, and she was planning to destroy the remaining link to her son. After that was done, she would turn Columbus in to the police, with whatever proof she found at his house to support her accusation.

Thomas would need therapy, and she would make sure he got it. But she was fiercely determined that his life wasn't going to be ruined by his encounter with Columbus.

PJ wiped her prints from the original house key, returned it to the pocket of Columbus's jeans, and drove herself to work. She allowed herself to be fussed over because of her sickly appearance and told that she should be home in bed. She listened to Dave, Anita, and Schultz discuss the results of interviewing the kids who had been students of all three teachers. They were very earnest, and debated bringing the forty-two kids in and sweating them. Interrogating children was a legal field of land mines. PJ offered little input. She knew the whole direction of the investigation was a waste of time, even though she had originally suggested it. She knew it because Columbus's name wasn't on the list.

The main accomplishment of the workday was to obtain a pair of latex gloves, the type that Schultz produced at a moment's notice to handle evidence. She had long suspected that the gloves bred in some orifice of his clothing, or in her less benevolent moods, of his body. She had always depended on him to provide the gloves whenever she needed them. Getting her own required cruising through a laboratory she normally didn't frequent during lunchtime.

PJ got through the evening by pleading illness again and retiring to her room early. She listened for the sound of the boys' voices, although she couldn't make out their words. The unremarkable hum of their conversation was reassuring. As long as Columbus didn't leave the house, she didn't need to take any action. If he went out somewhere, she'd have to call Schultz.

She tried to read, but that was no use. She ended up dozing in the chair in her room, waking up to the fear that she had failed in her vigil, that Columbus had gotten out of the house. She went down the hall to check, and behind the closed door she found two sleeping boys.

At three A.M., when the house was still and she felt that their bodies would be sluggish and their minds well into the cycle of restoration, she pushed Megabite off her lap and got ready to leave. She checked the boys and found them both with chests rising and falling rhythmically. She flushed the toilet of the hall bathroom to see if either boy was easily roused, and checked the results of her experiment.

In her son's bedroom, no one was stirring, not even a killer.

PJ could leave and return in an hour or so and no harm would be done. She thought about taking Schultz into her confidence. He could watch the outside of her house. But could she tell him what she intended to do? In the Washburn case, there had been the implication that he condoned tampering with evidence in Rebecca's cause. It hadn't come to that, so there wasn't any confirmation that he really meant it. He could have been just blustering on the way he sometimes did. In Thomas's case, there was no blustering, only direct action. She had dragged Louie the A/V tech along on a poorly-thought-out scheme earlier, and gotten him in trouble. No, she couldn't tell Schultz what she was doing. It was all on her shoulders.

She drove to Columbus's house but parked around the corner and walked half a block to get to it. The moon was full, or perhaps one night away from being full, so there was ample light to guide her along the sidewalk. She had brought a small flashlight in her pocket, but didn't need it.

At the corner there was a storm sewer. She took out the erased disk she had been carrying, and bent it back and forth in her hands until the plastic case came apart. Inside was a flat, flexible doughnut with a metal hub. She removed the hub and crumbled the floppy disk in her fist. She tossed all the pieces down the sewer. She heard a small but reassuring splash.

PJ slipped on the gloves she had brought from work and inserted the key in the front-door lock. She had to jiggle it a little. Apparently it wasn't a perfect reproduction. Inside, in the entry hall, she stood in the shadows for a couple of minutes, letting the racing of her heart subside.

The place smelled stale, as though there hadn't been a household cleaner used or a window opened in a long time. On all but the coldest nights, PJ liked to sleep with a window open in the bedroom. Snuggling under the covers with her nose cold was something she had enjoyed since childhood.

No snugglers here, evidently.

There was a lamp on in the living room, most likely on a timer, trying its best to make the house look occupied although Father was dead, Mother was in the hospital, and Son was on the road to hell, if not there already.

She should head directly upstairs, locate and search his bedroom, but she turned aside and veered into the living room. The lamp beckoned somehow, and that was where she had last seen Mrs. Wade. PJ wanted to learn more about the couple who had raised a brutal killer. She wanted to make sure she wasn't anything like them.

In the living room there was an entertainment center fronted by his and hers recliners. An uninviting couch, shoved off to one side, made it clear that the couple hadn't had company often, if at all. There were slippers on the floor by one of the chairs, a man's pair of slippers left waiting in case Norm came back, sat in his accustomed spot, and picked up the remote control as usual. The Sunday *Post-Dispatch* lay in a disordered stack near the slippers. She noticed by the headlines that it was the newspaper from last Sunday, the day before Norm died.

There was a bookcase in the corner of the room, and in it were several photo albums and a larger one that she took to be a scrapbook. Mindful of the passing time, and not wanting to leave Columbus unguarded too long, she picked up only two of the albums and the scrapbook. She automatically headed for the woman's chair. She wouldn't dream of disturbing the slippers and the newspaper.

The first album contained pictures of the happy couple before they became parents. On a beach, on a cruise ship, skiing, standing in front of the Christmas tree, first one of them, then the other. A picture of the car, freshly waxed. A beautifully set Thanksgiving table, with only two place settings and a ridiculously large turkey. Norm and Vicky looked happy enough. The pictures could have been of PJ and Steven before their son was born.

The second album turned out to be one of those remembrance books, "Our Child From Birth to Twelve." PJ had one of them, too, given to her by her mother. In PJ's case, she had never gotten around to filling it out. She opened the cover, curious how Vicky had done.

The woman had started off with commendable enthusiasm. The birth announcement was on the first page, the one that she had cut out of the newspaper. On the next few pages were tiny footprints, no bigger than PJ's palm, a baby picture taken right in the hospital crib, and, tied with a blue ribbon, a lock of Columbus's hair. PJ fingered it. Even through her glove, she could tell that it was soft, and the strands were so light in color as to be almost transparent. Thomas's hair had been thick and black from the day he was born.

All the comment lines were filled in, where the new parents were supposed to record their reactions. Duly recorded were the homecoming trip and Columbus's first night at home. The pages of "First Visitors" were packed with names, all of them with notations next to them indicating that they were either Vicky or Norm's work associates. Evidently their social life centered around their jobs. Milestones were noted, such as first smile, rolling over, sitting up, and the big ones like the first step, first tooth, and the first word, which was "Nanny." All of them were accompanied by pictures. In the second year, the pictures thinned out a little, but it was clear that the Wades wouldn't be accused of neglecting their infant son.

In the toddler years, there were only a scattering of pictures. In one of them, the person taking the picture was captured in a mirror above a dresser. It wasn't Norm or Vicky. Most likely it was Nanny.

By the fifth year there was nothing.

Had the Wades become too busy to take pictures of their son? Had they lost interest as the chubby thighs and cute, pinchable cheeks gave way, leaving them with a boy who wasn't even average looking? PJ had seen it before, in her practice—parents who loved the baby but couldn't stand the child the passing years revealed.

The scrapbook that she turned to next was the oddest thing PJ had seen. It wasn't about Columbus's accomplishments, or even those of the parents. It was more like a wish book. There were pictures and articles cut from newspapers and magazines, all of them about other children. Awards given, team pictures for Tiny Tot soccer, Boy Scouts, gymnastics, spelling bees, music performances, essay contests, artwork on display in local malls. PJ didn't know if the children in the clippings were strangers or the envied children of the Wades' acquaintances. Either way, it was a clear statement that their own son was a disappointment. If Columbus had seen the scrapbook, and it was openly displayed in the living room, it certainly would have been a slap in the face.

The dates on the clippings began when Columbus was four. It must have been about then that the Wades realized their son wasn't especially athletically, musically, or artistically gifted. He was going to be an ordinary kid, bright maybe, but not in a demonstrable way that could be shown off in their circle of shallow friends. PJ figured that they had only added a child to their lives because it was the expected thing to do. All the other couples were having kids, so why not jump on the bandwagon? Norm and Vicky Wade had expected a bright star, and had gotten, from their viewpoint, a dull rock.

There was more to it than that. PJ thought back to her brief encounter with Vicky. There wasn't a normal parental concern there, it had been more like . . . fear? If what she suspected was true, PJ didn't think it was farfetched at all that the Wades were frightened of their own son. He must have shown some behavior at home which would alienate if not terrify them.

She snapped the scrapbook shut. Enough speculation. She couldn't be gone from the house very long, and the minutes were ticking by. Tomorrow she would visit Vicky Wade in the hospital and learn more about Columbus. Tomorrow Columbus would be in jail. If she couldn't get any meaningful information out of Vicky, PJ had a feeling that the woman in the early photograph—Nanny, who had taken her own picture in the mirror over the dresser—would have some interesting things to say. No doubt the police could track her down.

If she's still alive.

She put the albums back in the bookcase and glanced quickly into the kitchen. Nothing out of the ordinary. She gathered her courage and climbed the stairs.

It was dark, as there were no more lamps on timers and only a little light filtered up from below.

There were several doors off the upstairs hallway. They were all closed except for one which yielded a glint of a bathtub in the dim light. It symbolized the family to PJ, having all those doors closed like that. The first door she tried was a study. Moonlight came in the double windows and she could clearly see a desk and bookcases. Nothing worth spending time on.

The next was clearly Columbus's bedroom.

The light coming through the window wasn't bright enough for a thorough examination, so she flipped on the overhead light. The room was large, about twice the size of Thomas's room, and she had considered his a good-size bedroom. Every surface was strewn with clothing, books, or papers, just as Columbus had begun to do in her own home.

She turned to the right and began systematically going around the room. There wasn't time for a genuine search, as she had seen done by detectives and evidence technicians. No spiral patterns, no marking the room off in grids. It was all up to her, and, seeing the clutter she would have to get through, she regretted the time downstairs going through albums.

The first piece of furniture she came to was a six-drawer dresser, the low kind that were generally found in a girl's room, topped by a mirror. PJ wondered if the Wades had expected—or later dreamed of—a girl. The top of the dresser held nothing of interest. She went through each drawer, but found nothing but sloppily folded clothing and a package of sixty-watt light bulbs. One of the drawers resisted her tug until she figured out that it still had the toddler-proof catch that prevented it from being opened more than an inch. She slid her fingers inside and released the catch, releasing the breath she had been holding at the same time. Nothing.

She patted the bed, feeling under the pillow and between the mattress and spring. The flashlight revealed nothing more than lint and a few forgotten toys under the bed, until the light reached the far corner. There was a flat storage box which she struggled to remove. Inside was a safety ladder, with aluminum steps strung on light chain supports. Instantly it reminded her of the delicate string shapes she had taught Thomas to make with his hands: Jacob's Ladder, Cat's Cradle.

The metal framework and lightweight steps of Columbus's safety ladder were neatly arranged in their storage box and looked new. It was a good idea, she thought, something she should get for her own two upstairs bedrooms. She was about to close the lid when she noticed small tufts of green caught in the chain. Leaves, and fairly fresh ones. The ladder had been used since new foliage had appeared this spring.

Had there been a fire at the Wade house? Unlikely. PJ shoved the box under the bed and levered herself up to her feet. She went over to the only window in the room and inspected the sill. There were scratch marks on it that could have been made by the hanging hooks of the ladder, but not conclusively. The window opened easily. She put one hand on the sill to steady herself and leaned out with the flashlight held in the other. The beam of her flashlight was barely powerful enough to reach the ground. It looked as though the ladder would be long enough to allow Columbus to drop to the ground, and to jump up slightly to reach it in order to get back into the house. It appeared that the dirt behind the bushes beneath the window was trampled, but she'd have to inspect that from below to be certain.

So the boy had a way in and out of his room without being observed by his parents.

She tried to remember what she had been reading in the handbook Lieutenant Wall had given her about the MOM principle—Motive, Opportunity, and Means.

She could put a check mark in front of Opportunity.

She looked at her watch, and figured that she had another twenty minutes at most before she had to be walking out the front door. There was nothing ironclad so far.

She moved to the desk and flipped on the computer, chiding herself for not starting with it. She wasn't thinking clearly, and that would have to stop if she was going to help her son. As the computer booted, she opened the desk drawers, her anxiety growing as she rapidly checked the contents.

They were crammed with computer disks, shoved in every which way, and most of them were unlabeled.

She searched the computer's hard disk, her fingers flying over the keyboard. As far as she could tell, there were no simulations at all on the hard disk.

Frantically, she yanked out the drawers and dumped the disks into a pile on the floor. She sat down next to them and started going through them, tossing the unlabeled ones aside. There was no time to examine them individually in the computer, which was the only way she'd find out what they contained.

There! A familiar label. It was the one she had found in Thomas's room, the one she had copied. Breathing hard, she got to her feet and replaced the disks in the drawers, without regard as to what went where. She slipped the disk into the computer and displayed its directory. The Loring file was there, plus a few more she hadn't seen before. She discarded the contents of the disk and then started the reformat utility.

When the computer had followed her directions and reinitialized the bit patterns on the disk, she wiped the outside of the disk carefully, because Thomas's fingerprints were undoubtedly on it. She tossed it back into the drawer with fifty others that looked the same. Then PJ turned her attention to what was left of the bedroom.

She thought that the bookcase to the left of the door would yield nothing. There were toy cars arrayed on top and books in disordered rows on the shelves. Nothing unusual, until she spotted the diary.

It was a blue girl's diary, complete with the little lock on the front. She'd had one just like it when she was a child. Another piece of evidence that the Wades had wanted a girl?

She pushed the button on the front, not really expecting the diary to open, but it did. It was unlocked. She scanned the entries rapidly, starting at the most recent date and moving backward. She was horrified as she skimmed page after page of descriptions of death and torture, including accounts of the murders of the teachers. Only a most depraved soul could have written it, gloried in it as the text did, and it was all the more sickening to her because the author was the same age as her son. She closed the diary and put it back on the shelf.

Trying to get a grip on herself and make use of her last few minutes in the house, PJ opened the closet door. She stepped in and felt something brush across her face. Stifling a scream, she moved back and aimed the flashlight inside. It was only the string hanging down from a ceiling light fixture which had touched her face.

She put her hand on her chest, feeling her heart bounding. She had retrieved the original disk—and hoped to God there wasn't another copy—but there was still the second part of her mission. The diary and the leaves caught in the safety ladder were strong. What she wanted was something iron-clad. She wanted the murder weapons.

The closet smelled, an odor that flowed from the open door like bad breath from a derelict's mouth. She stepped back in and pulled the light chain. At the far end of the closet was a haphazard stack of food wrappers, used napkins, and greasy paper plates. A half dozen cockroaches ran for cover, surprised by the ceiling light. Nearby was a pile of dirty clothes, including worn shoes and items typically cleaned out of boys' lockers during summer vacation by a janitor wearing HazMat gear.

She turned away from the smelly heaps in disgust, and found her eyes riveted on a baseball bat standing in the corner. She went to it, touched it, turned it, and found a dark stain on the wood. Shining her flashlight on it, she saw hairs caught in the grain of the wood, where small splinters had formed. Excited and repelled, she knew she had it. All she had to do was get the police to search the room and match those hairs against Loring's.

Why hadn't Columbus gotten rid of the bat? Obviously he didn't expect his mother to come in here. Vicky Wade hadn't been in his closet for months, maybe years. She was probably frightened of what she would find, or in denial that she'd find anything worrisome at all.

PJ, who had been trying to take shallow breaths because of the smell in the closet, reached to pull the string. It was time to go.

Her eye caught the toy chest along the side wall of the closet and her brows knit, wondering what was wrong with it. She figured out that the reason it looked odd was that there were no clothes draped on it, which was something that happened to anything that held still for more than two minutes in other parts of Columbus's room.

She knew her time was almost up, but she stepped over to the toy chest, and, heart in her throat, raised the lid.

Nothing but a bunch of used toys.

She stuck the flashlight into the toys and stirred a little. Stirring harder, she bent over and pushed her arm in up to the elbow. The flashlight snagged on some cloth. She reached in with both hands and dragged a heavy, cloth-wrapped bundle to the surface of the sea of toys.

Inside, she found a hammer, a hacksaw, and a camera with a built-in flash.

PJ was stunned. It was the hacksaw that did it, that made everything real. Its teeth still held dried blood and bits of tissue. A smell wafted up to her, and it wasn't leftover French fries. There was nothing else to do in Columbus's room. The evidence was overwhelming. All that was missing was the motive to have a complete MOM, and she'd have to think about that later. She hurriedly covered the killing tools—a camera?—and prepared to shove them back into the toy chest.

And heard something on the stairs. Or someone.

CHAPTER

40

Schultz was on his third mug of coffee. He knew that wasn't the brightest thing to do when he couldn't sleep. Getting up and drinking coffee wasn't going to get him any more beauty rest. He figured it was too late for that, had been for about twenty-five years.

He sat at his kitchen table and thought about Julia. If she hadn't had the courage to take off, to move out and go live in Chicago, he would still be married. But what did a marriage mean if there was no love left in it? Somebody to glance at over the morning newspaper. Somebody to use up all the hot water before he got up for his shower. That was the extent of it, and even those things had lost their comfort value.

Julia had found a lover, and that didn't bother him, or at least it no longer bothered him. She had realized that, at age fifty, she wanted more than someone to take out the trash. She wanted romantic love, and she had gone out looking for it. She hadn't been complacent, wasn't sitting around on her ass waiting for old age to spin its cobwebs. He would never have had the balls to start over without Julia pushing him out the door.

He could stay lost in the past, or he could use the chance Julia had given him. He had to find a way to make things work with Helen. He was a resourceful man. He told himself that all he needed was confidence that he would win her over.

And about this thing, whatever it was, with PJ. That was cut off, effective immediately.

CHAPTER

41

PJ froze, with the crudely wrapped bundle still in her hand.

Another noise, like a creaking stair.

She pushed the bundle back under the toys as quietly as she could and closed the lid. She pulled the light chain, and turned off her flashlight.

In the shadowy rankness of the closet, she listened again.

Hearing nothing, PJ glided across the bedroom floor and snapped off the light switch. She waited until her eyes adapted to the dimness of the light in the hall, and then looked up and down the hallway.

Hoping that her heartbeat and breathing weren't as loud as they sounded within her own body, she stepped out into the hall. As she walked toward the stairwell, she passed a heat grate on the floor, and noticed that heat was pouring out. The furnace had turned on, and the old house was creaking and snapping with the heat. That was what she had heard.

PJ could breathe again. She went downstairs, and in the entry hall, checked her watch. Late. She should have been home already. She hurried out onto the porch and locked the door behind her, satisfied that she had left everything as it was, with the exception of the computer disk. She squelched the sudden flare of worry that there was more on the unlabeled disks she hadn't had a chance to examine that would incriminate Thomas.

As she passed the sewer on the corner, she tossed in the duplicate house key.

She started the engine of her car but left the headlights off. She planned to ease away from the curb and then turn them on when she was down the block.

There were eyes in the rearview mirror, and then a cloth was placed over her mouth and nose. Frightened, she thrashed her arms and gulped in air, drawing the sweet fragrance deep into her lungs. Too late, she recognized it as chloroform. The anesthetic took hold, and she slumped against the steering wheel. Her last conscious thought was of Thomas.

CHAPTER

42

PJ opened her eyes and saw only blackness. Her face was pressed against something and her body was painfully contorted, with one leg twisted under her. Her temples throbbed and her stomach threatened to empty. She tried to open her mouth to scream, but found that she couldn't. There was a strip of tape across the lower part of her face.

She desperately tried to control her nausea, because if she vomited with the tape across her mouth, she could aspirate fluid into her lungs. After a minute or so, she thought that she was over the worst. She shifted her weight, hurting her leg even more and sending pain shooting through the side of her head. She rested for some time, until the pain receded. When she was able to think clearly, she examined her surroundings. The noise and movement were familiar; she was in a car. She could see a narrow opening in front of her face. The car must have passed beneath a streetlight, because she got a quick glimpse into the opening. She was looking underneath the seat of a car. Her own car, because there were the gloves she had misplaced before Christmas. Her face was mashed against the floor, and her body was wedged between the front and rear seats.

She tried to straighten out to give her bent leg some relief and to lift her face off the floor.

"Stop wiggling around back there," said a voice from the front seat. It was Columbus. She remembered seeing his eyes in the mirror, then the smothering cloth over her face, then blackness. Experimentally, she wiggled a little more, and discovered that her hands and feet were immobilized also. Her feet were fastened together at the ankles. She twisted around until she was able to look down at her wrists, and saw that they were crossed and then wrapped in so many layers of duct tape that she wouldn't be able to free herself quickly. If the layers had been fewer, she would have been able to bite at the tape and then rip it. As it was, she'd have to have the incisors of a beaver and considerable time to work. The first step was getting the tape off her mouth, and that had to be done by her captor.

Judging from the ache in her side whenever she breathed, she had been tipped over the front seat and unceremoniously dropped into the position she was in.

The car moved on through the night. There hadn't been a streetlight since the one which had shown her the gloves under the seat. She struggled to raise herself up onto the rear seat of the car, and after several attempts, managed it.

Sitting up made her dizzy, so she lowered her head between her knees. Mistake. Pain shot from her temple into an area deep behind her eyes, and everything whirled around her. She raised her head again and waited out the dizziness.

When the car interior stopped spinning, she saw something which would have made her speechless even if her mouth wasn't taped.

Columbus was driving.

There was enough moonlight coming in the windows to make out his narrow, sloping shoulders and oversize head that looked like it was too heavy for his neck to support. His hair stuck up in the back, and when he briefly turned toward her, she recognized his profile. He seemed artificially tall in the seat, so he must have been perched on a pillow in order to see out over the steering wheel. He was sitting forward, hugging the steering wheel, but even so, it must have been quite a stretch to reach the gas and brake pedals.

"Looks like I got the dosage just right," he said. "I tried it out on a couple of dogs, but I couldn't find anything your weight to practice on. The tricky part was that I only wanted you out for a short time."

PJ mumbled something in response which it was probably lucky that Columbus couldn't make out. The tape over her mouth turned anything she said into a muffled grunt.

"What was that?" When she didn't answer, he went on. "I hope you don't mind me driving your car without a license," he said, looking quickly back over his shoulder. "Doing this in real life isn't much different from doing it in the simulations. Did you know you can buy computerized driver's training courses? Amazing what you can get with a computer and a credit card."

They were on a two-lane road lined with trees. He swerved sharply to the right, and PJ saw a tree coming up fast. Was this the end? Killed in a car accident while trussed up and being driven around by a psychotic twelve-year-old?

Columbus brought the car back into the driving lane.

"Of course, when you smash into a tree in VR, you get to try again. Scared you, didn't I?"

He brought the car to a stop right in the middle of the road. She had seen several cars go by in the opposite direction, so she knew there was traffic even at this hour of the night. An unsuspecting driver could come upon them from behind.

Then he turned off the headlights.

"I'm going to take the tape off your mouth," he said in the sudden darkness, when even the moonlight seemed to have dissipated like fog under the warm gaze of the sun. "Don't scream, or I'll put it back on and then I'll tape you down onto the road so you can wait for a car to come by. Maybe a big truck. I've done it before, but never with a person. Should be interesting. Well, you decide, scream or not. Lean forward."

She scooted up and leaned toward the front seat. In a moment she felt his fingers lightly touching her face. It felt like spiders crawling across her in the dark.

They were still in the middle of the road with the lights out.

He found the edge of the tape and yanked it off. It hurt, and she stifled a yelp. But she knew he was within her reach, so there was no time for dithering.

She quickly brought her arms up and swung her hands in a sideways arc above the seat back. With any luck she could disable him long enough to get out of the car. Her blow brushed against the side of his head, but he was already moving away from her. The contact wasn't hard enough to do any good.

He pressed something against her arm which gave her a searing electric shock, throwing her against the backseat.

"Don't try that again," he said. "Did you know there are web sites that sell farm supplies? I haven't had this cattle prod long, but already it's one of my favorite things. I believe it was set on medium. I wonder what high feels like."

PJ's right arm hurt and quivered. She wondered if there was a burn mark, then thought that was a silly thing to worry about, given the big picture. Noticing that it was growing brighter in the car, she stretched her neck to look in the rearview mirror. Headlights. She started to scoot across the car seat, hoping she could reach the door, open it with her taped hands, roll out, and get off the road.

"I see them, too. How close should we let the car get?"

She fumbled with the door latch, only to find that he had taped it shut. She could get it open eventually, unwrapping the multiple layers, but not rapidly. The boy was a walking advertisement for duct tape.

He started the engine and accelerated, leaving the other car behind. PJ didn't know whether to be relieved or not. At least he'd turned on the headlights. But he was traveling fast now, too fast for the curvy, hilly road. On the turns, he crossed the center line in order to hold the road. She closed her eyes and tried to block out a vision of the car smashed against one of the rocky bluffs they were passing where the road had been blasted through the hillside.

"What do you want?" she whispered.

Columbus slowed down to a reasonable speed, if any speed driven by a maniac with thirty minutes' experience behind the wheel could be considered reasonable.

"I'm going to take that as a serious question and not just small talk," he said. "No one's asked me that in years."

PJ thought of the examples of Columbus's handiwork she had already seen, and knew that if she didn't turn things around, seize control of the situation away from him, that she was going to end up in a body bag. Or bags.

The fact that she was still alive was a good sign. He

wanted her to talk. She just had to figure out what he wanted to hear.

"I'm asking," she said, trying to keep her head from spinning. "I care."

The headlights went off again. "Sshhh," he said. "We have to sneak past the ranger's house. We don't want to wake anyone up, do we?"

In the silver light outside the car, she could make out a long, low building in a clearing by the side of the road. Then there were a few dusk to dawn lights, a small parking lot, and finally a house that looked like a log cabin. The setting jogged her memory. She thought it might be the visitor's center in Rockwoods Reservation, a state park in west St. Louis County. She'd gone there with Thomas last fall. They'd gone through the center and hiked one of the trails.

The residence had its porch light on. It looked so inviting. Safe.

The sleeping occupants wouldn't hear her through the car windows if she yelled. If she could only get out the door, the car was traveling slowly enough that she could roll without hurting herself too much. Her feet were taped together, though, so she couldn't move fast. She doubted if she could get away from Columbus by doing the bunny hop.

Too late. They were past the museum and ranger's home. Columbus turned the headlights back on, picked up speed, and picked up the conversation where they'd left off.

"If you cared," he said, "why would you have all those rules? Pick up this, put away that, lights-out time, get your own dinner?"

A boy who'd been without rules, she realized, wouldn't recognize loving discipline when he saw it. Wouldn't know that everyone contributed to a family to make it work. "You don't have to do those things if you don't want to," she said. "They were only suggestions."

"You're not talking to a baby, you know. I can tell when you're lying. You're just trying to make me think everything's peachy, so I won't kill you."

That thought had entered my mind.

He pulled the car into a parking lot on the left-hand side of the road. "Here we are," he said lightly, as though they were arriving at an amusement park. "A bunch of us came here last fall on a field trip. Everybody wrote a paper about the same dumb stuff, the lime kiln and the quarry where they blasted all the rocks away to make a big cave. Local history crap."

"Why are we here, Columbus?" she asked. "Why don't we go back to town? I can help you."

"Bullshit! The only thing you can do to help me is disappear. Poof! Gone from my life."

"I care about . . ."

"You don't care about anybody but your own son! That's clear to me now. I don't know why I thought it would work."

There was no use arguing with him, trying to convince him that she cared about what happened to him. She'd have to work hard to convince herself, too. She'd skipped over the concern she was supposed to have as a psychologist and gone straight to survival mode. She was prepared to say or do anything that would change the balance of power.

Power. That was crucial to him, she was certain.

"Thought what would work?" she asked. "What was the plan?"

The more he talked, the better. If enough words came out of his mouth, maybe he would give her something to work with, a lever to pry herself out of this situation.

He reached back and unlocked her door, then got out and walked around to open her door from the outside. He stood far enough away that she couldn't kick at him with her feet.

"Listen, I'm going to take off the tape on your feet. Lie down on the seat and don't move your arms. Remember, I've got the cattle prod."

She did as she was told. His palms were sweaty when they came into contact with the skin above her ankles.

"Now sit up. We're going to walk up to the quarry."

There was nothing to be gained by trying to stay in the car. Outside presented more chances for escape. She complied, standing up and shaking first one foot and then the other. Her feet had fallen asleep while they were taped. She eyed the woods across the street from the parking lot.

"Don't try it. If you make a move that's not what I say, I'll jab you in the leg." He hefted the prod so that she could see it. "You'll fall over, and then I'll stick you again for being bad."

"I'll walk. You don't have to worry about me. What was the plan, Columbus?"

He gestured toward a trail that angled uphill. The first portion of the trail was steep, and neither of them spoke. PJ concentrated on picking out safe footing on the trail, which was treacherous at night with projecting rocks and tree roots. At some points the trail paralleled what looked like sheer rock bluffs. The moonlight didn't provide enough light to make out how far the drop was, but she stayed as far away from the edge as possible.

It didn't help that her head was alternately spinning and throbbing from the anesthetic.

"You might as well know," he said when the trail leveled out. "I thought you'd take better care of me. After I moved into your house, all I had to do was get Tommy-boy out of the way. And my mom had already had one accident. She could have another one."

"And the two of us would live happily ever after," PJ said.

"Yeah, except I changed my mind. I decided my mom wasn't so bad after all. She gives me money, leaves me alone, and we don't have any stupid rules. So I came up with Project Fairy Tale, Plan B. I get rid of you instead. Thomas can move in with me and my mom."

She stopped suddenly. "So you want a brother."

Someone his own age to have power over, twenty-four hours a day.

"Kind of. I want somebody to do things with. . . . Keep moving."

"Things don't work that way, Columbus. If I died, Thomas would go to live with his father in Denver. A court would see to it."

"I don't want to hear anything about that! I'm in charge. What I say goes!"

He pressed the cattle prod into the small of her back. Her back arched as pain traveled in both directions, down to her feet and up to her head. She swayed, dizzy from the shock and the aftereffects of the chloroform. She sat down abruptly, before she fell down. The rocky trail jarred her tailbone. Columbus was so close behind her that he almost stumbled into her. Almost. If he fell, she could try to yank the cattle prod away from him. There were a couple of places she'd like to use it on his body.

"What are you doing? Get up."

Perhaps she could wrest control instead. She didn't feel like a woman in authority, but it didn't hurt to try. "No."

He came around in front of her. "Get up now!"

"Or what?"

"I'll just kill you here," he said flatly. "It'd be more fun in the cavern. I was hoping to study the echoes."

There was a flash in the moonlight, a silver edge. He had a knife.

The skin of her back, behind her right shoulder, crawled in remembrance of the knife. A memory of another time and place, another knife in the hands of a madman, made it impossible for her to think for a moment.

"I'll walk," she said, shoving aside the memory. "Give me a minute to get to my feet." She maneuvered herself up clumsily, since she couldn't use her hands. She noticed that he had moved back away from her. That chance in the car, when she had first swung her arms at him, had alerted him to the possibility of her defiance.

Thank God it's me here with him and not Thomas.

She tried to calm herself and think clearly. Another shock with the cattle prod and she wouldn't be functioning at all. No one else knew where she was. She wished that she had gotten Schultz's help, or at least let him in on her plan. If she was going to get out of this alive, she had to come up with something. She decided to try another tack.

"What happens when the police catch up with you, Columbus?"

"Nobody's going to catch me. Who'd suspect a little kid?"

"I did. All the detectives on my team did. They'll catch you."

"They don't have anything on me, and you're going to be dead soon. Not too soon, though." He chuckled.

PJ didn't want to say anything about the evidence she'd uncovered in his room. She didn't want him to destroy it. She knew Schultz would get this kid. He was already highly suspicious, and he'd figure out a way to get into the boy's room and find the damning evidence—the evidence that she hoped no longer contained any hint of her own son's involvement.

If she turned up missing, Schultz would just let himself into the unoccupied Wade house. It probably wouldn't be the first time he'd shortcutted the legal process. She just hoped that she could stay alive long enough to benefit from it.

Then it hit her, through the fog in her brain: How would Schultz know where to look for her?

"You saw the computer simulation of the Mitchell killing," she said, grateful that some small inspiration had struck. "The one I worked up. You saw it at my house the first night I took it home, when you were there with Thomas. That's why you killed Harquest. You saw the flashes from his camera at the end of the simulation."

"Yeah, so what? It was nice of you to let me know about him, so I could clean that up."

They were at the top of the hill. The trail continued on into a huge man-made opening in the rock face. The moonlight penetrated only a few feet, and all beyond was blackness.

"Inside," he said, pushing her forward with his hand.

CHAPTER

43

Thomas awoke with a start. He was lying down, but he wasn't in his bed. The ceiling was too far away, the shadows cast by the night-light were different from what he was used to seeing. He brought his hand up and found his face wet. He tasted a drop caught on his finger, and found it salty. He had been crying. He rolled over and discovered why everything looked strange to him. He was in a sleeping bag on the floor. Waking up and seeing things from floor level was a disorienting experience.

Megabite wandered toward him, her tail stiff, pupils wide in the low light, probably wondering what he was doing down at her level. She nudged his chin with her forehead and he automatically reached out to stroke her. He remembered she wasn't supposed to be in the room. Columbus had closed the bedroom door last night, saying he didn't want Megabite jumping up on him.

The door was open.

Just thinking of Columbus caused a flood of emotions that brought fresh tears to Thomas's eyes. At one time he'd thought his new friend was so cool, so grown-up. If he was a little spooky, well, Thomas could handle that. As Columbus pulled him further and further into his violent inner world, Thomas found himself trapped. He didn't understand the hold the boy had over him, and he didn't know what to do about it. He longed to talk to his mother, and several times had come close. But Columbus had been there, a nudge here, a push there, and somehow Thomas never had a chance.

Until last night, Thomas had thought he still had some sort of control over what was going on. Last night blew everything away.

The latest project—Thomas felt a pinch in his stomach as he thought of it—had been the worst of all. Pulling a man apart. Jeez, how could he have participated in something like that? It was wrong, and yet he got some kind of thrill from seeing himself doing those things in the simulation. What would his mother think if she knew about it?

Then Thomas had learned that it wasn't just a simulation. He nearly sobbed at the thought of it. The TV news had been full of Mr. Loring's murder. There hadn't been much detail, but one thing stood out clearly: the murder had been committed at an auto repair shop.

The victim in the simulation hadn't looked like Mr. Loring, but the conclusion was still obvious. The two of them had planned and practiced a horrible murder, and Columbus had actually carried it out. The boy he'd thought was his friend was a monster.

None of the other simulations they had done together resembled any of the other teachers' deaths. Only Mr. Loring's. But Thomas couldn't help thinking that Columbus was responsible for the others, too. It was as though Columbus hadn't trusted him earlier, but Thomas had gained his confidence somehow, so Columbus let him in on the real thing.

If he went to the police now, what proof could he give? The computer disk under his mattress was gone. Columbus must have taken it and hidden it after the murder was on the news.

He was sickened with powerful feelings of guilt and fear. His body shook. He was alone with something—and someone—he couldn't handle. There didn't seem to be a way out.

The door was open.

Thomas looked over at his own bed. Columbus wasn't there. He must have gone to the bathroom and left the bedroom door open. Remembering that Columbus had said he didn't like Megabite in the room, Thomas took the cat into his arms and got up. He quietly carried the cat to the top of the stairs and urged her to go down. She wouldn't, rubbing on his leg instead. Figuring that Columbus would be back any minute, he pinched the cat's tail to make her move. Surprised and indignant, Megabite took off down the stairs and disappeared safely into the kitchen.

He hurried back to his room, got into the sleeping bag, and turned his back to the door. He pretended to be asleep, and soon he was.

CHAPTER

44

"The police have a photo of you," she said. She didn't want to enter the cavern. It looked too much like a one-way trip.

"It was dark. The old guy was across the street. Couldn't be much of a photo, or they would have picked me up by now."

"You have a jacket with a chameleon on the back," she said.

"Shit," he exploded. His smugness had slipped, like a Halloween mask that didn't fit well. Suddenly he was a small boy whose plans were being thwarted. She felt a surge of hope. Small boys she could handle.

He kicked at the rocks underfoot. "Shit, shit, shit! How do you know that stuff?"

"I can help you, Columbus," she said, as smoothly as her tattered voice would allow. "Just hear me out."

"Who else knows about that?" he asked sullenly. He sat

down on a boulder, looking like an elf in the moonlight. She had to close her eyes to remember that he had killed at least four people.

"Everyone," she said. "I told them all at the police station. It's only a matter of time before they catch up to you. That's where I can help."

"Stop dancing around and tell me. I'm getting cold anyway."

"Okay. Give yourself up. Go with me to the police. Tell them everything."

Let them into your bedroom, your personal Museum of Horrors.

He didn't react. Was that good or bad? She rushed on. "You're young, Columbus. It would be ridiculous to try you as an adult in court. Missouri doesn't have a death penalty for something you did before you were eighteen, if that's what you're worried about. You'll get sent to some juvenile detention center and get psychological treatment. It'll be a breeze. When you turn eighteen, you'll get out and your records will be sealed."

He was still listening. She lowered her voice conspiratorially. "I'm a psychologist, Columbus. I can help you through the whole thing. I can be your coach, and I can make sure that you're considered cured by the time they're ready to release you."

His eyes gleamed in the moonlight.

She decided to lay every card she had on the table. "Those kids in juvie wouldn't be any match for you," she said. "You'll have them all wrapped around your thumb in no time. So you'd spend the next few years not just with one brother but with a whole lot of them."

"Do they have computers?"

She tried to keep the rising optimism out of her voice as she spun her web. "Of course they do. In fact, you won't have regular school at all. You'll learn everything by computer."

"Why would you want to do all that for me? Be my coach?"

"I told you. I care about you." She swallowed nervously, wondering if she was about to overdo it. "You're smarter than Thomas, and I like the way you always take charge of things."

There was no answer. He was still sitting on the boulder, his head slightly above hers. She wondered if she should make a break for the woods. Maybe by the time he jumped down and went after her, she'd have enough of a head start. It might be her last chance, if her appeal didn't work.

He jumped down, careful to remain far enough away so that she couldn't kick or trip him.

"Turn around."

"What?"

"There's nothing wrong with your hearing. Do it." She hesitated. Columbus turned the control dial on the cattle prod all the way up and brandished it at her. For all she knew, a maximum shock could stop her heart.

Holding her breath, she turned away from him.

A knife in the back?

"Walk back down the trail. I'll tell you when to stop."

She exhaled. *Not yet.*

"Where are we going?"

"Shut up! Start walking."

PJ went back the way they had come. Were they going back down to the car? After only a hundred steps—she was counting—he told her to stop. A beam of light played across the bushes to her left so suddenly that she jumped. She hadn't known he had a flashlight.

There was a side trail, barely discernible, probably used by deer. She had passed it on the way up and not noticed it. Before he could get the idea to prod her in the back, she moved toward it. The footing was even worse than on the main path, and branches whipped her face.

The narrow track ended abruptly at a steep bluff. She was sure they were far enough from the main trail that they couldn't be seen in daylight. Many of the trees had leaves already, and the path had taken several turns. A good place to hide a body?

There were piles of rubble at the foot of the bluff, formed by chunks of rock that had been dislodged and rolled down. He pointed the flashlight to the side of the trail, revealing a narrow crevice that began partway up the bluff, reached the base, and ran across the rocky ground for several feet like a miniature Grand Canyon. Columbus traced it with the flashlight. She couldn't tell how deep it was.

"I need some time to think about what you've said. You'll have to wait in there while I make up my mind," he said.

PJ was horrified as she grasped what Columbus had in mind.

"I can't do that," she said, her voice rising with fear. "I'm not going in there."

"I'm in charge, remember?"

He lunged forward and jabbed the shock stick at her. Pain exploded in her belly and she doubled over. At the edge of her vision, she saw Columbus moving in with the knife. Then her knees buckled and the rocky ground rose up toward her face.

CHAPTER

45

The first time Thomas was shaken, he mumbled and tried to turn over.

"Go away," he said the second time it happened. Then he was poked in the ribs.

"Wake up!" said an insistent voice. "I've been trying to tell you that your mom is gone."

He opened his eyes to find Columbus squatting over him. Thomas sat upright so fast, he conked the boy in the head.

"Way to go, jerk," Columbus said, holding his head. "Next time I'll just let you sleep through everything."

"What did you say?" Thomas shook his head, clearing away the remnants of sleep. He must have been really zonked. Then he remembered that he had been awake for a time in the middle of the night. No wonder he had overslept.

"Your mom's gone."

Thomas got up quickly and went down the hall, Columbus trailing a few feet behind him. The door of his mom's bedroom was open. Her bed was mussed, but not as badly as it usually was. She was a restless sleeper and knocked some or all of the blankets off the bed. She had told him it runs in the family, since he did it, too.

Columbus stood in the doorway but said nothing. Thomas turned to face him.

"How long have you been up?" Thomas asked. He remembered waking up and thinking Columbus was in the bathroom. He hadn't looked at the clock, so he didn't know what time that was.

"About ten minutes. I went out in the hall to use the bathroom and noticed her door open. I thought that was strange, since last night she slept with the door closed. I checked the kitchen and computer room downstairs. She's not here."

Worry began as a cold feeling at the base of Thomas's spine. Anxiously he moved back into the hallway, to the top of the stairs. There was no smell of coffee as there usually was when his mom woke up early. "Is her car here?"

"I don't know," said Columbus. "I didn't think to look. What's wrong, man? Where could she be?" The boy looked upset, but Thomas had the oddest feeling that Columbus was reflecting back to him the emotions Thomas was already feeling. It was eerie, like looking in a mirror and not seeing his own face.

"Go look for the car, both in the backyard and out front," Thomas said. "I'm going to check for her purse. It's usually on her dresser."

Thomas tried to calm himself as he hurried back down the hall. In his mother's room, he went to the window to see if she was working in the flower beds outside. No luck. As he turned away from the window, he caught sight of something tangled in the covers on her bed. He bent over and picked it up.

It was a ragged piece of fabric, a couple of inches across, which he recognized immediately as coming from Mom's favorite sweatshirt.

There was blood on it. He dropped it and screamed.

Columbus came dashing in, breathless from running up the stairs. "What? What is it?"

Thomas couldn't speak. He pointed at the scrap of cloth and sobbed.

Columbus came over and inspected it, but didn't pick it up. "Holy cow, it looks like something really bad happened. You better call the police."

Thomas was scared, as scared as he'd ever been in his life. There was a noise in his head, like static, that made it difficult to think. His heart felt as if it was pounding against his rib cage and his skin was clammy. He looked at Columbus blankly.

"Call the cops, man." Columbus pointed to the phone on the nightstand.

Somebody had to get his mom back. Had to. Thomas went over to the phone and pressed the speed-dial button with Schultz's name next to it. He was the most dangerous man Thomas knew, and if anyone could help his mother, Schultz could.

"Schultz." The voice on the other end of the phone was an anchor, the only one he had.

"Um, it's Thomas."

"Yeah?" Instantly alert.

"Mom's gone and there's blood," Thomas blurted out.

"Christ. Oh, Christ." There was a slight pause. "Where are you now?"

"In Mom's room."

"Is Columbus with you? Just say yes or no."

"Yes."

"All right. Christ. I'll have a unit there in five minutes. Listen carefully. Keep an eye on Columbus, but if he leaves, don't try to stop him. You hear me? Don't argue with him, don't do anything to thwart him. Answer yes that you understand."

"Yes."

"When the officers arrive, go downstairs and let them in the front door. Then you and Columbus go out and sit in the patrol car. Someone will wait with you until I get there. Got all that?"

"Yes." A sob burst from Thomas.

"Hang in there, son. I'm on my way." The connection was cut off.

Thomas replaced the handset. He turned around, and found himself inches away from Columbus, who had probably been trying to eavesdrop on the conversation.

"Her car's around back," Columbus said. "You think she's dead?"

Thomas sank to the floor and put his head in his hands.

CHAPTER

46

PJ woke to a nightmare of suffocation. She was lying in the crevice, and the rocks Columbus had put on top of her squeezed the air from her lungs and the rational thought from her mind.

She pushed hysterically against the weight, opening cuts on her arms and legs from sharp-edged fragments. She couldn't scream because of the tape on her mouth, and the muffled noises that she was able to make caused her terror to feed on itself. After the first struggle, she fell back, a dozen fresh wounds stinging from the salt of her sweat and mindless with fear.

When the flood of adrenaline passed, she tried to take stock of her situation. Her feet and hands were fastened tightly, she was wedged into the crevice she had seen in the beam of Columbus's flashlight, and there were fist-size rocks piled on her, enough to keep her immobilized. She was able to turn her head about two inches to the right.

When she did so, she saw a dim light. There was a bundle of branches sticking down through the rocks and up into the space above. They formed an irregular tunnel through the rocks that brought her air and a patch of light. She froze, fearful that if she moved her head any more she would shift the branches and collapse the small tunnel. She was lucky she hadn't done so already, in her first panic. If the branches were dislodged, the rocks would press tighter on her face . . .

She focused on the light and told herself over and over that she wasn't in a grave.

Her body ached, especially in the midsection, and she remembered Columbus stabbing at her with something. She remembered the glint of the knife, and new panic swept over her as she thought that she might be bleeding from a knife wound. She would quietly die from blood loss. Gradually she put together the events of her last few minutes with him. Mentally she felt along her body, taking stock, and realized that she was dazed from the cattle prod, but not bleeding in any great volume.

No one knew where she was, and there was no way she could help herself. Columbus was out there, maybe back in the house with Thomas. Tears rolled down her cheeks, mingling with the sweat and rock dust.

It might as well be a grave.

CHAPTER

47

When Schultz got to PJ's house there were already two patrol cars at the curb. It was six-thirty in the morning and birds were chirping, full of themselves in the springtime.

He cursed himself for allowing PJ to take Columbus into her home. He had been opposed to it, but faced with her determination, he had given in and gone along. It pained him to think that he had talked himself into seeing something good in it.

He knew Columbus was guilty. The cord told him so. It was no longer slender, with the far end casting about. It lanced from his chest to the boy's, a brilliant streak of accusation, and it was a wonder that Columbus wasn't impaled on it.

That wasn't enough to convict him. Hell, it wasn't even enough to get him off the streets. Schultz couldn't see himself getting an arrest order for a minor on the basis of a hunch, no matter how much that hunch glittered.

Schultz had thought that if PJ was watching the boy, had him under her thumb, that at least no more people would die while he gathered evidence against him. A breather, that's how he had seen it. A chance to halt the body count.

It had backfired on him, and he was dead certain Columbus was the cause of PJ's disappearance. She must have said or done something to challenge him. They hadn't pinned down Columbus's motive yet, so how could they know what would set the kid off?

He wondered where and how they'd find PJ's body. He didn't think his heart could stand it. Already the thought had filled him with deep sadness, and, floating on top of it, like cream on milk, rage.

If there was a chance she was alive, he was going to save her, and he was going to wring the information out of that boy if it was the last thing he did. And considering Columbus's track record so far, it just might be.

On the drive over, he had worked on transforming the heat of his emotions into calculated purpose. The dashboard of his Pacer had made a convenient target for his physical frustration and he had battered it with his right fist even as he controlled the car with the other hand. But by the time he rounded the street corner onto Magnolia and saw the blue-and-whites, he was ready.

The boys were in the rear seat of the second car. A young officer sat in the front, turned sideways so that he could watch them, but following Schultz's instructions, he wasn't talking to them. Schultz passed the car and watched Thomas's eyes fasten on him anxiously. Columbus looked straight ahead. Schultz's shoulders sagged as he took on the added weight of Thomas's fear.

In the house there was little to see. The first officers to

arrive had secured the scene and, at Schultz's radioed request through Dispatch, already summoned assistance and an ETU, an Evidence Technician Unit.

He was able to look at the blood-soaked swatch of cloth with no outward reaction. *Cold. Frozen. Save it for later.*

Approaching the car with the two boys again, he didn't have the slightest idea what he was going to say. He just had to trust that whatever it was, it would be right. He cleared his throat and started, and the words surprised even him.

"There's nothing much I can do here," he said. "I'm going to take the two of you back to my house. We can wait for news there."

Columbus nodded. He was playing his part well, concerned but going with the flow.

Anita Collings and Dave Whitmore had arrived while Schultz was in PJ's house. He went and talked to them briefly, explaining that it was necessary for him to leave the scene and asking them to take over. It was unusual, but the grim look on his face didn't invite questions.

Schultz put Thomas in the backseat of the Pacer and Columbus up front where he could be watched. There was little conversation on the ride over to his house. When they got there, Columbus needed to use the bathroom. As soon as he left the room, Thomas came over to Schultz.

"I need to speak to you alone," Thomas said. "There are some things you should know that might help Mom."

Obviously Thomas wasn't admitting to himself the likelihood that his mother was dead.

"I'll get us a chance," Schultz said. "Wait until I set it up."

When Columbus came back, Schultz took both boys upstairs and installed them in his bedroom. He'd be sleeping on the couch, if it came to that. But he doubted that the situation would carry on that long. He pulled some blankets and a pillow off the top shelf of the closet. "One of you can sleep on the floor and the other can have the bed. You can flip a coin if you want."

"I'll take the bed," Columbus said quickly.

Power-hungry little freak. Stay cold. Frozen.

Schultz glanced at Thomas, who didn't protest, and shrugged his shoulders. "Okay by me. I need some help in the kitchen fixing breakfast. Who's the better cook?"

"I always burn the toast," Columbus said.

Thomas took his cue. "I help Mom all the time. I can do it."

As they were leaving, Schultz saw Columbus walk over and turn on the TV, then flop onto the bed. Schultz pulled the door closed. The boy didn't seem to notice.

Downstairs, Schultz rattled around in the kitchen, getting out a pan and a couple of bowls.

"All right, I'm listening," he said to Thomas. He turned around and found Thomas gripping a spatula, his knuckles white, face as pale as pancake batter.

"It's Columbus," Thomas said. "I think he's done something to Mom, and if he has, I swear I'll kill him myself."

CHAPTER

48

Left alone in the bedroom, Columbus immediately got off the bed and went over to the window. He unlocked it and was pleased to find that he could raise it easily. Sometimes windows in old houses got stuck or were painted shut. He looked out and considered.

There was a branch of a large tree about seven feet away, but it might as well have been seven hundred feet. He couldn't jump the distance. If he could get a running start and throw himself forward, windmilling his arms and legs, he'd make it. But jumping from a squatting position on the windowsill, there wasn't a chance. He turned his attention back to the room. He wanted out, and he had to shake the two downstairs, especially the detective. The man was old and fat, but on a much deeper level there was something about him that was threatening.

Columbus had made his decision, and he needed to get back to Rockwoods Reservation to get Thomas's mom out of where he'd stashed her. It wasn't going to be easy, but that didn't faze him. He was sure he was up to it. He had setbacks sometimes, but, on the whole, things went in the direction he wanted them to go.

First he had to get past Schultz. Then he had to steal a car, which he'd never done before. The drive wouldn't be easy in daylight. Cops would be on the lookout for him, and he couldn't hide the fact that he looked too young to be driving a car. A certain element of luck would enter in, and that bothered him. He hadn't yet achieved power over luck.

There was nothing apparent in the room that he could use to get over to that tree. He even checked for slats in the bed, but the box spring sat on a metal frame that, in addition to being too heavy for him to maneuver, wouldn't fit out the window. Then he noticed the closet door.

On one side of the narrow walk-in there were men's shirts and pants, haphazardly put on hangers. Some had slipped to the floor. There were half a dozen pairs of shoes in a jumble underneath, most of them looking as if someone had forgotten to put them in the trash. On the other side was a neat row of women's clothing. Blouses, then skirts, then the longer items, the pants and dresses. A few things in dry cleaner's wrap, and, at the end, a zippered garment bag. Underneath was a neat line of shoes, ordered by heel height, with walking shoes on one end and the dressy ones on the other. He noticed that some items were missing; there were gaps in both the hanging clothes and in the line of shoes. The clothes could be in the laundry, but the missing shoes were a puzzle.

Columbus thought about the meaning of the clothes. Either the old fart wore women's clothes sometimes—he had heard of that—or Schultz had a wife. A wife who was unaccounted for. A wife who might at any time open that bedroom door.

Columbus left the closet and turned down the TV. Cracking open the bedroom door, he listened for the sounds of someone fixing food. He heard cabinet doors closing and soft voices. So far, so good. He'd have to take his chances on the wife.

"I understand how you feel, son," Schultz said, "but you can't seriously threaten someone with a spatula. You won't get a thing out of him that way."

Thomas lowered the kitchen tool, but his chest heaved and his resolve was plain.

"You have a seat at the table and spill your guts, kid. I'm going to keep moving around the kitchen, rattling a pan here and there. Start talking, from the beginning."

The story tumbled out. After ten minutes, Schultz took a break and went upstairs to check on Columbus, just to make sure the boy wasn't listening to them. The bedroom door was closed, and when Schultz put his ear to it, he heard the TV playing softly.

Columbus's search of the closet had been interrupted by discovering the women's clothing and going to the door to check for another person in the house. He went back to it for a better look. On the floor behind the women's shoes he found exactly what he needed. It was a coiled rope, thick, at least an inch and a half in diameter, and there were knots in it at intervals. He knew immediately what it was. On the box that his fire safety ladder had come in, there had been a picture of someone trying to use such a rope to escape a burning house. The picture had shown the top of the rope dramatically on fire, and it had a big circle around it with a line through it. It meant "No rope ladders," and it was supposed to be an incentive for buying the new, improved metal ladder that wouldn't catch on fire at an inconvenient time.

He dragged the heavy rope out of the closet. One end of it had a loop formed by doubling back the rope and fastening it with a metal band. He slipped the loop over the post at the head of the bed that was nearest the window and tugged. The bed didn't move. It would hold him. There were some advantages to being a skinny little kid.

He raised the window, and, faster than Santa sliding down the chimney, he was gone.

CHAPTER

49

Schultz sent Thomas up to get Columbus to come down to breakfast. He thought it seemed more natural that way. After a few rough minutes, Thomas was a lot more composed. Resolved was a better word for it. He knew he had a role to play, and he could handle it.

Schultz spooned out eggs onto three plates and retrieved the stack of frozen pancakes he had zapped in the microwave. Butter, syrup, orange juice. Mr. Domestic himself.

As he went about his tasks on automatic, his mind turned over what Thomas had told him. He was worried about Thomas's involvement but thought it was nothing that a little firm guidance couldn't rectify. That, plus grounding for about five years. Thomas had been on a greased slope to hell but hadn't recognized it because it was cool to have a secret life that his mom didn't know about. Schultz could understand that. He had a secret life himself, his sex fantasies, and he certainly wouldn't have told his own mom about it.

Thomas was salvageable. On the other hand, the kid upstairs was a grade-A looney. PJ's life, if there was still one to consider, depended on Schultz figuring out a way to get the boy to go pay her a visit, with Schultz following but not detected. A tall order. He needed help, and he intended to get it. After breakfast, he'd get in touch with Anita and Dave. The three of them could work something out.

Or PJ could already be dead, in which case he'd smash that boy's brains out, slice his belly open, and have his heart for lunch. In no particular order.

Frozen. Stay frozen.

Thomas came back into the kitchen. Alone.

"He's gone."

"Can't be."

"He went out the window on some big rope."

Schultz looked at him blankly, then sat down heavily at the table and put his head in his hands. "Oh, Christ. The fire rope."

"What do we do now?"

"Shit, shit, shit."

"Schultz! What do we do? We have to get my mom back."

Schultz looked up at Thomas. He recognized the desperate heat in the boy's eyes. If Columbus had been in the room at that moment, it would have been a toss-up which one of them would have been at the boy's throat first.

Schultz called Dispatch and was put through to Anita. He gave her the two-minute version and asked for an immediate search of the neighborhood.

"Can do, Boss, but he could be pretty far away by now."

"On foot?"

"Kids steal cars. Haven't you ever heard of joy-riding?"

"Christ. He could be holding PJ anywhere, then."

Anita cleared her throat. "You're assuming the killer is heading for PJ. She could already be dead. Or he could be heading in the opposite direction, making his escape, abandoning her wherever she's being held."

And she'll die, alone.

"Yeah, well, I'm ruling out those two scenarios. He's on his way to her and we're going to find the little bastard."

"Amen to that, Boss."

"You or Dave get over to whatever hospital Mrs. Wade is in and put that woman on the rack. Break a few of her fingers first. Find out anything she might know about favorite places, anywhere that's meaningful to him."

"Will do."

He hung up the phone forcefully. Before Thomas could ask him again what they were going to do, Schultz sat him down at the table.

"Okay," Schultz said. "The situation is this. We think Columbus kidnapped your mother and is holding her somewhere. You're going to tell us where."

"Me?"

Schultz asked every leading question he could think of. He asked for details that Thomas didn't think were important. He snapped his fingers impatiently, knowing that every minute was important. He went over every word of his own conversations with Columbus, including the day they went to the science museum.

"What exhibits did you two see there while PJ and I were resting our butts?" Schultz said. Thomas was holding up well. He wasn't wringing his hands yet. Schultz admired him, and figured he'd grow up to be a hell of a man.

"Geology. Migration of the continents. Earthquakes.

Volcanoes. Igneous rocks. Sedimentary rocks.'' Thomas's eyes widened.

"Tell," Schultz demanded.

"The seventh graders went on a geology field trip last fall. Half of us went one day, and the other half the next day. I was in Columbus's group. I didn't know him well then, but I remember it because he got in trouble for sneaking away from the rest of us. The chaperones were ticked off when the bus count wasn't right. We waited almost an hour before he showed up. There's something else." Thomas's brow furrowed as he tried to remember. "Oh, yeah. Even before that, one of the rangers caught him putting rocks in his pocket. You're not supposed to take natural items out of the park."

"Why would he want the rocks?"

"Because they were limestone. They fizz when you put them in vinegar. There's a limestone quarry where you can see the holes in the sides that were drilled for the dynamite. It's a neat place, like a big cavern that goes into the side of a hill. You can hear echoes inside it."

Schultz sighed. He was itchy to get moving, to do something, and all he needed was some plausible spur to action. Fizzy rocks would have to be it. After all, Columbus had been a chemistry lab monitor. What had he been doing during that hour he had stolen away from the group? It was weak, but it was enough to get him on the road.

"We're going to hop in the car and drive to this place. We can talk more on the way. Is it far?"

"Nope. Less than an hour."

Schultz let Dave know where they were going. He also asked to be put through Dispatch to Barnesworth, whom he knew was going to hold a press conference that morning on the progress of the case. It should be quite a song and dance, because from the official viewpoint there hadn't been any progress.

"What the fuck do you want?" Barnesworth said.

"Hey, you'll hurt my feelings."

"Oh, it's you, Schultz. I don't have time to talk. I'm on the air in a few minutes."

He was probably getting his hair styled and his face powdered. Or vice versa.

"Yeah, I know," Schultz said. "Listen. Wall's sending you out there with nothing but your dick to wave. You don't feed the sharks, they'll take a bite out of you, if you get my meaning." There was a pause.

"So what's your point?"

"My point is, I got a hot tip. You want it or not?" He could practically hear Barnesworth salivating on the other end of the phone.

"Why would you be doing me any fucking favors?"

Schultz drummed up some indignation. It was easy. "Hey, we're all on the same team. You want to see this asshole caught?"

"Fucking right. This from usually reliable sources?"

The fish is wriggling on the hook.

A couple of minutes later, he hung up the phone and saw the quizzical look on Thomas's face.

"Nothing you need to worry about," he told the boy. "Consider it a little present for your mom."

It felt good to be in the Pacer with a destination. The streets were deserted. The residents were still having their morning coffee and wondering how the hell they were going to make it through another day. He stomped on the gas. The car sputtered and sluggishly accelerated. By the time he got to the first stop sign, he was up to about sixty. There weren't any other cars around, so he sailed on through, bottoming out the springs as he cleared a small rise in the road.

"You didn't see that, did you, son?"

"No, sir."

He glanced over to see the corners of Thomas's mouth turned up in a tentative smile. Schultz himself was grinning like a maniac.

CHAPTER

50

PJ became aware that the weight on her was lessening when she was able to suck in a deep breath through her nose and let her chest expand. When the bundle of branches was withdrawn, a shower of pebbles fell on her face, and she blinked rapidly to keep the dust from her eyes. The light grew brighter, and in a moment the sunlight dazzled her. She was looking up at a patch of blue sky surrounded by the bright new canopy of the woods in springtime.

Rescued!

A face hovered over hers. "Yuck! You pissed in your pants."

It was Columbus. The terror of being buried alive was replaced by the terror of being helpless in front of a dispassionate killer. He pulled the tape off her mouth and she gulped in the fresh air. She frantically tried to collect her thoughts. He had come back. Was that good or bad? At least she wasn't totally helpless anymore. With the tape off, she had a chance to use her words to save herself.

"Well, what did you expect?" she said. "The line at the ladies' room was too long."

He laughed. She imagined herself placing her hands around his neck and squeezing. Columbus pulled up on her hands and PJ was able to sit up. Her hands and feet felt numb. She was sitting neck-deep in the crevice. She hadn't been buried very far down.

He squatted down next to her. "No screaming. I still have the shock stick, in case you're curious. I buried it right in the hole with you. Now climb out."

It was a struggle, but he didn't offer to help. She got her elbows on either side of the crevice and scraped her way up. Finally she gave a last heave and flopped over the edge and down on her face. Gravel bit into her cheeks and forehead. PJ rested, and he didn't rush her. When she was able, she turned over on her back.

"What about our deal?" she asked. Her lip was split and she swished the blood around in her mouth and swallowed it. "You go to the police and I make it easy for you in juvenile detention."

No answer. From her prone position she couldn't see him. There was a squirrel on a branch overhead that was chittering and flipping its tail.

"It's not like a real jail. It's more like camp," PJ said, hoping she wasn't rambling too much. "You spend a little time at camp and then you go free. Start all over again." She left ambiguous exactly what he would start over again.

"I went back, and nobody arrested me," he said. "I was right in the detective's house. I was testing them. They don't have a thing on me, or I'd be in jail now."

She heard him approach, crunching on the gravel.

"We're going to walk back up to the cavern," he said.

"Stay put, and I'll cut the tape on your feet. Stretch your arms above your head and keep them still."

She complied, and in a moment felt him sawing at the tape that held her feet. She fumbled with her hands and grasped a fist-size rock. She had heard the decision in his voice, and had nothing to lose.

CHAPTER

51

Schultz pulled into the parking lot in Rockwoods with Thomas gesturing excitedly that it was the correct one. He parked on a slant, blocking in the only car that was there. Its front bumper was pressed against a heavy timber railing, so the car couldn't make a quick exit. Thomas wanted to hop out, but Schultz put a hand on his shoulder and called in the license number. His heart leaped when he heard the report that the car had been reported stolen earlier in the morning.

His hand still firmly clamped on Thomas's shoulder, Schultz called for backup and asked Dispatch to notify the park ranger's office and the police of whatever the hell jurisdiction he was in. Not that he planned to wait until they arrived. Columbus had as much as a half hour's lead on them.

He got out of the car. Thomas was ahead of him.

"No way, kid. You're staying here."

"Who's stopping me?" Thomas said. He took off up the path.

"Come back here," Schultz said to the boy's retreating back. He shrugged as the boy continued on. "Or don't." There wasn't anything he could do about it. Thomas was ahead, and putting more distance between them every second.

The path was a steep climb and had switchbacks. Schultz could see Thomas several curves ahead. Muttering under his breath, he cursed the arthritis that hampered him and the extra forty pounds on his frame that he was lugging up the hill, not to mention the forty years the boy had on him. He couldn't shout at him without alerting Columbus that they were coming. He didn't have the breath to spare anyway.

The knife cut through the last of the tape and PJ's feet broke free. She sat up, bringing her arms in an overhead arc. She saw Columbus's startled look as he tried to dodge. The rock struck him on the side of the head. It wasn't enough to knock him unconscious, as she'd hoped, but it did knock him over.

He had dropped the knife. Her momentum carried her forward. PJ reached for the knife and closed her fingers around the handle. She forced herself to her feet and staggered a few steps, her legs numb. Columbus hadn't gotten to his feet yet. Was he hurt more than she thought? She took a step toward him. What to do? Beat him again with the rock? The shock stick was lying next to his right hand. If she approached, he could reach for it, and once it was in his hand, she would have lost the advantage of adult over child.

The weight of the knife in her hand was seductive.

PJ could end it, kill him while he was down and make sure that he would never take another life. Her story about juvenile detention and sealed records wasn't completely farfetched. She hesitated, then took another step toward him.

Columbus moaned, and all thoughts of justice fled her mind. She took off down the path, heading for the main trail. She stumbled once as she regained better use of her legs, but she didn't hear any pursuit.

Her heart pounded and her breath slipped in and out noisily through her parted lips. She reached the main trail and turned downhill, and then she heard him coming after her. She didn't know how far behind he was, and couldn't turn her head to look. She needed all her concentration for the trail. One treacherous tree root could allow him to catch up. It was a critical disadvantage that her hands were still fastened together in front of her. She couldn't pump her arms.

She was fleeing for her life from a child young enough to be home watching *Lassie* reruns, and there was no time to decide what she was going to do when she got to the bottom of the hill.

She had to plan. Had to think ahead. He must have gotten here in a car. But it was probably locked and the key was in his pocket. Something she could have checked out while he was down and dazed, but it was too late for that now. Stay away from the car.

She skidded on some gravel and nearly lost her footing. A new threat occurred to her. If she fell, she could injure herself on the knife she was carrying awkwardly out in front of her body. She risked a glance behind her as she recovered. He wasn't more than fifty feet away, and was running as though oblivious to the obstacles in the trail.

If he got close enough, he'd use the shock stick on her from behind.

She could run for the ranger's residence they had passed during the night, the one with the porch light. How far back was it on the road? Her legs weren't hampered by numbness anymore, but there was a sharp pain in her right heel every time it hit the ground, and her chest ached as she pulled in air. She couldn't stop running long enough to use the knife to free herself of the tape binding her wrists. Her physical conditioning wasn't good, and he probably had more stamina than she did.

What if he got in the car and tried to run her down like a scared rabbit on the road?

That settled it. At the bottom of the hill, she'd have to fight, even with her hands tied. She put her head down and focused on the next few feet of trail in front of her as she moved.

Something barreled toward her on the path, startling her. She thought it was a deer and veered to the side. Too late, her mind registered what had passed her. Who had passed her.

Thomas.

Dear God, her son was running toward the killer.

CHAPTER

52

PJ skidded to a stop. She stabbed the knife into a tree at the side of the trail, with the sharp edge up. Slipping her wrists over it, she sawed at the tape with furious motions. When her hands were free, she worked the knife loose.

Someone was yelling at her. She thought it was Schultz, but it seemed to be coming from far away.

PJ turned and headed up the hill. She heard shouting ahead, and one of the voices was her son's. She ignored the burning in her lungs and ran faster, arms swinging. Around a bend, she took in the scene immediately. Thomas was lying on the ground, his head against a rock, and there was blood. Columbus stood over him with the prod, about to press it against his chest.

She hit the boy at full speed, ramming him backward away from her son. The impact drove the breath out of her and sent the prod spinning into the air. It clattered onto some loose rocks where the trail hugged the bluff.

Columbus tumbled and rolled to a stop against a tree. He wasn't badly injured. He was alert and starting to rise, although he had one arm pressed to his side, probably where she had smashed into him. PJ looked at her boy lying on the ground, blood on the rock next to his head, and her reason left her. She went after Columbus with the knife.

Columbus saw her coming and moved faster than she would have thought he could. He was scrambling for the shock stick, the symbol of his control and his only weapon against her.

Schultz caught her from behind, clamping her arms against her sides in a bear hug. He said something close to her ear, but she struggled against him and didn't want to hear. She struggled, and if she could have slashed his arm with the knife to make him let go, she would have.

Columbus ran and dove for the shock stick, got his right hand on it and tried to dig his left hand into the loose rock to stop his slide. It didn't work.

He went over the bluff head first. There was a thin cry and then silence.

PJ could feel Schultz's heart thumping, his chest to her back. He kept his hold on her, as though he was afraid she'd go over the cliff after Columbus. By the time he let her go, the sounds of the forest had started up around them again.

EPILOGUE

PJ watched her son sleep. She tipped the last of the M&M's into her palm, tossed them back, and crumpled the bag.

Schultz came into the hospital room.

"How is he?"

PJ stood up. She took a few nervous steps and ended up at the foot of the bed. "The doctor says he'll be fine. It's only a concussion, a severe one, but the CAT scan shows no hemorrhage or swelling. One night of observation and he can go home. Assuming no change."

Schultz nodded. She could see the relief in his face. He'd just come from the scene where Columbus's body had been recovered. It had been hours. She didn't know what time it was. A nurse had brought her the pack of M&M's, and she had downed the whole bag in about thirty seconds.

"It's time to take care of yourself, Doc."

"I have to stay here."

"Anita's right outside. She's got magazines and drinks. Christ, I think she's got a picnic table. She'll be camping out here while you get cleaned up and get some rest. You've got to get those cuts taken care of, too."

After a quick exam out at the park, PJ had refused any additional treatment until she knew her son was all right. She ached all over, and when she stopped to think about it, she could feel every one of the cuts she had sustained. One of them, on her arm where Columbus had cut away a piece of her sweatshirt, was especially deep.

Anita came in. She set down a couple of tote bags, walked over to PJ, and hugged her. PJ didn't even mind the pressure on her ribs.

"I've got a change of clothes and some shampoo and soap. There's a shower in there," Anita said, gesturing at the bathroom in the corner of the hospital room, "and you're going to use it. I hate to mention this, but you don't smell sunshine fresh."

Schultz plopped into the bedside chair and waved the two women into the bathroom. "Go do your stuff," he said, "and remember, I'm not the one who said anything about the smell."

PJ stayed in the shower for a long time, letting the water wash away the blood and dirt that streaked her body. It felt indescribably good to be alive, to be above ground, and to have a son sleeping right outside the bathroom door.

Schultz had told her what Thomas had revealed, how he had been led on by Columbus. PJ was ready to help her son, and to see that he got outside help, too. She was tremendously relieved that his involvement hadn't gone any further than it did.

What of her own efforts to delete the computer simulation in which Thomas appeared? Clearly unethical. Criminal, maybe. She had done it out of love and protectiveness, but did that make it right?

Her rigid standards of right and wrong had been demolished by personal experience. PJ had a feeling that when she had some distance from everything that had happened in the past few days, she would find that the change was permanent. She'd have to construct new standards, grayer ones that took into account compassion and desperation. Ones like Schultz had.

When she got out of the shower, Anita tsk'd over her assorted wounds. She wrapped PJ in a hospital gown and took her to a doctor who examined, bandaged, stitched, dispensed painkillers, and advised rest.

Clean clothes felt wonderful. Schultz drove her home, after she had checked on Thomas and spoken to his doctor again.

On the way, he told her about Barnesworth and the news conference. The Big B had announced that conclusive evidence, including a corpse of another victim of the Schoolhouse Slaughterer, was buried in Cahokia Mounds across the river in Illinois. He'd said that the Mounds would shortly be dug up, and the case would be solved in a matter of days. Cahokia Mounds was both a national historic site and a world-renowned Native American archaeological treasure. Lieutenant Wall had made himself scarce, and Chief Wharton's office had been fielding angry phone calls from preservation groups all day. Rumor had it that the White House had called and demanded an explanation.

It felt good to laugh, even though it made her ribs hurt more.

At home, he sat her down in the kitchen and fixed her

a cup of hot cocoa with marshmallows. She swallowed a couple of Toradols she'd brought home from the hospital. After Schultz cleaned the pan he'd heated the milk in, he sat next to her at the table. There was something on her mind, and she didn't know how to broach it. She settled for the direct approach.

"I almost killed that boy," she said, dunking her marshmallows with a spoon. "I could have knifed him right there in the woods. No one would have known it was deliberate. If he'd gone to trial, who knows what would have happened. Sometime during his life he might have gotten out. What if he'd killed again? It would have been my responsibility, wouldn't it?"

She looked at Schultz and saw shadows in his eyes, of guilt, of impossible choices, of loss.

"Sshhh," he said. "You talk too much." And he closed her mouth with a kiss.

Read on for an exciting preview of Shirley Kennett's
new novel, CUT LOOSE—coming in November
from Kensington Books.

PJ Gray smashed the buzzing alarm clock with a righteousness worthy of a pulpit-pounding preacher. It was six A.M. Monday morning, and it seemed like her head had just hit the pillow. She turned over onto her side, closed her eyes, and indulged in wishful thinking.

Her cheek was lightly brushed by something that registered as spider legs. Popping her eyes wide open, she found herself with a close-up view of honey-colored feline eyes: Megabite, responding to the sound of the alarm and the expectation of the meal to follow. Still inert, she was bumped on the nose by the cat, who clearly wasn't satisfied with progress made.

She had just about convinced herself to sit up, promising herself a long shower and a leisurely breakfast, when the phone rang.

"What?" she barked into the phone. It was all of Monday morning pared down to a single word.

"Take it easy, Doc. After all, I waited until the alarm went off."

"Just how do you know when my alarm goes off?"

"Deduction. I'm a dee-tective."

"Not so anyone would notice."

"Christ. Okay, I'll call back after you have your coffee. You can explain the delay to Lieutenant Wall."

"Let's start over," she said in the best apologetic tone she could manage.

There was a pause as Detective Leo Schultz unrolled himself and flattened his quills.

"Got a call from Dave," he said. "Tenant complained of a bad smell from an apartment next door. Dave didn't get too excited, since this time of year we get a fair number of those calls. People go on vacation, leave the family pooch in a locked up apartment. 'But I left plenty of food and water out,' they whine when King the Wonder Dog turns up looking like a well-done roast."

"Could you get to the point?"

"Yeah, anyway, this call turns out to be a corpse of the human variety. Male Caucasian. Weird setup in the room, plastic, bondage, must have been something kinky. Dave wasn't too specific."

"Good for him."

Schultz gave her the address and she wrote it down. It was on the way in to work, so she'd stop there without going to her office first. It looked like a shower and breakfast had moved further away. In fact, over the horizon. She told Schultz she'd be there before him, and to let Dave know to expect her.

PJ slipped on a pair of linen trousers that were draped over a chair. They were supposed to go to the dry cleaner's that afternoon but would have to get another wearing.

Remembering with a groan that she had intended to do the laundry yesterday, she knew there wasn't much hope of finding any clean clothes in her closet.

The only summer blouse left had large orange and red flowers and a deep V-neck. It was that or go with long sleeves on a day that promised nearly a hundred degrees by afternoon. She slipped the blouse over her head, figuring that she had been possessed by the Demon of Poor Judgment when she purchased it.

PJ made her way down the hallway to her son's bedroom. Sitting on the edge of Thomas's bed, she admired his unlined forehead and angular tan cheeks, and couldn't resist running her fingers over the soft, barely-there mustache on his upper lip. Impulsively she bent over and tickled his nose with the tip of her shoulder-length hair. He snorted, wiped his nose with the back of his hand, and looked sleepily up at her.

"I got a call from Schultz and I need to go to work. What's on your schedule, T-man?"

He yawned. "Winston and I are going to bum around the house and then ride our bikes over to the rec center after lunch."

"Swimming?"

"Yeah."

"Tough life," she said, thinking about she had savored her own childhood summers in Newton, Iowa. "Be home by four. I don't want you out during rush hour on your bike."

"Geez, Mom, it's not like we're riding on the Interstate."

"By four." She kissed him on the forehead. He was almost back to sleep. She noticed that his alarm was set for nine-thirty.

Envy swept over her.

In the kitchen, PJ poured Megabite a dish of dry food. The cat sniffed it and decided to wait and see what Thomas offered.

PJ was surprised to find a trio of HazMat vans parked in front of the apartment building on Lake, and a crowd of people who must have been tenants clustered in small groups. Some were hastily dressed, some still in night wear, a few men stood on the sidewalk in their boxer shorts. They had been rousted out of the building.

The HazMat teams were packing up to leave. When PJ got out of her car, a faint smell of ammonia wafted over to her. She had a short wait at the door of the building as her ID was checked and her name entered onto the log of people entering and leaving the scene. The walls of the tiny entry vestibule were dark, dirty green and seemed to press in on her.

Climbing the flights of stairs to the third floor of the building where the murder had occurred, PJ was reminded in the clearest way that she had recently celebrated her forty-first birthday. The twenty extra pounds she carried weren't defying the laws of physics, either, and by the time she reached the top, she was breathing hard. The ammonia smell had grown stronger as she climbed. It lightly stung her nose and throat, and there were tears poised in the corners of her eyes by the time she got to the third floor.

The door with the yellow tape was down at the end of the hall. There were three doors on each side, painted the same shade of green as the entry hallway, and a run of patterned blue carpet down the center. Decals were used to number the apartments, and the lettering was comically crooked, as if put on by a drunk. There was a small window that hadn't seen a washrag and a spritz of glass cleaner in years at the end of the hallway, but it wasn't open. The heat was oppressive. She closed her eyes and tried to pick up the bad odor reported by the tenant, but the ammonia overrode everything else, even the smell of the ashtray at her feet, crammed with butts. Evidently a smoker in 3A was exiled from the living quarters and used the hall as a smoking lounge.

There was an officer planted in the center of the hallway, controlling access to the apartment. The young woman looked as if she had been dipped in starch and blow-dried. Every hair was in place, her uniform was neat, and not a drop of sweat was in sight. The only concession to humanity was the fact that she had edged her way down the hall, presumably to escape the source of the odor, the end apartment where the door was standing open. The officer's eyes were locked onto PJ and narrowed in disapproval.

It must have been the orange and red flowered blouse.

PJ strode purposefully down the hall and identified herself again. Officer Erica Schaffer informed her that there had been cyanide gas in the end apartment, which had condensed, evaporated, and left a film of acid. The HazMat team had washed down everything with an ammonia mixture and then sucked up the liquid with powerful vacuums. A few minutes ago, the place had been declared safe for entry, and the tenants would be let back into the building soon. It was obvious, though, that none of the curious were going to get past Officer Schaffer.

At the sound of their voices, Dave Whitmore's head popped around the corner of the doorway. One look at his face and she knew that he was seriously upset. Dave had a reputation for squeamishness, but what he was feeling must have been far beyond that. It set off alarms in every part of PJ's body.

"What is it?"

"Boss, the victim is . . ." Dave said. "My God, it's Rick Schultz."

PJ exhaled, and tried to draw shallow breaths instead of gulping the foul air. "Can't be. He's in prison."

"He was released last Wednesday. Assistant ME says the decomposition is accelerated because of the heat, but she estimates the body's been there four days or more. Probably won't be able to be more precise than that, but the general time frame fits."

"How do you know it's him?"

"He had the release papers in his pocket, along with some letters addressed to him. His clothing was cut off and searched by the HazMat team before they bagged it. You might find a dead guy with somebody else's wallet, but not his prison release, for God's sake. He looks bad, real bad. Someone tied him up in a homemade gas chamber. There's no positive ID yet, that'll come later, but it's him all right."

She could read the certainty in his voice, and a numbness settled over her like a cold fog descending from the ceiling of the hallway.

"Schultz is on his way here," she said flatly.

"Go on back down and see if you can intercept him. He shouldn't be up here."

PJ pivoted and headed for the stairs. She hoped to catch Schultz outside the building, but she was too late. She heard his booming voice in the front hall, stepped up her pace, and met him on the second floor landing. She put her arms out, her hands touching the walls on each side, forming a barrier to block his way. He towered over her five-foot-three height, and was still a powerful man although the years and poor habits had taken their toll. He could easily charge right past her. He stopped and melodramatically shielded his eyes.

"Christ, Doc, you ought to hand out sunglasses when you wear a blouse like that."

"Schultz . . ."

He came up close to her and dipped his eyes toward her neckline.

"Nice view, though."

"Leo, there's something I have to tell you."

He nodded his head toward the stairs. "Let's go on up, and we'll talk. You have some ideas already? This place smells like the world's biggest cat litter box."

She was silent. He studied her face and took a step back. "Tell."

There was no way to sugarcoat it, and Schultz wouldn't have wanted that anyway. She put her hands on his shoulders, feeling the warm skin beneath his light shirt.

"The victim is Rick."

His eyes went wide. "He's in . . ."

"No, he's not. He was released last Wednesday."

His body slumped, and he leaned against the wall. She watched his face carefully, and saw waves of emotion pass over it like an earthquake and aftershocks.

"I've got to see him," he said. "Move, Doc."

"Dave thinks it would be better if you weren't involved right now," she said. Her words sounded hollow. "So do I."

"Shit," he shouted. He shoved her roughly aside, and she banged her shoulder into the wall. "Get out of my fucking way!"

* * *

Schultz had taken a lightning bolt through the heart. Looking at PJ, hearing her words, he was transfixed. Then everything seemed to come loose inside him, whirling out as though chunks of his body were flying away into space. His knees gave way and he sagged against the wall. He couldn't seem to find the center of himself, and his vision faded around the edges.

The victim is Rick.

He pushed PJ aside angrily. At the top of the steps, he saw an officer in the hallway. She put her arms out toward him, then backed off as he showed no sign of stopping. Toward the end of the hall he was met by the unmistakable smell of death, ripened by heat.

Christ, that stink has nothing to do with Rick. Nothing.

He blundered into someone at the doorway, and pulled together enough focus in his eyes and mind to recognize Dave.

"Tell me what happened," Schultz said hoarsely. It seemed as though he hadn't used his voice in a long time. "It's not Rick, is it?"

Schultz held Dave's eyes and saw his own agony reflected there.

"Boss, you should wait downstairs. You don't want to remember him like this."

Schultz lowered his head and lunged forward. Catching Dave off guard, he rammed his junior detective in the center of the chest, sending him staggering backward. Dave was a big bear of a man, tall and broad, but Schultz had desperation on his side.

There was a photographer in the room snapping away, and the Assistant ME was off to one side. They looked over in surprise at the commotion at the door and assessed the situation rapidly. Deciding to wait out in the hall, the two nearly tripped over themselves, and then over the recovering Dave, trying to get out in a hurry.

Schultz took a few steps toward the center of the room. There was a chair, an old wooden one that had been painted green at one time.

A man's body was fastened in a sitting position in the chair with leather straps at the wrists, ankles, and around the chest. His clothes had been cut off him, though the straps hadn't been removed yet, and he was naked. Someone had draped an opaque piece of plastic sheet across his groin as a modesty cloth. Not approved investigative practice, but they had probably guessed Schultz was on his way. It was a small kindness, and he was grateful for it.

The tissues of the man's body were swollen, and the bands of leather dug in so tightly they were practically buried. His mouth was taped, and there was crusty dried blood on his chin that had dribbled out from underneath the tape. His eyes were open, and there were so many broken blood vessels in them that the whites looked red. Patches of skin had begun to slide off, as the skin of a ripe tomato can be neatly removed after immersing it in hot water.

Rick Schultz had been slowly suffocated from the inside, his flesh and heart and brain starving, as hemoglobin carried the cyanide through his blood vessels in place of oxygen.

In a gas chamber, it could take ten minutes to squeeze the life from a convict. In the uncontrolled amateur horror show in apartment 3F, there was no telling how long it had taken for his son to die.

He couldn't draw breath, and his heart felt as though it had blown apart in his chest. His roving eyes landed on the right hand. There was a silver ring deeply embedded in the flesh. A ring that Schultz recognized. There were initials RVS on the face of the ring, and on the inner band, Schultz knew, was the inscription *Love from Mom and Dad.*

Schultz was struck down by the sight of the ring like a giant redwood felled by a saw. He dropped to his knees, covered his face with his hands, and sobbed.

Special Note to Readers

Shirley Kennett warmly welcomes your comments on the PJ Gray series and answers all correspondence personally.

Send e-mail to: SAKennett@aol.com or
visit her web site at http://members.aol.com/kennettsa.

BOOK YOUR PLACE ON OUR WEBSITE AND MAKE THE READING CONNECTION!

We've created a customized website just for our very special readers, where you can get the inside scoop on everything that's going on with Zebra, Pinnacle and Kensington books.

When you come online, you'll have the exciting opportunity to:

- View covers of upcoming books
- Read sample chapters
- Learn about our future publishing schedule (listed by publication month *and author*)
- Find out when your favorite authors will be visiting a city near you
- Search for and order backlist books from our online catalog
- Check out author bios and background information
- Send e-mail to your favorite authors
- Meet the Kensington staff online
- Join us in weekly chats with authors, readers and other guests
- Get writing guidelines
- AND MUCH MORE!

**Visit our website at
http://www.pinnaclebooks.com**

THE MYSTERIES OF MARY ROBERTS RINEHART

THE AFTER HOUSE   (0-8217-4246-6, $3.99/$4.99)

THE CIRCULAR STAIRCASE   (0-8217-3528-4, $3.95/$4.95)

THE DOOR   (0-8217-3526-8, $3.95/$4.95)

THE FRIGHTENED WIFE   (0-8217-3494-6, $3.95/$4.95)

A LIGHT IN THE WINDOW   (0-8217-4021-0, $3.99/$4.99)

THE STATE VS.   (0-8217-2412-6, $3.50/$4.50)
ELINOR NORTON

THE SWIMMING POOL   (0-8217-3679-5, $3.95/$4.95)

THE WALL   (0-8217-4017-2, $3.99/$4.99)

THE WINDOW AT THE WHITE CAT
                    (0-8217-4246-9, $3.99/$4.99)

THREE COMPLETE NOVELS: THE BAT, THE HAUNTED
LADY, THE YELLOW ROOM
                    (0-8217-114-4, $13.00/$16.00)

ON THE CASE WITH THE
HEARTLAND'S #1 FEMALE P.I.
THE AMANDA HAZARD MYSTERIES
BY CONNIE FEDDERSEN

DEAD IN THE WATER   (0-8217-5244-8, $4.99)
The quaint little farm community of Vamoose, Oklahoma isn't as laid back as they'd have you believe. Not when the body of one of its hardest-working citizens is found face down in a cattle trough. Amateur sleuth Amanda Hazard has two sinister suspects and a prickly but irresistible country gumshoe named Nick Thorn to contend with as she plows ahead for the truth.

DEAD IN THE CELLAR   (0-8217-5245-6, $4.99)
A deadly tornado rips through Vamoose, Oklahoma, followed by a deadly web of intrigue when elderly Elmer Jolly is found murdered in his storm cellar. Can Amanda Hazard collar the killer before she herself becomes the center of the storm, and the killer's next victim?

DEAD IN THE MUD   (0-8217-156-X, $5.50)
It's a dirty way to die: drowned in the mud from torrential rain. Amanda Hazard is convinced the County Commissioner's death is no accident, and finds herself sinking into a seething morass of corruption and danger as she works to bring the culprits to light—before she, too, ends up 6-feet-under.